OPENED UP & DIRTY DEMO

EVA MOORE

OPENED UP

OPENED UP

Sofia Valenti dreams of designing beautiful homes. Stuck doing office work for Valenti Brothers Construction and stress eating her weight in chocolate, she wants more than hand-me-down responsibilities. When her father signs up the whole family for a reality TV show, Sofia sees a chance to grab the spotlight for her dream. What she doesn't count on is the sexy head contractor knocking down her ideas and her barriers like it's demo day.

Adrian Villanueva has spent his life on the outside looking in. When Adrian sees his chance to finally buy his way into the company he helped build, he's certainly not going to let the inexperienced designer daughter with expensive taste and mouthwatering curves stand in his way. Ignoring his old crush on Sofia the girl will be easy. It's the appeal of Sofia the woman that threatens to bring him to his knees.

When hidden attraction flares into open desire, they must decide if a chance at love is worth giving up on a lifetime of dreams.

For K~
May you always listen to your dreams and stay brave enough to chase them.

CHAPTER 1

IF ONE MORE THING HITS MY DESK TODAY, I'm going to snap.

Sofia Valenti cradled her aching head in her hands and questioned the wisdom of working with family once again. Joining Valenti Brothers Construction had always been her dream. But since Gabe's death, that dream had become a nightmare.

She pushed aside the stack of time cards she needed to process for payroll to give the contracts her cousin Seth had dropped off a first read-through. Dropping her cheater glasses down from their perch atop her head, she squinted at the fine print. Seth and his best friend, Nick Gantry, were incorporating their custom woodworking business into the larger family firm, and the details of the deal fell, as usual, onto Sofia's desk. The thought of woodworking drew her mind to the purchase order for cabinets that had landed on her desk late in the day. Needing to get that done so it could be filled first thing, she pulled it from the stack and laid it on top of the thick folder of legalese. The contract could wait.

Perfect. The order form was only half filled out. She clicked her computer screen awake and opened the supplier's website, while she let a soothing stream of curse words flow through her mind. Now she'd waste precious minutes looking up part numbers that damn well should have been filled in. This was not how she envisioned using her double degrees in Business Administration and Interior Design. Her thoughts drifted to the naïve but tempting dream she'd shoved into the back of her mind the day after Gabe died: the pretty, airy design studio, a waitlist of clients eager for her services, her father's respect. All of these goals had taken a back seat when her mother had lost her eldest son and fallen apart. She carefully tucked the dream away and turned her mind back to the pain-in-the-ass order.

Someone had needed to step in and keep the place running while her parents had dealt with their grief. Bills and contractors needed to be paid, and she'd needed a temporary job while she got her design business up and running. That had been three years ago. Truth be told, the mind-numbing work had gotten her through the worst of her grief after Gabe died, but now she needed more.

Basic cabinet package, bulk drawer pulls, the same retractable faucet kit they put in every house. The list never varied much. Valenti Brothers stood for good work at affordable prices, and their orders reflected that ethos. Though it hurt her creative soul, at least the part numbers were easy to find bookmarked on the site. With a few clicks, the order was entered, approved, and in queue for payment. If she was going to be stuck doing the office work, at least she could do it well.

As her mother and father, Josephine and Domenico Valenti, argued over how to pull back from the company and retire, the bulk of the day-to-day responsibilities fell on Sofia's shoulders. It had been months since she'd played with a design. No one even knew that she was available for design consults, because Dad never told anyone. Frustration weighed heavily on her mind as she tucked the PO into the appropriate file and pulled the contract back in front of her.

The legalese began to blur, and her glasses fogged over. She pushed the glasses back into her hair and blinked away the tears. God, she needed a break. A week at the beach would do. Hell, even a weekend over in Monterey would work. The soothing waves and brisk sea air would clear out the cobwebs in her mind. Since that wouldn't be happening any time soon, she hauled in a deep breath and reached into her emergency drawer. Her stash of snack-sized candy bars was flush, and she chose one with care. Almond Joy. She could certainly use a little joy today. She unwrapped the candy and popped the whole thing in her mouth.

She wouldn't mind a little action involving nuts either, but she'd have to get out of the office regularly for that to happen. What had seemed like a temporary drought of male interest was turning into full-on climate change. The Almond Joy disappeared before she had a chance to taste it, so she reached for a mini 100 Grand. This time she focused on the chocolaty, sugary goodness filling her mouth and soothing her scrambling mind.

A hundred grand would certainly be nice right about now. If she had some reserves, she could finally get out from under her father's thumb. When she'd started, having everything wrapped up with a neat little bow had seemed ideal. The plan was simple: work for the family business, live in a family property rent-free, pull a small salary to cover expenses but not drain their coffers, with the understanding that someday she'd have equity in the firm and would make commissions from her design work. Now that little bow was pulling tighter around her neck every day, and her father didn't understand that she was suffocating.

If she was ever going to make a name for herself, she needed capital to invest and time to design. Right now, her bank account was crying by the end of the month. As long as she was stuck at this desk, trudging through paperwork and indulging in pity parties, her account was going to keep weeping.

Enough. She slid the drawer closed and double-checked her planner. Two more hours before she could knock off for the family meeting her dad and Zio Tony had called. At least she knew she wouldn't have to rely on her freezer for dinner. Family meetings always took place around her mother's table, laden with food. She put her head down to focus on her remaining tasks, despite the images of her mom's lasagna triggering her salivary glands and tempting her to open the drawer just one more time.

Giving up on the contract until her brain was fresh, she rearranged her desk for the eighteenth time and began the rote task of entering payroll. In all her years of being the older sister, she had learned that she needed to leave on time. Enzo and Frankie would inhale more than their fair share if she was late. After the day she'd had, that was *not* happening.

ADRIAN VILLANUEVA HEARD the muttered curses as he pushed open Sofia's office door. That didn't bode well for his request, but he didn't have a choice. The tile that had arrived at the Chu project wasn't right, and he needed Sofia to call the supplier and sort it out before the warehouse closed for the weekend. He couldn't fall behind on that job, or it'd set off a chain reaction of delays and angry customers as his other sites suffered. He protected the Valenti Brothers' reputation as if he'd earned it himself.

Taking his life in his hands, he strode up to the prickly office manager's desk with a grin on his face. It wasn't a hardship to smile at Sofia Valenti. For years, he'd had to remind himself that, no matter how touchable her soft blonde waves looked or how her blue eyes twinkled at his jokes, she was off-limits. When he'd started working for her father as a teenage dropout, she'd been a sixteen-year-old stunner, and she'd only improved with age. Despite the fact that she was now old enough to choose her own partners, she was still the boss's daughter. He wouldn't do anything to jeopardize his relationship with Dom Valenti, certainly not while he worked up the courage to ask for the keys to his future. But in this case, his smile was wasted. She hadn't even looked up. He tried a different tactic in his charm offensive.

"Hello, beautiful."

"Ugh." She rolled her eyes, her manic fingers still flying across her number pad. The stack of time cards rapidly moved from one pile to another, her rhythm unbroken.

"I need your help."

"Get in line." He knew the snark was meant to be sarcastic. That was the usual tone she took with him, but the furrow between her brows looked like it was carved in granite. He wanted to smooth it away with his thumb, but he had a firm no-touching rule. The last thing he needed was to lose his precious restraint around her, and giving in to his impulse would trigger exactly that.

Focus on the problem. Get in, get out.

"The tiles on the Chu project are wrong. I need you to straighten it out with the supplier."

She closed her eyes and let out an ear-piercing scream. It surprised him into stepping back.

"What was that for?"

"Long story." She finally looked up, her slate-blue eyes brimming with anger and frustration. *Damn.* Nothing in his arsenal was going to smooth over whatever else was making her scream. His best option now was to muscle through the details and get out of her way.

"Here's the original order form and the packing slip. It looks like they switched the final numbers. We need to catch them before they leave, or we lose three days on this project, and I'll have to pull crews from scheduled work at other houses to finish."

"You've got to be kidding me! I need to be out the door in half an hour. I'm not a miracle worker."

"Could have fooled me."

"Yeah, yeah. Flattery will get you nowhere. Give me that." She snatched the paperwork from his hand and grimaced.

"So, got a hot date?"

Her head snapped up, eyes wide with surprise and...offense?

"Excuse me?"

"You said you had to leave. It's Friday night..."

"Screw you. When's the last time you saw me leave this office before eight p.m.?" She gestured to her small room, walls covered in mismatched sample cabinets and drawer pulls for the clients to see, and desk layered in papers.

"Just trying to make conversation. So why do you have to leave, then? It's well before eight, as you say."

"Dad called a family meeting. He's got something he wants to talk to us about."

Jealousy clenched briefly, even as he clenched his own fist in response. It was always this way. Family first. He'd started working for Valenti Brothers in high school as a general laborer. After his father had been deported, he'd been forced to become the man of the house far sooner than intended, working any and all hours to keep his mother and sisters safe and sound.

Over the last twelve years, he'd worked his way up, learning, apprenticing, proving his worth. He now led his own construction team, with Dom and Frankie leading the other two since Tony had officially retired last month. He'd always expected to work alongside the old man until Gabe had finished college and was ready to step in. But Gabe had chosen a different path, one that led him to the army and Iraq. One that hadn't led him back home.

He could see the opportunities, his own potential to fill that role. He wanted it so bad he could taste it: the stability, the power over his destiny, the sense of finally belonging. But as long as business was decided over family dinners, he was stuck, always on the outside looking in. He needed to get his ass in gear and ask Dom the question he'd been choking on for months. As casually as he could, taking care to bury his frustrations deep, he asked, "Oh, yeah? Any idea what about?"

She raced a highlighter across the invoice and reached for her phone, already tackling his problem.

"None. And if you don't get out of here, I'll never finish so I can find out. Shoo! Hello? Yes, can I speak to Javier? Thank you."

She continued entering numbers while she calmly reamed Javier a new one and wrangled a guarantee that the tiles would be delivered to the site by Saturday at ten a.m., no extra charge. He had no idea how she juggled it all, but better her than him. He backed out the door, wondering why that prim tone of voice turned him inside out.

PHONE CALL DONE, payroll half entered, contracts still waiting, Sofia lowered her swirling head to her desk. *What nerve that guy has!* Calling her beautiful, asking if she had a date... She knew she wasn't beautiful, not by a long shot, but she didn't need to be teased about it at work. Once upon a time she'd dreamed she was a lovely princess in a beautiful castle just waiting for Prince Charming. But little girls' dreams often fade in the face of cold, hard reality, and hers was no different. Now, she was an overweight, underappreciated servant approaching thirty, trapped in a mismatched dungeon, and no one was coming to save her.

She hated that in spite of Adrian's insulting endearments and rude questions, the man still had the power to awaken the yearnings she kept carefully suppressed. There was no use getting turned on if there was no one to enjoy it with, so she tried to avoid it at all costs. But there was something about him...

His dark, chocolate brown hair, his peanut-butter-colored eyes, the perfect combination of sweet and nutty... She reached back into her drawer and pulled out the big guns, a double pack of Reese's cups. She slowly chewed the sugary treat and pretended that it filled the aching hole in her chest.

She'd watched him during her shy teen years, afraid to approach the boy who was already a man. He'd intimidated the hell out of her with his confident, cocky air. When she'd come back to the company after a few years of experience in college, she'd been ready to pursue the strong tug of attraction, but every minor advance crumbled against the firm wall of physical distance and relentless teasing he kept between them. If he'd pushed her away when she'd been young and beautiful, she could only imagine he'd run screaming if she approached him now. She'd packed on weight in the months following the funeral, and her sedentary job and borderline depression were keeping it there. She'd let herself go, and now she could barely find herself in the reflection in the mirror. She didn't have a chance in hell with a guy like him, so she did her best to keep her inappropriate longings well contained. Humor and sarcasm were her defensive weapons of choice.

She had to laugh or she'd cry. Adrian was a trusted employee and a minor jerk, no matter how attractive she found him. She could handle him and this pesky response he provoked. He probably had no idea that his words had wounded. Most men didn't. It likely didn't occur to him that words like "beautiful" or "gorgeous" *could* hurt. He would never imagine that his casual conversation rang like a condemnation in her mind. He had no clue, and that was why he could never know that his broad shoulders and strong arms made inner Sofia weak in the knees.

He would never know because she'd die sitting behind this desk, all alone. She was well and truly stuck. The futility of her situation weighed on her heart. It wasn't fair. This wasn't how her life was supposed to go. The anger she tried hard to keep hidden from the rest of the family flared hot in her chest, lashing out at the one person who couldn't defend himself.

Damn it, Gabe. Why did you have to go and change everything? I want the life we had planned. I wish you were here.

But wishing would not make it so.

She shut the chocolate drawer firmly on her feelings and grabbed her purse. Time to see what Dad was up to.

CHAPTER 2

"You're late."

"Bite me."

Seth had opened the door to her childhood home, and pulled her into a one-armed hug. "Careful. I hear karma's a real bitch."

"I'm really not in the mood. It's been a hell of a week."

He pressed his glass of red wine into her hand.

"Well then, I'll cheer you up. Zia Jo held dinner for you. The antipasti plates have been devoured, but really can you blame us? You're late."

Sofia had to smile at that. It did indeed make her feel better to know that, although her family created ninety percent of her headaches, they were also there to help put her back together. She knew she was loved, even if the heathens had eaten all the marinated mushrooms. But really who could expect restraint around Ma's antipasti plates?

Sofia often wished that she had inherited some of her mother's culinary genius, but aside from a few staple recipes, she made do with prepackaged frozen meals. She was too exhausted to cook by the end of the day, and making her mother's recipes designed to feed the masses felt like a waste for just her. She relied on nights like this to satisfy her cravings. So yeah, she was bummed about missing out on her favorite mushrooms, but she could still feel the love.

"Lead the way, and thanks for the wine." She took a deep sip and swirled her glass in the light. The nearly black wine glinted with ruby highlights, while bright berries and tart cherries burst on her tongue. The Montepulciano cleansed her palate of her lingering sugar binge and called to mind her mother's red sauce, which included a generous glug of the dark wine. "Did you screw up again?"

"No!"

"Then why are we drinking Ma's favorite wine?"

"For once it's not me. It was open when I got here," Seth whispered over his shoulder as they headed for the kitchen. "Maybe we'll find out now that our slowpoke has arrived."

Sofia jabbed him in the ribs with a hard finger, his yelp supremely satisfying.

The warmth and noise of her mother's kitchen wrapped her in a hug even before Jo left the stove to do the same.

"I was getting worried. You should have called." Josephine Valenti's frown managed to contain disappointment, frustration, humor, and love, all at once.

"I got caught up at the office." Sofia leaned in to kiss her smooth cheek out of long-standing habit.

"That office… Enough, I won't get into that now. I hid some mushrooms in the fridge for you."

"You are the best mother ever. I am sorry I was late. Last-minute snag on the Chu project that I had to untangle."

"Bah! Nothing is more important than family. Come. Sit." She turned and yelled, pitching her voice toward the raucous family room. "Time to eat! Everyone washes." This last was said with the same stern tone of warning with which it had been delivered

17

since Sofia was a toddler. In a home full of children and construction workers, it was one of Ma's golden rules.

Her father entered the room first, followed by Enzo and Frankie. The trio had obviously been biding their time with the preseason baseball game on the family room TV, but the lure of Josephine Valenti's table was stronger than any team loyalty. Good-natured tussling broke out as they all attempted to wash up in the kitchen sink. Sofia found herself in the middle of a whirlwind of damp hugs, arguments, and laughter. Family.

She sat in her chair at the table, the same space she'd occupied since she'd left her high chair. Few things brought her comfort in the swirling chaos of this world. The soothing repetition of waves at the ocean. A glass of good red wine. Her seat at this table. Chocolate was another, so she was hoping her mother had splurged on dessert.

To her right, her mother sat at the foot of the table. Or rather, she would sit there once every dish was arranged to her liking and everyone had a full plate and glass. Enzo and Frankie, matching chocolate brown heads bowed together, arguing over who would get the first slice of lasagna, sat across from her. There was another comfort in knowing that her younger siblings had bickered since birth and would continue to the death.

Her father sat at the head of the table, his smile benevolent if a bit weathered as he looked down on the family he'd created. Stocky and broad-shouldered, skin a tough leathery brown after years in the California sun, he looked as immovable as the mountains outside her window. Unlike those bare peaks, his own crown was sporting more frosty gray than it used to. Sofia couldn't help but wonder if today was the day he'd feel his age and announce that he was retiring.

Next to her dad sat her cousin Seth, who'd recently needed convincing that he did, indeed, deserve his seat at the table. The only one who shared her own golden features, he looked more like her brother than her own. He joked with her like he was another big brother, too, and in truth he was the closest thing she had to that anymore.

Which brought her to the empty chair on her left. The chair no one had the heart to move, or the courage to speak of. Gabe's chair.

When her big brother had decided to join the army for a few years before settling into the family business, Sofia had been jealous. Sure, she'd been at college, but it was only San Jose State. With campus only half an hour away, she'd lived at home in Menlo Park, while Gabe had been off seeing the world. His deployment had left a hole in their family unit. A hole that had become permanent when he'd been killed in action three years ago. The resentment she'd felt around him leaving had solidified into righteous anger that he was never coming back. Three years later and the hole in their family was just as large, and she was still struggling to make sense of the new normal. But nothing was getting solved on that front tonight.

Sofia brushed aside her melancholy and reached for her own slice of lasagna and garlic bread. As one of four children, she'd learned that if she didn't move fast, she'd end the meal hungry. Seconds were for the quick and the bold. She had even better chances if she kept everyone else talking.

"Hey Seth, where's Zia Elena and Zio Tony?"

"They decided to extend their European holiday by a week. Apparently Spain was too tempting to miss."

"And Brandy?" Seth's girlfriend had become a regular fixture at their family dinners. How long would it take Seth to make things permanent? Sofia was betting under a year.

"She's working the evening shift at Flipped to cover for someone out sick. She's sorry to miss this."

"You'll take her a plate." Josephine scooped a square of lasagna onto a plate and set it aside, thereby decreasing the amount left to be fought over. Seth wiggled his eyebrows knowingly.

"Yes, ma'am. I sure will." There was bold avarice in his gaze as she moved the plate, and it gave him away.

"I will call her tomorrow to ask how it was."

His tone dropped comically like a scolded child. "Yes, ma'am."

Tucking in with vigor, Sofia moaned in delight. Her mother's signature spicy red sauce, made with only the freshest Gilroy garlic and the favored Montepulciano wine, burst on her tongue. The creamy ricotta soothed the fire in her mouth and the crispy brown edge bits crunched delightfully between her teeth, leaving behind a nutty goodness.

"God, Ma. This is delicious."

"Thank you, sweetheart. I wanted to do something a little special for your father's announcement." She raised her glass with a secret smile for her husband of forty years.

So that *was* it. Dad was finally going to join Ma in retirement. Ma had been office manager since Frankie had started kindergarten. After Gabe's death, she hadn't had the heart to keep the business going. Losing Gabe had brought her mortality into fine focus, and she wasn't going to waste another minute. She was determined to enjoy her retirement, preferably with Dad by her side. At least that's what Sofia had gathered from snippets of overheard conversations and not-so-whispered arguments.

Unfortunately, her mother's abrupt retirement had caused the bulk of her duties to fall into Sofia's lap. She could wish it wasn't so, but she certainly didn't begrudge her mother the time off. Losing her oldest child had shaken her badly. Sofia hoped she'd never see the day that something else shook Josephine Valenti to her core. Her father might bluster and bark, but everyone knew who ran this family. When the bedrock shook, no one was safe from the aftershocks.

About a year after Gabe's death, her mom had begun to work on her dad. Domenico Valenti was not an easy man to persuade, and these two years had passed with little change. Though Ma couldn't stop talking about all the travel she wanted to do, Dad had been no closer to letting go of the reins. Apparently, Jo had made some progress on that front.

"So, Ma, made any travel plans lately?" Sofia teased.

"You know I won't go anywhere without your father. But I was talking to Elena the other day." She switched her gaze to Seth as she spoke of his mother. "She was filling me in on all the details of their time in Italy. She was quite taken with all the vineyards. It sounds beautiful in the springtime. We'll see."

Dad cleared his throat, immediately drawing the attention of everyone at the table. He was a man used to being listened to and obeyed.

"I'm officially calling this family meeting to order."

The only sound breaking the silence was the occasional scrape of fork against plate.

"You all know that Jo and I have been talking about retiring for the last few years." Sofia looked down the table at Ma and saw the wide, warm smile that she reserved for her husband alone. Sofia was happy for her mother, but she couldn't help but think that this would mean even more duties would fall to her. Maybe if she positioned herself right though, she could convince him to leave her in charge. If she were running the show, she could hire more office staff, freeing herself up to return to her first love, interior design. As the oldest now, it only made sense for her to take the reins. Of course, Frankie and Enzo would still have a share of the company, but if she was the CEO, so to speak, she could turn it in the direction she'd been dreaming of. A kernel of hope warmed in her chest.

"I'm not convinced that the business is in a strong enough position for me to walk away. People come to us because of the reputation Tony and I spent our lives building. If we just leave, I worry that the work will drop off."

"But Dad, the Valley is booming!" This outburst from an impatient Frankie was cut off with a firm slice of Dad's hand.

"I also can't see a clear successor to take over running the business. So I've decided to kill all the birds with one stone. We're doing a TV show."

Forks halted halfway to their intended mouths. Wine glasses clunked back down to the table, un-sipped. Judging by the complete shock around the table, Dad had kept this secret well. The open bottles of Ma's favorite wine were beginning to make sense.

"What do you mean a TV show?" Her mother's smile was gone, and her voice had gone shrill, a tone usually reserved for broken vases and calls from the principal.

"A producer approached me a few weeks ago."

"A few WEEKS? You've been thinking about this for weeks and didn't see fit to discuss it with me? Does Tony know?"

Her father knew the futility of responding to this line of questioning from his wife. There was no good answer, so he simply continued talking as if the question had never been asked. "You know that HomeTV network? Well, they heard about our price guarantee, and saw some of our work at that director's house in Los Altos. They want to do a show about us. The concept is that we are a family business, helping families move into properties that they can afford in Silicon Valley. Because everything is so damn expensive, we are going to work on a tight budget and timeline to make these houses livable again. We're calling it Million-Dollar Starter Home. The couple buys the house. We do basic renovations, kitchen and bath, that sort of thing, on time and under budget with a blind reveal at the end."

"Why do we need a show?" Frankie piped up defensively. "What's wrong with the way we do things now? You know I want to run the business."

Really? This was the first Sofia was hearing of it.

"You're too young. You need more experience, and the pressure of the show will give you that, while bringing new clients in the door based on your reputations, not mine."

"So I'm basically out of this?" Lorenzo, Enzo for short, was their landscaping genius. He didn't seem too upset about this at all. He'd never been one to search out the spotlight. He'd never voiced an interest in running the larger business either, no matter how many times Dom had hinted.

"Not true. They want to feature easy curb appeal fixes."

"Damn it." Enzo's face fell.

"Where does that leave me?" Sofia was almost afraid to ask.

"Well, I'll need you to read through the contracts and make sure—"

"No, Dad. On the show."

"Well..." His pause said it all. He didn't have an answer she was going to like.

She pushed down the disappointment and anger and fought for her place. She could tend to her wounds later. "I want the design piece. I want to consult with the clients and create beautiful homes."

"The concept calls for simple but solid renovations under budget. This isn't the place to showcase your *creative* designs."

"You don't think I can do it. I can be creative *and* frugal."

"The network mentioned having approved designers..." Dom let his sentence finish with a deep sip of wine.

"And you don't approve of me? You said this was a family show. Why not let me use my skills?"

"How would you keep up with all of the day-to-day needs of the business? I don't think you have the experience to handle something of this scale."

"And whose fault is that?" Sofia muttered under her breath. He would never let her out of the corner he'd so lovingly backed her into. It was up to her to break free.

"What was that, young lady?"

Sofia looked to her mother for backup and found a blank frown where her smile had been. Still stunned by this betrayal, she would be no help arguing Dad down. Sofia knew she was pushing her luck, but if she didn't stand up for herself, she'd always regret it. She hadn't graduated at the top of her class to file receipts. This was just the challenge she needed to get out of her rut.

"Dad, I can make these basic houses into beautiful homes. You order paint and fixtures in bulk. You can't remake each house the same way on a TV show. Plus, if you hand over control to Hollywood designers, you know they're going to mess up the budget. I could really make them shine for the same cost. Give me a chance."

He sat back in his chair and crossed his hands over his chest. She knew she'd probably offended him, but this was too important to tiptoe around his fragile ego.

"We'll talk about this later."

Damn it. That was Dom Valenti code for *I'm done talking about this*, but at least it wasn't an outright no. She sat simmering in her seat in silent frustration. Seth stepped into the conversational gap.

"Is there a role for us? Nick and me?"

"Of course. We'll feature one of your custom pieces in every home."

Sure. Of course there was a plan for Seth. He'd get featured even though it had been a scant three months since he'd gotten his shit together. Sofia's blood boiled, and she shoved back from the table.

"Thanks for dinner, Ma. I just remembered. I need to be somewhere else." Not strictly a lie. Her mother didn't respond, still glaring at her husband, her meal untouched. Sofia dropped a kiss on her head as she walked by. "I'll see you tomorrow."

"Sofia, sit back down. We're not done with this meeting."

"I am. You don't have any plans that involve me, and I'm sure all the details will get dumped on my desk in the morning anyhow. So there's really no reason for me to sit here and listen to you dismiss my dreams. Good night, everybody." She strode into the dark, her heart a twisted bundle of anger and determination. She would find a way to take her rightful place, in the company and in this harebrained scheme, if it killed her.

CHAPTER 3

WHACK! WHACK! WHACK!

There was little better for working out frustrations than demolition day, and starting one on a Monday morning was perfect. Adrian wielded his sledgehammer with repetitive ease as he took down an old brick fire pit in the Nguyens' backyard. So far this morning, his sister had needed more money for college expenses since she'd be doing the summer semester as well, his mother had needed coffee, so he'd had to run to the store early, and his favorite pair of work jeans had split at the knee. On the bright side, they hadn't fallen behind on the Chu project thanks to Sofia's wrangling, so he could shift his crew easily to help Enzo with a little landscaping gig. They'd gotten the tiles down Saturday and let them set up Sunday. They could get back in this afternoon. He hoped his crappy morning would be the end of his bad luck. Dom and his crew were counting on him.

"Hey, man!" Enzo yelled from behind him, breaking his swing.

"Hey. What's up?"

"I'm trying to save as many of these bricks as possible for a reuse project. I don't know what's got you so pissed off, but don't take it out on my poor fire pit." Enzo laughed, lightening the dark mood that had gripped Adrian since Friday night. Speaking of...

"No problem. How did the big family meeting go?"

"Ugh. Shit show."

"That bad?"

"The worst, but I told Dad I wouldn't spill the beans. He wants to tell everyone himself."

"Jesus, Enzo."

Was he getting fired? Were they closing the firm? Would he be back at square one? In his position as crew chief, he'd been able to support his mother staying home to raise the girls, and put his little sisters through college. True, they'd gone to local state schools and community college, and he'd be paying off the loans for the next twenty years, but his job with Valenti Brothers had qualified them all for financial aid. Financial aid that his baby sister still needed. If he lost this job, the intricate web holding the family's finances together would unravel.

And it wasn't just his immediate family who would suffer. He'd also found work for his cousins and friends looking for stable jobs. Half of his neighborhood depended on Valenti Brothers for some part of their income. His fear must've shown on his face, because Enzo was quick to reassure him.

"Don't panic. It's just a big change. He's on his way here now, so you can ask him for yourself." Enzo bent to sift through the rubble for his precious bits of bricks.

"Thanks, man. Sorry about the bricks."

Adrian handed off the sledge and strode around the edge of the house, tugging off his leather work gloves and safety glasses as he went. Perfect timing. Dom's truck pulled into the drive and the boss man himself honked jauntily. He climbed down from the cab of his Ford F-150 and clapped his hand into Adrian's for a hearty handshake.

Passing Adrian a steaming cup of takeout coffee, Dom Valenti stood beside him, surveying the work site while having a no-eye-contact conversation in the manner of busy men.

"This yard is gonna be a showpiece."

"Yes, sir. Enzo has the touch."

"All cleared up on the Chu tiles?"

"Yep. We'll get them grouted today and the toilets installed this afternoon. Might need a little overtime, so we don't fall behind."

"Sounds good. We can afford a little overhead to keep the customer happy. Keep your two best guys late if you need to. No more than four hours though."

"Shouldn't even need that many, but sounds good."

A silence descended between them as a noisy backhoe trundled past. The yard was a well-organized hive of activity, a thing of beauty. Adrian was the first to break the peace. He had too much riding on this conversation to let the opportunity slide.

"So…is there anything else?"

"Enzo talk to you?" Dom's face revealed nothing.

"He said I should hear it from you."

Adrian turned, forcing the older man to face him or be rude. Even though at six feet two inches Adrian was taller than him, Dom Valenti was a man he looked up to. If he was getting the axe, he wanted to hear it face to face.

"You know Jojo's been after me to retire ever since…she stepped back from the business."

Adrian had been around long enough to hear what hadn't been said. *Since Gabe died.* Since everything had changed. Since the Valenti clan had lost their eldest son to the war in Iraq.

"I've been wanting to talk to you about that." Adrian gathered his words carefully around his fledgling dream. He had a feeling it was now or never. "I want in."

"How so?" Dom locked eyes with him. He definitely had the old man's attention now.

"I want to buy in. I've worked my entire adult life for this company, and you couldn't leave it in better hands."

"We'll see how you feel after you hear my announcement."

"It's not that you're retiring?"

"Not yet. I wanted to give the company one last boost before I step down. Your idea has merit though. I'll have to think about it."

"That's fair. What's this boost?"

"We're doing a TV show, and I need you on board. We're gonna have film crews crawling all over the Shah project when we break ground, to film the pilot and a sizzle reel, whatever the hell that is."

"TV? What the hell do I know about TV?"

"Probably as much as I do, but you know good construction, and you're good at explaining things to our younger guys. Just talk to the cameraman like he's a grunt, and it'll be fine. The idea is to explain how we do renos that look good without going over budget."

"Jesus, Dom. I thought you were going to shut down the business or lay me off. This is making my head spin."

"Let it spin awhile. You think about my idea, and I'll think about yours. Fi should be done going through the contracts soon. I'll tell her to walk you through it. If this takes off, it could be a big win for everyone."

If Dom needed Adrian on board, there was very little to think about. He might be uncomfortable with the idea of being on camera, but he'd do it anyway.

After his own father had been deported, he'd had to grow up fast. The first man to give him a chance had been Domenico Valenti. If there was anyone in the world who deserved his loyalty outside of his family, it was this man. He'd become something of a surrogate father in the years in between, giving Adrian a taste of the approval and stability he'd craved.

Adrian could see the potential. And if business boomed, well, that was good for everyone. If he could just see his littlest sister through college, he'd be free and clear to start his own family. Obviously, he'd need to find the right woman first, but he hadn't even been looking. Time for that to change. Maybe.

His mom was comfortable in her house, which he owned outright. When the foreclosure had gone up on his block, he jumped at the chance and bought the dump cheap. Renovations made possible by Valenti Brothers' overtime paychecks and his own hard labor had made the house livable, and as the girls began working, he'd had more cash to pay off the mortgage. It was small and not in the greatest neighborhood, but it had ridden the rising tide of home prices in the area anyhow. He'd already gained enough equity to consider approaching Dom about buying in. He loved his mom and sisters, but he wanted his own place, a wife, kids in the yard. He was thirty, and feeling the pinch to get started. He'd delayed as long as he was still needed to play big brother for his sisters, but the prospect of more money pulled his own dreams into sharper focus.

"I'll talk to Sofia. Thanks, Dom, for thinking about it."

"If there's anyone in the world who's earned it, it's you. But I'm not the only decision maker. We've always been family first, but there's no reason that can't change."

EVERYTHING WAS CHANGING, and Sofia could barely keep up. As she'd predicted, the contracts for the show had landed on her desk with a disheartening thud. Her father had dropped them off Monday at the end of the day, and she had deliberately not looked at them or him. Tuesday morning, though, they were still waiting. Armed with her coffee and fast food breakfast sandwich, she dug in, looking for any opportunity to turn this tide in her favor.

The contract for the pilot and sizzle reel seemed pretty

straightforward. The crew would follow them around job sites, the office, and family functions. The production company would retain rights to use any footage gathered. Each main actor would receive a per diem payout, but ancillary talent wouldn't be compensated beyond a normal salary. They'd negotiated a twenty-five percent fee paid back to the production company on any branded merchandise lines they might do, but since they didn't have anything of that nature going, Sofia wasn't too bothered by it. The ten percent of increased business profits was more worrisome, and she made a note to discuss it with her dad. The production staff would approve the homeowner's designer for the projects, and Valenti Brothers would handle the construction.

Sofia drew a line through that part of the contract.

"Sofia Valenti will do the initial designs for all properties and have first right of refusal, subject to approval by the production company and homeowners," she muttered as she wrote. This was it, her window, her chance to shine. To show her dad that she had the chops to do more than paperwork. To reclaim her creativity. If she had to be sneaky to get her shot, then so be it.

When Adrian knocked on her partially open door, she jumped like a teenager caught cheating on an exam. *Guilty much?* She wouldn't have to do this if only her dad would listen.

"Adrian! You startled me."

"Sorry, *querida*, I didn't mean to. Dom said you'd walk me through the TV contracts. Is now a good time?"

She pushed aside her irritation over the casual endearment. She spent her days around construction workers. She'd certainly gotten worse. She wasn't going to let him fluster her, even if those golden brown eyes had a tendency to throw her off. It was criminal for a man to have lashes that long. He folded his long, rangy frame into the chair across from her desk before she'd even summoned an answer. When he crossed his arms and his biceps

31

flexed beneath the short sleeves of his T-shirt, Sofia's mouth went dry and her thoughts scattered.

Down, girl. He's not for you. The truth of that statement helped her find the thread.

"Sure, make yourself at home." Her sarcasm was wasted. He just grinned at her.

"Got any coffee?"

"Yes, I do." She raised her full mug along with her eyebrow and took a lukewarm sip. "If you want a cup, there's some in the kitchen."

"Good to know. I'm dragging today."

All she wanted was to win one point with him, one little jab to land home so she could feel like she'd stood up for herself. He hit all of her nerves, and he didn't even seem to notice. Maybe he was just used to women jumping to do his bidding. She let her irritation creep into her voice. Otherwise it would build up inside until she snapped at some poor, unsuspecting whipping boy. No, much better to point her anger where it belonged. "Oh? Late night? You should know better than to go out partying on a work night." *Damn it. Where had that thought come from?* Now she had a picture of him out with some beautiful, faceless woman with an itty-bitty waist and mile-long legs at some club. Of course that's the kind of woman he'd date. His beauty equivalent. Not that she was jealous or anything.

Damn it, again. Sofia's subconscious kept betraying her. Her own recent drought was weighing on her heart, but that wasn't his fault.

Not his problem to solve either, she firmly reminded her racing pulse.

"No, just family stuff, and then finding out about the show, and pitching my proposal to your dad. Yesterday was a roller coaster."

Sofia rummaged in her snack drawer for a second and tossed a Kit Kat in his lap. His eyebrows rose in question.

"Gimme a break..." Sofia sang the Kit Kat theme song. "You looked like you could use one. Now what's this proposal?"

He grinned and snapped into the crispy chocolate. "I told Dom that I want to buy in when he retires. I want to help run this place. He said he'd think about it."

Shock pushed Sofia back in her chair. She'd always assumed Valenti Brothers would stay in the family. It was a family-owned and -operated business, after all. She had been counting on her siblings and cousin understanding when she hired on office staff so she could tackle more design projects. Would Dom sell the business to Adrian outright? Would Adrian become her boss? Or would they have to learn to run a business together as part of a five-way split? She couldn't deny that Adrian was an extremely talented and loyal employee, but if he had more control of the company, it would change the dynamic drastically. Would his casual "baby" and "beautiful" endearments take on a different tone? And since when did her father make big decisions like this without consulting the family first? Yesterday a TV show, today a new partnership? What was going on? Why was he changing so many things at once?

"Do you have a problem with that?" His deep voice pulled her from her scrambling thoughts.

She grasped at anything she was thinking that would be appropriate to say out loud. "Uh, no, but isn't this kind of sudden?"

"I've been working here for twelve years. I'm good at what I do, and I want to own that. Again, is there a problem?"

Sofia knew she looked like a fish out of water, mouth open as she gasped for the right words. "You never mentioned this to me. I'm just surprised. Give me a minute to catch up."

"If this is about me not being family—"

"It's not." She answered too quickly, and he finished his sentence with a grin.

"We could always fix that." He wiggled his eyebrows comically, and she wasn't quick enough to suppress the laugh.

"Don't be an ass. It's just a lot to think through. We've done things one way my entire life. Fresh ideas aren't necessarily a bad thing. I just need to think things through before I give an opinion." Maybe this could work for her after all. If she was the one in favor, backing him up, would he do the same for her? Or would he continue to be oblivious to her inner struggles? *Hmm.*

Adrian cleared his throat, pulling her back from her plotting.

"So about this contract. The one that actually exists…"

"It's pretty straightforward. You agree to allow cameras to follow you around job sites, the office, and home. This is just for the pilot and a teaser short, so it's a short-term contract but it includes an exclusive option on the larger contract if it gets picked up. You walk the viewer through the steps of the renovation." She flipped to the pages involving his particulars. "Included is a supplemental bonus to your current salary."

A bonus she wouldn't get since she wasn't listed on the main talent list. That burned, but she wasn't going to argue. She was already pushing her luck to get listed as the designer. And if that side of her career took off, the money would sort itself out.

"Well, babe, I gotta say, more money always sounds good to me."

Ugh. It's like he does it without even thinking. She passed him the paperwork and pointed to the pertinent sections.

"I just started going through this. Give it a read-through, and tell me if you see any red flags. I'm going to refill my coffee."

She needed a minute to calm her swirling thoughts, and sitting in a small room with a man who simultaneously generated a low-level buzz of attraction while also making her want to punch him in the stomach was not helping. His proposal had stunned her, and she'd not responded well. She pulled down another mug out of force of habit and filled it before topping hers off as well. She added one sugar and a healthy dollop of cream to his, fake sugar and cream to her own.

All done, but nowhere near ready to return, she braced her hands on the peacock granite countertop, stretched her arms long and dropped her head between them. She lengthened her spine and took a deep breath, aiming for some of the peace she'd felt when she'd dropped into a yoga class with Brandy.

Change itself was nothing to fear. So what if most of the changes in her life had been awful? That didn't mean these changes were going to be bad, too. She could handle whatever needed handling. She'd managed before, and she could do it again. And she was absolutely full of crap. She was three seconds from panicking, and her deep-breathing exercises were getting trapped in her clenching throat.

"Hey, are you okay?" Adrian's deep, husky voice skittered up her spine, leaving a trail of goose bumps that didn't subside when she jumped and squealed.

Why did this man have the power to make her feel like a twelve-year-old girl? She spun to face him, only to find that he'd invaded the space she'd cleared and was reaching for her shoulder, as if to steady her. She backed away swiftly, bumping into the counter and rattling the cups. Remembering why she'd come to the kitchen in the first place, she handed him the coffee she'd made him, being careful not to scald herself with a brush of his fingertips. She could pick apart the ridiculousness of her response later.

"Yeah, I'm fine." She retreated into a fortifying sip of her own coffee.

He mirrored her sip and stepped back as well. *Message finally freaking received. Good.*

"You know how I take my coffee?" He grinned as if this detail somehow meant something special.

"I know everyone's coffee order. Have you not noticed who keeps the lists for meeting coffee runs? Or who is constantly being charged with stocking the kitchen? Or did you just think a magical caffeine fairy came in at night and brought lattes to all the good little boys?" She tried once again to take him down a peg while setting him straight. She couldn't have him thinking that she'd been watching him, paying attention to his personal preferences. Even if she had.

Once again, her sarcasm flew right over his head. He raised the contract in his hand and held it out to her.

"Listen, I tried to read through this, but it might as well be written in Latin. Can you walk me through the specifics?"

"I just got it myself. Give me a day or two to really pick it apart, and I'll fill you in."

"Thanks, angel. That sounds good." He tossed the contract on the break room table, supremely confident, coffee in hand.

She'd wager he hadn't even heard the "Sure thing" she'd managed through clenched teeth. How could she be so attracted to someone who pissed her off so royally?

Good thing he didn't know, or he'd be insufferable.

CHAPTER 4

Two days later, Sofia's reaction was still troubling Adrian. He shifted in the driver's seat of his pickup truck. His wipers flipped the early spring rain aside as he reached for the paperwork he needed to complete for her. Why was she so skittish around him? She almost seemed nervous to be alone in a room with him? He'd tried to put her at ease, by calling her sweet names, by joking, by being as non-threatening as possible, but still she backed away.

It didn't bode well for becoming a partner if the woman who ran the show couldn't stand to work with him. Sure, Dom might be the man with the name on the sign, but Adrian knew who kept the lights on and the paychecks coming. How could he convince her to back his plan? He drew a blank and tried to turn his attention back to the order forms in his hands.

It also didn't help that he had trouble keeping his mind strictly on business when she was around. He'd walked into that break room and nearly swallowed his tongue. She'd been bent over at the waist, stretching her rear toward the door in what he was sure she considered sensible leggings. He thought they were the sexiest item of clothing he'd ever seen, and was jealous that they got to touch the luscious curve of her ass, while he had to keep his hands to himself. It had taken all of his control to remember that he'd gone in there to ask for help, not to push her against the cabinets and show her exactly how much he wanted her.

She had the same good girl face she'd had since high school, all innocence and smiles, but her body had changed. No longer a girl, she was a woman built to drive a man insane. When she opened her mouth, and the sass and sarcasm came spilling out, he was tempted to grin. But he reminded himself to play nice and keep his distance. But just because he was determined not to act didn't mean he couldn't still look. She wore these sweaters he was sure looked conservative on a hanger, but when they were stretched over her mouthwatering curves... *Jesus Christ. I'm daydreaming about her sweaters...* As his mind helpfully supplied a montage of all of the sweaters she'd ever worn, he struggled to put his attraction away.

When he'd started with the company, she'd been in high school, the daughter of his boss, and firmly off-limits despite being only two years his junior. He'd crushed hard, and if he'd met her while he had still been in school a few months earlier, he would have asked her out. But dealing with his father's deportation and having to drop out to work, he'd put girls on the back burner. Besides, he couldn't afford to screw up the lucky break he'd gotten working for the Valentis. While she'd gone away to college, he had put his head down and worked his way up to crew boss. Now, she was a woman, with a quick mind he admired and a curvy body he desired, and she was more off-limits than ever.

He sat back in the chaos of his truck and ran a hand over his face, as if that could erase the naughty thoughts that kept pushing to the forefront. He needed to tackle the paperwork Sofia would need for the next big bid, and the rain gave him the perfect window. He hovered his hand over the stack of papers on the dash, moving left and right, before diving into the stack and coming out with the exact form he needed. To the outside eye, organization was not his strong suit, but he could find anything he was looking for. He just needed to see everything so he could remember where things were. As busy as they were, filing was a waste of time that was better spent hanging drywall.

He blamed the busy season, the constant interruptions, the second-language factor, the stupid vendor websites that wouldn't load on his phone—but he just plain hated paperwork. He was good with his hands and had an eye for detail. Ask him about any open job, and he could tell you anything you needed to know, from dimensions to finishes. But words and numbers did not like to go from his brain to the page easily. He'd play to his strengths, thank you very much. He tossed the unfinished bid form back on top of the pile and ran his hands through his hair, unable to focus with Sofia still on his mind.

He spooked her somehow, and no matter how much he longed to run his hands over her lovely hips, no good would come from hitting on and striking out with the boss's daughter. Too many people were depending on him to make the most of his career to risk her rejection. She could crush his goals with a well placed "no" at the dinner table. She worked with contractors all day. Given that she was built like a fucking brick house, Adrian was sure that she shot down unwanted advances all day long. He wouldn't put himself in that position no matter how many more pleasant positions he imagined her in.

His phone buzzed in his hand and her name flashed across the screen, as if his dirty thoughts had summoned her. He let it ring twice while he pulled himself together.

"Hey, I put together a cheat sheet on the TV contract. Do you have time to go over it today?"

"I'm all the way down in Almaden Valley. I wasn't going to go back into the office before I go home." He certainly didn't want to see her in his, uh, current state. Just hearing her voice was making things harder.

"Can I meet you halfway? I really need to get these signed so we can get the ball rolling. The producer keeps calling me. I guess they're really excited."

"Okay, sure. Have you eaten?"

"What?"

"If I'm making you drive a half hour out of your way, the least I can do is buy you dinner. Do you know the Black Bear Diner? On El Camino?"

"Yeah, it's a favorite of mine." He knew that but wasn't going to say so for fear of going too far.

"Great. I'll see you there around six."

See? He could keep it professional if he tried. And now he'd gotten a dinner date out of it.

No. He got firm with his inner horny devil. *Not a date. A business meeting. One I can't afford to blow.*

∽

WHEN SOFIA finally got to the Black Bear Diner after battling Bay Area rush hour traffic, Adrian was already seated at the table. She pulled her hair back into a fresh ponytail after the drive and tugged her sweater back down over her hips. She had nothing to be nervous about. This was just coffee and contracts. He had his hands curled around one of the two cups of coffee before him, and she briefly envied that stoneware mug before pushing away those unprofessional thoughts. He rose to meet her when she approached the table.

"Hey, gorgeous. I'm ashamed to say, I don't know how you like your coffee so I left it black, but asked for everything."

Sofia rolled her eyes at both the endearment and the idea that anyone would know how she took her coffee. He was after something, and she wasn't in the mood for his bullshit, no matter how prettily delivered.

"Cream, one fake sugar, the green one if they have it."

She reached for the coffee, but his hand closed over hers and she jerked back, singed.

"Please, sit down. I'll do it." She sat and watched, faintly stunned as he prepared her coffee just right. When was the last time someone had taken care of something as simple as making her coffee? Too long ago to remember. She had to remind the flutters in her belly that it was a simple gesture, certainly nothing to read into, but she appreciated it all the same. He slid the drink in front of her, and stood while she sipped.

"It's perfect."

"Good." Apparently satisfied that he'd done the job well, he sat back down and sipped his own coffee. "So, contracts?"

Right to business. Of course, because this isn't anything but a work meeting. She bent to dig the papers out of her massive purse and when she rose, Adrian's gaze was significantly lower than her chin. She was usually very careful about keeping her 40DDs covered, but her V-neck sweater must've given him quite the show when she'd leaned over. Her cheeks flushed crimson, but she couldn't tell if her blush was the usual one of embarrassment over her body or one of pleasure over the blatant male desire she saw in his eyes. Maybe a weird combination of the two? She sure as hell didn't know how she felt about that. She fell back on her defensive habits honed over her years working with construction grunts. She crossed her arms across her chest to symbolically block his view. Her cough and raised eyebrow drew his eyes farther north.

When he did look her in the eye, the desire was carefully banked, and Sofia could tell she had his attention where she wanted it.

"The contracts. Basically, you agree to play nice for the cameras and explain what you're doing to the viewers at home. You also have to agree to work within their timelines and shooting schedules. They have certain dates they need certain

41

footage by, etc. Then we pay your wages, insurance, retirement, as usual, plus an added stipend from the show."

"So what happens if the project goes over forty a week? Do my guys get paid overtime?"

"Hmm, I'm not sure. Let me check." She pulled her cheater glasses from her purse and perched them on her nose before scanning the documents in the dim light. "No, it doesn't cover that. They are considered ancillary and do not get any increased stipend. I assume Dad would continue to pay regular overtime hours though."

"You assume? Would my crew have any hour limits? Like max ten a day?"

"No. They'd agree to work until the required task was done."

"I can't sign this."

"What? What do you mean?"

"You are asking me to sign away their rights and protections. These guys will be taking the brunt of the workload, and this doesn't even guarantee they will get paid what they're making now. Did you talk about any of this with Dom?"

The truth rankled, but she hadn't seen this pitfall, and she hadn't seen hide nor hair of her father since he'd dropped off the contract on Monday.

"I'm sure it's just an oversight."

"I can't sign this without his assurances, and I need to talk to the guys first."

"Damn it." She pinched the bridge of her nose and calculated delays. "I can't imagine your guys will be called on to do all that much overtime. Your projects always run on time."

"But this contract says that if we do run late, we have no choice but to stay until it's done. These men have lives, families, and second jobs that may suffer. They deserve the right to choose." His voice had gone hard, and she realized she'd sounded pushy and petulant. Just because she wanted to move the contracts through quickly and without too much scrutiny didn't mean it was the right thing for everyone involved. That realization didn't make it any easier to tamp down her frustrations.

"You're right. Of course they do. I just thought I'd be able to get these contracts done today."

She looked up and took off her glasses. An almost wistful grin stretched his face, and that damn dimple that made her knees weak was winking at her.

"What? Do I have something on my face?" She wiped her upper lip.

"No, *querida*, I just like the way you look in glasses. I've always had a thing for smart women."

Jesus, laying it on a little thick... Enough was enough. "Listen, you don't have to do that."

"Do what?"

"Compliment me, call me beautiful or gorgeous or *querida*. It's crap and you know it."

He paused for a moment, and in that silence Sofia watched confusion turn to frustration.

"But it's what I see."

"Oh, please. Look at me." She gestured to the body she loved and hated daily. Since Gabe had died and her well-organized world had fallen apart, she'd gained thirty pounds. On her already petite frame, this had pushed her from curvy to overweight. She hated not fitting into her cute clothes anymore, but buying new ones in a larger size felt like giving up. She couldn't let herself get comfortable at the weight she was now, and the pinching waistbands and gapping shirts made sure she felt every unwanted inch. Sweaters were the only thing that covered her well enough to hide her ill-fitting jeans.

She needed to get serious about losing the weight. Tomorrow. Next week, for sure. But right now, she just needed him to stop reminding her of everything she'd lost.

"You can't fire me, right?"

"No, I can't."

43

He sat silent for another moment, and she could almost see him weighing his words.

"Then I will tell you exactly what I see when I look at you. I see tempting blue-gray eyes that sparkle with intelligence and humor behind glasses that make me dream about naughty librarians. I see sexy blonde hair that you wear pulled back in a tight ponytail too often, making my hands itch to let it down. I get distracted when you walk into the room. Every curve makes me want to look, to touch, to savor. I see a pretty girl I used to know who has grown into a beautiful woman I'd like to know better."

She had no words, no response, no idea that those thoughts had been hiding behind his casual endearments. She had no script for this situation because never in a million years could she have seen this coming. Her mouth dropped open but nothing came out past the lump of lust in her throat.

He shook his head. "I knew I shouldn't have said anything. Forget it, and I will call you Fi like everyone else. No. No, I can't give you the nickname of a poodle. But I will watch my words." He rose from the table and gathered up the papers she'd brought for him. "I didn't mean to make you uncomfortable. I'll talk to my guys tonight, and let you know about the contracts in the morning."

Before she could marshal her whirling thoughts into phrases, he was gone. *Damn it!* He'd gone and crossed her wires, but he hadn't given her a chance to untangle her tongue.

She turned her glasses over in her hand. Would she ever look at her specs the same way again?

He'd probably been insulted that she hadn't flirted back or at least said thank you, but she'd been too busy swallowing her own tongue in shock.

Maybe it was for the best. She couldn't deny that she found him attractive, too. But knowing he felt the same didn't change the fact that they worked together. It was still a bad idea.

"Can I get you anything to eat, hon?" The waitress looked at her with pity in her tired eyes, and Sofia caved to impulse. She deserved a little pick-me-up after letting that piece of man-candy walk out the door.

"One of your chocolate cream pies, please."

"You bet."

Sofia smoothed a hand over her tight ponytail, the images he'd painted still vivid in her mind. Dating him might be a bad idea, but his fantasy intrigued her, and Sofia was certain she'd be dreaming of the library later.

CHAPTER 5

"I GUESS you're all wondering why I called you over here tonight."

Adrian sat at his mother's table, surrounded by anxious faces. The last-minute call had produced more anxiety than he'd intended, but it couldn't be helped. His mother, God bless her, had responded by raiding her freezer so at least everyone had a plate of her famous enchiladas to soothe them. Graciela Villanueva never let a friend go hungry.

Children up past their bedtime chased each other around the living room packed with well-loved furniture, while their mothers chatted in the homey kitchen and brought more shared dishes that had been intended for their own tables into the dining room. The men, ranging in age from seventeen to fifty-six, were gathered around the table, waiting for him to speak. The weight of responsibility felt heavy on his shoulders tonight. This was his crew, his community, and he knew they were counting on him to lead them straight.

"So, you've heard about this TV idea?" Heads nodded solemnly as he scanned the room. "I talked to Sofia today, and I have some concerns. You will have to decide if you want to sign the contracts or not."

"Tell us." This came from Alonzo, an older man who said little but had seen a lot.

"They have strict timelines and filming dates. The work gets done on camera, and we have to follow their direction as well as Dom's. Your pay will still come directly from Valenti Brothers at the same rates you get now." He paused and waited for the questions to come.

"So we have to work all the hours they say?" Rico raised his voice above the murmurs.

"We have to get the jobs done on their schedule. It doesn't say we all have to stay."

"And they don't have to pay us overtime or extra for the show?"

"No, you still get overtime from Dom, but nothing extra for the show."

"It sounds like a lot of extra work for no extra money. I mean, we don't stand to benefit if the show does well either. What if we say no? Do we lose our jobs?" Rico was quick to tease out the problems Adrian had foreseen.

"For now, I could try to switch you to Frankie's crew or keep you on the other projects we have running. But if the pilot gets picked up, and we start doing only TV houses? I can't say."

"Man, you know I'm busting my ass on two jobs already. I can't be late because of some bullshit director!"

A chorus of agreement rose up in response to Rico's comment. Adrian raised a hand and quiet slowly fell.

"I know, man. I know. So here's what we do. One, don't panic. Two, bust our asses to get our shit done on time like we always do. Three, if we do need to stay, it will be me and anyone who can afford to stay. Even if that means it's just me."

"That's not fair to you though," Alonzo pointed out.

"If it means everyone keeps their employers happy and their families fed, I don't care. I can handle it."

He pushed aside a vision of a wife and children who suddenly

47

had startling blond hair. He'd find the time for his own family eventually. Somehow. The needs of his found family were more important right now.

Conversation continued as his guys hashed out how to make this work with their crewmates and spouses. Angry grumbles and soothing reason flowed back and forth, as partners figured out the details and made plans for their futures together. Sitting in silence, waiting, Adrian felt jealousy creep around the edges. He would do what was best for his family, as he always did, but being the guy in charge was getting old. He was ready for a partner to help shoulder the load.

This TV deal had been an unexpected complication to his plan, but as any good builder would say, complications are just part of the business. And if approached correctly, they become opportunities. If he could make this work, it could really benefit his entire community. More demand meant more work meant more jobs, and he was the guy hiring.

His mom came and rested her head on top of his.

"¿Està bien, mijo?"

"*Si, Mamá*. It's a solid deal, if we can make it work."

"You're a good boy, Adrian. A good son. Always fixing things for everyone else. Who will fix things for you?" She ran her hands down over his hair to rest on his shoulders as she had for as long as he could remember, and he leaned into the comfort.

"I'm fine, Mamá. I don't need anything fixed." The reassurance rolled off his tongue even as the image of a stunned Sofia floated through his mind. Nothing to fix except a few scratches to his pride. He would be just fine.

~

WHEN ADRIAN STRODE through the door of the office an hour early Thursday morning with a mocha in hand, he was firmly in fix-it land. He had his contract requests figured out and his apology for what he'd said memorized. He was prepared to say and do what ever he needed to get Sofia to agree. He had a packed day ahead of him so he was hoping to get in, apologize, convince her, and get out.

His plan to wait in her office and surprise her backfired when he opened her door and found her already sitting at her desk, although slouching was a better word for her posture. It wasn't until she failed to respond to his *"Buenos dias"* that he realized she was asleep in her chair. Setting the coffee down on her desk, he took a moment to watch her. She was so rarely still. How had he missed that sexy little mole high on her cheek or the way her lashes, much darker than her hair, brushed her cheek when they closed? He fantasized about making those lashes flutter closed with his kiss and sighed. Sleeping beauty, indeed, but he was no prince.

Pushing aside his desire, he ran a hand down her arm to wake her.

"Princesa, wake up..."

Those lashes fluttering open was just as sexy as he'd imagined in reverse, and his pulse leapt in response. He jerked his hand back from her arm and leaned on the backs of his hands against her desk, as if that would keep his desire to touch in check.

"Adrian? What are you doing here?" Her voice cracked with sleepy confusion. Why the hell did he find that sexy?

He pushed the coffee toward her. "I brought a peace offering."

She took a sip and sighed her pleasure, yet another image that he was sure would haunt him later.

"Were we at war?"

"No, but we do have a difficult conversation to have."

"So this is a bribe?"

"More like stacking my deck for a good mood before we get started."

She took another sip and moaned again. "Your strategy is sound. This is definitely improving my mood. I came in early to try and get ahead on the day, but I must have fallen asleep." She stood and stretched, raising her arms high over her head, her breasts showing him a hint of their fullness above the neckline of her T-shirt. She addled his brain without even trying, which was the reason his next words slipped past his filter.

"You looked like Sleeping Beauty resting in her tower."

"Sleeping Beauty, huh? So where's my magical kiss?"

He knew she was being flip and sarcastic, but desire made him stare at her lips and second-guess. Did she mean that? Had Sofia Valenti just asked him for a kiss? The silence between them stretched. The tension pulled between them, like a rubber band being cranked tighter and tighter until it twisted in on itself, drawing him in. He took a step closer so that they were inches apart. The heat coming off her skin, the smell of sinful coffee and chocolate on her less-than-steady exhale, the banked desire in her eyes—all combined to sink the last of his resistance.

"As you wish." When she didn't back away, he threaded his greedy fingers through her golden hair, anchoring her where he needed her, and poured all of his desire into the kiss. This was no polite peck, no gentle exploration. This was a dam breaking beneath the weight of years of repressed attraction. This was a flood of greed, rushing to discover the plump texture of her lips, the rich and toasty taste of the mocha on her tongue, the melody of her sighs.

Part of him hoped that the kiss would wake her up to the potential between them. The other part of him worried that he was screwing everything up. That was the part he muzzled when she moaned and sagged against him, her spine going limp. With one hand still in her hair, he wrapped the other around her waist to pull her in close, to give her the support of his body and permission to use it. If she felt how much she turned him on, even better. This kiss was quickly outpacing his imagination, and all he could think was *more*.

When her hands speared into his hair and gripped tightly, he lost his own battle for balance and slid both hands down to her ass as he fell back against her desk, holding on for dear life. He kneaded her ass with his fingers, pulling her hips tight against his and helplessly tilting his pelvis forward.

The pressure of her belly sliding against his cock was divine but short-lived, because she gasped, breaking the kiss. Sanity returned to her eyes as she stepped back from him and stumbled, falling into her chair. She couldn't get away from him fast enough. Damn. He'd let his cock do the thinking and had fucked it all up. Time for damage control.

"What was that?" She couldn't even look him in the eye. Her gaze darted from his belt buckle to her desk to the door and back. He could read the panic and regret on her face.

Shit. He needed to recover, and fast. Which tactic did he choose? Humor? Charm? Ignorance? Anything but the truth, which was she'd just ripped a healthy chunk of his heart out with her retreat. "Just your good morning kiss, *princesa*. Feeling more awake?"

"I'm not the only one who *woke up* with that kiss."

She glanced at the tent in his jeans. A blush colored her cheeks, before she hid her lips behind the mocha. He'd never been jealous of a piece of plastic before, but watching her lips, still rosy and slick from his kisses, caressing the edge of the cup nearly sent him over the edge. He had to get some space between them so his big head could take over the thinking again.

He backed away from her, despite every fiber of his being protesting, and sat in the chair across from her, putting the big wooden desk between them. He watched the concerns she wasn't saying out loud cycle through her mind, as she shuffled and stacked papers together on her desk and fidgeted with the hem of her shirt. He couldn't deny that it gave him a little buzz of pleasure to know he'd made her nervous. He could work with that.

"We can't do that again." She still wasn't looking at him.

"Why not?" The question was out before he could think twice about whether he actually wanted to know the answer.

"We work together. We have a lot of things happening right now, between the show, your proposal, my plans... I just don't think it's wise."

"How did your parents ever manage?" He could understand where she was coming from, but the pulsing in his lap had yet to subside and his frustration came out as sarcasm.

"They aren't managing very well right now, because this business got all twisted up in their marriage."

"We are not your parents."

"You're the one who brought them up. I just think it would be smart not to rock the boat while everything else is already up in the air."

"One question—did you enjoy that kiss?"

Her blush deepened, and though she didn't speak, he caught the slight nod of her head.

"So, this isn't a no. It's a not-right-now. I can work with that."

"No, no, no. This isn't some challenge for you to work on. I need a truce." She held up her hands as if she could stop the train of thought he was on.

"A truce. Are we negotiating terms here, Sofia?"

"Sure. I need your help making sure this pilot episode is a success, and your promise not to distract me with more of that." She fluttered her hand in the direction of his lap, and he couldn't suppress his grin.

"I need your help convincing your dad about my proposal, and taking care of my crews in the contract. In return, I promise to keep all of this"—he fluttered his hands over his lap—"away from that." He wiggled his fingers at her chest and earned a laugh.

"I'll think about it."

"Not good enough, Sofia. If I'm going to ignore the way I feel about you, I'm going to need a powerful motivation."

"Okay, deal."

"I also need a deadline. How long does this truce last?" *Please don't say forever...*

"Until things settle down. This...thing...between us, it took me by surprise. I'm not saying I didn't enjoy the hell out of that kiss, just that I can't handle anything else right now."

"Okay, Sofia. You have your truce. I'll help you get this pilot to succeed, and you'll help me convince your father that I deserve a chance to buy in. I'll keep my hands to myself until you ask me not to." He paused and leaned closer to her, gratified when her eyes focused on his lips. "Just know that every time I see you, I'll be thinking of this kiss, waiting for the day I get to do it again." He reached across the desk and offered his hand to shake on it. When she took it, warmth raced up his arm at her touch, and he couldn't resist pulling her hand to his lips for a quick kiss to seal their bargain.

With that, he stood and walked out the door. He'd call her later about the contract details. If he didn't get some distance and quick, their truce wouldn't last the next three minutes.

CHAPTER 6

Three weeks later

"Sofia, I need your help." Jake Ryland cornered her in her office and shut the door.

"With what?" She slid her ever-present stack of papers to the side and gave him her full attention.

"It's your dad."

Leaning back in her chair, Sofia let out a sharp bark of a laugh. "If you think I've got any influence over that man, you're crazy."

Jake dropped into the chair across from her desk and handed her his tablet. "This is the sizzle reel."

Sofia tapped the white triangle and saw their recent construction projects come to life on the screen. Punchy music overlaid the introduction shots of her parents, Frankie, and Enzo. It even showed a clip of her talking with Adrian. Damn, the camera loved him. He looked good enough to eat, and she let her mind wander down that pleasant path a moment.

"Here it comes." Jake drew her attention back to the opening scene. Her father stood at an angle with the Shahs in his office. Had he tweaked his back again? She'd never seen her father hold himself so still unless he was in pain.

"Hello." His voice was as flat as paint primer.

"Hello." The Shahs replied together, all smiles.

"We will give you a great house under budget and on time. Great house. No problem."

Maybe he was in pain. This was certainly painful to watch. He was reciting the show pitch and stumbling over it. Dom Valenti, family patriarch and veteran contractor, was pale and shaky. He looked seconds from passing out.

"Breathe, Dad," Sofia muttered aloud.

"I don't think he did for that entire segment." Jake braced his elbows on the desk and cupped his head in his hands. "What a mess!"

When the shot shifted to her and Adrian joking, the sizzle reel found its sizzle again. Was the attraction between them that obvious to everyone else, or was she seeing more than she had before? The rest of the extended commercial looked fine, until Dom came on screen again.

"And that's why I think you should make Million-Dollar Starter Home a show. Thank you." He sounded like the end of every bad third grade persuasive essay. He did not sound like the confident owner of his own construction firm who deserved to have millions invested in his show idea.

"So he needs some coaching..." Sofia tried to minimize what was clearly a fiasco. If Dom couldn't perform on camera, this show was going to tank. He was Valenti Brothers. This was his baby.

"That *was* with coaching. Listen, Sofia, now that you're doing most of the design work, I think it would be best for you to be the voice of the company. You seem comfortable on camera, and..."

"And anyone would be better than that," she said.

"I was going to say, and it gives you a chance to showcase your brand. But yes, that too."

Sofia could see the potential. If she got bumped up to a major role, her designs would have to take center stage. Dom wouldn't be able to dismiss them if they were key to the show. Plus, she'd be in a better position to negotiate what she wanted in the next contracts if the show got picked up.

"Who's going to tell Dad?"

"Let me figure that out. But you'll do it?"

"I'll do it."

～

"AND HERE IS YOUR NEW KITCHEN!" Sofia forced enthusiasm into her voice. Why had she agreed to do this? Farha and Gautam Shah sat kitty-corner across the table from her at an awkward angle and oohed and ahhed for the third time as she walked them through the Virtual Design CAD rendering of their new space. Again. Apparently the lighting had been off in the first take, and her hair had looked funny in the second. No wonder, since she'd taken to tugging on it in frustration. Instead of her usual ponytail and basic eyes, they'd gone all out to make her "camera-ready." She was ready to dunk her head in a bucket of cold water, but she clamped down on that urge and excitedly listed the kitchen's design features one more time.

They had hustled to reshoot all weekend, and the revamped sizzle reel had been sent off to studio execs. What she had been assured was a "bare-bones" crew had descended into her life bright and early Monday morning to begin filming the pilot. Two camera operators, two sound techs, one lighting engineer, three producers, three furiously scribbling assistants, and a gopher were crowded into the Shahs' outdated dining room. Dom stood just off camera, attached to Jake's elbow and scowling ever since he'd been told he wouldn't be needed for this segment. The only person not in the room was the hair and makeup artist, Natalie, and that was only because her setup was out in the garage. Trina, one of the camera operators, had her large black camcorder up on her shoulder and moved with the grace of an acrobat while she captured their reactions around the framing of the still cameras. Sofia tried to act normal, but the lens zooming to focus on her face made her feel self-conscious. She felt her smile stiffening on her face. She could understand why her Dad had struggled. He was such an honest, straightforward guy. A great trait in a contractor, but not so much for a show where he needed to convincingly fake emotions several times in a row. She was much better at pretending to be happy, and even she was struggling here.

"We'll knock down this wall and extend the kitchen into this formal dining space, nearly doubling your cabinet space while opening up this whole side of the house. You'll still have room for the large dining table you mentioned as well. Colorful reclaimed wood cabinets on the large island, midrange rustic for the rest, and a white countertop and backsplash to allow your colorful collection of serving dishes to pop. Antique copper farm sink and fixtures. Eclectic, homey, with splashes of color and fun."

This design had come together during her conversations with the couple who craved a mix of modern functionality and high-tech amenities, with personal touches from home and their travels. It looked nothing like the cookie-cutter fixes her dad usually slapped on a remodel. Sofia couldn't be happier with the result.

"Are you sure we can afford this? We only have a hundred thousand dollars to spend out of our home equity loan, and we haven't even seen the master bedroom, bathrooms, or the nursery…" Gautam's eyebrows furrowed in concern.

Sofia hesitated a split-second before reassuring them.

"Trust me. We'll give you your dream house under budget and on time. That's what Valenti Brothers are famous for."

Producer Jake Ryland's head popped up at this, but Sofia held her smile firm and confident. True, she'd cut it close on the budget, and if there were any unforeseen complications, it might be difficult to deliver. But if that happened, she'd handle it. Especially with Adrian on her team.

They'd managed to keep their hands and lips to themselves, but the truce was getting harder to maintain. Sofia spent as much time trying not to think about him as she did failing miserably. But she wasn't ready to revoke it yet, because she was absolutely getting slammed by the production schedule on top of her regular workload. She needed him focused on the reno. She had no doubt that he would help her make this work. He had the skills and know-how, and she trusted his work implicitly. She just prayed that her strength held, because she was starting the most important project of her career, and she couldn't afford to be distracted by pretty words and a pair of fine eyes. On that thought, she forced her attention back to the design in front of her.

When she'd first met with the Shahs about fixing up their Cambrian bungalow, the consult had gone well. They had a clear design aesthetic and were eager to work with her. The walk-and-talk session through the house had been very productive. Gautam and Farha had both worked in tech in Silicon Valley for eight years and had been frugal with their stock awards, which put them in position to buy a nice three-bedroom fixer-upper in advance of the birth of their first child.

They still seemed excited with her digital mock-ups in front of them, but the technical glitches of filming were wearing down everyone's enthusiasm. It didn't help that they were sitting at a prop table in the still-awful late seventies dining room complete with harvest gold sea-grass wallpaper, surrounded by people staring at them. She knew in post-production they would overlay the decor with her CAD designs for maximum impact, but right now it was just depressing.

Farha was fading and rubbing her belly. When Jake yelled cut,

Sofia rose to stretch and casually went to check the take. "How was that one?"

"There's no sparkle. We lost it after that first take." Jake grimaced and rubbed his forehead.

"I've got an idea." Sofia said. "You can overlay to any room, right?"

"Yeah, our graphics gal does it in post."

"And the lights in the rooms are already set for the stills, right?"

"For the stills, sure, but not for people. What are you thinking?"

"Can we have the walk-and-talk camera follow us into the back bedroom? I want to do the nursery reveal in there. Farha needs to get up and move, and I think you'll get the sparkle you're looking for."

"Hmm, it's not a bad idea, Fi. Give me ten."

Sofia turned back to her clients with a satisfied smile. "Is she kicking?"

"Like a champion footballer." Farha winced and pressed on her rounded belly as if she could remove the tiny foot from its spot pressing into her ribcage. "We won't have to worry about a scholarship."

Sofia couldn't help the mushy grin that spread across her face. She'd always loved children and hadn't quite given up hope that she'd have some of her own someday.

"I'm sure all of this sitting isn't helping. We're going to try something else for this next shot. I'm going to show you the design on my laptop in the room, so you can picture it in the space. They'll do some cool graphics work later that will make it look magical, and most importantly it gets us up from this table."

Gautam laughed and rubbed a hand across his wife's lower back. The way Farha leaned into his touch with relief came perilously close to pushing Sofia's envy button.

"Anything to stretch a little. I'm game."

"Okay, folks. Let's head to the back bedroom. Trina will lead with the camera rig." Jake rounded them up and expertly placed them where he wanted them.

Sofia snagged her laptop and followed Trina. More setup. More fidgeting. More tedium. This was going to get real old, real quick. She hoped this was just beginning-of-production kinks getting worked out. If everything took this long, there was no way they'd stay on track. At Jake's nod, Sofia opened her laptop and began again.

"This is going to be the nursery. By the time you're ready to bring your little girl home to this room, it will be completely transformed. I worked with the corals and neutrals you chose as the color scheme. Over here," she gestured to the longest wall, "we'll have this beautiful crib and the reading nook here in the corner with a comfortable rocker for bedtime stories. I can already picture you cuddled up with *Goodnight Moon.*"

She could tell by the glowing look on her face that Farha was picturing the same thing. Sofia grinned in response. *Nailed it.*

"The changing table and custom toy chest will go here under the window, and we'll be swapping out this carpet for the darker hardwood you've chosen for the rest of the house…" She trailed off as Farha and Gautam looked back and forth from her laptop to the dirty white walls with tears welling in their eyes.

"It's going to be beautiful. Thank you, Sofia. It's exactly what I wanted." Farha wrapped Sofia up in a hug made awkward by her large baby bump, and Sofia beamed.

"Cut! That was great, everyone! Let's try the same format in the master. Archie, help me get the lighting set up in there."

Sofia grinned at the now glowing couple. Maybe this TV thing wasn't so hard after all.

ADRIAN FROWNED at the blueprints in front of him. This TV show was going to kill him. He could see Sofia's vision quite clearly, but he had serious concerns. As he walked through the house, he tapped walls, pulled up carpet, and peeked into attics. Trina was following him with her camcorder, filming his every wince. She'd told him he wouldn't have to speak since she was just filming for background and he wasn't miked for sound, so he didn't, but this was still going to look bad on screen. The good news was that the Shah family hadn't moved in yet, so he had plenty of room to explore and work. This wasn't always the case on their renovation jobs. The bad news was that the Shahs had ignored a lot of warnings from their inspector when they bought the house, and he wasn't a good enough actor to hide his concern.

Housing was so scarce and so overpriced that he couldn't fault them for pouncing on the fixer-upper, but a house in this condition always had hidden problems. Sofia's complicated plans didn't have a shot in hell of becoming reality on time or under budget. If he was going to convince Dom to trust him with his company, he couldn't deviate from their mission statement: make the house comfortable and safe on time and under budget. There simply wasn't money for all of the fancy extras she wanted to incorporate.

He hadn't even opened any of the walls, and he could already tell that most of the electrical would need replacing, which meant extensive drywalling, not to mention the cost of the wiring and electricians. While they had the walls down, it made sense to pull out all of the old galvanized plumbing and replace with copper, too. Galvanized pipes were only meant to last forty years, and this house was going on fifty. It wasn't as sexy as Carrera marble, but it was a hell of a lot better use of the money. He couldn't in good conscience let this family move their new baby into a pretty house just waiting to break down. To add insult to injury, the wall she wanted taken down in the kitchen was load-bearing. The header they'd need would eat another five thousand from her budget, not to mention the cost of installing it... What a mess.

And he'd promised his crew he'd try to avoid having them work unscheduled hours. He'd also promised Sofia he'd do what he could to help her make this a success. He could see a lot of late and lonely nights in his near future.

As Trina ducked out for uploads, he pulled his cell phone from his back pocket and called the office.

"Hello?"

It was ridiculous that the sound of her voice made everything go still inside, quiet and waiting for more. The rest of the world fell away as he got lost in her voice, which was a problem because she clearly expected him to speak.

"Hello? Is anyone there?"

Get it together, man. You called her, remember? Bad news? Right.

"Hi, Sofia. It's Adrian. I'm over at the Shah project... Have you got time to talk about these plans?"

"I'm still stuck at the office. Is there a problem?"

"Why are you still at the office?" He glanced at his watch, wondering how he'd missed that it was six o'clock, well past his usual knock-off time.

"Surely this doesn't come as a surprise to you, but I had to get caught up on all the order forms after a full day of filming design reveals."

"Shit. They've already seen your plans?"

"Yes, and they got final approval, too. You're starting to scare me, Adrian. What's wrong?"

"We should get dinner."

There was a pause on the line. Adrian tried to figure out why his brain wasn't putting the right words in the right order... He'd been careful to keep his longing concealed at work, and they hadn't had much time to be together outside of work because of the crazy prep for the TV show on top of their full client load. His filter was clearly slipping under the strain.

"The truce is still on. We just need to talk with the plans in front of us. I haven't eaten yet, and I assume you haven't either if you're still there. Let's meet in San Jose at Vino Vino in half an hour? Does that give you enough time to wrap up?"

"No, I was planning to stay late tonight. But as you say, I need to eat. I'll meet you and come back."

"See you soon."

Why on earth had he named a date restaurant? He knew she preferred wine to beer, but she wasn't even going to be able to enjoy herself if she had to go back to work. *Idiot.* His stubborn subconscious was leading him astray, and he couldn't afford to follow. This was a work dinner. He had bad news. This was NOT a date.

His pep talk worked through the drive, into the restaurant. He chose a larger brushed aluminum high-top inside. No intimate table for two on the fairy-lit patio. He set the tube of prints in the middle of the table. All business. Up to the moment she walked in the door, he believed he could keep their precious truce. Then, all hope was lost.

She'd done something different with her makeup, likely for the filming, but her usually beautiful face was stunning. The teal sweater made her eyes glow a brilliant blue, and sweet Jesus, it didn't hide a single curve. The pencil skirt was new, too. He knew she'd never worn it before. He'd have remembered. And heels. She never wore high heels, but tonight she was, and as she made her way across the room to him her hips swayed and swung in the tight skirt, hypnotizing him. With her hair twisted up into a bun, and her glasses pushed up on her head, she was his librarian fantasy in the very tempting flesh.

She walked in as if she hadn't just stolen all the air from the room. She was speaking, and he could barely drag in a breath. He could hear her voice, but the words weren't making any sense. She stepped too close, and his brain slammed to a halt and his hands reached for her of their own accord. With a quick jog step and some heavy side-eye, Sofia avoided his hug and put a table between them. He still hadn't managed to say a word.

"Hello?" She waved a hand in front of his face to break the trance. "What's the matter with you?"

"You look different."

It was as close as he could come to the truth and maintain their truce. He was pretty sure that telling her she was a walking wet dream would cross her invisible line in the sand. And the discussion they needed to have was difficult enough without bringing his sexual tension into it. But when she licked her lips and rubbed them together self-consciously, his mind helpfully supplied the memory of their soft and supple texture. He could swear he smelled chocolate.

"Ugh. It's all the stage makeup. I feel like I'm wearing a mask. So what's so bad we had to talk in person?"

She grinned playfully at him, and Adrian struggled to remember what he needed to say. *Work.* It was something about work…but it was bad news, and he didn't want to chase away her smile so quickly. Thankfully, the waiter came at that moment and interrupted for their order, giving him a few precious minutes to wrangle his brain cells and get his priorities in order. They agreed to share a flight of local red wines. She ordered the garden salad and the burrata, and he settled on the chicken pesto panini and the bold truth.

"Your plan is not going to work."

There, he'd said it. Like tearing off a Band-Aid, sometimes it was best to say it fast, even if he did come off sounding like an ass.

"My design is great. It got approved by the homeowners and the network's design consultants."

"It didn't get approved by me."

"I wasn't aware I needed your approval." Her tone went ice cold, and her walls came up.

He couldn't blame her for being pissed off, but he had to get it

64

all out. He laid the plans on the table between them. "There are structural concerns. We need to replace all the pipes with copper. I'm shocked the galvanized is still holding. That means kitchen and both bathrooms. Easy enough to do while we have the walls opened up, but copper is expensive."

"How expensive?"

"Ten thousand dollars expensive."

"Do we have to use copper?"

"It's the better choice, but we could also go with PEX flexible plastic piping. That would bring it down to five, but it's not as reliable as the copper long term. But that's not the only hurdle. I found Romex wiring that had been chewed by rodents in the attic. I think we need to rewire with BX to make it safer for the Shahs down the line." He watched her absorbing his words like individual punches to the gut. He hated hurting her. *Band-Aids. All at once.* "And then there's your wall."

"My wall?"

Her face went gray. Or he imagined it had from her expression because he couldn't actually see her real skin beneath the makeup. He wondered if he'd be able to see her blush through it.

"Which wall?" she asked again.

"The one you want down between the kitchen/living/dining room. It's load-bearing. To get rid of the entire length you need a special timber header to maintain the stability of the house. But it's going to cost you as well. Less if we can keep the portion of the wall that goes around the corner, but still a hefty price tag."

She dropped her glasses to her nose and leaned forward to peer at the blueprints as if she could magically find the savings she needed to keep her designs intact. The motion pressed her gorgeous tits into the table, putting them on display. He leaned closer, ostensibly to point out the wall in question, but really because he was helpless to stop himself from getting a better view of heaven. Keeping this truce was getting harder and harder, along with another pertinent part of his anatomy. He was having a real difficult time remembering why dating the boss's daughter was such a bad idea.

"How much?"

"A lot." He wanted her a lot.

"Specifically, for all of those things you mentioned?"

God, he had to snap out of it. "Ten for the pipes, eight for the wires, five for the header, a few other little fixes, minimum twenty-five K if there are no other surprises."

"Fuck me." His cock leapt at the suggestion even though he knew it was metaphorical. "What are we going to do?"

He couldn't deny he liked the way that "we" sounded.

"We'll have to get creative. This is why we keep things simple. It's easier to handle any surprises."

"Easier is not always better."

"Well, next time, we plan together, after I do my inspection. But these fixes are non-negotiable. I won't put them into an unsafe house."

"Agreed. But shit, how creative can we get and still deliver?"

"I guess we're going to find out."

While they sipped their Pinot Noirs, they tossed ideas back and forth. Adrian pushed to downgrade the door package, and Sofia countered with swapping concrete for the counters. When she suggested changing the wall removal to a cased opening, he wanted to kiss her. Maybe, just maybe, they could make this work.

By the time their dinner arrived, the conversation had turned personal.

"So you grew up here?" Sofia took a sip of her wine, and Adrian watched her lovely neck as she swallowed, wanting to press his lips just there. His throat had gone dry, so he took a sip of the Petite Syrah sampler, and managed to answer.

"I was born at Good Sam, grew up in San Jose. My mother still lives with me in the house downtown."

"And you have sisters right?"

"Yep. Three."

"And your dad?"

"He's gone."

She set down her wine with a clink and grabbed his hand across the table.

"I'm so sorry."

"It's okay. It's a long story, but he got deported my senior year of high school. I was seventeen when I started working for your dad to help support the family. The separation was stressful on everyone. He had a heart attack about three years later, before his appeal was even processed, and he died because he was too far from a hospital to get help. I never even got to say goodbye." Her hand squeezed his tighter, and he wondered if she realized it. She usually went out of her way not to touch him.

"Oh my God! I had no idea."

"You were just a kid when I started working for your dad."

"So were you."

"Yeah, not for long. At least I got my GED. My mom, even though she's got her green card now, has anxiety so bad she's afraid to leave the house. Someone had to make ends meet. I'm proud to say I paid off the house and helped all three girls get through college. My baby sister is finishing next year."

He looked up from his plate and found her staring at him, eyes warm with...admiration?

"No wonder," she murmured.

"No wonder what?"

"No wonder Dad respects the hell out of you. You're a modern-day superhero."

He couldn't find the words of denial when she was looking at him like that. Like she believed the words she said wholeheartedly. Like she saw him as a hero. Like he could be her hero.

"What are we doing here?" The words were out before he could think better of spoiling the mood.

"Having a nice meal and talking shop?"

67

"This feels like more. I know we've been pretending it didn't happen, but I can't stop thinking about that kiss."

"I've been thinking about it, too." *Excellent.* "I don't know what to do with you. This doesn't make sense." *Not excellent.*

"What about attraction needs to make sense?"

"Adrian. Look at you. Tall, dark, handsome, body made of steel." She ran her hand down his arm, tracing the curves of his bicep, so lightly that he shivered. "A literal Superman." He felt his own blush starting, before her next words killed it. "Then look at me. I used to be okay, but now I don't even recognize myself in the mirror."

"Hey, I can see you clear as day, and I like what I see. I thought I made that obvious in your office when I couldn't keep my hands off your ass. More than that, I like who you are. Dedicated daughter, smart and sexy, willing to compromise and problem-solve when others would have thrown a tantrum. There's a lot to like."

Her face remained pale, but he watched the flush spread downward from her neck toward her cleavage. He had his answer about that blush. God, he wanted to see how far it spread. Turning her hand over in his, he traced her palm, marveling at her softness against his rough calluses.

"Just think about it, and next time you look in the mirror, try seeing the person I see. When you walked in here, I lost my words."

She didn't respond, but she didn't pull her hand back either.

CHAPTER 7

SOFIA WAS knee-deep in discount websites, trying to pull off her looks at a fraction of the original cost. In the last day and a half, she'd called every marble supplier in a hundred-mile radius and had tracked down an off cut large enough to do a modified island. She hoped Adrian could help her get it here from Fremont. She'd downgraded the cabinets from custom to prefab, and she'd replaced the original countertops with poured concrete, but she'd still only managed to trim about ten grand. At least that would cover the pipes.

When Jake popped his head in her doorway, she quickly put on her "Me stressed? Never!" face. She couldn't let him see the extent of the problems, or this pilot might crash before it even got off the ground. She refused to be the weak link that made the project stall out.

"Hi, Jake. What can I do for you this fine Wednesday?"

The classically handsome man, with perfectly coiffed hair and a smile an orthodontist would love, came farther into the room. Why didn't her heart go pitter-pat for him? He was every bit as attractive as Adrian, albeit in a different way. She had a feeling she wouldn't like the answer, so she pushed the unspoken question aside.

"I just spoke to the Shahs. Is there room in the budget to touch up the curb appeal? I know you were close to their upper limit, but I think it would be great to highlight Enzo's talents a little in the pilot so we can build it into future episodes."

"I'll be honest. It's tight, but I'll see what I can do." She scribbled the note in her project binder.

"I may be able to get another thousand out of the production budget."

"That would go a long way." She'd twist Enzo's arm to do it cheap anyway. But that extra grand might save her light fixtures. "I'll talk to him about it."

"I'm really glad you're here on the ground, doing the design and helping manage the team. I don't think things would be flowing as smoothly without your guidance. Watch! This pilot is going to get snapped up in a heartbeat!"

Sofia soaked in his approval and hoped he was right. If this whole thing tanked because she screwed up the budget, she could kiss her chance at designing full-time goodbye.

Not to mention, she'd screw up her dad's plan to retire. She didn't think her mom would forgive and forget that level of mistake. Jo hadn't spoken of Dom's crazy TV plan with anyone since the awkward announcement meal, which had to be some kind of record. Sofia had never known her parents not to talk about a problem. Bicker, argue, yell? Sure. But silence? Never. Even when they fought they managed to come out the other side laughing and in agreement.

For the first time she could remember, she was worried about her parents' marriage. They'd always been her rock, her role models. She'd often judged her own relationships against theirs and found hers wanting. How would a relationship with Adrian compare?

She shook her head. *Well, I made it a whole half hour without thinking about him. Call the Guinness people. We're setting records left and right this week.*

What would a relationship with him look like? Given the way he talked about her body and her personality, she'd built up some pretty high hopes. The fact that she did indeed hear his voice in her head, telling her all manner of lovely things, when she looked in the mirror had her absolutely considering asking for a real date. She was still nervous and not at all confident after three years out of the dating game, and this was the most professionally stressful moment of her career. She had every reason to wait.

But the little voice inside of her, so long ignored, kept whispering, "Give him a chance," in her quiet moments.

She needed to talk to him about the changes in the plans anyhow. Before she could talk herself into an email, she picked up the phone and called him.

"Hello?" His deep voice on the line sent a shiver of pleasure from her ears down the back of her neck. How did he do that?

"Hey, it's Sofia. Do you have a minute?"

"Sure, we are between takes. What's up?"

"I have some updated changes to the plan. I'd love to get your thoughts on them before I commit. Can I drop by the site?"

"I'm in the middle of demolition day on the Shah project. Everything is a hot mess, and the cameras are rolling…"

The idea of him sweaty and dirty, his T-shirt clinging to his chest, flipped every last switch. She crossed her legs and pushed caution aside. "And if I said I missed seeing your face?"

"I'd ask you why you aren't over here already." She heard the grin in his voice.

"I'll see you at the lunch break."

"Sofia?"

"Yeah?"

"I miss your face, too."

∽

71

SHE WAS as good as her word. Sofia walked into the chaos of demo day seven minutes before they were scheduled to break for lunch. Not that he'd been looking at his watch every five minutes since she'd hung up or anything. She looked fresh and bright in her flowy top and tight jeans, and he wanted to drop everything and have her for lunch instead of the leftovers in his cooler. Adrian shook his head at his own ridiculous behavior. He was completely gone on her, and they hadn't even had a real date yet.

"Cut! Hey, Sofia. What are you doing here?" Lorena, the assistant producer, hustled over.

"I just came to talk to Adrian about a few tweaks to the plan."

"That's great. When we get back from lunch we can do a quick makeup blitz and film a walk-and-talk. Get it on camera. I know Jake is still playing with the plotlines, so the more feature shots we can get before he goes into editing, the better." She spun away from them without waiting for a response. Adrian supposed she didn't need an affirmation because they'd both signed contracts saying they'd play nice. "OKAY, EVERYBODY! BREAK FOR LUNCH!"

Adrian winced. How that huge voice came out of that tiny body, he would never understand. Lorena might be little, but she was a force to be reckoned with. The image of her as a miniature Napoleon in full costume leading an army into battle flashed fully formed into his mind, and he grinned. He turned that smile back to Sofia and gestured to the door. "Shall we?"

He followed her out to her car, so it wasn't until they'd gotten in that he noticed her smile had dimmed.

"Hey, what's wrong? Is it the plan?"

"No. Nothing. It's nothing." She put her hands on the steering wheel but didn't start the car.

"I have a mother and three sisters. 'Nothing' is never nothing. Spill."

She shook her head and reached for the ignition. "I'm being stupid. Leave it alone."

He covered her hand gently and waited until she looked up. "I can't. Not if it's something I can fix. What can I do?"

She loosed a deep sigh and hid her face in her hands. Speaking between her fingers, she muttered a curse.

"I didn't catch that."

"I said, 'God save me from persistent men.'"

"No, you didn't." He grinned.

"God knew what I meant."

"So are you gonna tell me?"

She hauled in a deep breath and sighed. "I saw the way you smiled at Lorena. It didn't feel very good."

"That is a problem."

Her eyes went wide, his answer clearly not the one she was expecting. "It is?"

"Yes. You see, I don't want to ever hurt you, but I may smile at other people. I'm a happy guy, and I smile a lot. But I can't look at another woman the way I look at you." As he spoke, he leaned across the console. When her focus shifted to his lips, his heart leapt in satisfaction. "It's not possible. There is no other woman I want the way I want you. So this look? The one that is begging for your smile in return? The one that keeps dropping to your lips because I miss how good they taste? That look is all yours." He raised one hand toward her cheek, needing to touch her, connect with her. He stopped just shy of her soft skin, not wanting to sully her with his dirty hands. He dropped his hand and hesitated, a breath from touching her lips with his own. "I've missed you. May I?"

Waiting for her to decide, to close the distance, to choose him back, nearly killed him, but it was worth every tortured second when she nodded. She leaned into the kiss, as eager as he was.

From the moment their lips touched, all notion of the outside world disappeared. His existence narrowed to the one spot where his body was touching hers. The power, the heat, the intensity of her kiss blew all of his good intentions away, their truce incinerated.

He lost himself in her. Tongues tangled, and he was thoroughly caught in her web. Moreover, he was content to let her wrap him up nice and tight and feast away.

When she jerked back from the kiss, his first instinct was to pursue and resume. Her hand against his lips was the only thing that stopped him. That he didn't exactly remember where they were or what they were supposed to be doing didn't alarm him as much as it probably should have. His brain was still struggling to engage through the warm haze of arousal.

"We're in my car, parked at a client's house. We can't do this here."

"Hmm, so we can do this somewhere else?"

"Now is not the time for semantics." She tried to start the car multiple times, her nerves making her jittery enough to stall out. She pulled back behind her defenses and away from the house. "We need to get lunch and get back. I can't afford to get distracted." Her eyes trained on the road and her hands gripping the wheel, she drove them to her favorite take-out burger joint in silence.

Damn. Hadn't she enjoyed that as much as he had? And how the hell was she able to find words like "semantics" after a kiss like that? What did that even mean? He sat back in the passenger seat, trying to navigate the right path but lacking the map of her mind.

CHAPTER 8

How could a cheeseburger be awkward?

She'd eaten a million of them in her lifetime. She loved the special magic of the thick, juicy meat topped with fresh lettuce, tomato, onion, melty cheese and special sauce that her favorite chain was famous for. But now that she was eating one in front of the man who'd kissed her like he meant it, it felt completely weird. Was the juice dribbling down her chin? Was he judging how many fries she ate? Holy hell, if she kept this up, kissing Adrian would be the best diet she'd ever tried. She set down her food and pushed the tray away. Apparently, embarrassment killed her ability to eat and converse like the grown-ass woman she was.

She sat and stared at her half-eaten food, unable to swallow past the lump in her throat. He'd kissed her, and she'd freaked out when she'd started to lose control. *Why did I break the truce? Where is my self-control?* And what if someone on-site saw the kiss? Then she'd have to explain everything to everybody even though she didn't have a clue what anything was, because that was just how her family worked! Sometimes working with the people she loved was a real pain in the ass. She couldn't believe she'd caved to temptation, but even now, with Adrian covered from head to toe in dirt and grime, his hands and face hastily scrubbed clean, she wanted to climb in his lap and let him kiss her until her brain quit this incessant worrying.

"Is your food okay?"

Startled from her rapidly spiraling thoughts, she answered on the defensive.

"Of course. Why?"

"You're not eating it. I don't think I've ever seen you turn down a cheeseburger."

Heat flashed to her cheeks, and not the good kind. Of course, he'd never seen the fat chick turn down food. That lump in her throat grew as shame joined the party and threatened to choke her.

"Whatever you're thinking to put that look on your face, stop. All I meant is I know you like In-N-Out, so if you're not enjoying it then it must be because of what happened in the car."

"What did happen in the car?"

"You were sad because I joked with another woman. I speak to women every day, but I didn't want you to be sad. I missed you and your smile. So I kissed you to bring it back. I thought you were enjoying it, too, until you weren't. What did you think happened in the car?"

Though she felt ten times a fool, Sofia gave him an honest answer. "I think you took pity on me because I got all twisted up and kissed me to make me feel better. But you did it in front of an entire work site of our employees."

"So it would be better if I kiss you while we're alone?"

"Yes. No. Don't twist my words."

Sofia shook her head with an exasperated sigh. He took her chin between his fingers and waited for her to look him in the eye.

"I'm not. I'm trying to understand. You think I took pity on you, but you're the one ashamed to be seen kissing me. How does that work?" She could hear the annoyance creeping into his voice.

"That's not the point."

"What is the point?"

"Neither of us seems to know what's going on here. I'd rather not face the Valenti Family Inquisition until we do."

"So does this mean the truce is over?"

"My brain is so scrambled right now, I don't know what to think."

His irresistible grin spread over his face, and his dimple made an appearance. Sofia struggled to stay mad. Why was she mad again?

"So my kisses scramble your brain?"

"They make me stupid. It wasn't a compliment."

"You don't get to decide what I take as a compliment. Turning that impressive brain off with my lips is something I'm very proud of."

"I do get to decide when I want to kiss you."

"Yes, you do, just as you decided to kiss me in the car."

"Clearly, the truce isn't working, but I'm going to ask that we keep our kisses away from the workplace while we figure things out."

Now that she'd spilled her worries, she felt her anxiety spiraling. She nibbled a fry.

"I just don't want everyone jumping all over this," she said around another fry, "before we see if it's really going to be a thing." She grabbed three fries and tucked them into her mouth. "I mean it could be bad for your proposal, for my credibility, and oh God! The show! What if someone caught us on camera?" She reached for another handful of fries, and his hand covered hers. Taking it in his, he raised it to his lips and kissed it, silencing her thoughts with frightening ease.

"Don't worry, beautiful. We will go as slow as you need to, but be clear. There is an *us*. And this is definitely a thing." His phone chirped a text alert. He glanced at it and frowned. "We should head back. We need to film your walk-and-talk, and I need my guys to finish this demo day on time."

Head still spinning that he hadn't walked away from her melt-down, she climbed back into her car in silence. There had been something she'd wanted to talk to him about…

~

ADRIAN RAN a hand through his hair as a camera-ready Sofia walked into the rubble of what used to be the kitchen and stole his breath. Was it her beauty contrasting with the wreckage he'd caused that made his heart stutter in his chest? Or was it something more? He had to get a grip, or he'd look like a fool on film.

"Okay, you two, just walk side by side and talk to each other. Try to keep a steady pace, because I'll be walking backward." Trina prepped them. "I'm pretty nimble, but things are all torn up today. Good job on that, Adrian." Trina was friendly but focused as she talked them through what she needed for the shot.

"What can I say? You've got to break things before you can fix them."

"Let's start here in the kitchen. The demo is mostly done, and it makes a great backdrop. I'm going to keep filming so if you blow a line or need to repeat yourself, just say it again, and we'll edit it in post. Ready?"

"As I'll ever be," muttered Adrian.

"And…go!"

"Hey Adrian, the demo looks great!" He barely recognized the girl he'd had lunch with. When she put on her camera mask, she was a different person.

"Yeah, we had a fun morning. You'll see your wall is mostly gone. We've got the cased opening framed in, which let us avoid the header beam."

"That's fantastic. I've got a few changes I need to talk to you

78

about in here. Instead of the custom built-ins, I found some gorgeous ready-mades for less, but it means I have to change the layout a little..." She turned to gesture to the empty space beneath the window. "How hard would it be to move the main sink a foot and a half to the right?"

"The plumbing? Maybe an extra hour. But then it isn't centered under the window." Where was this coming from? Why was she making changes to the blueprints now?

"That was my next question."

"We can't move the window." He crossed his arms as if that would help him hold back his frustration. It didn't help. He couldn't tear apart the back of the house just so she could keep her fancy plans. It went against everything Valenti Brothers stood for.

"But the cabinets won't work right if we don't."

"If we move the window, we'd have to completely tackle the back exterior of the house, replace siding, fix any surprises we find when we pull off the back wall, plus extra permitting and the cost of a new window because the old one isn't energy-efficient..."

"So that's out. Shoot." He hated the way her shoulders fell along with her smile, but he had to be clear. Sometimes trying to save on cheaper materials cost more in the end, and changing blueprints midstream always fucked things up.

"Why are you changing the plans now? I thought we had everything approved."

"I'm just trying to keep the clients happy."

"Leave the sink. Seth and I will make the new cabinets work. What else?"

"The island is going to be smaller."

"Wait. Isn't the island why we knocked down this stupid wall? Who makes an island smaller?"

"Someone who found a deal on a smaller slab of marble and needs to stay under budget." She raised her eyebrows and tilted her head toward the camera.

Screw the camera. Her plan to save money was to shrink everything down? Would they be building a dollhouse by the end? Her father had built his reputation on affordable quality, but he was always up front with clients about what they could afford. If he wanted to stay in Dom's good graces, he had to toe that line. This was not going to end well. "There has to be a way to keep the size or the proportions will be all off."

"I'll see what I can do." She pressed her fingers to her forehead and winced.

He regretted pushing back, but she needed to be realistic. He might as well get all the bad news out on the table at once. "While we're in here, there's something else I need to show you."

"Oh, God. What now?" She snapped her head up, eyes wide with panic.

He wanted so badly to touch her, to soothe her, but he knew how she'd feel about that getting caught on camera so he kept his hands to himself while he added another straw to the camel's back. "The old fridge had a water line that was slowly leaking for who knows how long." Adrian knelt by a dark spot on the subfloor and pushed his thumb through what should have been solid plywood. "It's a miracle the thing didn't drop into the crawl space when we pulled it out."

Sofia's jaw dropped. "How did the inspector miss this?"

"He didn't have to pull out the appliances, just note if they were working. And there's a note that he couldn't get into the crawl space because he was too broad in the shoulders so he did a visual inspection from the trap door."

"So we don't know about the supports underneath?"

He could hear the panic in her voice. He wished he didn't have to be the bad guy here.

"I don't know the damage yet. I told the guys to wait to rip a hole in the floor until we were done carting everything out." He held out a long-handled sledgehammer, hoping to give her a bit of control back. "Do you want to do the honors?"

Sofia gripped the sledge and dropped her sunglasses down from their perch on top of her head. He watched her gather her courage and grinned. She looked beautiful and fierce wielding that sledge in full makeup, but he hoped to God they weren't opening another can of worms. She lifted the sledge waist high before dropping it down onto the ruined panel. It sank through the weakened wood without a hint of resistance and dropped the foot and a half to the bottom of the crawl space.

"That can't be good." She tugged the hammer back up through the hole, and a bigger chunk of subflooring fell down. "Can you see the joists yet?"

Adrian took the hammer from her and widened the hole with a few punches. He took the flashlight and dropped his head and shoulders into the dark space below. He surveyed the beams for damage before pulling back out, gratified that Sofia had to move her eyes from his ass to his face when it reappeared.

"Good news? Bad news?" Her shoulders were brushing her ears as she braced for another hit.

"Hang on a sec!" Trina moved to reframe the shot, climbing halfway up a ladder to get a better angle. "Now, angle your shoulders toward me a little…perfect. Okay, go ahead!"

Adrian tried not to feel self-conscious, but it was hard standing so close to Sofia and trying to keep his impulses under control. "Both. Bad news, two of these joists show signs of water damage."

"Da—darn it! How much?"

"That's the good news. The damage seems localized and minimal. So I think we can dry them out and reinforce this section with two-by-six sister beams. We won't have to replace the whole thing."

Sofia let out a heavy breath, and he rubbed a filthy hand on her shoulder.

"Not as bad as we thought, babe."

She deliberately stepped out from under his touch and glared. *Damn.*

"We talked about this," she hissed. He couldn't help but think about the rest of that conversation, the part where they'd talked about kissing and more. "Watch it, *babe.*"

Her sarcasm slapped his hand away, and she brushed the dirt off her shoulder. Damn it, he'd slipped up already. Keeping his hands to himself now that he'd had the privilege of touching her was going to be harder than he thought.

"Shit, sorry."

"Let me show you the other changes."

He tried to keep the Valenti Brothers' mission at the forefront of his mind, but then she walked in front of him in those jeans and shattered his concentration. He was tempted to give her whatever she asked for just to bring back her smile.

Shit.

CHAPTER 9

SOFIA SAT where she always sat, behind her desk piled with papers, trying to make sense of the chaos that had landed there while she was out at demo day on the Shah project. After a full day of filming and emotional turmoil, she'd returned to the office to tackle her day job. The influx of paperwork hadn't slowed just because she was designing and filming now. Purchase orders, catalogs, and the day's mail had all been tossed haphazardly on her desk. Could no one see the in-box she'd labeled and placed on the corner of her desk? The one that was still empty, gathering dust? *Why do I even try?*

Taking a sip of hours-old cold coffee, she winced and began to restore order to her world. She'd just gotten everything into its appropriate pile when her dad popped his head in her door.

"Hey, princess. Still here?"

"Well, these bills aren't going to pay themselves."

"No, they won't. Found that out the hard way when your mother quit working."

"I know. I remember."

After Gabe's funeral, Mom had embraced the *carpe diem* philosophy with open arms, determined to make the most of every day remaining to her. Sofia had stepped into the chaos left behind. Three years later, she was buried while her mother went wine tasting. *Damn you, Gabe. Why did you have to leave and change everything?*

If he were still here, at least she'd have one more voice in her corner. He'd always supported her ideas, even letting her paint on the walls of his tree house. True, he'd hidden her pink and purple paints, but he had opened his hideout to her. He'd recognized, even at the age of ten, that creating made her happy. She'd been counting on that understanding to help her make a space for her talents at Valenti Brothers.

If only she'd had a chance to really prove herself as a designer before the world had come crashing down, maybe she wouldn't be spending her evenings entering data and writing checks. Her dad would have hired someone else, or maybe Mom wouldn't have shut down. But Gabe's death had made Dad overly cautious about spending money. It seemed to make him realize how tenuous his stability really was. Every time she brought up hiring someone else, the answer was that there wasn't enough design business to justify hiring someone else to take over the desk duties. The catch-22 was infuriating.

Oblivious to her internal musings, her dad leaned against her doorjamb, clearly settling in for a conversation. Great, now she'd be even later.

"I want to talk to you about Adrian."

Do not blush. Do NOT blush!

"What about him?" She surreptitiously pressed a palm to her neck. *Whew, still cool.*

"Last time we talked about his proposal, you walked out."

Proposal? Her mind flashed to Adrian on bended knee with a black velvet box in hand. The image was oddly tempting, and she made a mental note to revisit it later, before pulling her wits back to her current conversation. Domenico Valenti was not one to suffer quiet long, and he was already filling her pause with more words. Clearly, he'd been saving up.

"I know you two don't always get along, but I'm seriously considering saying yes."

Sofia's temper flashed. True, she'd promised to help Adrian get his proposal approved, but how could her dad keep making these decisions without talking about it with any of them?

"Dad, I know he's been a loyal employee, and he's a great contractor. But how would that work? We've always been a family company, yes, but you and Zio Tony own this place. The rest of us just work here. Zio Tony is already retired and can't move on with selling his part of the business until we figure this out. Does he sell out to Adrian? Or does he give his half to Seth? Does that leave Seth with a fifty percent share, and me, Enzo, Frankie, and Adrian fighting over what's left? Or is it just going to be Seth and Adrian running things and me, Enzo, and Frankie stay on as employees? Have you thought about any of this? Because if you have, I sure haven't heard about it. Is Adrian going to step into Gabe's seat at the dinner table, too?"

Sofia tried to keep her voice even, but by the end of her rant she knew she'd gotten fast and shrill, her emotions spiraling out of control. *Where did that rant come from?*

"Why do you always have to fight everything?"

"I'm not trying to fight with you, Dad. I'm trying to protect our future."

"Jesus, Fi. Don't overreact."

"You want to take what I thought was my inheritance, what I thought I was working to build and expand as a family legacy, what I sacrificed my dreams for, and sell it without a thought to the details, and I'm overreacting?"

"What have you sacrificed, Sofia? You sit here in this office pushing papers and signing checks. You've got it easy. Adrian understands what it means to sacrifice to build something that lasts."

The question hit her like a slap to the face, stealing her breath. Pushing aside the fact that she had let go of her social life and her creative outlets to save his ass, she focused on the detail he'd most likely value.

"Do you know how many job offers I had coming out of school? And I said no, I'm going to work for my own business. Except it's not ever going to be mine, is it? Have you talked to Frankie about this?"

"Not one-on-one."

"Coward. You know it's been Frankie's plan for years to take over as head contractor. What now? Is Adrian going to be that guy?"

"Frankie is too young and inexperienced to take over as head contractor right now."

"Ah, but not forever. Have you thought about that, Dad? Do you have a plan?"

His silence answered her more clearly than words.

"And you wonder why I left the other day. Do you think I'm doing this," she gestured at the papers on her desk, "because I like earning an hourly wage? No, Dad. I care about this company, and I want it to be solvent when I inherit my part. I also want to get the hell out of here before midnight. Come back and talk to me when you have an actual plan." She couldn't quite believe that she'd just spoken to her father that way, and apparently he couldn't either.

"I don't know why you're so angry about this. If the job is too much with the designing and the show—"

"Don't even say it." Sofia couldn't let him suggest she give up her dreams a second time. For as much as she'd just stood up to him verbally, actually going against something her dad told her to do felt nigh on impossible. "I didn't say I couldn't handle it. I said I want to be working my ass off for something that's mine, not someone else's. I don't want to take orders from a boss, and if you're going to sell the company out from under me, I'd like to know so I can make other plans."

"What other plans?" He seemed genuinely baffled by this idea.

"Dad, I'm a designer. I am not going to enter time cards forever. Don't take me for granted."

"I don't, Sofia."

Oh, but you do. And you don't even realize it. Her face must've telegraphed her disagreement, because he got defensive.

"I appreciate the work you do."

"As long as it's the work you want me to do. Listen, Dad, it's been a long day, and I can tell I'm not saying what you expected me to say. Why don't you go home and talk things over with Mom? We can talk more tomorrow."

"I can't."

"Okay, then the day after."

"No, I can't talk to your mother. She won't speak to me."

Sofia sat back in her chair, stunned. She couldn't remember a time in her life when that had been the case. Her parents' marriage had always seemed rock-solid. Sure they argued, but they did so briefly and at top volume, and then it was done and life went on. Her mother had never shied away from an argument, never kept her opinions to herself. Sofia wanted to be just like her.

"I thought she just didn't want to talk about the show. How long has this been going on?"

"Not a word since the family meeting."

A whole month? This is serious.

"Well then, go home and think about what your plan is. Talk to Enzo and Frankie, and see what they say. And then we'll talk again. Like I said before, I'm not against it in principle, but I can't agree until I know the specifics of what you want to do."

Her email chimed from her computer. Another message from Farha Shah.

"Sorry, Dad. I need to read this. We'll talk soon."

"Don't stay up too late." She rolled her eyes at the ridiculousness of that command just as she had at age nine when he caught her reading after bedtime. It earned her a short laugh. "I love you, princess."

"I love you, too, Dad."

At least that part of their relationship hadn't just changed. But now that she'd spoken her concerns and frustrations aloud, Sofia didn't think she could go back to being biddable. As he left and locked the front door behind him, Sofia turned her attention to the email.

From: Farha Shah
   To: Sofia Valenti
   CC: Jake Ryland
   Subject: Chandelier

Hi Sofia,

   I know you've been making changes to the design plan. If it's not too much trouble, we would love to have a fixture like this over the kitchen island. Let me know what you think.
   Farha

She'd attached a picture of a geometric figure made of connecting bronze bars and antique Edison-style bulbs. Gorgeous and perfect for the slightly modern, slightly eclectic vibe she wanted. Price tag? Three thousand dollars? No way! She clicked to reply and realized that Farha had included Jake Ryland in the email chain. Shit. She couldn't say no. Maybe she could find a knockoff for cheaper. One more thing to add to her ever-growing list of things to figure out. She noted it in the design plan and made an entry on her calendar to research it in the morning. Finally, she pulled the stack of purchase orders back in front of her. The mangled, half-complete paper on top sent her already aggravated blood pressure skyrocketing.

Damn it. She did not have time for this. Why couldn't he fill out the damn paperwork the way she'd asked?

She had changed the order form three years ago, needing more info than her mother who had been dealing with contractor crap for thirty years. *Some people* decided to ignore this fact and continued to expect her to figure out what the hell their chicken scratch meant. The order request from Adrian had a supplier name scrawled across the top and notes on amounts and dimensions.

No part numbers. No prices. No respect for the extra time she'd spend filling in the blanks so she could place the damn order. And Dad wanted to give him the company? Frankie never pulled this shit. Her blood boiled. The spaces were on the freaking form for a reason! If he couldn't handle minor forms, how on earth would he manage to run the company? And how much more crap would fall into her lap?

Before she could flip her filters back on, she pulled out her phone and tapped his number. She'd given her dad a piece of her mind. Why not give a little more to the guy who deserved it?

CHAPTER 10

"*¡Hola, Mamá!* I'm home."

"*Mijo*, it's so late. I was worried."

"I know. That's why I called you. Twice."

"Yes, but the worry doesn't leave until you come through that door."

Adrian leaned over and pressed a kiss to his mother's forehead. She had always told him that his kisses kept the wrinkles away, so he'd made it a point to kiss her anytime he came or went since he was a child. He'd keep her forever young if he could. She was the only parent he had left. When she passed, he'd become the official head of the family. Just the idea of her being gone snapped his throat shut, so he pushed it ruthlessly away. He could still make her smile with a simple kiss, so he would take every opportunity to do so.

"What's for dinner? I'm starving."

In a routine as familiar as his own face in the mirror, he took off his work boots by the front door and walked into the tiny bathroom off the kitchen to scrub the day from his hands and face. By the time he'd worked the grime and sweat from his pores, his dinner would be hot and waiting for him on the table.

The comfort of this routine soothed him after his rough run-in with Sofia that afternoon. He'd thought they were making progress, but then she'd wanted to change everything while the stupid cameras were rolling. They'd spent the rest of the afternoon arguing. He didn't know why the cameras put him on edge, but they did. He hated the feeling that he was being watched. Probably a holdover from his childhood of being told to put his head down, obey, don't cause trouble. But it hadn't made a difference in the end. His father had still gotten caught up and hauled away.

He'd have to find some way to make it up to Sofia. In hindsight, he realized she was probably scrambling to cut money from her design budget after his bombshells. Why hadn't she said something about it at lunch? Because he'd scrambled her brain. He allowed himself a small smile over that particular victory. He would make amends. He'd won the bigger battle that day.

He strolled into the kitchen and dropped his exhausted body into his chair.

"Mmm, *pollo en mole. Mamá*, you're the best."

"You deserve the best, *mijo*." She bustled around the kitchen, putting food away, packing plastic freezer bags with the leftovers, moving pans to the sink. Though his sisters had all moved out now, his mother still cooked like she was feeding a brood of four hungry teenagers. She couldn't seem to scale down her recipes, so the neighborhood benefited from her abundance. Since Adrian knew the creation brought her pleasure, he was happy to spread her wealth to his friends and neighbors. As long as he got his plate first.

"Come! Sit and eat with me." He tugged her down into the chair next to his, knowing she'd likely eaten at five o'clock when the food had been ready. "How was your day?"

"Oh, you know. I talked to Mahalia today." His older sister called almost every day since she'd moved up to Oakland with her husband, Rey.

"How's the baby?"

"So sweet! Look how big he's getting! She sent me pictures." She pulled her smartphone from her apron pocket to show off his only nephew. As the first grandbaby, every moment of Jeremiah's life was being documented. Today's pictures featured a red face and tears.

"He looks less than happy."

"Still not sleeping well. Poor little guy."

"Poor Mahalia. She's never done well on little sleep. Remember high school?"

"Trying to get that girl out of bed..."

"Do you want to go up there for a couple of days to help out?"

"No."

No explanation, just no. Same as every other time he asked if she wanted to get out of the house. When his dad had been taken, she'd stopped seeing friends, afraid of who she could trust. She'd let her driver's license lapse, and had gradually stopped doing the daily errands that had filled her day with familiar faces and routine. While his sisters had lived in the house, there had been more than enough hands to get the job done. But since his baby sister was living on campus, it was all falling on his shoulders, unless one of the older girls dropped in to help. He would keep trying to encourage his mother to get out more, but if the lure of her first-born grandchild wasn't enough, he doubted he'd succeed. When was the last time his mother had used the front door?

"Marielena picked up our groceries while she was out today, so you don't need to stop tomorrow."

Adrian cringed. Marielena was a good friend to his mother and often included her in her daily errands, but he hated imposing.

"I told you I'd do it, Mamá."

"Don't fuss at me. She offered, and I'm making my *arroz con leche* before her mother-in-law comes next week. It's fine. How was your day?"

"Ugh. This show is going to kill me. Demolition took twice as long as it should have, and Sofia showed up with changes to the plan. So we had to film all of that as well. I had to explain why we tore up the floor five times!"

"Sofia?"

"She's done the interior design and remodel plans for this one."

"I thought she just did the paperwork."

"She does, but she does designs, too. I don't know how well it's working out. She seems to be in over her head, and the budget is spiraling."

"She's a good girl, that Sofia."

"Mamá, don't start. You've never even met her. What makes you think she's so good?"

Even though the Valentis had extended invitations to his entire family for summer company picnics and winter holiday parties, attending would require his mother to leave the house, so he'd always gone with his sisters. While his mother knew everyone he worked with by name and reputation, she'd never met them face-to-face.

"She drives you nuts. She must be smart and strong to stand up to you and get what she wants."

"She's also the boss's daughter."

"Bah! Love is love. When I met your father—"

"You married him in three weeks despite Abuela warning you not to. I know, but I just talked to Dom about buying into his company. I don't want to do anything to rock the boat." That was part of why he hadn't pushed for more of her time outside filming. He was going slow, because he knew it could all blow up in his face. They'd managed a few flirtatious private conversations, but it seemed like her private time was increasingly scarce.

"Boats always rock, especially if you're enjoying yourself."

"Mamá!" Adrian covered his ears and laughed. He couldn't deny that it was getting harder and harder not to think of that aspect of things with Sofia. The woman turned him on by breathing. Before his mind could travel down that well-worn path, he was pulled back to the present by his mother's voice.

"Well, I'm glad you finally talked to Dom. You deserve to own part of that business."

"Thanks, Mamá. We'll see what he says."

"He will say yes. And then you can date this Sofia."

"Enough meddling! I'm going to watch the game upstairs." He rose and put his now empty plate in the sink. "Do you need anything before I go up?"

"No, *mijo*. Go relax. *Te amo*."

"*Te amo tambien, Mamá*. Good night."

He trudged up the wooden stairs to the second floor addition he'd added to the bungalow five years ago. His mother would check the locks, pick her books to read in bed with a cup of tea, and be in for the night. This had been her routine for as long as he could remember. He'd go down later and double-check the locks before he fell asleep, just to reassure her, but other than that and meal times the main floor was all hers.

Needing to escape his sisters, he'd built the second story apartment for himself. Dating while still living in a house with three teenage girls had been awkward at best, and there was only so much noise he could take.

His retreat came complete with a balcony and outdoor access, though he rarely used it. But it was nice to have if he wanted to come and go unnoticed, or if they ever needed to rent the place.

Given the way his mother worried when he left the house, he made a point to let her know when he was leaving, so his private door stayed locked most days. Although he'd sponsored her green card, she was terrified that someone was going to come and take her away to a Mexico she barely remembered. All four of her children had been born in the US, but still she worried that the government would ignore that and send them away, or that the police would shoot first and ask questions later, or that they would be victims of a violent crime... Her list of daily anxieties was endless. And Adrian knew them all, because he did his best to talk her through them every day.

Never leaving the house only exacerbated her fears about the big, bad world. Adrian did his best to respect those fears and let her know where he was and when he was leaving. The home-cooked meals waiting for him didn't hurt to reinforce the habit either. He could have moved out a long time ago, but this arrangement worked for everyone. His apartment had everything he needed, and he saved money by not paying rent since he owned the house.

He walked in his door and eyed his comfortable brown leather recliner with longing. It had been the first piece of furniture he'd ever bought on his own, and it was perfect. Comfortable and durable, it accommodated his long frame easily. He'd arranged it the perfect distance from his flat-screen TV. He turned on the A's home game against Texas and grabbed a beer from the minifridge he'd installed in his efficiency kitchen before heading back to finish cleaning up. Now, the bathroom he'd added up here was a different story. Efficiency was not a word that applied to this space. This was his retreat. Being able to escape sharing a bathroom with his sisters *and* design it to his specifications had been a double bonus.

He placed his beer on the tile shelf in the corner of his travertine-clad shower and turned on the water to heat while he stripped down. The tankless water heater he'd installed made that wait quick, and he grinned with pleasure as he stepped beneath the rain showerhead. The water beat heavily on his head, massaging away the stress of filming, the aches of demolition, and the frustrations of having to keep his growing feelings for Sofia in check. He sipped his cold beer in a steaming hot shower and let his cares flow down the drain. There were few pleasures in life better than this. He sudsed his hair briskly, enjoying the scratch and the feeling of clean before turning his attention to scrubbing away the dust and plaster from the rest of his body. Switching the spray over to the side jets, he scrubbed himself clean with his bar of soap, ready to relax and fall asleep in front of the TV.

Although he'd built a functional bedroom/office space, most nights he fell asleep in his perfect recliner, too sore to move and too tired to care. There certainly wasn't anyone luring him into bed. He was free to do as he pleased. Why did that detail, which his married friends envied, always make him so sad?

He shut off the water and thought about that. Since he'd gotten honest with Sofia about wanting her, he'd begun to notice the places in his life where she wasn't. His once-solid normal now felt full of Sofia-shaped holes.

He dried off and tugged on a pair of gray sweatpants and a T-shirt he'd worn down to nearly threadbare perfection. He snagged his second beer and sat down in his sacred chair, ready to just be still for a while.

And then his phone rang.

CHAPTER 11

SOFIA GRIPPED her cell phone till the edges pinched her fingers while she waited for Adrian to pick up. She was tired of waiting. And at the end of this marathon day, she was just plain tired.

"Hello, beautiful."

"Don't you 'hello, beautiful' me!"

"¡Ay! What's got you ticked off?"

"You and your inability to do what I asked. You turn in these order forms half filled out and mostly illegible and expect me to track down all the freaking details for you. It's bullshit, and I've put up with it long enough."

"You're calling me after eight o'clock on a work night to complain about the way I do paperwork after twelve years?"

"Technically, I've been dealing with this shit for three years, but it ends tonight."

"That's not why you called me."

"Yes, it is."

"No, it isn't. We aren't children, and you don't need to make excuses to call me."

Sofia resisted the urge to chuck her phone at the wall. As

satisfying as that would be, she simply didn't have time or funds to replace it. She settled for yelling her displeasure into it.

"Argh! You arrogant bastard! I'm not calling to flirt with you. If I were, I wouldn't call you an asshole for wasting my time. Let me guess. You're sitting at home, watching the game with dinner and a beer resting in your belly."

"What, are you spying on me now?"

"Guess where I am. The office. I sure as hell haven't been able to turn my brain off for the night and relax. After a full day in the office and a surprise afternoon on camera, I'm still here placing orders from your half-assed form. I haven't eaten since lunch, and I still haven't solved the budget crisis. Thanks by the way for throwing me under the bus on camera with that. What the fuck? So yeah, I'm gonna call you and interrupt your evening, because I deserve better than this."

Sofia let all of her frustration vent into the phone. When she ran short of breath, she paused and waited for his response.

Crickets.

He'd hung up on her. Son of a bitch! All of the warm and fuzzy feelings she'd been considering nurturing shriveled and snapped in the fire of her rage.

Five minutes later when the phone rang, she let it go to voice-mail. She was afraid she might say something she couldn't take back. Her anger had temporarily disabled her filter. When it rang again, she turned off her ringer. When he called a third time, she turned the music in her office up to eleven. She'd given him enough energy today.

She pushed his orders to the side for later. The music would keep her awake and focused so she could finish the other requests in her pile. She would have ignored them completely just to spite him, but they were for the Shah project. She couldn't afford to have things arrive late, but she was too mad to deal with his shit right now. She put her head down and buried her anger in the classic alternative rock she was blasting.

So when the door to her office swung open, she screamed and grabbed her stapler as if she could use it to ward off an attacker or the zombie apocalypse. When she could draw breath again, she used it to shout.

"What the hell? Don't you knock?"

"I did. I also called you three times after my phone died to tell you I was coming to fix the papers," Adrian yelled back, competing with Dolores O'Riordan wailing about tanks and bombs and guns.

Sofia slapped the keyboard to turn off the music. Charged silence filled the room, neither willing to be the first to break it. Sofia gave in to her curiosity. "Your phone died?"

"Yes. I forgot to plug it in when I got home."

"Huh. I thought you hung up on me. How much of my rant did you catch?"

"Enough to know I'd better show up with a peace offering. Would you put the stapler down?"

Sofia looked at the stapler in her hand still held raised to strike and wondered who she thought she'd be maiming with a Swingline. She carefully put it back on her desk.

He passed her a sealed Tupperware. "Trade? Paperwork for dinner?"

She eyed him suspiciously. "What's in there?"

"Pollo en mole."

Sofia moaned deep in her throat, her mouth salivating at the words and flat-out drooling once the smell hit her nostrils. His freshly-showered clean man scent snuck in behind it and her rage weakened.

"Deal. That smells incredible." She shuffled the papers again to find his POs and shoved the papers into his chest to remind him that she was angry. That he was here to work. That they had established boundaries. That she absolutely wasn't going to kiss him again.

When her every impulse screamed for her to put her lips back on his, she clutched the Tupperware to her chest to keep her hands from reaching out and grabbing him. Who needed reminding of the boundaries?

He looked so good, his T-shirt wet with droplets he'd missed with his towel. She imagined that he'd thrown on those clothes intending them to be his pajamas. He'd be going to bed soon. Hmmm, Adrian in bed. Adrian in *her* bed. *Damn it! I'm angry. Not horny. ANGRY!* This took the term "hangry" in a whole different direction.

"Here are the orders. Do you see all the little boxes? Believe it or not, I need the information in all of them to fill out the order online. I'm going to reheat this." She hid behind sarcasm and ran, pushing past him to the office kitchen. She put the chicken and rice dish into the microwave and timed her breath to the countdown of seconds. She needed to regain her equilibrium before she went back in there. Ever since that kiss, she felt like he kept knocking her off-balance.

She grabbed a fork from the drawer and washed the few dishes that were left in the sink, so that their clients wouldn't think they were slobs, while she waited for the chicken to cool enough to eat. Returning things to order soothed her, when she wasn't busy resenting the fact that she was the only one who did it around the office. She wiped off the countertops again for good measure.

She took one more deep breath, and this time her head filled with the rich spicy scents of the mole. Her walls trembled a little. She'd been cross and bitchy with him on the phone, and he'd brought her food. That definitely earned him a few points. True, his mother had probably made it, but he'd brought it to her when she needed it. It was getting harder to hold on to her mad. Unlike the other men in her life, she'd told him she had a problem and he'd shown up to help. She carried the plastic bowl back to her office.

Adrian had taken her seat at the desk and had a pen in a death grip. His tongue peeked out between his lips, his concentration at once cute and fierce. He used the mouse to navigate down the screen, muttering part numbers under his breath.

She stood behind him and leaned over his shoulder, pointing with her fork at the screen.

"You know, if you use the search function here, it will go faster than trying to navigate around using the menus."

"I'm used to seeing this page on my phone. I can barely find what I need there. Here, everything is in a different place."

Sofia leaned back on the counter and took a bite of the chicken and moaned as the gorgeous blend of chilies, cocoa, nuts, and spices melted with the soft, tender meat on her tongue. This was the best Mexican food she'd had in ages, and she was going to savor it. She licked her lips, not wanting to miss a drop of that sauce.

When she realized Adrian had stopped typing and was staring at her, embarrassment flooded her face.

"What? It's delicious. Where did you get it?"

"Uhhmm, my, uh, my mom made it." He had turned to watch her over his shoulder, and he couldn't get his work done if he wasn't even looking at the computer.

She moved, resting her rear against the edge of her desk so she could face him where he sat. "Darn it. I'm going to have to steal her away from you. This is amazing."

"Yeah, good luck with that. It might be the only way to get her out of that house. I'll tell her you liked it." He scribbled a few numbers on the order form in front of him.

"Loved it," she corrected as she took another bite.

He leaned back in his chair and set down his pencil. His intent gaze unnerved her.

"What?"

"I just like hearing that word from your lips." He shifted in her chair, drawing her attention to his lap, and the fact that his sweatpants hid none of his excitement. What was it about an erection under gray cotton that made her thirsty? Good Lord, she wanted him without any of these barriers between them. She'd been angry and frustrated, but the combination of his caring actions and his gorgeous body were quickly eroding her determination to keep things all business at the office.

He hitched his hips again, and she knew she'd been caught staring. Chuckling, he put his hands on her hips and rolled the office chair over so he was seated directly in front of her, deliberately in her space.

"You know, I'm still a little hungry. I did have to smell that goodness all the way over here. Can I have a little taste?"

She searched for the perfect piece, intending to tease him. She held the morsel of chicken suspended in front of her mouth.

"Come and get it."

He stood and leaned into her space, his lips open to receive the bite, his eyes full of laughter. She grinned and popped it into her own mouth, chewing with dramatic appreciation. She'd expected him to laugh. When his eyes narrowed to focus on her lips, she was toast, slowly roasting in the heat of his gaze. She dropped the fork back into the plastic bowl and barely managed to swallow before she moved in to give him his taste fresh from her own lips.

Adrian followed her lead and kissed her senseless. The only place they touched was lip to lip, and it wasn't nearly enough. So when Adrian paused just long enough to remove the fork and Tupperware from her limp fingers and boost her up on her desk so she was fully supported, she didn't complain. She let go of her good intentions and held on tight to his hips instead. He smelled deliciously clean from his shower, and she had a moment's worry over her own scent after a full day of work. But only for a moment, before he drove every thought out of her head.

Framing her face with his hands, he tasted her cheeks, her

forehead, her eyelids, before returning to her mouth. Her hands were free to roam, and she let them explore the impressive muscles that lined his spine, all the way down to his very fine ass, which she gripped to pull him flush against her between her spread legs. Even through layers of clothing, feeling his hard erection pressed against her clit sent waves of heat through her belly. After months of self-service, she was ready to hand over control. She wrapped her legs around his hips, trapping him against her while she rocked her hips toward his. This had escalated quickly, but she couldn't bring herself to care. Keeping herself from mounting the man was taking all of her restraint. He moaned and slid his hands around her waist.

Sofia cringed and reached her hands under his, raising his to her upper back. She tried to lose herself in the kiss again. He pulled her in close, making her feel cherished and protected. When he slid his fingers forward to graze the sides of her breasts, her awareness of her body focused to that narrow point, allowing her to ignore the parts that she wished she could hide. But when he slid his hands down her sides again to grip her hips and lift the hem of her shirt, her focus shifted with them. She wished that the desire this created would be enough to shout down her self-consciousness, but it wasn't. She reached down to block his upward momentum, and this time he definitely noticed. He stopped kissing her altogether and stepped back.

"Why did you stop?" she asked. *Please, let it be any other reason...*

"You keep pushing my hands away when I touch you. I didn't think you wanted me to keep going."

"No. I... That's not..." She sighed. "Never mind. Let's just finish so we can go home."

He reached for her again, one hand heading for the space between her legs, and she clenched them shut tightly, trapping his hand on the edge between heaven and hell. She'd taken care of unwanted advances since middle school when she'd gotten breasts ahead of everyone else. She hadn't needed her brothers or her cousin then, and she didn't now.

She gritted her teeth and corrected his assumption that she wanted him to finish *her*. "I meant the purchase orders."

"Right. Sorry. Of course." He raised his hands in the universal sign for surrender, before gesturing to her chair.

She sat and struggled to find the offending papers and her outrage to go with them. He stood stiffly, arms crossed, behind her. He was frustrated, and she couldn't blame him. She was too busy berating herself for screwing up a hot-as-hell kiss to remember why she was supposed to be mad. All she could find was the sad. The shame of her reaction. The remorse over losing something she'd never had in the first place. That loss of potential pinched her heart harder than she expected, but she had to protect herself. Once he got his hands on her, once he saw what she was hiding, he wouldn't want her. And when he backed away, it would hurt even more if she'd let him get closer. The sadness and pain she'd bundled up in her weight gain threatened to break free, so she clamped down on it hard. Tears in her eyes, she turned back to the form he'd tried to fill out before they'd gotten distracted.

"Okay. This…is better. Please, just…fill it out…next time." *Damn it.* She was losing the battle to keep her tears out of her voice. His hand brushing down the back of her hair, offering comfort even after she'd pulled away, broke her.

All of her combined stresses poured out of her heart and down her face. She dropped her head onto the desk and gave up the fight.

Adrian continued to smooth his hand over her hair while making a shushing sound, as if she was a child with a skinned knee instead of a woman with a bruised heart and a stressed mind. Her pains were not easily fixed with a Band-Aid and a kiss. She couldn't deny that it brought her comfort though. How long had it been since someone had cared enough to comfort?

She turned in to that comfort, and he was there, kneeling next to her, arms open wide. His strong shoulder caught her tears as she let herself be wrapped up in his hug. She'd been so strong for everyone for so long... She'd borrow some of his strength for a while and put herself back together.

"It's okay. I've got you. Let it all out." His deep voice rumbled through her, breaking the last walls around her heart. So she did.

"It's just...everything. I hate this part of the job, but I do it because my family needs me to, and if I don't nothing gets done and no one gets paid. Now that I've got the designs, too, and the show, I resent the time it takes away from doing what I love. And then I started missing Gabe, and then I got mad at him for leaving me with this mess, but that gets me nowhere. It's not like he can come back and fix it. This crap takes even longer when the order forms are only half filled out, and I know more are coming tomorrow. And I still haven't gotten the show budget back on track. I really don't want to screw this up. I need this, and Mom and Dad need this, and you need this... and...and then I argued with Dad because he was being Dad, and then I blew things with you... I just... It's been a bit of a day." As her words ran dry, her embarrassment swamped her and she reached around him for the peanut butter cups in her candy drawer. Adrian must have thought she was reaching for her work, because he intercepted her and pulled her back in close.

"Just leave it a minute. I don't know what to say to most of that, but you didn't blow things with me. I don't know what I did to make you back away, but I'd like to. I don't want to screw up whatever this is either."

"What exactly is 'this'?"

"I don't know, but I'd like to find out."

Could she trust him? Did she dare hope that he would still want her once all of her walls were opened up, revealing her hidden flaws? He'd risen to every challenge she'd thrown in his path so far. The caress of his rough fingers down her arm tempted her, but the gleam of truth in his eyes convinced her.

She summoned her courage and met him out on that ledge, ready to take the leap alongside him.

"Me, too."

CHAPTER 12

ADRIAN FINISHED TIGHTENING the last screw to brace the final beam to the damaged one, fixing the damage caused by the leaks. By supporting the weakened beams with sister beams, the kitchen floor would be stabilized, and there would be no further risk of the refrigerator ending up in the crawl space.

He wished all foundations were this easy to shore up. After Sofia's rapid retreat the night before, he hadn't been able to stop thinking about how he could help her. If she had less stress in her life, maybe she'd be more open to starting something with him. It never hurt to be the guy who fixed things. He'd had no idea that she was feeling all those stressors so deeply. She hid it well. So often, she was the loud and confident business manager ribbing him. He hadn't realized that her snarking wasn't a joke and that he needed to change his habits. He seldom got to see her softer side. It was easy to forget that it even existed.

She needed a little support while they navigated these changes, and he was going to be right there for her every step of the way. It wouldn't hurt if he could keep her happy about the partnership proposal, too. He had a deep, driving desire to be the man this strong woman leaned on. Her tears last night had unlocked that goal, making him feel like a goddamn hero when they'd stopped.

He could get used to being her hero. Going home alone had taken every ounce of heroism he'd had left, but earning her trust was worth it.

He laid down the fresh subflooring and screwed it into place. One more hiccup handled. That should make her smile. He would also make more of an effort to fill out those damn order forms better. It was a pain in the ass to try and track down part numbers on his phone when his hands were covered in spackle, but he didn't want to be the reason she was in the office until nine every night. Not when he could be the reason she was in his bed at nine. Maybe they could figure out a shortcut or some middle ground that worked for them both, but until then he could make this work.

Now that the floor was repaired, he could install the cabinets and then start tiling. He liked the part where everything started to look finished best. He would love to see what finishing with Sofia looked like. He shook his head at his own rambling thoughts. He was getting turned on over cabinet installations.

I've got to stop thinking about her. These cabinets aren't going to hang themselves.

"Hey, handsome. The strong, silent type might work for your dating game, but it makes for shit TV. Pull your head out of the clouds, and talk me through what you're doing."

Adrian looked up at Trina and grinned. She was an attractive woman who dressed like a twelve-year-old boy, swore like a sailor, and handled that camera rig like a professional wrestler. He couldn't help but like her. He realized he'd gotten caught up in his thoughts again and wondered how much had shown on his face. He explained his next steps for the camera.

"Now that we've got the supports reinforced and the subfloor down, we can hang the cabinets and install the island. Seth and I were able to alter the prefab cabinets to make them fit the existing space by cutting down the door widths and reassembling the trim, creating a custom cookie sheet drawer next to the sink. Once we get the island installed, we'll start laying tile in here. This space is really starting to shape up."

"Did I hear something about an island?"

As if his thoughts had conjured her, Sofia rounded the corner of the kitchen door, all smiles.

"Yeah, you did. I hear Hawaii is beautiful this time of year. Want to go?"

"Ha ha. How's the floor?"

"All fixed. I'm going to hang the cabinets now, and we should be ready for the island by tomorrow. Then we can start laying the tiles."

"You're moving along faster than I expected."

Was it him or did she look nervous? They had the island, right? He'd seen it on her cut sheets. Something wasn't quite right, but he wasn't going to call her on it on camera. He'd learned that lesson yesterday. Trina was right there catching the whole conversation. "So, what's on your schedule today?"

"I was coming to check on your progress in here, and meet up with Trina to go do a walk-through of the Shahs' current house to see if there are pieces worth moving or repurposing before I stage the house."

"She's all yours. I'm going to break for lunch and then hang cabinets with the crew. Will you..." He paused, unsure if he should ask. But he couldn't help her if he didn't spend time with her. "Will you be coming back here after that?"

"I think so. I might have pieces to transport. Why?"

"I had an idea I wanted to run past you, but it can wait until later."

"Okay, if you're sure..."

"I am." He was absolutely sure that he wanted to spend more time with her.

"Then I guess I'd better get going. Trina? Are you good?"

"Sure thing. I'll round up some grunts to follow us in the moving van and swap batteries real quick. I'll meet you at the car."

～

"So what's up with the sexy head contractor?"

The non sequitur from Trina as she buckled her seat belt threw Sofia for a loop.

"I don't know what you're talking about."

"Uh-huh. Sure. The camera doesn't lie. There's something going on between you, and I can't tell if it's good tension or bad. All I know is that Jake is eating it up with a spoon. The sparks between you are a major plotline of this pilot."

Sofia squirmed in her seat, not sure how to take the news that her tension with Adrian was visible enough to be a plot point. "But there's nothing…" No, she couldn't lie. There was *something*, but damned if she would put a label on it and sell it on TV. "I don't know what it is, but you're right about one thing. He sure is hot."

"I have to tell you, this is one of the best reality shows I've ever gotten to work on. No flies in the jungle or mud races, and watching these guys swinging hammers all day is no hardship."

"I envy you."

"Why? You get to work with them all the time."

Sofia rolled her eyes. "Exactly. Water, water everywhere, and not a drop to drink. I'm the boss's daughter, and I'm in charge of everyone's paperwork and payroll. No one wants to mess with that."

"That sucks. So then you and Winston never?" Trina was fiddling with her camera and avoiding eye contact.

"Winston? No. Never. He's kind of a loner, but does solid drywall work. We use him on a lot of jobs. Why?"

"Just curious."

"Just curious, or just interested?" Sofia prodded as she turned onto the Shahs' street.

"Oh, look here we are!"

"So you can dish it but you can't take it?"

"There's a reason I'm behind the camera, honey, not in front." Trina hustled out of the car the minute it stopped moving, and Sofia chuckled before she let it drop.

If the camerawoman had the hots for one of her guys, she didn't care. Good for her. As long as it wasn't *her guy*.

Trina got her camera up and rolling to catch Sofia approaching the door. Farha Shah answered the door on the first knock.

"Hi. It's good to see you. Are you ready for the furniture walk-through?"

"I'm a little nervous. I tried to get everything cleaned up, but I can't reach under the sofas anymore." She ruefully rubbed her belly.

"Don't worry about that. I promise no one will be judging. Why don't you take me on a tour of your house? Tell me which pieces you love, which have sentimental value, and which you want to pitch in the dumpster."

"That's easy enough. Let's start in here." Trina sprinted ahead of them to set up the shot as Farha led Sofia into the living room.

"What pieces in here really fit your style?"

"I love the TV cabinet. We took an old wooden sideboard and repurposed it. But it's looking old, and I'm afraid to keep the flaking paint around the baby."

"But if we could redo it, would you want to keep it?"

"I'd love that. Gautam and I picked it out together, our first piece of furniture together. I just want it to be safe."

Sofia cheered internally. If Seth could work miracles, she'd just solved the kitchen island problem. "Is there anything else in the room that you like?"

"I like the sculpture in the corner. My roommate from college does metal work, and she made it for our wedding." The geometric twisting form definitely spoke to two lovers entwined. Sofia could see exactly where she'd put it in the new house.

"I want her number. That is stunning. What else?"

"Nothing else. I hate the couch. I hate the coffee tables. The dog has peed on the rug more times than I can count. I want it all gone."

"I can do that. I'm thinking a darker neutral, maybe with a pattern on the couch since it's going to be well-loved by children in the coming years. Do you like the style of the couch? Maybe I could recover it…"

"No. I hate the whole thing. It doesn't fit our style at all. It was a hand-me-down, and we are ready to upgrade."

Damn. There went that idea for saving money. Thank goodness she had her game face on today. "No problem at all. Why don't we see if there's anything worth salvaging in the dining room?"

"Cut!" Trina called out. "That looked great. Let me go get set up in there so I can get a good shot. I'll call you when I'm ready."

Farha turned to Sofia and put a hand on her arm.

"I can't thank you enough for taking on this project. I know it's kind of hectic with the show, but you've been so great to work with. When Jake showed me the pictures of the chandelier, I just fell in love with it. Thanks for taking our style into account with the design plan."

Her mind stuttered. Why was Jake encouraging Farha to change the design plan in the middle of the project? She kept her show face on, and smiled through her reply.

"Every good designer makes the plan with the client in mind. I'm just sorry that the production schedule on this is twisting things around. Normally, we'd have had this conversation back when we did the initial consultation. But it's okay. We are going to give you a beautiful home no matter what. I promise."

"Okay! Come on in!" Trina's voice cut into their conversation.

"Ready?" When Farha nodded, Sofia pushed aside her concerns and turned on her TV voice. "So, tell me about the furniture in here."

~

AFTER THE WALK-THROUGH WAS DONE, Sofia asked the production crew members to help get the TV cabinet packed into the back of the van. While they broke down cables and figured out how to carry it out, Sofia called her cousin Seth.

"Hey there, cuz. How's it going?"

"Great! I've got a project for you."

"Oh no. You're using that fake perky voice you use when you want me to do something I'm not gonna like."

There was no use denying it. She was asking a huge favor.

"Listen, it's for the show. I'm at the Shah house, and they've got a TV cabinet that I want to turn into their kitchen island."

"What?"

"No, really! It's a sideboard they were reusing, so it's got a ton of drawers."

"What's the catch?"

"I need to add two legs to support the overhang of the marble countertop for the breakfast bar, and I need to add two deep storage cabinets with doors on one end to make the dimensions work for the section under a butcher block countertop. Oh and we need to sand down the old paint, and repaint it all to match and look like weathered paint."

"That doesn't sound too bad. I can get it to you in...two weeks."

"I need it in two days."

"Sofia Amelia Regina Valenti. Have you lost your damn mind?"

"Please? I need to cut costs and stay on schedule, and the only way I can see to do that right now is to return the island I bought,

113

and repurpose what she has. And I might need you to donate your labor…" She trailed off into a mumble.

"What? Are you kidding me? I get why you need it fast, but you can't not pay us. That's not right, and you know it. We've got bills to pay too, and this is a rush job."

"Family discount, then?"

"Fi…"

"Think of it as an investment in your business. If the show takes off, we'll get more business through our doors. More business equals more money. I can't afford to screw this up on the pilot."

"Well, whose fault is that?"

"This stupid filming schedule! I had to submit plans for this before I even got to see the inspection report, so I overpromised, and now I'm scrambling. Adrian kept finding more problems behind every wall and floor he opened up. You know how that goes."

"I do. Don't you? Why didn't you plan for this?"

"I thought I had. Do you really want Dad's retirement to get screwed up because I messed up my first project budget in three years? Come on, Seth. I need your help. What will it take?"

Her cousin was silent, and Sofia's nerves began to twitch. She really needed Seth to come through on this one. She could ask Adrian to delay by a day, but she couldn't put him off much longer than that without tipping off the production team that there was a problem. She had no doubt that he would be able to pull this off, but she was wary of what it would cost her in return. She also knew he loved nothing more than busting her ass. He knew the quiet was killing her. Finally, he spoke.

"Two full days, to make up for the two days I'm going to spend busting my ass to finish this. You will do dinner duty/carpool/babysit Brandy's brother and sister for two days, so I can surprise her with a long weekend away."

"Done. You're the best, Seth."

"And don't you forget it."

"I'm driving the piece over to you right now."

"I'll be here."

"Thank you, Seth." She did a quick happy dance. She wasn't out of the woods yet, but this would go a long way.

"Don't thank me until I pull it off."

"Deal. Love you."

"Love you, too. Most of the time."

CHAPTER 13

ADRIAN STOOD up at the sound of the front door opening in the early evening. In the now empty house, any sound drew his attention. But it was her sound, her movement, her energy that had him rising and watching the doorway with anticipation. She did not disappoint. She looked amazing today in her TV-ready outfit and makeup. The violet sweater skimmed her curves, and her jeans showcased the ass that made his mouth water. She was still in her filming fuck-me heels, and they clicked across the new tile flooring he'd laid in the entry yesterday. She was stunning, but he saw through the façade to the real her. Her shoulders were slumped and her smile was for the cameras.

"Rough day?" he asked as she strolled into the dining room he was flooring with hardwood laminate.

"No, filming was fine."

"Everyone else has gone home for the day. Cameras off. So, rough day?"

Her shoulders dropped even farther and the smile disappeared.

"You could say that. I need an extra day on the island, but I found a solution that's going to fit our budget if Seth can make it work." She leaned up against the doorframe and crossed her arms.

"That's great! Why aren't you more excited?"

She turned to face him, her heart in her eyes.

"Have I bitten off more than I can chew? Nothing is going right, and I feel like it's my fault that we aren't better able to handle it. I'm running out of corners to cut. I just asked Seth to do me a huge favor to make this work. Is it worth it?"

Adrian needed to touch her, to console her, so he reached out a hand and placed it on her shoulder. When she didn't shrug it off, he counted it a win.

"Listen, we are all juggling crazy expectations to make this work. You've never done TV before, and it's been years since you've designed anything. You're doing fine under the circumstances, and next time we will work it out together. Just don't forget the unofficial company motto. Keep it simple. Is there any way to scale back on your designs?"

"I'm trying, but the whole point was to make a wow statement."

"A wow on a budget and a timeline."

"If I take it too bare-bones, it will look like crap on TV, and I'll never convince Jake and Dad to let me design full-time."

"Screw that. Focus on this client, this house. It'll come together."

"Easy for you to say. It's not your company that might go under if this backfires."

The smart-ass comment hit him right in the heart. He knew he shouldn't let it bother him, because she was right. Until Dom made his decision, it wasn't his company, not even a little bit. He was just an employee, trying to look out for his crew. "You're right. It's not."

"That's not what I meant..."

"But I still care about it, and your dad, and you. So don't you go second-guessing yourself. Own the plan, and make it happen."

She placed a hand on his arm, and he turned to look her in the eye. "I don't know much about this partnership plan, but you know I didn't mean it that way, right?"

"I know." But did he know? Did he know that she was on his side for the partnership plan? He wasn't a fool. He knew Dom's children had just as much say in the business as the patriarch. What if she wasn't on his side? He needed to spend more time with her, convincing her that he was the right guy for the job. He could think of one way to do that. "Come home with me."

"Excuse me?"

"Come to my home. You're done working now, right?"

"Yes, but I'm exhausted and covered with hairspray and makeup from the show. I just want a hot shower and my bed."

"I have a shower and a bed at my place." He wiggled his eyebrows, hoping to make her laugh but only half joking. If she wanted to get in his shower or his bed, he certainly wouldn't argue. Ever since she'd agreed to figure out what was growing between them, all he'd been able to think about was the next step. He wanted to spend some time alone with her. He wanted to figure out why she'd backed away from his kiss. If she didn't open up to him, he was bound to make the same mistake again. He'd waited for her to elaborate on her "It wasn't your fault," but she'd remained stubbornly silent. She'd shared her words and opinions all day long with everyone on the site. He closed the door behind them and set the alarms. Now that work was done and the cameras were off, he wanted her all to himself.

"I think it's a little soon to be talking showers and beds."

"Simply trying to be a good host. Come to my place. We can talk, relax, watch a movie, maybe make out a little on my couch. What do you say?"

"My, after an invitation like that, how can I refuse?"

"Good. Grab your coat. It's chilly." He deliberately ignored her sarcasm and took her hand in his.

The night cooled around them, the scent of freshly turned earth and juniper floating in the damp spring air. It was fairly dripping with dew, waiting to paint the lawn now that the sun had dropped behind the mountains. He inhaled deeply, hoping that the blast to his lungs would help cool his blood, to no avail. They walked hand in hand out to the curb, and Adrian couldn't remember the last time the simple pleasure had felt so right. But when he opened the door to his truck cab, she turned and headed for her own car.

"I'll follow you. That way I can get myself home if it gets late."

Damn it. Logic scored another point. At least the quiet ride home would give him time to think. He needed to convince her to give this flicker a chance to flame. He had spent too many years quietly waiting for it to burn out due to lack of fuel.

A girly movie. A glass of wine. A little snuggle on the couch. He plotted his strategy to give her a relaxing evening. She had earned a break from juggling basically three full-time jobs. He felt a little guilty for the extra work his paperwork had caused her and for all the mishaps on the project. First with the inspection fixes, then with the leak repairs, he'd added more to her stress than he'd ever intended. Time to fix that.

He had a twenty-minute drive to plan his strategy. When Sofia pulled into his driveway a few seconds behind him, Adrian was waiting to open her door for her.

"Thank you."

"You're welcome. It's just this way."

He led the way around to the back of the house, and realized that she was a good five feet behind him. She warily walked through the back gate. He laughed.

"I promise there's nothing weird or creepy."

"I'm sure that's what every weird or creepy dude says."

"Am I weird or creepy?"

"I'm reserving judgment."

"Ouch." Adrian rubbed a hand where her arrows of snark hit him square in the chest. "I have the second floor apartment, and the stairs go up the back."

She exhaled audibly, and he prayed it was good nerves and not the bad kind making her short of breath. He wasn't really scary, was he? Was she having second thoughts about getting involved with one of the crew? To his knowledge, she had never dipped a toe in that pool, though she certainly could have. She'd always kept a careful distance. Was she going to try and back away from him, too? Was she worried about his proposal? To be so close to what he wanted and still doubt that he would ever truly belong pinched at the heart beneath his hand. But fortune favors the bold, so he pushed ahead.

"It's just up here."

He offered his hand and was reassured when she took it. He led her up to his deck and opened the dead-bolted door to his apartment. The door creaked as it opened, giving its best imitation of a haunted house after weeks of neglect.

"Nope. Not creepy at all." Her laugh cut through the night air and hit him square in the throat. At this rate, he'd need a medic by morning. But she walked inside, and that was all that mattered.

"Wow! There's a lot more space up here than you'd think, looking at the house from the outside. Did you build this?"

"I did, a few years ago. I needed my own place that wasn't overrun with little sisters, but Mamá still needs me too much for me to move far away."

"I know all about that headache. Dad bought an apartment building as an investment property about fifteen years ago. Frankie, Enzo, and I all have apartments side by side. It's a freaking Valenti dorm!"

He liked hearing her joke and watching her explore his home. He'd worked hard to make it his.

"You've got a way with design. The way you tucked the kitchen under the eaves with floating shelves is genius. And I love the dormer window over the sink."

Adrian felt his face warming. Blushing? Was he blushing over a little compliment? Time to get his plan rolling, before she turned him into a panting puppy. "Thank you. Would you like something to drink? I've got wine…"

"Actually, I'd kill for a cold beer right now."

He was surprised, but pleasantly so, that he'd pegged her wrong.

"That I can do." He dramatically opened his small refrigerator like some game show host, and she laughed again. So far, so good. "Ladies' choice."

"I'll have a Pacifico, please."

As he opened their beers, he heard telltale footsteps on the stairs.

"*¿Mijo?* Is that you?"

"Yes, Mamá. I'm home. Come on up and meet Sofia." He had no qualms about this. He loved his mom, and he knew she didn't get much company, so he always invited her up to meet his friends. His mom had been hearing about her for ages, and he was hoping that Sofia in his apartment would be a frequent occurrence. Then again, Sofia was more than just a friend.

He flashed back to his conversation with his mom earlier… Okay, maybe one qualm. Make that two. His mother was a loose cannon around women she wanted him to date. All of the mothers on the block with daughters of marriageable age had been called in and vetted over many cups of coffee. She could be intimidating, but it was too late to turn back. He didn't want Sofia to think he didn't want her to meet his mother. He'd just have to bulldoze through it now.

"Mamá, meet Sofia Valenti. Sofia, my mother, Graciela Villanueva."

"It's so nice to meet you." Sofia reached for his mother's hands and held them in her own while she spoke. "Adrian brought me some of your *pollo en mole*. It was divine."

"Did he, now? Well, I'm glad you enjoyed it. He's a good boy, my Adrian. Strong but thoughtful."

"She's a good woman, my *mamá*. Sweet but meddlesome."

"What? I'm not telling her anything she doesn't know." His mother let go of Sofia's hand long enough to pat him on the cheek.

"Enough, Mamá."

Sofia laughed along with him, and warmth flooded his chest. He'd heard more laughter from her tonight than he had in the last year in the office.

"You sound like my mother. She likes to list my attributes to any single man who will stand still long enough to listen. You don't have to sell me on Adrian though. I already know he's a great guy."

Adrian watched this woman charm his mother, and desperately hoped she'd be *his* woman soon.

"I'm sure your mother wants the best for you, too. My Adrian..."

"Mamá, stop!" He laughed along, since Sofia was laughing, but he knew his mother was deadly serious and would not be deterred. "We are going to watch a movie and relax. I'm in for the night, so you can lock up."

"Okay, I can take a hint. I'm glad to put a beautiful face with the name. Good night, you two."

"I could say the same Mrs. Villanueva. Sleep well."

Adrian leaned over and kissed his mother's forehead. "Night, Mamá. I'll be down to double-check the locks later."

"Don't worry about it tonight. You have a guest."

"I'll be down later. *Te amo, Mamá.*"

"Te amo tambien, mijo."

As he closed the door behind her, he let out a sigh of relief with the breath he'd kept trapped in his chest. That had gone well. Or at least, as well as could be expected, when one had a nosy mother with no filter.

CHAPTER 14

"THAT WAS SWEET. I'm glad to finally meet her. Why didn't you ever bring her to one of the company picnics?" Sofia tucked her hair behind her ear, and deliberately kept the small talk rolling as she wandered down his hallway. Her nerves were nipping at her heels, and she was afraid to slow down in case they caught up with her and ruined everything.

"I would have had to drag her."

"Wow. Are the picnics that bad?"

"No." He chuckled. "She hasn't left the house in years. Even her doctor comes to her."

That caught her attention, and she turned back to face him. "So when you said stealing her might be the only way to get her out..."

"Yeah, I meant it. She's terrified of the outside world. Ever since Dad..."

Wow. What would it feel like to be afraid of the outside world? Her mother had reacted to losing Gabe by chasing life. What if she'd chosen to hide instead? Sofia had a hard time picturing her mother hiding from anything, but wasn't that exactly what she'd done herself? She could tell herself that she'd stepped into the office to help out and gotten stuck, but she hadn't done anything to get unstuck either, before this whole TV thing. She'd spent three years hiding from life. It had been safe, but safe wasn't enough anymore.

"I get that. The world seemed like a pretty scary place after Gabe died, too."

She turned away again, afraid of sharing too much, opening too many dark closets. Instead she opened the door in front of her. His bedroom. Seeing his large bed covered by a smooth expanse of navy blue comforter, just begging to be messed up, took her mind down a much more pleasurable path. She slammed the door shut before she got herself lost in the forest. Didn't the story with the wolf warn of straying from the path? But oh how she longed to step into temptation and let herself be taken...

His voice in her ear startled her.

"You seemed to handle it pretty well."

Handle what well? What had they been talking about? *Gabe. Right.* That pulled her back into harsh reality fast enough. She moved back toward the safety of the living room.

"Did I? I'm glad it looked that way from the outside. Inside, it's been a bit of a dumpster fire for the last three years."

"Hey, didn't you want to shower?" He stood poised on the threshold of the bathroom she'd skipped.

She froze. Should she? Shouldn't she? She absolutely wanted to wash off the layers of product she was covered in. She peeked inside the doorway and saw the most tempting shower she'd ever seen, but the idea of getting naked anywhere near Adrian made her gut clench. "Um, I don't know if that's such a good idea."

"Your choice. I need to take one quick, because I'm filthy. Why don't you make yourself comfortable on the couch, and I'll be right out."

Sofia took her beer and sat on the couch, which conveniently left her with a view of the bathroom door. She would like to say that she didn't picture Adrian naked in the shower, hot water sluicing over his fine body. She would love to claim that she didn't think of all the ways she'd like to get him filthy, before she helped him get clean. But she wouldn't lie, especially not to herself. She might not know how she felt about his interest in her, but her own interests were shockingly clear. When he emerged from the shower with a skimpy white towel wrapped around his waist, she nearly swallowed her tongue. Drops of water still clung to his bare arms and shoulders, and she was dying of thirst.

Needing a minute to pull herself together, she ducked into the bathroom he'd just left. His scent in the steam filled her head and made her dizzy. Her reaction to him was potent, but it wasn't her reaction she was worried about. She borrowed his shower soap and scrubbed her face clean. It took some effort to get the thick makeup off.

When she'd succeeded and her own pink face stared back at her in the mirror she almost wished she hadn't. The woman staring back at her looked far too vulnerable, but she didn't want to hide behind a pretty mask anymore. If she was going to take a chance on him, he needed to see the real her. No makeup was a good first step. If he backed away now, it would hurt but she'd be able to recover.

When she came back out, she found him in the kitchen. He was wearing those damn gray sweatpants that made her mouth water, and a white T-shirt. He was bent over, pulling a foil-wrapped package out of the freezer, and she tried and failed to not stare at his ass. He unwrapped the foil and tossed the contents on a plate and into the microwave.

"Tamales."

"Huh?" She looked up to meet his smiling eyes.

"I've got tamales for dinner, if that's okay."

"Sounds great."

"So besides the show making things crazy, how are things at work?"

Sofia sat down on the couch, and Adrian took the opposite end. It seemed he really was looking to get to know her better. She didn't know what it said that she was a little disappointed by that. "It leaves much to be desired."

"How so? You've done a great job taking over for your mom as office manager when she needed to step back. I think most days you are the glue holding that place together."

"Yeah, but Gabe was supposed to be the glue. I took responsibility because there was no one else who could. I'm the oldest now..." Her voice thickened and cracked, but she bit back the tears. "I never wanted this. Three years of all work and no play. Between work and being sad, I haven't managed to have much of a life."

"No play?"

"Nothing beyond a few lackluster first dates. But that isn't the worst part. I was doing all this so I'd have a chance to chase my dream. I miss design so much. It's all been a dead-end. Finally, with this show I have a chance to get back to that. So even if I have to keep working crazy hours to hold it all together, I will." She peeled the yellow paper label off her bottle, worrying it into little balls.

"I had no idea you hated the office side so much."

"Looks like I'm better at hiding my feelings than I thought."

"I'll have to remember that."

What was wrong with her that the cockiness in his voice made her grin? "Oh, you think I'll have feelings for you that I'll need to hide?"

"I think you already do. And if I'm doing this right, there will be more." He slid closer to her on the couch and dropped an arm around her shoulders.

"Smooth."

"As Skippy. So, what do you want to watch?"

"Listen, I know how this Netflix and chill is supposed to work, but I'm not... I mean... I'm still trying to figure out why I agreed to come over here tonight."

"So you're saying you weren't driven out of your mind by lust over my hot body?" There was that confident humor again, the one that shook her and made her want to laugh at the same time.

"More like the idea of sanding more drywall was going to push me over the edge," she teased.

"I am disappointed in your imagination. I'm definitely a better choice than drywalling."

"We'll see." Sofia snuggled closer to his side, her actions at odds with her words.

"Listen, we can just watch a movie and relax. We'll see where things go."

"Yeah, it's where we might go that's tripping me up."

"Pick a movie. I won't do anything you don't want me to."

"Okay. How about the original *Fast and Furious*? I haven't watched that in ages."

Adrian's face blanked with shock, and she laughed as he reached for the remote.

"What? You expected me to say *Pride and Prejudice* or something? Actually, the version with the zombies was pretty funny. We could watch that instead."

"Just when I think I have you figured out."

At least I'm not the only one off-balance here...

ADRIAN SETTLED back into the couch and started the movie, watching Sofia out of the corner of his eye. He'd gotten used to seeing her in her full makeup. She looked younger and more real without it. His protective and possessive instincts were battling for control, but he was determined to give her the space she needed. He clearly had some figuring out to do, too. He couldn't believe he'd missed how much she hated her job. She definitely hid that well. What else was she hiding?

He rubbed his fingers over the shoulder of her super-soft sweater, and she snuggled closer. Okay, so shoulder strokes were okay. He tried to focus on the movie and go slow, but with her warmth pressed up against his side and her lovely breasts just a glance away, it was hard. So hard. He shifted slightly to readjust the pressure in his lap, and she took that opportunity to snuggle deeper.

Oh God. I'm going straight to hell.

His fingers gripped reflexively against her shoulder as he fought for control. Slow might kill him, but he'd honor his promise. He slid his hand farther down her arm, giving her time to decide if she wanted to settle into the side hug or retreat.

He felt a ridiculous leap of pride when she pulled her feet up beside her on the couch and leaned her head on his chest. She was blocking his view down her shirt now, but the scent of her hair flooded his senses and he forgot to care. Close enough to kiss. He hadn't been this physically excited by a cuddle since high school. The wave of well-being that washed over him was completely new.

Slow. Down. Think glacial. He had a better understanding of the threat to the Arctic now. What chance did a glacier have of withstanding this persistent rise in heat?

About the time Paul Walker's car blew up, she leaned forward to place her empty beer bottle on the floor.

His lap was momentarily filled with warm, beautiful Sofia. His mind flooded with wicked thoughts, and he couldn't stop the groan and involuntary cock twitch. His sweats weren't doing much to help hide his situation. She froze, and so did he, determined to make good on his promise.

She looked up at him over her shoulder and grinned. "You okay there?"

"Mmhmm." The mumble was all he could muster. She put a

hand on his thigh to push herself up, pulling the gray cotton taught over his erection. She tried to hide a gasp, and his quads spasmed in response. "Jesus, Sofia."

She chuckled like a goddess confident in her power over her mere mortal man.

"Is there a problem?" She slid her hand farther up his thigh, and it was all Adrian could do to keep his hips from arching off the couch.

He nodded, unable to find words.

"What is it?"

He took her hand and removed it from his thigh so he could think again. Holding it loosely in his own hand, he leaned back to look her in the eye. "I promised I wouldn't do anything you didn't like."

"Yes, you did. Is that a problem?"

He nodded. "I don't know what you don't like. Or if you'll like what I think you'd like."

She considered the problem carefully and he barely breathed. There was no way she was as turned on as he was, but he was hopeful that she was a little curious. Enough to give him a chance.

"Why don't you tell me what you think I'd like, and we'll see?"

He raised his other hand to her face, needing to see her eyes, to read her emotions as he laid his hopes and needs bare. "I'd like to kiss you."

"I'd like that, too," she answered quickly.

Adrian shook his head. "I'm not done." He brushed his thumb over her bare lips. "I'd like to kiss you here and here."

He moved his thumb with his words, tracing her cheek and down her neck, where her pulse beat madly beneath his fingers, despite her calm expression. So she *was* good at hiding her feelings.

"I'd like to take my kisses even lower." He didn't break eye contact as he moved his hand lower to toy with the edge of her sweater against her ample cleavage. He moved his thumb to the nipple he could feel hard as stone even through the layers and teased her, flicking back and forth. "I'd like to pull off your sweater, take off your bra, and kiss your gorgeous breasts."

Her eyes flickered away at that. First barrier. He took his hand away, and she looked back, questions and unspoken uncertainty in her eyes.

"You didn't like something about that, so I won't." He clarified his intentions, and moved his hand back to her cheek and safer ground.

"I liked most of that. I just... I don't..."

"Whatever it is, tell me. I want to make this good for you."

"I don't want to take my clothes off." She blurted it out. He could see the shame filling her eyes, and he hated it with a passion he didn't fully understand. "I don't want you to see me."

How could she feel ashamed of any part of her beautiful body? Maybe if he could pull her back into the heat of her own response, she'd forget long enough to let him show her shame had no business between them. "So me kissing your breasts, licking you, squeezing you, teasing you, is okay if I leave your sweater on?" She nodded, and he resumed his verbal seduction. "Can I pull your sweater down for that? If I leave it on?" She nodded again.

He hooked a finger into the low neckline of the sweater that was keeping her hidden. God, she tempted him. He planted teasing kisses on her chest before continuing his verbal mission.

"And if I wanted to touch you here? Kiss you here? Could I?"

He slid his hands lower to her hips and the top of her thighs, letting his fingers tease the space where her thighs compressed tightly together.

"If I wanted to run my hands over your beautiful ass to pull you closer to me, would you like that?"

She lowered her lids, and he couldn't tell if she was overwhelmed by the image or if she was hiding again. She hesitated to answer.

"If you're not sure, would you let me try to convince you?" Her eyes snapped open, and the wariness was written all over her face. He had to erase it. "I'd like to show you how every inch of your body turns me on."

"I'd like to see that, too."

That approval was all he needed. Clothes stay on? No problem. He was up for the challenge. Literally. Straight up and throbbing. He went back to the beginning, taking her lips in a gentle kiss that he poured all of his longing into. He'd been waiting years for this. His kisses down her neck drew shivers of pleasure in response, and he tried to chase them with his tongue. When she sat up and reached behind her to undo her bra strap, he knew he'd won.

"*Dios mio, querida.* You are so..." He couldn't help but gasp as he tugged her sweater and bra down low enough to expose one of her breasts.

"Big?" she supplied with a grimace.

"Gorgeous, beautiful, sexy. None of these words are enough." He'd always admired her breasts, but now that he'd seen their natural magnificence, he was a confirmed fan. He wanted to rip the sweater off so he could see all of her at once, but she wasn't ready for that. So he'd take what she'd allowed and adore it. She didn't like the way her body looked, so he'd take the time up front to convince her to see things from his perspective. Which was that she was a smoking hot goddess who could slay him with a twitch of her hips or a bounce of her tits. He sucked her nipple into his mouth, holding her firmly with one hand. Using his tongue, he pulled all manner of delicious sounds from her lips. She was so lost, she barely hesitated when he reached his other hand around to her ass.

So far she hadn't done anything but kiss him back, and he was already hard as a rock. When she slid her hands up into his hair to grip his head, he groaned and buried his face in her chest, enjoying the hell out of her willing touch.

He rolled and slid off the couch to kneel between her legs as she sat back on the couch. He tugged her sweater back up over her beautiful breast and was pleased by her obvious chagrin. But he didn't let her linger in disappointment long, tugging the offending sweater back down on the opposite side, determined to be fair and impartial. Both of her breasts were magnificent and deserved to know it. His new position allowed her to tighten her grip on his head, and he let her lead the way, guiding him where she wanted more. It had the added benefit of aligning their pelvises perfectly. He found a small measure of relief, even through the layers of denim and cotton separating them, as he rocked forward to kiss her lips. She moaned and arched her hips against his, encouraging him.

Soothing her fears had made him feel strong before, but the way she was responding now made him feel damn near barbaric. He was tempted to toss her over his shoulder and haul her off into bed. But a firm voice in the back of his head warned him to keep his promise of control. Making out on the couch would have to do for tonight.

He hadn't tried to make a girl come with her clothes on since high school. Same rules still applied. *Follow her lead. Read her cues. Stop when she stops enjoying it.* His father had been more open than most and had made the rules abundantly clear from an early age. He pulled back from Sofia's wicked kiss to make sure he was on the right track.

"Do you like that?" He rolled his hips again, and her eyes rolled back in her head.

"Yes, Adrian. God, yes. That feels so good."

It was as if she'd broken the seal on her resistance with that yes. She gripped his head and kissed him hard before guiding his head back to her chest.

"You do this to me, Sofia. I watch you walk through a job site

133

barely contained in your tight sweaters, and I want to take you into the nearest dark corner and set you free."

He needed little encouragement to match her frantic pace. Every lick, every tug, every pull of his lips drew him in closer to her fire. He took her hand and guided it to his hard length, and she gripped him firmly as he thrust into her hand.

"This is what you do to me. You sit behind that desk of yours like a queen, and I want to kneel at your feet and lick you here." He moved his hand between her legs and almost got burned by the heat. She shifted hers back to his shoulder and held on tight. "I want to hear you come for me, before I lift you onto your desk and finish the job."

Each sound he drew from her lips, each twitch of her body was driving him mad. The thought of how she'd feel beneath him, surrounding him, nearly pushed him over his edge.

"I want to slide my hand inside these jeans and see how wet you are for me." He moved his hands to the button keeping him from heaven and waited.

When she nodded frantically, he leaned her back on the couch and slid the button free. His fingers slid along the bare skin of her hip and dipped below her cotton underwear. Searching for her hooded clit, he reached lower until he found the spot that made her hips twitch off his couch. He took her nipple back into his mouth while he slid even lower to discover that she was indeed dripping wet for him. Still kneeling, his hips moved of their own volition, sliding hard against the edge of the couch as he tried to hold on to his sanity.

"I want..." He panted, trying to find the breath to keep weaving his spell. "I want my fingers inside you, Sofia."

He explored between her lower lips, tracing and teasing, until she tilted her hips, encouraging him inside. With every finger thrust, he pictured his cock enjoying the same exploration. He was seconds from coming without her.

"I need you, Sofia. Come for me." He pressed his palm against her clit and pleasured her tight pussy with two fingers now. Her gasps were coming closer together, and he tugged her nipple hard with his lips in time to her labored breathing. A long, shattered wail emerged from her throat as everything clenched. Her hands on his head, her legs around his hand, her grip around his heart. He was flung into his own orgasm by the aftermath of her pleasure.

That was beyond anything he'd expected. Making out with Sofia was his new favorite pastime. Sorry, baseball. He laid his head against her chest to catch his breath and reveled in the rapid drumbeat of her heart.

Whatever *this* was, it was off to an excellent start.

CHAPTER 15

OH, GOD. THIS WAS TERRIBLE. What had she done? How could they go back to work and not be weird with each other? She'd agreed to the movie date in a weak moment, and now she had his O-face seared in her mind. She couldn't lie though. If he'd been terrible, this would be easier. He'd been amazing, attentive and exciting, and she'd been powerless to resist. How on earth was she going to keep a stupid grin off her face while they were filming now? Her control was good but not superhero good.

It had been so long since someone else had taken charge of her orgasms that he had left her undone, raw nerves exposed, despite obeying her request to leave her clothes on. Sweet Lord, what would this man do to her if she were naked? She tried to snatch her defenses, but her mind was a swirling mess of pleasure and pain.

Thank God he'd listened though. The thought of this gorgeous man seeing her stretch marks and belly rolls was scary. She didn't want to see the disappointment overtake the desire in his eyes. Maybe next time, they could turn off the lights—

What was she thinking? Next time? They couldn't do this again, no matter how much her body craved his touch. She'd been caught in his magic, frozen by his words, unwilling to break the spell. But once she'd decided to take a more active role in her own downfall, she'd been mighty tempted to pull his shirt over his head so she could run her hands over what she was sure were gorgeous abs. But fear had stopped her. What if he took it as an invitation to reciprocate? The idea of never seeing him naked almost made her cry. *Nope.* She was not going to be that girl who cried after she came.

She eased from beneath him, embarrassment beginning to spread its nasty, prickly venom through her veins. He lifted his head with a sappy grin that quickly faded when he saw whatever was making it through her shield. Damn it.

Fear, shame, guilt, anger—take your pick. It could be any of them. She tugged her sweater up into place. She had to get out of here before she did something stupid. Like stay.

"Well, that was fun." *Too late to avoid stupid.* She stood and buttoned her jeans. "I mean, thank you, but I need to go. Go home. Um, I'll see you tomorrow."

With every syllable she uttered, she felt more and more ridiculous. Not to mention the fact that her bra was dangling beneath her sweater, simultaneously making her feel awkward and aware, while doing nothing to keep her overly sensitive girls from bouncing against the cashmere, reminding her of where his tongue had worked its magic. She had to get away.

"Sofia, wait. Why are you rushing off? I thought we were having a good time." He glanced at the TV. "Look, Vin Diesel hasn't even hijacked the truck yet."

"It was good. A good time. But I don't think we should do that again."

"I agree. Next time, no clothes."

"Adrian, be serious."

"I am serious. Why wouldn't we want to do that again? I'd like to do that and more every day of the week. You're amazing, Sofia." He reached for her, and she stepped back before she gave in to the impulse to tackle him to the floor and ride him like a cowgirl. The image sent a flush to her cheeks, this one definitely desire. But no. She didn't belong with a guy like him.

They needed to work together. She could be friendly and totally forget that she had pants feelings for him. The alternative was too scary to consider.

"I can't." Before she could make the situation any worse, she ran.

Thankfully, she made it into her car and out of his driveway before the tears began. She pulled over around the corner so she didn't end the night in an accident with her bra unhooked. Tears ran down her cheeks, and she grimaced at the thought of the splotchy cheeks and puffy eyes that would follow. Adrian would back off fast if he could see her now, with her careful façade disintegrating. The cashmere sweater, the tight jeans, the hair and makeup—it was all a shell to make her palatable for the home audience. He'd been attracted to the artifice, not the real her, or he'd have made his move a long time ago. The tears overflowed her dam for the second time that week, weakened by the passion of the evening. She cried over her cowardice and her wounded pride. She cried over her fear that she'd just screwed up big time. She cried over what her life had become. By the time the tears wound down, she was utterly spent.

Sofia felt like a fool, but she was a fool who could recover from this. She just had to pretend like it never happened.

ADRIAN WAS STILL CONFUSED as hell the next morning. Sofia had torn out of his apartment like a bat out of hell after what he thought had been an excellent make-out session on the couch. What had he missed?

He'd replayed the evening in his head so many times, he had entire swaths of her dialogue committed to memory. And he still couldn't read between the lines. What would he say to her today? He felt like there was a bomb ticking down and he was the only one who could detonate it. And he had no manual, no wire-cutters, and no backup. He hoped his MacGyver skills were up to the challenge.

Using the excuse of needing more coffee, he strolled out to the craft services table set up in the driveway. If he scanned the street for her car while he mixed his cream and sugar, well, he was just being aware. Damn, even he didn't believe that lie.

"Hey, Adrian! Just the guy I was looking for."

Adrian forced a smile as Jake Ryland bounded up with his trademark energy. Did the man ever do anything with normal intensity? "Not sure if that's good news or bad."

"Good, I hope. I just wanted to give this to you. I borrowed it to check some timelines last night." Jake hefted the site binder into Adrian's arms.

Jeez. How distracted had he been to not even notice that the binder had been missing? "Thanks. I was, uh, looking for that."

Jake reached around him to fill his travel mug with more coffee, drank half the cup down, and refilled it again before turning his full attention to Adrian. Mainlining caffeine like that, no wonder the man was wired.

"So, how are things going?"

Great, now he wants to chat? Adrian tried to keep the chagrin off his face. He didn't trust Jake as far as he could throw him, and his "casual chats" always had a purpose. He was in no condition to filter his thoughts this morning. This guy's job was to find, create, and film conflict. The last thing he wanted was to have his feelings splattered all over the TV. Drywall and tiling? Fine. Deep emotional confessions? Hell no. "Things are good. We are clipping right along."

"And things with Sofia?"

Adrian felt the blood drain from his face.

"What things with Sofia?"

139

"Well, it seems like you two have very different perspectives on the job. How's that going?"

Whew. Bullet dodged.

"It's going fine. We had a few kinks to work out in the beginning with the budget, but now I think we are on the same page."

"If you say so."

Don't take the bait... Damn it. He couldn't resist that lure.

"Why? Did she say something to you?" Adrian tried to keep the curiosity in his voice professional, but he had a feeling Jake saw everything roiling through his mind anyhow.

"She hasn't said a word, but the cameras don't lie. Get you two in a room alone together and the gloves come off."

Jake's laugh made Adrian grit his teeth. That would be the only item of clothing coming off between them. He bit back the sarcastic retort. None of Jake's business. "I'll try to be more flexible."

"Oh, God, please don't! You two fighting makes for great TV. I don't know how you've managed to keep working together for so many years, but whatever you're doing, keep doing it!"

Jake slapped him on the back and walked away, but Adrian felt the sting of his words far longer.

CHAPTER 16

SOFIA PULLED up to the Shah project Friday morning. They had three days left to finish the house before the big reveal, and she needed to be there every step of the way for the finishing touches, despite her desire to avoid Adrian. Her punch list was flooded with details, and she couldn't afford to let a single one slip. As she got out of the car, her brother Enzo leaned against his shovel and grinned. At eight a.m., his brown hair was already plastered to his head, and he wore a smudge of dirt across his high cheekbone.

"You're out here early." She greeted him as she walked up the drive.

"Been here since six. I figured I'd get as much done as possible before the film crew slows me down. It's gonna be a hot one today."

"Cameras roll at nine?"

"Yep. Not your usual filming attire," he pointed out. She looked down at her torn denim jeans and her ancient college intramural basketball shirt, both splattered with a rainbow of paint, and shrugged.

"I'm not wearing nice clothes on a get-dirty day. How can I

help with the yard?" Her little brother loomed over her as he gave her a hug. As she wrapped her arms around him, she realized his skinny waistband was bare. He'd managed to avoid being miked yet. She let her guard fall just a little and hugged him tight. Enzo had always been a string bean, ever since he grew six inches the summer before sixth grade. He never had been able to hold much weight on his frame. Working in landscaping had helped him pack on some muscle, but he was still a wiry giant who loomed over his *big sister* when he hugged her. Not for the first time, Sofia wished she could share some of her padding just to fill him out a little. Her Italian grandmother gene was strong.

"I'm good. You don't need to get all dirty."

"Yes, I do, Enzo. You're covering the labor on this for free to keep us on budget. The least I can do is reduce your personal labor."

"Fair enough. Grab some gloves from my truck. You can run wheelbarrows of dirt from the truck to the beds, and then fill up with trimmings to take back to the dumpster from these olives I'm pruning."

"You've got it. I really owe you one."

"Yes, you do."

"Got any requests?"

"Just...keep an open mind over the next few weeks." With that, her cryptic little brother clammed up and turned back to his clippers.

Why would she need an open mind? Was he talking about the show? Or Adrian's proposal? Or something else? She hated not knowing, but she deliberately did as he asked and moved on. "I don't know if I said it before, but I love your plan for this yard. Simple, native plants with modern touches of wood and whimsy. They're going to love it."

"Thanks, sis. I'm glad you approve. You gonna get movin' or what?"

"On it." She leaned up and pressed a kiss on his sweaty cheek. "Thanks again."

"I'm doing it as much for me as for you."

They worked in companionable silence, and Sofia got caught up in thoughts of Adrian. He was here. She'd seen his truck. She wondered how he was doing, but she was too embarrassed over the way she'd left that she decided to let it be until after they finished the pilot project. As the pile of cut shrubbery grew and the pile of dirt to be shifted diminished, a comfortable numbness descended. So when Enzo interrupted her flow with a question, she was caught off guard and answered honestly.

"So what do you think of this thing with Adrian?"

"I don't know what I think. It all happened so fast."

"Not so fast. He has worked for the company for twelve years."

Ohhhh. The partnership. Right. Of course that's what he meant. Sofia looked around to see if they were being filmed, before she answered. She'd rather not have their private family business shared on camera.

"True, and he is a reliable contractor. But I just don't see how this is going to work. Has Dad given you any specifics of his plan?"

"Not in so many words, but I'm for it. If it gets him off my back about leading the company, let's do it. Yesterday."

"You don't have any qualms about handing over part of our family legacy to someone else? No concerns about who's going to be in charge?"

"Not really. I trust Adrian. I want him on the team." Enzo snipped more branches from the olive, making it look more topiary than tree.

"As a team member, for sure, but Dad can't seem to answer the question of what role exactly Adrian will be playing. Is he going to be your boss? My boss? An equal partner? A lesser partner?"

"All I know is that ever since Gabe died, Dad's been looking at me like I'm some replacement oldest son, and I'm sick of it. If he wants Adrian to step into that spotlight, more power to him."

The idea of anyone replacing Gabe in the family sat like a stone in Sofia's stomach. True, she was still angry at Gabe for dying and was desperate to move past the career block his death had become. But no one could ever replace her brash, brave, big brother.

"I mean, he's practically already family."

"What's that supposed to mean?" Sofia snapped at him, daring him to back that up. What did he know?

"Twelve years is a long time to learn about the running of a company. He's been with us through a lot of ups and downs, and if Dad trusts him to be the crew boss, so do I." Enzo tossed his pruners into his work bucket and picked up a shovel.

"I'll tell you one thing. He's not going to be *my* boss." Sofia spun to see Frankie strolling up the path in ancient cargo pants and a freebie shirt that had seen better days.

"Has Dad said anything to you?" Sofia was hoping for more details so she could craft her response before Dom jumped off the deep end and got everyone into trouble.

"No. But he knows I want to run the company. I've dropped enough hints, and I'm putting in the man-hours to become head contractor. This is our company, and I'll be damned if I let someone swoop in and nab it just because Dad thinks I'm too young." Frankie's crossed arms and scowl sent a clear message.

"No one said anything about making him your boss," Enzo argued while he jabbed his long-handled shovel into the ground, clearing a hole for his cypress to live in happily.

"So far no one has said that he won't be either. I wouldn't put it past Dad to pull some crap like that."

"Frankie, if he was family, would you have a problem with it?"

"If he was family, we'd have hashed out this plan together a thousand times during our childhood. We'd have made a pact to run it together. We'd have secretly teamed up to outsmart the middles. But he's not family, so yeah it's a problem."

"So if I'm hearing this correctly, we have one for and two against his proposal?" Enzo asked.

"One and a half for and against. Lord knows we're going to need some help if the pilot gets picked up, and I'm not against him being a part of the company. But until someone can tell me what part that would be, I'm withholding judgment. We should also talk to Seth about this before we go any further." Sofia was trying to hold to her impartial position, but her father's silence wasn't making it easy.

"Talk to Seth about what?" Her cocky cousin walked up behind Sofia and put his head on her shoulder to surprise her.

"Speak of the devil, and he shall appear."

"What plot are we hatching now? Are we gonna go egg someone's tree house again?"

"Hush! There is no evidence to suggest that we had anything to do with that. No, we're talking about Adrian's partnership proposal. Have you talked to Dad about it?"

"No. I figured it would work itself out. If he wants to buy in, I don't have a problem with it. Heck, Nick just bought in when we merged companies."

"Nick bought in but only retained the rights to decisions involving his custom furniture branch of the company. Adrian's situation is different. He'd be buying in to have a say over the building business, and equity. How does that work? Seth, do you get Zio Tony's part of the business and we four split Dad's? Do we reset the pot and do an equal split five ways? Does Nick want to get in on that and make it six?"

Seth shrugged.

"No, dammit. You can't shrug this off. Why am I the only one thinking about all this?"

"Well, you are the business manager."

"NO, I AM NOT! I'm the designer. And just because you all

don't pay the bills doesn't mean you shouldn't care about the structure of this company. Frankie, how would you feel if Adrian was your boss versus an equal partner?"

"Dad knows I want to run the building teams one day."

"He doesn't think you're ready yet, and Mom wants him to retire now."

"That's not going to happen, Fi."

"But it could, because who knows what Dad is thinking. Has anyone talked to him lately?"

"No. He's been avoiding us. He hangs out with Jake whenever he's here, and I definitely don't want to talk about this with that snake listening in. He gives me the creeps." Frankie shivered dramatically.

"Anyone talk to Mom either? How's she holding up?" Shrugs. Crickets. Sofia looked over her shoulder and saw Trina approaching with her camcorder rolling. "Okay. I'll check in on her. If anyone can corner Dad, share the details, okay?" She raised her voice and angled herself toward the front door. "Now, let's get this house ready to reveal. The yard looks fantastic, Enzo. Frankie, thanks for coming to pitch in. Can you finish the trim in the nursery? Come on, Seth. I'll help you carry in the island."

ADRIAN'S BRAIN hitched when he heard Sofia's voice in the entry-way. Just the sound of her was enough to distract him. He set down his box cutter and waited. Walking backward into the kitchen, Sofia didn't notice him right away. Adrian watched her carry in the island piece with Seth, admiring her strength and dedication. He couldn't lie. He also enjoyed seeing her fine curves from his position kneeling on the floor, unpacking the tiles. He'd wondered if she'd go out of her way to avoid seeing him after her hasty retreat from his apartment, and he wasn't thrilled that their first encounter would be in front of cameras. He had too many questions pushing at the front of his brain to trust his filter for long. He stood up and braced himself.

"Oh! Hi, Adrian." Her voice squeaked on the last syllable as she tripped over a box of tiles waiting for installation, finally noticing his presence.

"Hi, Sofia. You okay?"

"Yeah. I'm fine. Seth, can you install the island, or do you need a hand?"

So she was still going to try and avoid him, huh? Hmm, he'd really rattled her. He didn't know whether to be pleased or worried about that. He settled for a little of both.

"I've got it. Adrian can help me get the countertop on. It's pretty straightforward since there's no prep sink or gas range to install."

"Great. As soon as you get it done, Adrian is going to get the tile floor laid, right?" She was narrating for the benefit of the camera Trina had rolling, and he played along.

"Yep, I've got the slate right here." She stopped in her tracks halfway out of the kitchen.

"Slate?"

"Yeah. You didn't see it when you came in?" he teased. She didn't smile as he'd hoped.

"No, I clearly didn't, or I would have asked you what the hell blue slate tiles were doing in my neutral kitchen instead of the bathrooms?"

The terse tone of voice had his hackles rising. Damn it. He hadn't said anything about the cost of using real stone tiles because he'd been determined to back-off his "utilitarian" stance, but it seemed he couldn't win. "The cut sheets in the project binder say blue slate in the kitchen and the porcelain faux marble in the bathrooms."

"That's not right. Let me see that." She snatched the massive binder from his hands and scanned the page. "Da...rn it!" Trina moved in for a close-up with her camera mounted on her shoulder, and Sofia barely managed to catch the curse. "How the heck did this happen?"

"I'm sure it was just a simple switch error when someone was entering the details."

"But was it ordered wrong? Or just written wrong? And...oh God! Did you already tile the bathrooms?" She shoved the binder at him and sprinted to see for herself, not waiting for a reply. He chased after her, his temper rising. Rico was mixing the grout, but hadn't started laying the floor tile yet. "Stop! Hold on! That's the wrong tile."

He raised his hands as if he was being held up at gunpoint, his trowel dripping mortar back into the bucket. Adrian stifled a chuckle, knowing it would only piss her off more.

"Adrian. I need you to figure this out. Do we have enough tiles to finish the kitchen? Or did we order the wrong amounts?"

"I'll figure it out. Relax."

Aware that Trina was filming them intently, Sofia managed to keep her temper under control, but just barely. "Relax? We are three days from turning this house over to its owners, and I'm standing on a bare kitchen floor. I have a list a mile long of punch out work that still needs doing, and apparently a tile disaster to figure out. And you want me to relax? Figure it out, Adrian. I don't have time for any other mistakes." She looked him straight in the eye, adding meaning to her last two words.

His blood ran cold. Message received. He shrugged and turned to Trina. "Looks like I've got to track down some tile."

SOFIA DETOURED by craft services to snag a cup of coffee, hoping to restore her sanity before tackling the switch plates and outlet covers throughout the house as painters cleared the bedrooms. That man made her crazy on all the levels. Had she really just ranted at him about tiles in front of the camera? Did she look like a raging harpy or the sexually frustrated coworker? Damn. If she lost her chance at this show, at her dream, because she let herself get all twisted up over a guy, she didn't think she could forgive herself.

"I think that's all mixed in now."

"Huh?"

Jake Ryland stepped up beside her and yanked her from her racing thoughts.

"You've been stirring that coffee like a can of separated paint. What's up?"

"Nothing. Just a little mix-up. Nothing we can't handle."

"Don't stress over mix-ups. Trust me. They make for better television. No one wants to see everything go right."

"No one wants their house to turn out a mess either though."

"True, which is why I'm glad you're on top of it. I love the direction this pilot is heading. The tension between you and Adrian is a great plot arc. Keep up the good work." He walked away before she had a chance to respond. He had a bad habit of doing that.

Sofia was sure he was a busy guy, but she had a sneaking suspicion that he cultivated that perception to avoid having to deal with arguments against what he said. If he'd stayed, would she have told him she wasn't sure what kind of tension was arcing between her and Adrian?

Probably not. At least not until she figured that out for herself.

She took a quick tour of the house while she sipped her coffee, pleased with the overall progress. Tiling the bathrooms and kitchen were the last major projects. The flooring in the rest of the house was done. Drywall was up, sanded, and primed. The painters were in the back bedrooms, so they'd be ready to do the front rooms tomorrow.

She could see each room coming together as it had in her mind, details from her design sheets floating into place. If she could just get them to align this nicely during move in, she'd have done it. She'd have proven that she could do the job she loved and do it well. Maybe then she'd be ready to beard the lion in his den and pin down her father about what he wanted to do with the company when he retired.

She tossed her empty coffee in the trash, energy restored, and picked up a screwdriver and her bag of covers. Time to make her dreams come true, one switch plate at a time.

CHAPTER 17

A BEER. A SHOWER. A BED. In that order. After a hellish day like this, that's all Adrian wanted. It was nine o'clock, and he was D.O.N.E.

The tile fiasco had simply been a matter of the wrong numbers on the wrong lines. The order amounts had been correct, and it had only set them back about fifteen minutes. Everyone who had a stake in seeing this series take off had pitched in big time today. He'd seen everyone but Sofia tackling projects, whether it was their responsibility or not. He and Seth had gotten the repurposed sideboard and cabinets assembled for the island, and he had to admit, the mix of butcher block and marble countertops worked well. But Sofia hadn't even come in to see it.

After lunch, the rest of the day had been a struggle. Nothing major, just little hiccups that meant he spent the day putting out fires instead of knocking out his to-do list. His crew was solid though, and they'd gotten the tile laid so it could set before the moving crews started walking on it tomorrow afternoon. Frankie had handled the trim outs in the bedrooms, and then pitched in on the painting, so those rooms were done. Enzo and his guys had the landscaping roughed in, and they'd finish planting the annuals in the morning. Thankfully, that had been a lighter job, just a little curb appeal, no grading issues or major stump removal.

No matter how many times Jake had suggested he go ask Sofia a question, Adrian had resisted. Crown molding? He made the call to leave it out. It was a fussy detail and took too much time and money. The homeowners would never miss it. And if he was going to take more of a leadership role in this company, he should be able to make executive decisions like that.

Plus, the way Sofia had spoken to him didn't sit well, and he wasn't looking forward to doing it again. He knew she was worried about how this "thing" was going to impact their working together. He thought they could work around that. But if her response was to treat him like a grunt, when she was the one who was the unknown quantity, this was going to be over real quick. No matter that she turned him inside out with a blush. He'd give money to know what she had been thinking about before she tripped over those stupid tiles.

Flipping through the cut book, he made his mental to-do list for the next day before he left.

He could do painting touch-up and start the guys on grout in the morning, once he could walk on the tiles. And then a full day Sunday of lifting furniture and arranging it at Sofia's beck and call. That sounded fun.

"Last call! Anyone still here?" Silence answered him. He left a few of the lights on for security and pulled the door shut behind him. The camera crew had already left, and he'd sent his guys home at five, since they weren't getting paid overtime and he was perfectly capable of finishing tiling a floor on his own. When he was an owner, he'd make sure everyone respected the crew's time.

He locked the door and set the alarm code. Securing the site against theft was always his last step before heading home. If anything went missing, it would be on his head. He climbed into the cab of his truck and exhaled for the first time all day. He was bone tired. Getting a house finished was already hard, but doing it all over three times for the cameras and dealing with their external deadlines was exhausting. He, for one, would not be sad if the pilot didn't get picked up. If this became a show, this would only get worse.

He turned the key in the ignition, but before he even touched the gearshift, his phone was beeping an alarm. The motion detectors in the house were going off. *¡No mames! Can this day just be over?* Had someone seen the crews all over the house and been waiting for them to go? At least the raw materials had been installed so there was less chance of the pipes or wiring being stolen, but there was still a shit ton of electronic and video equipment in the house. He grabbed his long crowbar from behind the seat and dragged himself back out of the truck.

He disabled the alarm and began a room-by-room search. He'd say one thing for the new open concept kitchen and dining room: it was easy to scan from one end of the house to the other. That would come in handy once Farha and Gautam had little ones running around. Turning down the hallway, he pushed open doors to bedrooms and checked closets. The last room he checked was the nursery. And there she was, the thorn in his paw. Sofia, still in her baggy T-shirt and torn jeans. Her beautiful hair wasn't show ready. She'd tugged it into another goddamn ponytail on top of her head, and all he could think was how much he wanted to kiss her neck. Scratch that. How much he wanted to be welcome to kiss her neck.

She had earbuds in and hadn't heard him enter. She probably also hadn't heard him when he'd called out ten minutes ago to see if anyone was left in the house. What was she doing here so late?

"Hey. HEY!"

How loud were those headphones? He tapped her on the

153

shoulder and she spun, paintbrush raised, catching him across the chest.

"Oh my God, I'm so sorry." She brushed at his chest, simultaneously making his stain and his strain worse. "You startled me."

"I seem to have that effect on you. Why are you still here?"

"I wanted to work on the mural while it was quiet."

"Mural? That's not in the binder."

"I know. It's a surprise. I didn't want to tell them about it until I was sure I could make it happen. Since Frankie didn't finish in here until this afternoon, it was going to be close. But it's going to make the room so special for them." She pointed to an old photograph she'd taped to the wall. "See this? It's Farha when she was five, visiting her grandparents' house outside Mumbai. I'm going to paint it over here, next to where the reading nook will go."

A little girl in a full sari sat next to a reflecting pond full of floating lotus flowers and lily pads, reading a book.

"Do you know what time it is?"

"I do, but I don't mind a late night here or there to get the job done right."

Adrian's hackles rose. "Is that a dig?"

"What time did you send your crew home?"

"Five o'clock. Just like normal." He crossed his arms defiantly. He would not apologize for protecting his crew.

"Hmm." There was a wealth of meaning behind that one syllable.

"If you've got something to say, just say it."

"Nope, they are your crew and your business. I just hope that everything is ready for load-in tomorrow."

"They *are* my crew. Most of them are working extra jobs to make ends meet. If they don't need to stay late, I won't ask them to, especially since the contract you negotiated doesn't pay them overtime." His anger rose, and he tried to keep his voice calm but firm. He was pretty sure he failed.

"Are we back to that?"

"Apparently, since you have a problem with me tiling a floor by myself."

"I didn't say that." She wasn't saying a lot. Adrian wished she would knock that chip off her shoulder and admit that she was in over her head.

"My guys got everything done that they needed to do today. They put in a full day, unlike some people in this room."

"I wasn't just sitting on my ass filing my nails, you know." She pulled a folded sheet from her back pocket and shoved it into his chest. "Here's the punch list I knocked out today. All the outlet covers and switch plates are on, lights are installed and have bulbs, closet organizers hung, and rooms cleaned. I've spent enough time helping on crews to know what I can handle."

"Fine. Next time you 'pitch in,' let me know." He glanced at the list. This would free up a good bit of time tomorrow, but he was still pissed over her attitude.

His tone must have flipped her switch because her icy control flashed to anger. "I don't report to you. You can run your guys however you want, but I'm not one of your guys."

His eyes wanted to wander over her curves and confirm her abundantly obvious statement. He chose to make his point instead.

"Listen, if you've got a problem with the way I run my crew, talk to your dad. At least he respects the amount of work these guys put in to make your ridiculous designs happen."

"Ridiculous? What, in your opinion, was ridiculous about my plan?" Her voice rose, and she stepped into his space.

"Where do I begin? Crown molding in every bedroom, despite the cost issues? I vetoed that, by the way. Unnecessary demolition of walls that weren't bothering anyone? No, I know. Let's take the tiles." He held tight to his control, knowing it would infuriate her.

Sure enough, his calm condescension had her spitting flames.

155

"You mean the tiles that you had slated for the wrong rooms? The tiles I had to stop you from laying?"

"That was a simple mistake, easily fixed. You know what wasn't easy? Laying those huge square tiles on a diagonal pattern. Do you know how many extra cuts we had to make to fit the corners of every straight edge in that room?"

"I'm sure however many cuts, it was worth the effort. I peeked in there earlier, and it looks beautiful and wide open."

How could she not see that she was making this all way more difficult than it had to be? How could this woman he was falling for have so little respect for his time and talents? He lost his battle for control, and anger and frustration filled his voice.

"It would look just as wide open with straight tiles, since we took down most of a fucking wall."

"No, it wouldn't. But I don't have time to argue the point with you. I've got a ridiculous mural to finish. If you'll excuse me…"

"No."

"No?"

"I'm not leaving you alone in the house this late. It's not safe."

"You've got to be kidding me."

"Listen, we put alarms on the construction sites for a reason. Just ignore me and keep painting. I'll just start assembling the furniture for this room. If I'm going to stay, I might as well get ahead for tomorrow."

"You don't have to do that. I'm sure your mother is wondering where you are." She held up her hand. "And no, that was not a dig, just an observation. I don't want her to worry."

"I'll call her."

"You are really going to sit here and assemble a crib while I paint?"

"Get to it, *princesa*. I've got a beer at home with my name on it."

He walked back out to his truck and got his tool kit, and grabbed the crib packaging out of the closet on his way back in.

He couldn't figure it out. Even after all of the crap she'd dumped on him, spending an evening working late with her was more appealing than relaxing at home alone. He shook his head at his own stupidity. But he went back in anyway and tore into the plastic wrapping. She already had her headphones back on and was swaying her hips as she meticulously added brush strokes to the wall.

She had a point about the design. Even though he'd cursed her while using the tile cutter, he could see that the floors looked nice. But they would have looked just as nice the normal way. He wished that she could respect his time and his work more than she did. Just because something looked better didn't mean it was always worth the extra effort to be fussy.

He laid out the pieces of the crib and let his brain empty as he assembled. Slot A, Tab B. A couple of quick screws. If only a relationship with her was that easy.

Hours floated past as he completed first the crib, then the bookcase/window seat, and finally the changing table. He moved on to the master bedroom and built the headboard and bed frame, and the bedside tables. Buying everything in pieces was certainly cheaper, which he was positive was a motivating factor, but God, was it a pain in the ass. His eyes were crossing with exhaustion by the time he peeked back into the nursery to see how close she was to done.

Sofia sat on the drop cloth beneath her finished mural, head resting against the wall, fast asleep.

She had talent. He'd give her that. The image from the photograph had come alive on the wall through her paintbrush. Any little girl would feel inspired to read beneath it. He checked his watch and winced. He didn't know if it was worth working until one in the morning for, but he was sure she thought it was. Slipping an arm beneath her legs and around her shoulders, he lifted her and carried her outside. About halfway to his truck, she roused enough to realize what was happening.

"Put me down."

"It's okay. I've got you. I'm going to drive you home."

"I'm too heavy. Put me down. And I can drive myself home, thank you very much."

"If you were too heavy I wouldn't be carrying you. Stop saying that."

She couldn't argue with that logic, but that wasn't going to slow her down.

"I'm still not getting in your truck. I can get myself home. Plus, I need to be back here early tomorrow."

"You're exhausted."

"I'm fine."

"Quit being stubborn."

"Quit being an asshole."

That stopped him in his tracks. Here he'd been trying to do something nice for her, and she was going to call him an asshole? He set her down on her feet and stepped back.

"You want to drive yourself home? Be my guest. I forgot. You don't need or want to lean on anyone. You won't have to worry about me forgetting again."

CHAPTER 18

THIS WAS IT. Her day of reckoning.

"Okay, is everyone ready?"

Sofia knew that her ideas were good, that their work was solid, but would Farha and Gautam agree? Would they love the house as much as she did?

Saturday had been a marathon of work, and yesterday had flown by in a blur of furniture and accessories for staging. She hadn't had a chance to talk to Adrian at all. When she'd woken up in his arms, being carried effortlessly, she'd wanted to swoon. That kind of weakness was not allowed. She didn't like the way she'd left things with him, but she couldn't tell him that. So she'd spent another late evening arranging the Shahs' keeper pieces and the new furniture in each room, while shoring up her defenses. She wanted everything to look perfect for the cameras, and she needed to feel a bit stronger before she talked to him again. He'd knocked off with his guys once the crew was done with the last-minute grouting and clean-up. She'd missed her opportunity, and now was not the time to regret it.

No fewer than four cameras were aimed at her and the Shahs,

ready to catch the next thirty seconds from every angle. Not the best time for her to be angsting.

Jake gave her the thumbs up, and she turned to the couple holding hands and covering their eyes.

"Farha and Gautam, let me be the first to say, 'Welcome home!' Open your eyes!"

The simultaneous looks of shock and delight confirmed what she'd always known. This moment was what she worked for, and it was worth every hour of stress and trouble. The wide eyes and open mouths pleased her immensely. She began talking about the changes to give the lovely couple a chance to find their words.

"You can see that Enzo has removed the old scraggly shrubbery from in front of the house, so you can see the porch now. You've got some nice drought-resistant native plants that are hardy enough to survive our dry years and still bloom beautifully with a little care and attention. We also painted the exterior a light taupe for a brighter, fresher look."

"It's beautiful! Is that the same house?" Farha turned to look at the mailbox. "The numbers are right. This is our house!"

Gautam hadn't spoken yet, but his emotions were clear in his pressed lips and watering eyes. He hugged Farha close and planted a kiss on her temple.

Farha stepped into the gap left by Gautam's silence, understanding his loss for words. "We're home. This is more than I imagined could be done with paint and plants."

"You haven't even seen the inside yet. Let me show you."

"And cut." Jake's voice broke through the moment. "That's great. Gautam if you could be a little more verbal inside that'd be great. Break for fifteen, so we can set up the cameras for the living room/kitchen reveal."

Farha turned to Sofia and pulled her into a tight hug. "I am so excited! Not driving by the past few weeks has been so hard, but this is totally worth it. Please tell Enzo that he did a marvelous job. I love the yard and how eco-friendly it is. That floating bench built off the side of the porch is just begging me for a book and a big mug of tea."

"It's made of reclaimed redwood. I'll tell him you loved it."

"She mostly loves that this garden will be hard to kill. She has a bit of a black thumb." Farha hit Gautam on the arm, and he laughed. "Hey, if you don't believe me, go look at the herb garden she started at our last place."

"Shhh, or Enzo won't come back and do the backyard next year when we can afford it."

Sofia laughed along with them. "Just hire his crew to maintain them, and you'll be fine."

Natalie approached with her brushes and began touching up their powder while they spoke, to hide the fact that they were beginning to sweat in the bright California sunshine.

"Unfortunately, after everything we poured into this house, Gautam is our grounds crew for the foreseeable future."

"I know you've put a lot of your savings into this project. I think you'll be pleased with the inside. It has definitely added value to your house. You bought the place for $985,000, and put in just over $100,000 in improvements, but I think market value is closer to 1.3 million."

"The equity is great, but is it a home where I'll be happy to have my children grow up?"

Jake bellowed across the lawn and waved them in.

Sofia took Farha by the hand and escorted her to the front door. "Let's find out."

They closed their eyes once again, and at Jake's direction, Sofia opened the door and followed the couple inside.

Dropped jaws, squeals of laughter, and jubilant hugs filled her heart with satisfaction, even as the nerves threatened to overwhelm her mind.

"Look at this space! It's so open! I can see all the way into the kitchen. And look at all this light. I don't see our TV cabinet, but I don't even care. I love the new couches."

"Don't give up on your cabinet yet. Those couches were a steal from a showroom sale, and they are completely scotch-guarded so if the baby spills on it, it will wipe right up." Sofia ran a hand over the espresso brown tweed two-seater, proud that she'd found a couch set similar to the one they wanted for under a thousand dollars for three pieces.

"Is this the laminate that we picked? It looks so real." Gautam crouched down to inspect the floor.

She let them wander the room, pointing out details as they neared each feature. Their approval was apparent, so why didn't she feel happier? She felt like she had to justify every choice she'd made with their money. Was that Adrian's influence or was it her own insecurities bleeding through? *Enough.*

"I know you could spend hours in here, and you will because it's your house, but I really can't wait for you to see the kitchen!"

After a quick pause to position cameras, they rounded the edge of the framed entry to their new kitchen.

"Oh it's gorgeous. Look at the cabinets, and I love the mosaic marble tile in the backsplash, and oh! There's our cabinet!"

"I knew how much that piece meant to you and it went perfectly with the decor in here, so we repurposed it as part of your island. Seth added some side cabinets to expand the storage and some custom legs to help support the breakfast bar side of the slab. I'm so pleased with how it turned out."

Farha sat down in one of the new barstools and placed a hand beneath her belly for support.

"I'm not pleased. I'm freaking ecstatic! This is just how I pictured it, but better." She leaned back on her stool and looked up at the ceiling. "Oh look! You found the funky geometric chandelier. Wait, are there three?"

"There are three pieces hung together as an art fixture, with bulbs installed and recessed lighting above. Those were a gift from your friend who made the sculpture in your current house. I contacted her, and she took several pieces she had been working on and tweaked them as a housewarming present for you."

Tears were openly running down Farha's face now as she continued to swivel her head trying to take it all in.

Gautam was busy inspecting every nook and cranny. "This looks amazing. The finish work on this is so clean. You wouldn't believe the ridiculous things we've found in our old house. Drawers that can't open because of appliances, gaps between the tile and the cabinets they just left open, odd cuts of flooring that don't line up. I mean look at the attention to detail on the diagonal floor. Each cut is so precise. If it wasn't, it would drive me nuts! Please thank Adrian and his crew for me. His work makes my engineer heart happy."

"Are you ready to see more?"

"I think I need to sit down a minute." He dropped onto the stool next to Farha as if his knees had given out. "This is all so much to take in."

"Wait just a second. I've got the perfect place for you to rest." She pulled Jake aside and asked him to set up the smaller crew in the nursery. She made a cup of herbal tea at the craft services table outside and brought it in for Farha while they waited for the okay.

"This has been such an overwhelming day. I don't know how many more surprises I can take." Farha sipped the herbal tea and grimaced.

"Hang in there. We've only got a few more rooms to see and then you and Gautam can relax all you want in your new home. At least until you bring that baby home."

"That baby is kicking up a storm right now, likely because her mama's heartbeat is jumping like crazy." Farha took Sofia's hand and pressed it to the top of her belly near her rib cage, and Fi could feel a little foot firmly pressing back.

So moved, she rubbed the little bump until it receded, forgetting that she was also rubbing another woman's stomach. "Sorry, I got a little carried away."

"It's okay. You got her to stop pushing. I'll take it. Sometimes she gets stuck up under my ribs and ouch! And now, my back is killing me. I'm so done with being pregnant." Farha laughed as she said it, but Sofia could see the strain on her face as she rubbed her back.

Sofia leaned over to talk to the baby. "Hello, little girl. I know your parents are doing all they can to get ready for your arrival. What do you say we go see your new room?" The little foot kicked again, and Sofia gave the baby a little high five. "I think that's a yes."

She was very glad that she had chosen a soft reclining rocking chair, because the minute Farha walked in, she collapsed into it. Instead of darting her eyes around the room as she had in the kitchen, Farha's gaze fixed on the mural of the little girl reading that Sofia had painted on the wall. Tears filled the woman's eyes, and Sofia's heart swelled with pride.

"Oh! Sofia, it's perfect." Farha reached for Gautam's hand, and he was quick to give it, his smile stretched from ear to ear. "Where did you get that picture? How did you know?"

Gautam placed a hand on her shoulder. "You're not the only one who has design ideas. I wanted our daughter to grow up knowing where she came from and where she can go. She should see how brilliant her mum is every time she picks up a book, so she can grow up to be just like you."

Sofia's heart tugged. This couple was so sweet together, each so supportive of the other. With her professional hat, she was delighted to give them a house they could raise their family in. With her personal hat, she was deeply envious of that bond and wondered if she'd ever find it for herself. She sure didn't feel it with Adrian. He didn't support her in her chosen career. She doubted he'd ever say that she was brilliant or smart or important. It was more likely that he'd complain about her ideas being a pain to implement than offer a compliment. She sighed. Was it too much to ask to be seen for who she was and who she aspired to be? And be appreciated as is?

"Sofia?" Jake broke into her rambling thoughts. "Do you think we could talk about the rest of the room now?"

"Oh, yes. Of course." She gathered her thoughts and put her camera-ready smile in place. "You had chosen the coral and brown color theme based on the crib you picked out and the bedding you liked. You'll see we built the crib for you and got it all set up. You've got the changing table next to it that will transition into a toy caddy when the baby gets a little older. Nick and Seth, our custom builders, designed the window seat bookcase and Adrian built it in. And I made those custom coral and white cushions, so Baby Girl Shah will be cozy when she reads." She'd been over the moon to find the fabric on clearance and thanked the Lord that her mother had insisted she learn to use a sewing machine in her youth.

"That is all lovely, Sofia, but the mural... The mural is my heart." Farha clasped one hand on her heart and the other on her belly.

"We have a little more to do. Are you ready to see your bedroom, or do you need to rest awhile longer?"

"I think I'm done resting for quite awhile, as you said. These contractions are getting stronger, and I want to see it all before we have to head to the hospital."

"Oh my God! You're having the baby! We're having a baby!" Sofia turned to the film crew. "Let's go! You heard the woman. Go set up, so she can see her master bedroom and bath! Hurry!" She didn't wait for Jake's approval to hustle them along. Turning back to the expecting mother, Sofia's hands were shaking with adrenaline. "Do you need anything? Water? More tea? An ambulance?"

Farha laughed.

"No, I'm fine. The contractions are about ten minutes apart

still, so we have time to go home and get our bag and drive to the hospital."

"You are so calm. I can't believe you are this calm."

Farha laid her hand over Gautam's on her shoulder. "We've been waiting a long time for this. I'm ready."

"Well then, let's go!"

CHAPTER 19

STANDING OUTSIDE ADRIAN'S HOUSE with a ridiculous grin on her face, Sofia felt like dancing. Adrenaline was still coursing through her after the day she'd had. Filming with the couple had wrapped up quickly after the announcement of the impending arrival of Baby Shah. The film crew was still there taking their panning shots of the details in the finished rooms for the "after" scenes. Farha and Gautam were at the hospital, safe and sound.

Not even bothering to change out of her camera-ready leather skirt and button-down blouse, Sofia had grabbed Frankie and gone over to the Shahs' house with the spare key she still had from the movers. Who cared about keeping clothes clean in the excitement of a new baby? They had filled boxes with essentials from the kitchen, bathrooms, and dressers. Sofia found the stash of diapers, wipes, and baby clothes from Farha's baby shower and packed that up, too.

They spent the late afternoon moving the young family into their new home so that when they came home from the hospital, they could have a few days of comfort before they had to do the nitty-gritty moving of everything else. Sofia had done a quick grocery run and stocked the freezer with easy to heat-and-eat meals, while Frankie organized the kitchen cabinets.

Even after all that work, she was still revved from the adrenaline of the reveal. She'd pulled it off, succeeded beyond her expectations, and had very happy clients and a show that wouldn't fail because she'd screwed up. Now that the tension was gone, she wanted to celebrate.

She had also picked up a bottle of champagne. There was only one person she wanted to celebrate with. She couldn't explain it, even to herself, but she needed to see Adrian. Part of it was petty —a chance to gloat and say they'd loved it. But more than that, he'd worked just as hard as she had, and he deserved to know how the reveal had gone. It had felt strange to be showing off his handiwork without him after weeks of arguing about it side by side. And then there was the part she wasn't listening to that told her she just missed him.

So here she stood, at dusk, bottle of champagne dripping cold water down her leg, on his front porch. When she rang the bell, Graciela Villanueva answered the door.

"*Hola*, Sofia. How are you?"

"I'm good. And you?"

"*Muy bien, gracias*. Come inside. Let me close this door."

Sofia preceded her into the dark living room just off the foyer. She looked around the room, and her designer heart cringed. The heavy drapes at the windows blocked out eighty percent of the light, leaving the rest of the room feeling close and cave-like. The three couches were clean but old, clearly well used by the four teenagers who had grown up in the house. The one armchair in the room was a bright paisley patterned wingback with spindly legs, the matriarch's throne. A cup of steaming coffee and a book propped open on the tufted arm told Sofia she'd interrupted Graciela's reading time. How Adrian's mother managed to read in this gloom was a mystery to Sofia.

"You are here to see Adrian?"

"I am. We finished filming today, and I wanted to congratulate him on a job well done." She raised the bottle of champagne in a toast.

"He's not here right now, but he should be back soon if you don't mind waiting."

"I'd love to stay and chat with you. I don't want to interrupt your book though."

"It's one I have re-read a thousand times. It is a visit with an old friend. Now, I can visit with a new one."

"My mother protected her reading time fiercely. If her reading lamp was on, you'd better be bleeding to interrupt her."

"Nonsense. I love company. Can I make you a coffee? *Ven aquí*, sit with me in the kitchen. I have cookies."

Sofia followed Graciela as the older woman bustled into the kitchen, and within a minute she found herself seated with a steaming cup of coffee and a plate of *polvorones de canela*. She took a bite, and the buttery, sugary, cinnamon-spiced goodness melted on her tongue.

"Thank you. These are delicious." She tried to ignore the three other cookies on the plate and failed miserably three times.

"So, tell me! How did the last day of filming go? I have been so excited for you all. I cannot wait to see my son on television."

"The filming went well. The Shahs loved the house, and Farha actually went into labor during the final reveals. They headed to the hospital, and Frankie and I moved their baby things in so they can come home to their new house."

"You are a good girl. I'm sure your mother is very proud."

Sofia wasn't sure about that. She couldn't remember the last time she had spoken to her mother outside of a family meeting. She needed to remedy that, maybe take Mom for coffee tomorrow.

"The Shahs were so complimentary of the work done on the house, I wanted to tell Adrian right away, before the shine wears off. It's going to be a little while before we know if the pilot gets picked up."

"He'll be home soon. Rico, our neighbor, is sick, so Adrian is filling in for him on a landscape job he needed finished today."

Graciela checked the clock on the wall and her wristwatch. The older woman was fairly vibrating with nerves, her cookie a pile of crumbs on her plate. Sofia tried to distract her with idle conversation.

"Rico is on one of our crews. I didn't realize he did landscaping, too."

"His cousin runs a lawn maintenance service, and Rico helps out when they do big jobs."

"Do you have their card? Get them in touch with me. Clients of Enzo's are always looking for recommendations to take care of what he's built. He's gotten so busy with the landscaping side, he's had to stop taking on new weekly clients."

"Oh, that's wonderful, for everyone. I'll make sure Rico brings a card next week." She had worried her napkin to shreds, and Sofia could only be grateful she hadn't gone to find the business card.

Sofia cast around for anything to pass the time and distract Graciela from her anxiety over Adrian's absence. "While, I'm waiting, is there anything I can do for you? Adrian mentioned that you don't get out often."

"I don't go out ever, if I can help it. When the country you live in sees you as a criminal… When you have something precious snatched away…it gets harder and harder to trust the outside world not to hurt you."

So much for avoiding her anxiety. *Smooth move, Sofia.*

"I understand. Is it this hard any time Adrian is gone?"

"No, *querida*. Only when he's late." Somehow the endearment when heard from his mother's lips didn't get her hackles up, but it might explain where Adrian had gotten the habit.

"Do you need anything? I could run out."

"You are sweet. I have my children and my neighbors who make sure I have what I need. I wish I could find my courage though. My oldest daughter has just had my first grandson." She pulled out her cell phone and proudly showed Sofia a slew of baby pictures. "She had a C-section and the baby has colic, and I wish I could help her. But every time I try to walk out that door…I can't."

Sofia didn't know what to say to that. She couldn't imagine never leaving her apartment again. Living in the same dark rooms day after day didn't seem comforting at all. The open longing on the older woman's face as she gazed at her phone was breaking Sofia's heart. She had to do something to help. "Mrs. Villanueva…"

"Graciela, please."

"Graciela, do you like your living room?"

"*¿Perdóname?*"

"You said you spend most of your time in there, but I can't help but notice how dark it is. That can't be good for your reading." An idea was taking shape in Sofia's mind.

"Oh, it is fine. Adrian is so busy. I don't want to bother him with small things like painting."

True, he was busy. So busy that he was working even on his days off, not to mention the overtime for the show. But she didn't have to involve him, right? The things she was thinking of changing she could handle herself. She was mentally swapping out curtains for shades and painting walls. It would be so easy…

"But if you could have it redone, would you like that?"

"Maybe a new bookcase or two. A new sofa so friends who visit can be comfortable. Those things are ancient."

She heard the hope in Graciela's voice, and her decision was made.

"I tell you what. If you get up the courage to visit your daughter, I will come and make over your living room while you're gone."

"Why would you do this for me?"

"Because you are my friend's mother, and it hurts my heart to see good space not making people happy. That room could be so much nicer for you and still maintain your privacy."

"I will think about it."

"Let's take a walk through it right now." Sofia picked up her coffee and moved away from the cookies, re-energized. "Think out loud while we stroll. Then if you decide yes, I will know what you want done."

～

ADRIAN HAD RESISTED the urge to call Sofia all day. He wanted to know how the reveal went, but he was holding on to his mad. She didn't need him, and he didn't need her either.

Just because they'd been in each other's pocket for the show didn't mean that needed to continue now that the project was done. He didn't need to talk to her every day. A little distance was probably for the best. He'd gotten all caught up in her, and she clearly did not feel the same. Besides, he'd probably catch her mid-shoot and screw up a scene or something.

No, he'd see her tomorrow at the office. That would be soon enough. After all, she'd made it abundantly clear she didn't want him checking up on her, or taking care of her, or doing any damn thing for her.

Not to mention the fact that he was covered in dirt and grass clippings, and all he wanted to do was collapse in his shower. He didn't want to talk to anyone until he felt vaguely human again.

So when he pulled up to his house and saw her car parked in front, he sat in his running truck in the middle of his narrow street, mind spinning with questions. *What the hell?* A honk from behind him cleared his head enough to pull into his driveway. He climbed out of the truck, dusted off the dirt as best he could, and went in the front door.

"And these curtains, well, they came with the house— Adrian! You're home."

"*Hola, Mamá*. Sofia, what are you doing here?"

"That's no way to welcome a guest, Adrian. Sofia came by to see you, but was kind enough to keep me company until you got home. We were just talking about redoing the living room."

"What? What's wrong with the living room?"

"Nothing. It's fine." Graciela stepped back from the annoyance in Adrian's voice, but Sofia wasn't going to let his bad mood spoil his mother's joy.

"It's fine, but it's not great. It's dark and outdated. I was just talking to your mom about easy ways we could fix that."

Adrian felt his cheeks heat and his shoulders crept toward his ears. He only hit this level of embarrassment when Mamá chewed him out in front of his sisters. That Sofia could elicit it with a simple critique of his living room was not good. And didn't that just piss him off even more.

"Mamá, if you didn't like the living room why didn't you tell me? I will fix it for you." He bent down to unlace his boots, frustration turning the bows to knots.

"It is fine, and you have enough to do. Besides, Sofia offered to do it when I get up the nerve to go see Mahalia and the baby, so you should be happy I'm actually thinking about visiting."

That *was* a big deal. If it took Sofia dangling a reno carrot to motivate his mom, he wouldn't argue, but it still rubbed him the wrong way. Why hadn't she said something to him? He would have fixed the living room if she'd asked. He pushed away his guilt and focused on his mother.

"You tell me when you want to go, and I will clear the whole weekend." He crossed to his mother and kissed her on the forehead before heading into the kitchen. "If you want to talk about something, Sofia, can it wait until I've had dinner? I'm starving."

"Actually, I just…"

Sofia gestured to the kitchen, but Graciela cut her off while she bustled to the fridge.

"Here, *mijo*, take this upstairs. Put it in the oven for half an hour. There's enough for two." She pulled a ceramic baking dish from the fridge and pushed it into his hands. "Now shoo. You two have a nice night. And thank you, Sofia. It's been a long time since I had something to look forward to."

"It will be my pleasure, Graciela. I'm already getting inspired."

Good Lord. What was she going to do to the living room? Tear down a wall? Make an *outdoor living space* that would send his mother running to her bedroom? Lay diagonal hardwood floors?

"Come on." He jerked his head toward the stairs, in a move he knew he'd hear about from his mother later. But damn it, he was tired, hungry, and filthy, and now apparently was going to have his living room torn up because Sofia didn't like it. *What the hell?* She ducked back into the kitchen, and he didn't bother to wait, plodding up the stairs in his stocking feet.

Sofia didn't speak until they reached his apartment. He set the casserole on the countertop and scrubbed his face and hands in the kitchen sink. It wasn't until he dried his face on a towel that he realized she hadn't followed him into the space. She warily held out a bottle of champagne from the top of the stairs.

"Congratulations."

"What's this for?"

"I came by to celebrate the Shah project. They loved it, but I can tell you're not in the mood, so I'll just go."

"Stay."

The word was out before he thought about the implications, but he wouldn't take it back. Yes, he was in a shit mood, but he didn't want her to go.

"Are you sure?"

"I just worked an extra four hours shoveling mulch and manure to cover for Rico so that he's not out money because he got the flu. All I wanted was some dinner, a shower, and my bed. And I walk in to find you criticizing my home. I'm entitled to be a little cranky."

"I wasn't criticizing your home. I was trying to help. I came in, and your mother was reading in the dark. You can't tell me you like that living room. I've seen your taste." She gestured to his own apartment as she finally crossed the threshold.

"I ask if she wants me to fix anything up around the house. She always says it's fine."

Sofia looked at him, eyes full of pity for his feeble male brain, and it pissed him off. "When a woman says something is fine, it's never fine."

"Noted."

"Look, I don't want to make you mad. She just looked so sad when she talked about not seeing your sister and the baby, and then I had the thought, and then it was out of my mouth. I don't have to do it if you don't want me to."

"I'm okay with whatever she wants, and if it works to get her out of the house, I will kiss you." An awkward silence fell between them when she didn't respond. Dammit, he hadn't meant it *that* way. Well, he would like to mean it *that* way but she'd made it pretty damn clear that was off the table. This was why he shouldn't be around people right now. Why hadn't he sent her on her way? Maybe if she got out what she needed to say, she would leave and he could retreat with a beer to his shower. "So the Shahs liked the house?"

"Oh, I can't wait for you to see the video." She bustled around his kitchen, turning on the oven, grabbing two tumblers, and unwrapping the champagne as she spoke. Damn. She was planning to stay. "They loved everything. They had so many nice things to say about you and your crew. They really noticed that the details were done right. I guess they've lived in some places that could use your care and attention."

She popped the cork on the champagne with a grin, and he

175

barely noticed the wine bubbling over onto his table. His attention had gotten caught on her lips. Why did that smile make him think stupid things? Paired with the warmth of her words in his chest, she was hard to resist. She traded him a tumbler for the casserole of rice and pork, which she popped in the oven before raising her own glass in a toast.

"Here's to the end of a job well done and the start of a new adventure."

He clinked his glass to hers and drank deeply but wondered what she meant by that. What did she think was a new adventure? The pilot? The partnership? Them? It wasn't just the bubbles making his head swim.

"I'm glad it went well."

"I haven't even told you the best part. While we were in the nursery, Farha's labor started! They are at the hospital right now, so they will get to bring home the baby to the house we made for them. Isn't that wonderful?" She side-hugged him in her enthusiasm, and it took every ounce of control to let her go again.

"Glad we got it done in time. It would've been done faster without all the fussy stuff, but I'm glad they're happy."

"You party pooper." She laughed off his sarcastic jibe, and his throat clenched.

She didn't want him. She'd said as much the other night when he'd tried to drive her home. Why did her laugh still have the power to twist him up inside? Why was she here? His thoughts flowed from his lips like he'd forgotten to connect a shut-off valve. No filter, control gone. "Why are you here?"

"I told you. I wanted to share the good news with you, and celebrate being done with the pilot."

Nope. Not good enough. He crossed to stand directly in front of her. No hiding behind busy hands.

"You could have just called. Why are you here, offering to do favors for my mother, baking my dinner, drinking champagne in my apartment?"

"I don't know what you mean. Why shouldn't I be nice to your mother?"

"That's not... Don't twist my words. The other night you told me off in no uncertain terms."

"I told you I didn't want you to touch me without my permission. I told you I needed to drive myself home. I am allowed to say no when I choose."

"What am I allowed to do, huh? Am I allowed to do this?" He slid his free hand up the back of her head, letting her warm ribbons of silky hair thread through his fingers.

She closed her eyes and leaned into his touch. *Not good enough.*

"Am I allowed to tell you how beautiful you are?" He set down his glass on the table and rescued hers from her limp grip before it hit the floor. "Am I allowed to say that I missed you today? That I couldn't get your smile out of my head? That your laughter slays me? Look at me, Sofia."

She slowly opened her eyes, and they were glazed with desire. He stroked a finger over her cheek, and those beautiful blue irises hid again.

"I need an answer, Sofia. Am I allowed to fall for you or not? Because if the answer is no, you can't be here. It's too hard."

Her head snapped up at that, eyes wide open, and he let every emotion show on his face, the longing, the desire, the anger, the frustration, the entire tangled web of emotions he felt whenever she was near. She looked him in the eyes, long and steady, not saying a word.

Great. He'd stepped in it again. He dropped his head and began to turn away from her rejection, but she stepped in to him, bringing her luscious body flush against his, and slid her hand up the back of his head, mirroring his own position.

"Am I allowed to fall for you back?"

Adrian could barely manage a nod before his control slipped its leash, and he kissed her.

There was a heady freedom in knowing that his kiss was

wanted, desired as much as he desired to give it. She was actively kissing him back, welcoming his every foray, chasing each retreat of his tongue. God, she was sweet. Warm cinnamon and coffee flavors filled his senses, and his stomach growled loudly.

She pulled back and clapped a hand over her mouth. "I'm sorry."

"Why are you apologizing?"

"Because I'm jumping all over you before you've even gotten a chance to eat your dinner. I told myself I could wait, but clearly, I can't."

Adrian grinned at her admission.

"Well, yes, that was very rude of you, kissing me senseless in my own kitchen." He pulled her back in close and kissed just below her ear, where the scent of Sofia was the strongest. "Dinner will be awhile, but I'm hungry now."

"You also said you wanted a shower and your bed. Does the order matter?"

CHAPTER 20

"FUCK THE SHOWER."

Sofia gasped as Adrian picked her up again and carried her into the bedroom. When he did that so easily, like she was a light little flower, her heart fluttered. She tucked her head into the curve of his neck, inhaling deeply, wanting to remember every detail of this fleeting moment. When he sat her down on the edge of his bed, she held that breath, hoping it would give her the courage she needed for this next step.

"I want you right here, right now. Let me see you, Sofia. Let me have you." He knelt in front of her, hands tracing over her hips.

Doubt crept into her mind. Would he like what he saw? She clenched her thighs together and stiffened. He rocked back onto his heels.

"What? What did I say?"

Moment of truth. Did she want him more than she wanted to stay hidden? Did she trust him to try and understand? After all, he'd been paying attention. He'd noticed she wasn't comfortable and had asked. Gathering her courage and her words, Sofia decided to try and explain her paralyzing emotions.

"I'm afraid…"

"It's not your first time, is it?" Shock blanked his features and his hands stilled on her hips.

"No. No, it's nothing like that."

Adrian let out a deep, relieved exhale. "Thank God for that."

"It's just been awhile…"

He rose back up off his heels, scrambling her thoughts as he moved his hips between her thighs. When he whipped his shirt off over his head, she nearly swallowed her tongue. Each hard day of labor had given him the build of a god, and she wanted to trace every divot, dent, and curve. Preferably with her mouth. His arms alone made her drool. The strength she'd felt gentled for her tempted her to trust him.

"Don't worry, gorgeous. It's like riding a bike."

She stopped him with a hand on his chest, needing him to slow down and listen, but jerked it back, singed by the heat pumping off him. She had words. Somewhere in her brain. Words she had to say, before she started thinking with her hormones and let him do whatever he damn well pleased. She leaned back, away from temptation. She needed to be clear and open with him, so he knew what he was getting into. If he was going to reject her, she needed it to be while her clothes were still on.

"Wait." His hands dropped from her hips to fist around handfuls of the comforter beneath her. He tilted his head down and held her gaze, waiting as she'd asked. She cleared her throat and pushed her shame out of her mouth.

"It's been awhile, and I wasn't this heavy before. I haven't been with anyone since I gained all this weight, and I'm nervous to let you see me."

Sofia blurted her painful confession and then fixed her eyes firmly on the floor. She could feel the tears building at the corners of her eyes and prayed that she wouldn't embarrass herself any further than she already had.

"Hey."

Adrian hooked a finger under her chin and lifted, forcing her to face him and her fears in the same glance.

"Hey, there. It's just me. Let me tell you a little story and see if it helps, okay?"

Sofia nodded, caught in the warm sincerity in his eyes.

"Once upon a time, there was a boy. He was scared and lost, alone in the world of men, looking for somewhere to belong." His hands ran down her arms and around her back so he could pull her back to the edge of the bed to kiss her neck. "The king took pity on this boy and gave him a job carrying trash. One day, an angel walked across the job site."

He kissed his way across her collarbone and she shivered.

"She wore cutoff jean shorts that barely covered her ass." His hands skimmed down her back to squeeze his target. "And a tight tank top that clung to her in all the right places. When she walked, her high blonde ponytail swished and swayed." Adrian moved one hand down her ponytail, deliberately gripping and tugging lightly. "He wanted her instantly, the way a seventeen-year-old boy wants, all heat and little reason."

Wrapping her ponytail around his fist, he tilted her face up for a brutal kiss that left her lips throbbing and aching for more. She tried to follow his lips, but he leaned back and continued his story.

"But she walked right up to the king and said, 'Hi, Daddy,' and the boy's dreams crumbled."

He slid his hands down her neck, over her shoulders, down her back. She barely remembered being that girl, and his hands were making it very hard to remember anything at all.

"Then came the dark time, when the princess went away." He reached behind her and unzipped the back of her skirt, fingers dipping lower to grip her ass and pull her closer. When he reached around front and began to slide her tight skirt up her thighs, nerves compelled her hands to flutter over his. He steadied them and kissed them, grounding her in the moment. "The young man was sad, but he understood her need to grow her own wings. And when she came back, *Dios mio*, could she fly!" Her hands still caught in his, he moved them to slide up her thighs, pushing the skirt ever higher. She was twenty-eight years old and she couldn't remember the last time she'd touched her body and enjoyed it, shame free. She wanted new memories to replace the ones she couldn't find. "The girl had become a woman, and everything the boy had felt for her before magnified."

He bent his head and licked the hammering pulse at the base of her throat and she gasped as the pleasure shivered down her arms.

"She wore sweaters to hide her lush, perfect breasts." Adrian slid his hands over them reverently, before moving lower. "And jeans that molded themselves to her sexy hips. And lust tied the boy's tongue, because she was so smart and beautiful and he felt so dumb and crude next to her." He kissed his way to her ear and gently bit the lobe, then soothed it with his tongue. He whispered into her ear, "He had no right to think about putting his rough hands on such smooth skin."

How had she not known? Sofia was so entranced that she barely registered that his hands had traced back to her breasts. She gasped with sudden awareness when he squeezed them together and gently tweaked her nipples, sending waves of electricity through her system. She groaned with pleasure and broke the spell, and he released her.

"What happened next?" she asked breathlessly, needing to hear the rest of the story.

"He tried to better himself so she would find him worthy. But then tragedy struck. Her smile dimmed in the shade of grief, and he wished more than anything to find the way to make her happy again. He wanted her the way a man wants his woman, but he waited for the right moment to tell her."

He tugged her blouse free from her skirt and slowly slipped her buttons free, one by one.

"Every day. Every damn day, the woman walks in the door, and the man has to remind himself that he cannot touch her. Her body has curved and rounded in all the best ways, and it drives him crazy that she can't see it. He sees the girl she was and the woman she's become, and he wants her with his whole heart."

His voice wavered and he lowered his forehead to her sternum. She held her breath while he chose his next words.

"You slay me, Sofia. Let me make you happy." His eyes rose to meet hers, and the plea in them made her tremble. "I see you, Sofia. Better than you see yourself. The only thing I don't like about your body is that it makes you sad. Let me show you."

Her shirt hung from her shoulders, open but still covering most of her torso. He waited on his knees for her to decide. Did she dare to bare herself to him? When she tried to look away, he followed her, compelling her to look him in the eye.

"I see you. I've always seen you. And what I see keeps getting better and better. Do you trust me?"

Every nerve ending crackled, begging for his touch, and every doubt had burned away in the heat of the fire he'd kindled deep within her. She did trust him, and she found her courage in his story. She could take what she wanted and give what she could, and she would be safe in his arms. In answer to the question lingering in the silence between them, she shrugged her shoulders, letting the shirt fall behind her, and nodded.

"Show me."

She had expected him to pounce, unleashing his desire, but he surprised her yet again with his restraint. With both hands he framed her face and kissed her gently, insistently, until she was drowning in him.

She tugged her skirt up to her waist and wrapped her legs around his hips, pulling him with her as she leaned back on the bed. He followed, bringing his delicious weight on top of her. She rocked her hips up, needing to ease the ache against his hard length, and he gasped and rolled to his side, breaking the kiss.

"Be careful." He reached behind her and unsnapped her bra. "Or this will be over too quickly. I have wanted you for too long."

He tossed it aside and marveled at her. There was no other word to describe the wonder in his eyes.

"How could you think I would not like to see you?"

He bent his head to kiss her freed breasts, and she answered on a shaky exhale. "Those aren't the problem."

He deliberately held up a hand to silence her protests. She rolled to face him and he dropped that hand to her hip, impatiently pushing her bunched skirt down her legs. She inched back on the bed to help and to gain a little distance, but he rejoined her immediately. Nearly naked and lying on his bed, she felt strangely calm. Her nerves were suffocating beneath the blanket of desire he'd woven. He pressed a hand against her sternum, and she dropped onto her back before pushing up on her elbows to watch him.

"Now let's see here." He grinned evilly, and Sofia couldn't suppress a shiver. He ran his gaze over every inch of her exposed flesh, raising chills, and then soothing them with his warm hands and wet lips. "I was right."

She was so caught up in her own reaction that she had lost the thread of the conversation.

"Right about what?"

"There's not a single thing I see that I don't love."

His playful tone sparked her own to life. When was the last time she'd felt relaxed enough to tease a man in bed? Too long. She was done being passive and afraid. This was a man she could trust. This was a man she could be herself with.

"I wish I could say the same, but I haven't seen all of you yet." She raised an eyebrow and looked at his offending pants.

He grinned and tugged them off, kicking his feet free. His impressive erection strained against his boxer briefs, begging to be freed. He rolled toward her, intent on covering her bare body with his own. But Sofia wanted to enjoy the view. She'd been too afraid the last time they'd been together, but tonight she would be brave. He hadn't run away screaming yet. She playfully pushed his chest, and he leaned back.

"I'll show you mine, if you'll show me yours." She slid her fingers under the last scrap of lace covering her and sat up to tug it off.

His hands trembled gratifyingly as he traced from her thighs to her knees before spreading them, revealing her to his gaze.

"Sofia." Her name was all he managed to whisper before his lips were busy doing something else entirely. Her eyes fluttered closed as he licked and loved her most intimate folds, afraid that the visual of him going down on her would push her over the edge too quickly. When he added his rough, thick fingers to the assault on her senses, even her closed eyes couldn't save her and over the edge she went, shaking and clenching her thighs around his head. When the tremors stopped and her limbs went limp, he rose quickly and drew in a deep breath.

"*Dios mio*, Sofia." He stripped off his underwear with fierce determination.

She wanted him to slow down so she could enjoy the revelation of his body as well. She wanted to hold him in her hand and see if he tasted as good as she thought he would. But she couldn't find the energy or the words to object through her post-climax haze. Next time. *What a tempting thought...*

"Sofia." Her spinning thoughts stilled as he pressed the full length of his body against hers, setting off a chain reaction of trembling nerve endings.

"Hmm?"

He grinned at her sleepy response, and she mirrored his expression. Wrapping her legs around his bare waist, gripping her ass with his strong hands, he pressed her into the bed. As he rocked his hard length against her still throbbing pussy, he muttered a curse and a question.

Words? Did he honestly think words were an option?

She let her head fall back on a groan, but he didn't stop talking. Forcing her brain back into commission was hard, but so was he and he wasn't moving inside her yet, so she did her best to pay attention.

"Sofia, look at me, angel." She opened her eyes and her heart followed on his next words. "Let me love you. Say yes."

She managed a nod and a whispered, "Yes."

~

FINALLY.

He was nearly shaking with simultaneous relief and need. After so many years of watching and waiting, he was finally going to be with her. He'd earned every minute of this pleasure, and he was determined to remember every sweet second.

He'd been nervous earlier, revealing the well-kept secret of his crush, but she'd needed his words, his reassurance. He was helpless in the face of her need. Bringing her to climax almost had him shooting in his underwear like the goddamn boy who'd loved her first.

He pulled the blankets down and scooted her back until her head was on his pillow. He hoped he'd smell her hair there later. The sight of her naked and grinning in his bed made his heart clutch uncomfortably in his chest. His cock twitched in agreement. She was his. At last.

He grabbed a condom from his bedside table and climbed back into bed beside her. Even just touching side to side was threatening his control. He kissed her lips gently, reveling in her sleepy, sated response. She opened for him so sweetly. While she was relaxed, he took the opportunity to run his hands over every curve, committing her architecture to sensory memory. Neck, shoulder, collarbone, sternum, breasts, waist, belly, hips. Every place he touched her was beautiful to him, and he was determined to show her. He considered it a battle won when she didn't flinch until he reached her still sensitive pussy, breaking the kiss with a gasp.

"Oh, yes, Adrian. More." She tugged at his shoulders, and he let her pull him where she needed him.

His weight pressed her into the bed and her greedy hands on his ass were urging him to take what he so desperately wanted. What they both needed. "Hold on."

"I am." She flexed her fingers, her nails sending sharp spurs of pain straight through his ass to his cock, twitching his hips forward so the length of his hard shaft stroked over her clit. The pleasure was intense and reminded him why he needed to slow down a second.

"I mean, wait. I need to cover up."

"Don't tell me I'm not the only one with body issues," she teased. She ran her hands possessively up his back, and he enjoyed the chill running down his spine.

He could think of nothing he'd rather do than stay naked around her permanently. But he had to protect them. He pulled out of her arms and snagged the condom off the bed. "I meant this, smart-ass." He wiggled the foil packet between his fingers.

"Oh…right. Okay, I guess I can wait for that, but hurry up already. Talky, talky, talky."

He couldn't remember the last time he'd laughed in the middle of sex, but he loved that he could with Sofia. She was still chuckling when he slid his latex-covered cock into her sweet pussy. He could feel every giggle and gasp gripping him, guiding him deeper until he was fully sheathed.

And then the time for laughter had passed.

"Sofia. You feel so fucking good."

He tried. God help him, he tried. To go slow. To bring her back to the peak. To keep a firm grip on his sanity. But when she pulled her knees up to grip his ribs, moaning and rocking her hips to his rhythm, taking him as deep as he could go, any hope of restraint disappeared.

His need for her rode him hard. He pistoned his hips, slapping his thighs against her ass with every thrust. He knew his hands were gripping her shoulders too hard, but the thought of letting her go was obscene. She arched up, and he took her breast into his mouth, suckling hard, and sent her over the edge once again. Feeling her orgasm clenching around his cock was more than enough to send him chasing her over that cliff into oblivion.

When he came back into himself, he realized he was crushing her. He levered up on his forearms so he could see her face. "You okay?"

"I'm fine." The way she said it, with a laugh tickling the back of her throat, made him grin.

"Fine, huh? You know, a wise woman once told me that fine is never fine when a woman says it." He nudged forward with his hips, still buried inside her, on every repetition of the f-word.

"Then maybe you should try again. Practice makes perfect."

He chuckled into the crook where her neck met her shoulder and nipped her lightly. "A very wise woman, indeed."

When he pulled away and rose from the bed, she groaned and rolled after him. He disposed of the condom and turned back, committing the image of her draped across his bed, sated and sleepy, to memory. Those old art dudes knew what they were doing. She belonged framed in a museum, just like this. A goddamned masterpiece.

He tucked his arms behind her shoulders and beneath her knees, and lifted her to his chest. She wrapped an arm around his neck and burrowed in.

"Where are you taking me?"

"I believe I mentioned needing a bed *and* a shower."

"That sounds just fine."

CHAPTER 21

SOFIA SAT in the hard wooden chair at the café and squirmed. She was sore in all the best places, and feeling a little raw from Adrian's stubble during their shower adventure. It was a miracle no one had drowned. He'd given her two more orgasms and a renewed appreciation for the pleasures her body could provide. For the first time in years, she was aware of her body without a lick of shame. She smirked and replayed the way he'd knelt and hooked her leg over his shoulder while leaning her back under the spray. The combination of steaming hot water and his wicked tongue flowing over her clit had been mind-blowing. By the time he relented and let her go down on him, she'd lost all finesse, caught up in raw passion. She made him come all over her chest and enjoyed every second of cleaning up again. Even now, the mere memories were making her tingle.

So when her mom came up behind her and dropped a hand on her shoulder, Sofia leaped from her chair and blushed beet red as her mother laughed.

"Whoa! Easy. I didn't mean to startle you."

Sofia leaned in and kissed her mother on the cheek before gesturing to the chair next to hers.

"I was daydreaming." And what a fine dream it was. "Can I get your latte?"

"No, darling. I'll have a mocha, please."

"You look lovely today. What's the occasion?"

Josephine Valenti never dressed up without good reason. After years in the construction offices, jeans and flannels were practically her uniform. There were certain constants in Sofia's world. Her mother wore flannel, made a mean red sauce, and always drank skim lattes before lunch. So this polished version of her mother, complete with makeup and jewelry and ordering mochas, was cause for question.

"I don't need a reason to do the things that make me feel good. No time like the present."

"That's true." Sofia dutifully ordered a mocha for her mother and an Americano for herself. While her mother, still slender at sixty, could afford the calories of a mocha splurge, Sofia could not. As of this morning, she was taking back her life and going on a diet. She'd even gone so far as to clear out her chocolate drawer at work. It was killing her slowly. No one ever died from chocolate withdrawal, she reminded herself sternly. But man, that mocha smelled divine.

She set the tempting cup in front of her mother, who smiled and drank deeply.

"So, how've you been, Mom? You haven't come around the office lately to catch up."

"I'm not giving that place one more minute of my life." The smile dropped from her mother's face. The vehemence behind that statement set Sofia back in her chair. Her mother had certainly been more and more withdrawn from the business since Gabe's death, but she still popped in from time to time just to check up on things. Looking back, it had been a good six months since her mother had casually dropped by.

"Well, the pilot has finished filming. The Shahs loved their new home."

"That's nice, dear." Josephine took a sip of her coffee and checked her phone.

That was it? *That's nice, dear?* Sofia had spent the last month juggling the job her mother had dropped in her lap on top of this huge project. The casual disinterest felt like a slap in the face. Her mother looked up at her silence and Sofia's shock must've shown on her face, because Jo quickly followed up.

"You know what I mean. I'm sure it was challenging, and I'm glad it's done now. I didn't know how you were going to juggle everything. But honestly, I hope the show doesn't get picked up."

Sensing that she was stepping through a minefield of conversational topics, Sofia tried to pick a new path. Adrian was the topic on the tip of her tongue. She couldn't get him out of her head or her heart. Anytime she started dating someone new, her mom was the first to know. It felt strange that things had progressed so far without her mother's counsel. She should ask about bringing him to dinner Friday. Adrian had never been to a family dinner before, and she was nervous about how it would go. But with him by her side, Sofia felt she could handle her family's questions. Sofia wanted Adrian to be as welcome at her family table as she'd felt in Graciela's kitchen. Maybe they could get everyone together for a talk about the proposal. It was worth a shot.

"Are we still on for family dinner next Friday?"

"Yes." Jo had gone back to tapping on her phone. Who on earth was she texting? Since when did her mom text?

"Can I bring Adrian along?"

Jo sighed and turned her phone over. "I wish we didn't have to bring business to the table, but I suppose it's fine."

"It's not business, Ma. I'm seeing him."

Another awkward pause filled the space between them, accompanied by a searching and faintly pitying look from her mother. *Ouch.* Sofia rubbed a hand across her heart to ease the pinch. What was she seeing? Her daughter playing Icarus and

191

reaching too close to the sun? Did she just assume Sofia wouldn't be able to hold the attention of a guy like Adrian? Or was it the opposite, more of a "no guy is good enough for my daughter" thing? Adrian was a guy who worked in construction. Did she hold that against him? That couldn't be it. For goodness' sake, she'd married Dad, and she'd known Adrian for twelve years. He was a good guy, and Jo liked him. So, Option A: Sofia wasn't "enough" for him.

Her mother's unspoken critique flowed like rancid oil through her mind, coating every good thought with thick, sticky shame. Of course she wasn't good enough for a man like Adrian. Just look at him. Gorgeous, brave, successful. Everything Sofia wasn't. And whose fault was that? Her own, but she resented the fact that her mother had walked away and let the business fall into Sofia's lap. If she hadn't been stuck behind that desk for three years, maybe she'd have more to bring to the table. Pain and frustration pummeled her in waves and threatened to pull her under into the deep world of self-doubt and shame. She cast about, looking for a lifeline. Her mother might not approve, but Sofia wasn't going to let that sway her from her mission today. She'd told her siblings she'd find out what was going on between their parents. There would be time to tend her wounds later.

"So what have you been up to lately?"

"I've joined a group for older adults that plans outings to local sites of interest. It has been so fun! We got in for a tour of Moffett Field and the Rosicrucian Museum. We even helped prune back the roses at the San Jose Rose Garden. I've learned so much!"

For the first time since she arrived, her mother seemed like her old self, excited and full of energy. Sofia hadn't realized how long that sparkle had been missing until it showed up full force today. She was glad to see her parents finally starting to pull out of the grieving spiral. Maybe there was no need to worry about them not speaking. Dad was probably blowing things out of proportion again.

"Did Dad like being put to work on his day off?" Sofia could picture his gruff grumbling about pruning being Enzo's job.

Jo didn't look up from her mocha where she flicked the lid with her thumb. "He didn't come. He was too busy."

Sofia rocked back in her chair. Damn. But if Dad wasn't on set and he wasn't home with Mom, where was he spending his days?

Her mother picked up her phone and started tapping again. "In fact, I'm heading out for a tour of the Winchester Mystery House in a little bit, so I'm afraid I can't stay long."

"Oh. That's okay. I just missed catching up with you." Sofia couldn't help but resent whoever was on the other side of that text for taking her mother's attention. She wasn't a toddler who needed mommy all the time, but she sure felt like throwing a tantrum. She needed her mother's support and enthusiasm, not a casual brush-off in favor of a haunted house. Everything about this felt wrong.

"You're so sweet. How are things outside work?"

Finally, a bit of interest in her life. But how to answer that after her earlier silence? Adrian had been a large part of her life outside work. How could she explain any of that to her mother who clearly thought she was playing out of her league?

"Judging by your silence, I'm going to assume that you're still working your fingers to the bone for that damn place." Jo leaned forward and gripped Sofia's hands tightly. "Listen. Don't do what I did. Nothing—no company, no job, no man—nothing is worth sacrificing everything for. I gave that place thirty years of my life. I don't want to see you trapped in the same pit."

Sofia tried to hear the message of love behind her mother's words, but she *wanted* thirty years at the company, just not behind the manager's desk. To hear her dream condemned by her own mother sliced at her already wounded heart.

"That's easy to say when you're the one who walked away and left me holding the shovel."

"I never said you had to take over the office work."

"Who was going to make sure the bills got paid? Who was going to send out invoices and keep the place afloat? Who was going to make sure that our employees still got their paychecks? Dad? Enzo? Frankie? No. I was the only one stepping forward to do those things." Sofia's voice quivered with frustration.

"You always do this. You tear people down with all these questions. I don't answer to you, Sofia. I did what I had to do, and I don't regret it."

Sofia's heart took another hit and tears gathered behind her closed lids. She didn't tear people down, did she? Was that how people saw her? Sofia gripped her hands together, battling for control. Her mother's soft hand landing on top of hers nearly broke her. She was barely holding it together. This was not what she'd expected from coffee with her mom.

"No one is making you stay and do those things, Sofia." Her tone, as soft as her hand, was meant to soothe, but the condescension behind it pushed her into an angry retort.

"I am, Ma. I want my design business to be an integral part of Valenti Brothers. We have the reputation you all worked so hard to build, the opportunity to expand our brand through the show, and I am finally getting to do what I love. I can't walk away from the business side and let it all fall apart before I have a chance to succeed."

Jo pulled her hand away and checked her phone again before tucking it inside her purse. Her words were so quiet that Sofia almost missed the pain threading through them.

"I wish it would burn to the ground."

Sofia sat silent. She knew her mother had wanted Dad to step back, but this... This felt like more than that.

"He will never leave that company unless it is gone. I didn't

194

want to bring this up, but you should know. I am considering leaving your father."

"What? Does Dad know about this?" Sofia was in shock. She'd known her parents had fought over the company for years and the show more recently, but she'd always seen their marriage as rock-solid. This news was an earthquake, shaking her foundation.

"I don't know what your father knows. We haven't spoken since he announced that ridiculous television show. He knew. He knew I needed him, and he put that company first again."

Jo drank down the last of her coffee and set the white cup down carefully, while Sofia struggled to make sense of her words. Could her mother really toss aside a lifetime together? If Sofia had been asked yesterday, her answer would have been no. But today, the sadness and pain in her mother's eyes made the impossible seem plausible. Sofia needed to try and salvage this.

"So he could leave it in a strong position for the rest of us."

"Don't be naive. He won't leave until a backhoe loads his casket into the ground."

Was that why her dad wouldn't answer her questions? Because he had no intention of giving the company over to anyone?

Her mother's attention had shifted from her to a spot over her shoulder, before returning earnestly to her face. "I don't want to see what happened to me happen to you, too. I love you, Sofia. It's just not worth it. My ride for the excursion is here. I've got to run. Thanks for the coffee. Give my love to Enzo and Frankie."

Before Sofia had a chance to find her scattered words in the aftermath of the land mines she'd tripped, her mother had kissed her cheek and was gone, climbing into the car of a very attractive silver-haired gentleman who closed the door for her.

~

SOFIA TWISTED her hair into a bun for the third time and pinned it ruthlessly. She wanted everything to go perfectly tonight. Graciela had been so kind and welcoming all the nights that she'd stayed over, and she wanted Adrian to feel the same way at her family table. She also knew that her family could be ruthless in their teasing. Hopefully, the fact that they all knew him already would make it easier. But after her weird conversation with her mom the other day, who knew?

She hadn't shared her thoughts with her siblings yet, and that felt strange. She didn't know what was going on between her parents, and she prayed that whatever happened tonight, Adrian wouldn't be hurt. Her mom had always been a pillar of support and encouragement. She barely recognized the woman she'd had coffee with. Sofia had come away from that meeting battered and bruised at heart. Who knew what would happen at dinner?

She pulled her bun out and tried for a casual tousled look, as if looking relaxed was the same as feeling relaxed. She touched up her lipstick and mascara. *Nope, still not working.* Wielding her brush like a weapon, she ruthlessly tugged her hair back into her trademark ponytail so she could quit worrying about it and get a move on. When Adrian poked his head into the bathroom, she jumped and squeaked.

"Nervous?"

"Maybe. Are you?" She leaned into his hug.

"Hell, yes. I haven't talked to Dom in weeks because of the show, and the first thing I'm going to tell him is 'I'm dating your daughter'? Yeah, I'm a little nervous about how that's going to go down."

"Just don't tell him how I go down, and it'll be fine," she teased, more relaxed now that she had his strong arms wrapped around her.

He leaned his forehead against hers and chuckled. "You're sure it's okay that I'm coming with you?"

She let out a bark of laughter as her dirty mind followed that train of thought to Smutville. "So not touching that joke. You've really got to quit laying them out there like that."

"Be serious a minute." His voice trembled.

She pulled back and looked him in the eye. All of her own fears and nerves were reflected back at her. Taking his face in her hands she kissed him lightly.

"I'm sure it's more than okay that you're coming with me. I talked to Mom about it the other day."

"I'm sorry. I've just got a lot riding on tonight."

Eye to eye, Sofia pushed aside her own worries and gave him the support he needed. She nuzzled into his neck, kissing her favorite spot at the base of his neck where the soft met the sinewy strength of his shoulders.

It had been years since she'd been this happy. Three, to be exact. The process of filming the pilot had been stressful, but Sofia was grateful for the chaos. It had shaken up the routine of her life and opened all sorts of new doors. New challenges, new ideas, and new dreams. How long would she have ignored Adrian if it hadn't been for the show? She didn't like to think about it. He'd been right in front of her face for years. How much time had they wasted?

They were certainly trying to make up for it now. In the last week and a half since that magical first time, they'd settled into a cozy routine where she and Adrian would drive home to his house in their separate cars to sit and eat dinner with his mother. Graciela loved to tell stories, and Sofia learned so much more about this man she was falling for. His love for his sisters, his role in the community, his awkward teenage years—every story, whether embarrassing or told with pride, added pieces to the complex puzzle that was Adrian Villanueva. She had to admit she was falling in love with Graciela also. She was impossible to resist, with her laughing eyes, her relentless hospitality, and her fierce love for her family.

But her favorite part of the day was when Adrian would

follow her up the stairs to his apartment. The anticipation still tickled low in her belly, and made that moment when they finally joined together in bed even sweeter. They made love until dawn, when she'd drive home to get ready for the day. The thought that she could have had this in her life for *years* made her want to cry over their stupidity.

Maybe once things calmed down a little bit she could take him to her favorite cottage by the sea. The idea of spending time with her favorite person in her favorite place was tempting. The image of Adrian in board shorts made her mouth water. But she had no clue when they'd have time to indulge in a break.

No matter. They had here and now, and now was pretty darn spectacular. Not even a stressful family dinner was going to ruin her happiness.

"No matter what he says, no matter how this turns out, I've got you, and you've got me."

He closed his eyes and dropped his forehead back to hers. "Deal."

CHAPTER 22

From the minute they walked in, Adrian could feel the tension in the room. He was greeted with a friendly if cool smile from Jo, and Sofia barely hugged her mother. Damn it. Sofia had told him it was okay for him to be here. Clearly, it wasn't.

"Thank you for including me, Mrs. Valenti."

"I've been Jo to you for twelve years. I hope that won't change now that you're sleeping with my daughter." She turned away to put his proffered bottle of wine in the kitchen.

The awkward silence from the rest of the room confirmed his fears. They hadn't known, or if they had, they didn't approve. Adrian looked to Enzo for backup, but he just shrugged and took a sip of his red wine. Seth snorted his laughter through his hand, and Brandy smacked his bicep in reproach. Frankie at least poured him a glass of wine and offered it with a grin.

"You look like you could use this."

"Uh, yeah. Thanks."

He took a fortifying sip before he turned to look at the last man in the room, Domenico. Dom, who had been like a father to him after his own had disappeared. This wasn't how Adrian had wanted to approach the subject of his relationship with Sofia.

Dom just stared back at him, face blank and frozen for a solid minute, before he followed his wife into the kitchen, closing the door behind him with a snap.

Dom's raised voice echoed through the door, but no reply from Jo followed. The door was just thick enough that Adrian couldn't tell what was being said, but the tone was enough to extrapolate.

"Maybe I should go."

Sofia gripped his face and turned it from the door to face her instead. He was buoyed by the conviction he saw in her eyes.

"No, he'll have to get used to the idea, right? Because this thing between us isn't changing any time soon. He's just surprised."

Why hadn't she told anyone?

Jo came back into the dining room carrying a roast pork loin surrounded by broccolini. Placing it in the place of pride on a table already groaning, she went and sat in her spot without a word. Dom blustered in behind her with a bowl of pesto orecchiette. "...doesn't tell me a goddamn thing," he muttered as everyone took seats around the table.

Adrian stood to the side and waited while everyone sat, awkwardly nervous and afraid of screwing up his future in more ways than one. He took the empty seat next to Sofia and kept his head down while grace was said and bowls were passed. When he turned to hand the pasta to Sofia, he saw the tears in her eyes.

"What's...?"

She cut him off with a shake of her head and blinked back tears. Shit. He wanted to support her, but he didn't know how to in front of her family.

"Later."

Brandy dove into the silence around the table, and Adrian was thankful for her bravery. "So, I had a funny thing happen today."

While she recounted a story of someone passing out during an OB/GYN observation in her nursing program, Adrian tried to calm himself back down. Dom was just surprised. He hadn't been in the office much lately, and when he was on set he shadowed Jake so intently that he hadn't noticed the change between Adrian and Sofia. Where they once bickered incessantly, they'd grown downright cordial in the office. Paperwork was getting completed and flowing with ease. He couldn't remember the last time he'd felt compelled to tease her. Probably because he was getting plenty of her attention already.

As the laughter died down, Dom stepped into the conversational gap, clearing his throat. "I know this is supposed to be family dinner, but I do have a little bit of business to discuss." Jo rose from the table and headed for the door to the kitchen. "I thought you'd all like to know that the pilot got picked up. We will be on TV!"

The table erupted into excited squeals and clapping from nearly everyone—everyone except Jo and Sofia. Jo stood frozen in the doorway. Adrian could tell this news did not excite the family matriarch in the least, but he was surprised that Sofia was so quiet. He'd thought she'd be excited about the show getting picked up. Wasn't this her dream to jump-start her design business?

"Dad?" she asked, but only Adrian heard her. "DAD!" She yelled it that time and got everyone's attention around the table.

"What is it, honey?"

In a voice as sweet as the endearment, she asked a quiet question. Even Adrian could tell this was going to be bad.

"How can we be on TV if we haven't signed new contracts?"

"I signed them yesterday. We're all good."

"No, Dad. Not good. Did you read them?"

"Jake told me they were the same as the pilot contracts with a few more people added to it."

"What's the percentage cut on merchandise from the show?"

"Uh, I don't know. What was it in the other one?"

She ignored his question and asked another. Adrian could see the vein pulsing in her temple.

"Whose names are listed on the new contract?"

"Everyone in this room. Plus some of the regular guys on the crew."

Jo's head snapped up at this. "No way in hell am I going on that show."

"That answers my next question of whether you asked everyone or not. Have you thought about what this does to our project timelines? How are we going to handle the intake of new clients? Do they expect us to film our existing clients for upcoming projects in the pipeline? And have you gotten releases from those people? What's the revenue split between the people in this room? How can you have figured any of that out if we haven't even settled the roles people will play after you retire? Did you sort any of this out or did you just go with your gut and sign away our business?" Sofia's voice got louder and higher the more rapid-fire questions she aimed at her father. Without waiting for a reply she rose from the table and grabbed her cell phone from her purse.

Dom slammed his hand on the table, making forks and spoons jump as well as Sofia. "Damn it, Sofia. Enough with the questions! I thought this was what you wanted. Why are you so against it all of a sudden?"

"Dad, I'm not against it. But how can you say yes without knowing the answers?" She unlocked her cell phone and deliberately turned her back on her father.

"Who are you calling?"

"I'm texting Jake to tell him that you signed under duress and that the rest of us did not have access to the documents and that if he doesn't want a lawsuit on his hands he'll ignore your signature for a few days while we sort things out."

"Sit back down." The command in his voice didn't even faze

Sofia, and Adrian was reluctantly impressed. "You're overreacting, Sofia."

"No, Dad. The sad thing is I'm not. If you want me to be the business manager, you shouldn't make decisions like this without me. Oh wait, I don't hold that title, do I? I'm just the lowly office grunt."

Dom tried to strike a conciliatory tone, but Sofia was having none of it, her thumbs flying over the screen of her phone. "Sofia, you know I rely on you to—"

"To clean up your messes? Yeah, that's becoming abundantly clear." The phone in her hand began to ring. "Oh look, it's Jake. Imagine that. Excuse me, I have work to do." She headed out the back of the house.

"Don't worry, Dad. I'm sure she'll come around. Hey, after all, who doesn't want to be on TV?" Frankie's youthful enthusiasm wasn't enough to break the tension.

Dom eyed his wine glass, twirling it in his hand before pushing back from the table and following her out back. Adrian wondered if he should follow, but Seth shook his head.

"Better to let them sort it out, if you'd like to keep your head attached to your body."

～

SOFIA MANAGED to keep her voice calm as she talked to Jake on the phone.

"I'm sure it's fine, but none of us got to read through it, so the signature is at worst invalid, at best incomplete. Do you mind sitting on it for two days while I vet it?"

"No problem, Sofia. I'll be honest, I was surprised to get it back so soon without a mark on it. The first contract looked like my high school English papers. I'll bring it back by the office in the morning."

"Thanks, Jake."

"And in return, you'll do me a favor."

"Oh, really?"

"Yes. Convince your mother to be on the show."

"You've got a better chance of getting an appearance from a flying monkey."

"I want to get the dynamic between your parents for the full season."

"Trust me, that dynamic right now isn't going to reflect well."

"Just promise me you'll try."

"I'll try."

"Good. I'll get those papers to you in the morning."

Sofia hung up the phone, relieved that she'd dodged that bullet. She turned and realized she had another one barreling straight for her.

"Don't worry, Dad. He agreed to return the contracts and let me go over them tomorrow."

Dom pulled up short right in front of her and snatched her phone from her hand. His nostrils flared as he drew in a deep breath and struggled to keep his voice calm. "Whose company is this?"

"I don't know, Dad. Have you figured that out yet?" Her sarcasm would only make the situation worse, but she couldn't stop herself as she grabbed her phone back.

"It's mine. My company! I poured years of blood, sweat, and tears into it to make it what it is today. First, you kick me off of my own show. Now you think you can kick me out of my own company? You have no right to treat me like a child at my own table and embarrass everyone! How dare you question my leadership, especially in front of Adrian?"

Usually her father was all bluster and little bite, but today, Sofia knew she'd pushed him into true anger. But she couldn't back down now. She'd come too far to lose it all. She met his accusations with an angry one of her own. "How dare you determine everyone's future without thinking through the details?"

"Little girl, you watch your tone," Dom snapped.

"That's just it, Dad. I'm not a little girl anymore, and you can't keep treating me like one. For years, I've dreamed of running this company with Seth, Enzo, and Frankie. Is that ever going to happen? You need to nail down your retirement plan before we sign these contracts. Otherwise, you're locked in, and the rest of us can't move forward."

"I'm still running this place."

She hated when he yelled. It always brought the little girl who loved her daddy trembling to the front of her brain, afraid to do anything wrong. She fought to stay focused and stand up for herself. "Barely. Adrian and I have kept this pilot project afloat, because you couldn't handle it. All I've seen you do lately is peek over Jake's shoulder and raid the craft services table. I've been asking you for months to figure out what you want. The time has come. I want you to step back. I can hire an office manager to take over my duties there, with my supervision."

"Money should be handled by family."

"Then get someone else to do it. I think I've proven my business and creative chops, and I deserve a chance to keep designing."

"One over-budget house design doesn't make you a designer. Did you think I wouldn't hear about how your plan kept shifting to recoup losses? Or how you wanted to take out a structural wall just because? Or that you strong-armed Enzo and Seth into donating their labor for free? That is not how we run Valenti Brothers. You give the client a solid plan in their budget and you stick to it. We pay our employees what they're worth. If it's not broken, don't fix it."

"But Dad, if it is broken, why can't we fix it to be amazing? Did you see the look on the Shahs' faces? They love that house," Sofia pleaded. Why couldn't he see that she wasn't trying to kill the company, but expand it and make it better?

"Good work, safe fixes, under budget. That's the promise I've made for thirty years, and just because you want to play doll-house with people's lives doesn't mean I'm going to step back and let you." His angry words slapped at her pride, and she lashed back.

"Is that what you think I'm doing? Playing dollhouse?" She cringed at how shrill her voice had become but it was hard to stay calm when your father was tromping all over your dreams with his steel-toed boots.

"I don't have time to let you experiment with people's homes. I need you to take care of business."

"Is this how you treated Mom? Did you just dismiss her dreams and needs because they didn't line up with your expecta-tions? Because I'll tell you, it feels pretty shitty. I can understand why she doesn't want to be around you anymore. I don't either."

"Did she say something?" A hint of vulnerability teased the edges of his voice, but Sofia wasn't going to get sucked into this. This roller coaster ride of emotions was making her sick, and she was getting off. The fact that after everything that had happened for the show her father still didn't respect her skills had despair threatening, and she wasn't sure how long she could hold it together.

"No, if you want to know how Mom feels, you're going to have to ask her yourself. I'm going to go back inside and eat my meal, with my boyfriend Adrian, and enjoy myself, since I know this mess will be waiting on my desk in the morning."

"So you and Adrian are serious?" The doubt in his voice poked at her already tender heart.

"We're seeing each other and figuring that out. Is there a problem?"

"No, just that he's a good man. He's been through a lot in his life, and he deserves to be happy. I rely on him to keep the crews running. I don't want this to cause any problems."

"Business first. Right, Dad? How's that working out for you?"

He turned and went back into the house, and Sofia could do

nothing but stare after him. Lowering herself to the back stoop, she let her frustrated tears fall. Had he really just assumed that this relationship would fail? And he was more worried about Adrian than his own daughter? Where was her father who had always told her she could do anything she wanted for the first twenty years of her life? Where was her mother who'd always been her biggest cheerleader? And how had it gotten to the point that her parents weren't speaking? Had she been too wrapped up in her own grief to see that their marriage was disintegrating? The painful reality was that her parents were humans, just like anyone else. Her shiny image of their *perfect* marriage was tarnishing quickly. If they couldn't pull it off, what made her think she could? From seeing Adrian sitting in Gabe's chair to being dismissed professionally, she hadn't thought her heart could be hurt any more tonight. Once again, she was wrong.

CHAPTER 23

DOM RETURNED to the table a changed man. He looked tired. In all the years Adrian had worked with the man, he'd seen him worn out at the end of a big day, but he'd never seen him this soul-deep exhausted. Adrian almost felt embarrassed to witness the longing glance he sent across the table toward Jo.

Jo caught the look and turned away, leaving the table without a word. Dom's eyes followed his wife as she left the room, but he didn't go after her. Adrian didn't understand it. If his wife were mad at him, he'd chase her down and argue it out. You couldn't have make-up sex if you skipped the fight. He could picture himself and Sofia arguing fiercely over some future disagreement. Yeah, he'd really like to make up with her. Oddly, instead of worrying him, the image clicked in a fundamental place deep inside him as exactly right. He glanced at the back door, waiting for his partner to come back in.

"Zio Dom, I love you. We can talk more later, but Brandy's got an early morning. We should get going." Seth rose from the table as if on cue. Hugs and kisses passed between everyone before the young couple finally took their leave.

Dom gestured to the dishes left at the table. "Enzo, Frankie, you're on dish duty."

"But, Dad..."

Dom cut off the whine with a glare and a head shake. His remaining children left the table, leaving Dom and Adrian alone. This was it. They were going to talk about the proposal now. Why else would he have sent everyone away? Was Sofia giving them space for this conversation? Somehow he'd thought she would be by his side for this moment. Dom dropped heavily into his chair and drank down the rest of his mostly full wine glass.

"Adrian, you know I love you like you were my own."

Oh no. That didn't sound good. Adrian's gut clenched in anticipation.

"Yeah, Dom, I know. You've been a second father to me every step of the way."

"You make me so proud, which is why it kills me to say this."

Why wouldn't Dom look him in the eye? "Then don't say it yet. Let's talk about it."

"I've been turning over your idea in my mind, trying to visualize how it would work, but there are too many obstacles to see a clear path."

Adrian took the words like a punch to the stomach. It hurt like hell to hear it, but it wasn't going to knock him out of this fight. "Like what?"

Dom scrubbed his hands over his hair with a sigh before pulling them down his face. "For starters, what kind of role would you have in the company? Would you keep leading teams, or do you want to take over more of the management?"

"I'd like to do both. I'm happiest running teams, but I can take on some management duties if it helps spread the load." Finally, they were having a conversation about how this would work. Surely Dom wouldn't dismiss the plan without giving him a chance to compromise.

"How do you see the balance of power at the top?" Dom still

wasn't looking him in the eye. He intently pushed his pork roast around his plate with his fork.

"Look, Dom, I can't buy out the whole business, and I don't want to. I want to keep working with your kids and Seth to make Valenti Brothers strong. I just want to have a say in how it gets run. Like you said, I'm the one who best understands what Valenti Brothers is about. Quality work, under budget."

"Does your relationship with my daughter compromise your ability to work together rationally?"

That one hit Adrian a bit higher, right in his solar plexus, knocking the breath out of him. He was still fighting, but it was getting harder to breathe. He and Sofia were still figuring things out. Was Dom going to toss out this plan because he didn't like Adrian dating his daughter? That question slipped from his lips before he could stop it.

"Do you have a problem with me dating Sofia?" Even saying it out loud scraped at Adrian's heart, torn between affection for the man he loved like a father and the growing attraction he felt for his daughter.

"No, son. She couldn't do better than you. But I know how hard it can be to work alongside the woman you love. It's not for the faint of heart. Have you thought about how you'll handle that?"

"No, but I'm sure we can figure it out."

Dom looked up at that with a wistful gaze. "God, I wish I still had that optimism. Maybe it is time for me to step away. Adrian, it comes down to this. How can I make you a partner and take part of my kids' company away from them? I would in a heartbeat. You have to know that. I trust you to run the building side of the business more than any of my kids at this point, and I hope to God you'll stay, but it's not just my decision. I'm getting pushback on this."

Adrian had temporarily dropped his guard and the jab landed solidly, rattling his confidence. "Who is against it?"

"Sofia keeps butting heads with me whenever I try to talk with her about it. She just told me she wants to run the business with her siblings and her cousin. So as much as I hate to say this, I think the answer has to be no."

There it was, the knockout combination. Being told no was bad enough, but having the reason be the words of the woman he was falling for knocked him out. He scrambled to recover, but his back was firmly on the floor. How could Sofia turn on him like that? It couldn't be true. Surely Dom had misunderstood.

"Don't say no yet. Give me a chance to convince her. Let's pretend we didn't have this talk. I can't believe that she would say that."

"I'll keep an open mind, but she is pushing me to decide before we get the new show launched." Dom held his hands out as if they were tied, which pissed Adrian off. His were the only hands that *weren't* tied in this unholy mess.

Adrian could see his dreams slipping away, but he wasn't ready to give up yet. "Let me talk to her."

"Good luck, son. She takes after her mother. You're going to need it."

Dom quietly rose and headed for the kitchen, where his real kids were clanging dishes in the sink, leaving Adrian alone and still firmly on the outside.

Had he misjudged her completely? Had he given his heart to someone who didn't respect him? Was his dream of stability for his family and his friends going to blow up in his face because he couldn't keep it in his pants? What the hell was he going to do now? He knew how to build walls, so he steadfastly began to build one to protect himself while he figured out the answers.

∾

SOFIA WAS unnerved by Adrian's silence. When she'd come back inside, he'd been sitting alone at the table, quiet and withdrawn.

Waves of hurt were rolling off his hunched shoulders and crossed arms. What had happened while she was getting her shit together outside? Honestly, she didn't know if she had the emotional energy to handle one more round on the roller coaster tonight after her fight with her father.

She was a grown-ass woman. Why was it so hard to stand up to her dad when she knew she was right? If it had been any other boss, she'd have calmly and coherently laid out her argument. Sofia hated that her knees and her voice still trembled when her daddy got mad. It was exhausting.

And now here was another man in her life, clearly angry about something. They climbed into her car, and Adrian still hadn't said a word. When she couldn't take the wall of silence any longer, she chose humor as her hammer of choice. Hopefully she could get him to laugh off whatever her mom or dad had said, and get back to the happy vibe they'd had before they came.

"Well, you made it out alive. That's better than most."

Adrian grunted.

"Come on. It couldn't have been that bad."

He huffed out a breath and kept his eyes glued to the window.

"You know, that whole grunting instead of speaking thing is really only sexy when Tom Hardy does it."

No response. Not even a twitch of his dimple. So much for humor. She reached for the jackhammer of details.

"Are you worried about the contract? I convinced Jake to let me have it back. I think we can bargain for better compensation for your guys since it's going through the network this time."

Adrian stoically refused to look at her, flashing street lights illuminating his furious profile an eerie orange.

"What am I missing here? Why are you so mad?"

"It's what I missed."

"What are you talking about?"

"How did I miss that you never supported my proposal?"

Sofia barely managed to keep her eyes on the road. What was he talking about? "That's bullshit. Of course I support you."

"Oh really? That's not what your father said tonight. He said he hoped I wouldn't leave, but it was looking like I wouldn't have a unanimous vote. He said he couldn't see how to make it work around your reservations. What the hell, Sofia?"

"That's what he took away from what I said?" Sofia clenched her hands on the steering wheel, wishing they were around her father's neck instead. She could believe only too well that he hadn't really understood her point. She had to take her foot off the accelerator before she caused an accident.

"So you did say that? Jesus, Sofia. You know how much this means to me. How hard I've worked."

"I have reservations about it, sure. Has he talked to you about any details? Any numbers? Any structure of the deal?"

"No, not yet. If you had concerns, why didn't you talk to me about them?" Adrian was glaring at her now, and she kept her eyes on the road so she could say what she needed to say. She would not let another man intimidate her tonight.

"Because they weren't concerns you could address. Only my dad can figure out how he's going to structure the company. But yes, I asked questions about what would happen to my share of the company, and Enzo and Frankie's, too. It's our legacy. I need details, Adrian. How can I figure out how to support your proposal if I don't know what it is?"

"Because we are together. I thought you had my back."

Sofia pulled up to a stoplight and finally turned to face him. The anger in his eyes burned. She knew she'd hurt him with her questions, but she had to be true to herself. She knew her dad was impulsive, and she had to be the voice of reason. "I do, but you can't expect me to jump into a deal without knowing what's what."

"But you can design a house without the inspection, right?"

"That was different." Yes, she'd made mistakes, but with the pressures of the show, she'd thought he understood.

"That's bullshit. It's irresponsible and unethical to spend the client's money so recklessly."

"Excuse me?" A horn honked behind her, startling her into motion. How long had that light been green?

"You should have my back on this. I thought we were building toward something here. How can I be with someone who doesn't support my dreams?"

Sofia turned the corner onto her street and pulled into the drive of her apartment building. "All I said was—"

"That you don't believe in me or my plan. Yeah, message received. I thought we were on the same team. Don't worry. I won't make that mistake again." He was out of the car and stalking to his truck before she could do more than call his name.

"Adrian! Wait!" She fought her seat belt, frustration and fear making her fingers clumsy. She managed to fall out of the car and race to the end of the driveway as he slammed his door and peeled his truck off down the street, taking half of her heart with him.

THE SHOW DIDN'T STOP FILMING JUST because the pilot was done and her heart was broken. She had a full day of B-roll scheduled around the office. Sofia pulled herself out of bed and managed to strip out of the sweats she'd been wearing for two days straight. Friday night, she'd barely made it into her bed before collapsing into a mess of tears and snotty tissues. Now, after a weekend spent dissecting every last detail of that nightmare family dinner, she had two-day-old makeup caked on her face in oh-so-attractive rivulets and had to face the world. She hadn't realized that Adrian had managed to get inside her walls, so when he'd swung his words with the force of a sledgehammer, the damage was severe.

At least you held your own. The little voice inside was trying to offer comfort, but it wasn't making a dent in the sad yet. Yes, she'd pushed back against his accusations, defending her actions. But in doing so, she'd been forced to see just how little he respected her work, how little what they'd shared had meant to him. Apparently, his ego mattered more than making a reasoned decision. Honestly, it was for the best that things between them were over. She refused to be with a man who would treat her that way. She had to believe that or she'd crumble onto the floor of her shower, fragments of her soul rinsing down the drain.

She ran the shower as hot as she could stand and held her face beneath the stream, letting the water chase away her fresh tears along with her old mascara. If only the water could wash away the stain on her heart as well. She had really thought that things were going to be different with Adrian. Everything he'd made her feel was sharper and stronger than any man before. Unfortunately, that held true for pain as well as pleasure.

Enough. She had to push this aside and be professional. She soaped up on auto-pilot, towel-dried her body and hair, and put on a clean skirt and blouse. The routine of putting together her outer shell helped her shore up inside, too. Marginally coordinated, neat and tidy, she left her apartment and drove herself to work without waiting to see if Enzo or Frankie wanted a ride. Normally, living so close made it easy to spend time with her siblings, but today she needed the solitude to rebuild her defenses. She drove all the way to the office without turning on the radio, lost in her thoughts of how she would handle working with Adrian today. A day full of shooting filler scenes around the office would be hard, but she would handle it. She handled everything.

She pulled into the lot, aware that she was late, and prepared to make excuses.

"You look like hell." Jake called her out on her appearance the moment he saw her. "Where the fuck have you been?"

"Sorry, I overslept." She chose a technical truth over the whole story. If Jake found out about her breakup, he'd probably want to film her about it, and she was just too raw.

"Well, get into makeup. You can't go on camera looking like that. Luckily, your parents are stuck in traffic, so we are running behind anyway." He looked up from his clipboard and shot her a glare. "Why are you still standing here? Go!"

"Sheesh! What crawled up his butt this morning?" she muttered to herself as she obediently made her way to the makeup tent set up at the back of the parking lot. Natalie was there, finishing touch-ups on Frankie.

"Hey, I knocked this morning, but you didn't answer. Spend the weekend at Adrian's?"

Sofia sat back in her chair, casting a loaded glance at Natalie. She'd just as soon not have her breakup broadcast to the masses.

Natalie caught her meaning before Frankie did and laughed. "Oh, honey. I'm not miked, and unless you see Trina, there are no cameras here. I'm on par with your bartender or priest. We beauticians have an oath of secrecy as well."

Sofia had to laugh at that, and it broke through her resistance. Natalie had become a fast friend during the last month of filming, and she might as well get it out now before she got her face all fixed.

"No, I didn't see Adrian this weekend, and I'm not likely to again any time soon."

Frankie turned to face her, much to the annoyance of the beleaguered makeup artist. "What does that mean?"

"Please, Frankie. Hold still." Natalie swiveled the chair back to face the mirror.

"I don't see why I need this crap on my face anyway. I'm a contractor, not some freaking model."

216

"It's so you look normal on camera. Now, I'm almost done. Hold. Still."

"Fine." Frankie turned back to the mirror, but didn't let go of the question. "What do you mean by that, Fi?"

"It means that I think we broke up after dinner Friday."

"No wonder you look like hell."

"Thanks a lot." She flipped off the mirror they were both staring at and immediately felt better, then turned her attention to the makeup genius. "Do you think you can hide it, Natalie?"

"No sweat, honey. I'm a professional. If I can make this mug look normal, yours is no sweat." Natalie laughed and patted Frankie on the cheek. "That didn't hurt too much, did it?"

Frankie answered with a smirk and turned back to Sofia, like a dog with a bone. "So why did you break up?"

"Short story—he doesn't respect my opinions or my work. He expected me to fall in line with his plans just because we were sleeping together, damn the consequences to me or my family. If you want the longer version, you'll have to wait for the red wine tonight, because I cannot afford to start crying again."

"Well, if he was that much of an asshole, then good riddance. I wonder what this does to his plans to join the company."

"I don't know, but I'll be damned if I answer to him as my boss. If he's in, I'm out."

"Your turn." Natalie wrapped the paper bib around her neck. "It sounds like you need full armor today."

"Waterproof everything."

"You got it. Let's knock him on his ass."

Sofia closed her eyes, and relaxed as Natalie painted foundation on her face. She was definitely facing a battle today. It felt good to be pampered a little bit while she prepared her mental and physical armor. Even Frankie was quiet while Natalie worked her magic.

Sofia tried to pull her thoughts to the scenes they'd shoot today. B-roll, they called it, and they'd use it to fill in the transitions between big scenes and commercial breaks now that the pilot had been picked up. She wasn't used to doing everything out of order, but she was learning fast. She had always picked up on things quickly. She just wished her dad respected that ability more. Instead he just thought that her job was easy, and that's why she had stepped into the role seamlessly. After all, her mother had done it with ease as well. She hated what that said about her dad's opinion of both of them. His casual disregard of her achievements burned. To have Adrian talk to her in the same dismissive way was the last straw.

Natalie was working on her eyes when Frankie piped up again. "So, you really think things are over?"

"I do. I won't give myself to someone who doesn't respect me." Natalie's hand paused briefly before resuming her blending of eye shadow.

"Well, it's a shame that's how you see me." The deep voice rattled through her, and she kept her eyes closed out of mortification.

She'd been set up. She'd kill Frankie for this. Adrian sat in the chair next to her. She scrambled for a response. "What's a shame is that I didn't see that our relationship was dependent on your partnership deal."

"I never hid anything from you."

"What a crock."

"You're the one who went behind my back to convince your dad not to sell me part of the company. How is that not hiding?" Adrian stared her down in the mirror, and she wanted to cry at the anger and disappointment she saw there.

"I didn't tell him not to accept your proposal. I asked him questions and told him I couldn't decide one way or another until I had answers."

"Mascara. Open up."

Sofia blinked rapidly and raised her eyes to the ceiling, while the tiny artist expertly applied the finishing touches. She would not look at *him* and screw up all of Natalie's hard work with tears.

Frankie chimed into the conversation. "She didn't tell him not to sell, but I did."

"What?" they both asked in unison.

"I want to run the building side of the business. I have worked damn hard to prove my worth to this company, even if Dad refuses to see it. I'm not going to sit quietly by while he sells away half of my business."

"Lips." Sofia held hers still while Natalie painted them, giving her a good reason to refrain from stepping back into the fray. Frankie was doing just fine.

Adrian tried to protest. "That's not how it would—"

Frankie cut him off. "How would it? How exactly do you see this working?"

"I don't know. I've been trying to get Dom to talk about it."

"Ha. Good luck with that. I've been trying to get him to talk to me about the future for years."

"Camera in ten," Jake bellowed from outside the tent.

Sofia pulled the paper bib off her shirt and rose as gracefully as she was able to on shaky knees and stilettos. "I'll leave you two to hash this out. I've got scenes to shoot." Happy to escape the tension of the tent, she greeted Jake at the front door of the office with a firm and fake smile plastered on her face.

Let the circus begin.

CHAPTER 24

THREE WEEKS LATER

HOW LONG COULD she keep this up? Her brain was spinning, and her sketches were blurring before her eyes. She'd been at her desk since before eight, only getting up to go through makeup before filming two customer sessions at her desk. Even now, at four in the afternoon on a Wednesday, there was still no end in sight. In the three weeks since the show had started filming in earnest, her world had exploded. All of their active contracts were being converted to the show as the owners signed releases. Three crews would be filmed on separate houses to fill the season fast. New leads were being funneled through production assistants, too.

She was suddenly designing for three different teams, on six projects. They were hiring on an additional crew to handle the increase of work, too. On top of all the additional HR paperwork and design and ordering that needed to go through, she was lucky to see the light of day. It would all calm down. Soon. This was just start-up craziness.

She reminded herself that this was what she'd signed on for. After reworking the contracts to provide better compensation for the crews, better percentages on side-lines, and stipulations about designs in her name, she'd been able to get everyone to agree to the concessions that the production company wouldn't budge on, like timelines and overrun caps. It had taken all of her negotiating skill, but she'd done it. Three days later an expanded crew had pulled up, and she hadn't taken a full breath since.

She'd feel a lot better about her workdays if her nights were as blissful as they had been. But going home to an empty apartment had distinctly lost its appeal. She found herself staying later and later just to avoid the loneliness. Even though her heart was broken, she was proud of the way they were handling things. Post-breakup, she and Adrian had taken to avoiding each other as much as possible. She was determined that their split wouldn't interfere with their working relationship. She refused to prove her father right.

They had barely seen each other since filming started. Adrian was kept as busy filming at the houses as she was here in the office. And tomorrow payroll was due. It was going to be another late night for her. She printed and rolled up the three designs she'd fleshed out today and dropped them in a tube to go to Adrian for inspection. She was worried because she hadn't been able to wait for him to get to all of the inspections before starting because she had Jake breathing down her neck to film the client sit-downs. She had built more space into the budget and less detail into the plan this time. Hopefully, it would be enough.

When Enzo popped his head into her office, Sofia leaned back with a sigh.

"Now a good time?"

"As good as it's gonna get." She stretched her arms out in front of her. "What's up?"

"Dad wanted me to ask if you had the payroll done yet."

"Why doesn't he pick up the phone himself?"

"Because he's still pissed at you."

"Did you need something while you're here? Or are you just today's whipping boy?"

"I have pictures of the front elevations on the two projects that requested my services, but I wanted to see if you had already decided to make changes to the exteriors before I order the plants and pavers."

"Sure, which houses?"

"The Ong house and the Pichetti place."

"Perfect timing." She tossed him the tube. "I just printed them up. The Mitchell house is in there, too. In fact, if you're heading out can you take those to Adrian after you look at them? I need his feedback before I order, too."

"Are you two still not speaking?"

"I speak to him when I have to. I'm a professional. I'd just thought you could save me a step."

"Uh-huh. Sure."

"I need to get back to work. Since the answer to Dad's question is no, I don't have payroll done yet, it's doubtful I'll get out of here before ten."

"Sure thing, sis. Don't worry. It'll calm down soon. I've got to say I like your designs so far. You've got a real eye."

Sofia could feel the blush warming her cheeks. "Thanks, Enzo. That means a lot."

"What do you think you'll do after the show?"

"What do you mean?"

"Well, the show won't run forever, and Dad is going to have to retire sooner or later. Nick and Seth got me thinking."

"Thinking what?" As usual, pulling ideas from Enzo was like pulling teeth. Painful, and something she tried to avoid until she absolutely needed to.

"Incorporating separately from Valenti Bros. Just something I'm toying with. Thought I'd see what you think."

"I think that's a big step. Let me think about it a bit, pull together some data, once things calm down."

"No rush."

"No, there never is with you." Enzo was not known for his impulsive behavior. Always cautious, always wanting to consider all the possibilities, his slowness to action was a long-standing family joke.

"Hey, I resemble that remark."

Their shared laughter was interrupted by Natalie's knock at the door. The makeup artist popped her head in without waiting for a reply.

"Oh! I'm so sorry to interrupt." She blushed a fierce red.

The look on her face as she avoided meeting Enzo's eye was part embarrassment, part panic, with just a hint of...longing? *Interesting.*

"I was just on my way out. Sofia, we need to add you for one more scene over at the Mitchell house tomorrow morning. Jake asked me to have you put it on your schedule."

Almost before she had finished delivering her message, the tiny brunette had backed out of the office.

"Am I that scary?" Enzo's eyes followed her out of the office.

Very Interesting. "Hmm, maybe to those who don't know you're a complete marshmallow on the inside." Sofia pegged her brother in the arm, and he laughed.

"Very funny. See you tomorrow, sis. Don't stay too late."

"I don't have much of a choice."

ADRIAN GLANCED up as another truck pulled in the driveway of the Ong house. He'd sent the crew from the Hunter project home already. They'd put in a full day of work pouring a new concrete slab that would serve as the foundation for an outdoor living space.

He was dirty and exhausted and beyond done with having a camera in his face. He'd decided to try and squeeze in another inspection, so he could get it to Sofia before she started planning on this one. He refused to let their breakup get in the way of him doing the quality work Dom relied on him for. He was mostly finished, but he wanted another look under the house before it got too dark.

When Enzo climbed out of the truck, Adrian happily conscripted him into service. "Hey, man. Here, hold this." He tossed a powerful LED flashlight at the younger man.

"Sure. How's this place shaping up?"

"I'll tell you in a minute." Adrian lifted the grate from the side of the house and stuck his head into the eighteen inches of space under the house. "Can you shine that light at the back of the house?"

Enzo knelt down next to the hole and complied. "What are you looking for?"

"I saw a suspicious dip over beneath the kitchen when I looked in here earlier but there was a glare from the sun." Enzo helpfully angled the light toward the footprint of the kitchen. It was so nice to work with someone who knew what they were doing. "Thanks... Son of a bitch!"

"Hey. No need for name-calling. If you need me to move the light..."

"No. There's a leak. A long-term slow leak, if the area of discoloration is any indication. Who knows how much damage has been caused above it in the walls..."

He crawled back out, and made a note in his pocket journal to add to his report.

"So, what brings you over here after quitting time?"

"I wanted to look at the house one more time, this time with Sofia's plans, to see what will be changing before we get started ordering things."

"Sofia's plans? For this house?"

Enzo tossed the cardboard tube to Adrian, who caught it by reflex since his brain was currently spinning.

"Yeah, she asked me to bring them over to you. She said there are ones for the Mitchell, Ong, and Pichetti houses in there."

What the hell? They'd talked about this. She had promised not to do any more design plans without consulting with him first. This was why they'd had so many problems on the Shah house. And she'd done it, not once, but three times? He clenched his hands around the tube of prints, trying not to let his anger show and failing miserably.

Enzo held up his hands and backed away toward his truck. "I'm just the messenger."

"Are you gonna look at these or not?"

"Are you gonna punch me in the nose or not?"

"Not mad at you. Let's get this over with." Adrian briskly unrolled the plans for the house in front of him, mentally over-laying the existing structure onto the schematic drawings in front of him. He handed the front of the house drawing to Enzo and focused on what was left. She wanted to take down another wall between the kitchen and dining room and reconfigure the master bedroom to add an en suite bathroom. Damn. Given what he suspected was going to be extensive pipe replacements, changing the plumbing at the back of the house as well was going to be expensive. He really hoped she hadn't shown these plans to the homeowners yet. There was no way all of this was going to fit in the budget or the timeline for this house. "You good, man?"

"Yeah, I'm all good." Enzo handed back the front page. "Nothing too dramatic for me out here."

"That's good because we are going to be right up against the budget on this project."

"What's new?"

"The fact that it's your sister designing it, and I'm going to have to tell her no."

"Good luck with that." Enzo laughed and climbed into the cab of his truck.

"I'm going to need more than luck tonight," Adrian muttered as he tried and failed to suppress the urge to slam his truck bed closed.

~

HIS TEMPER HADN'T COOLED when he pulled up to the construction offices and saw her car out front. It was a slap in the face that she would just ignore everything that they'd agreed on. He knew he shouldn't walk through the door. He shouldn't talk to her while he was this angry. He shouldn't jump to conclusions. But too many of his buttons had been pushed today, and his shouldn'ts weren't as strong as his what-the-hells.

He pushed through the main doors and strode back toward her office. He paused outside her doorway when he heard her on the phone.

"Yes, that's right. I need to special order that porcelain tile. The timeline got moved up on a lot of our projects. If you can get it to me quickly, I'll make sure to feature your company name on the show."

She'd get what she wanted. She had a way of convincing people to bend over backwards to please her. Well, he was through contorting himself for very little reward. He had his crew and his reputation to think of.

Sofia looked up from her desk and held up a finger for patience. She had the nerve to ask him to wait, after ignoring his request that she wait for his reports? His simmering anger cranked up to a boil.

"Thanks, Ashley. You're the best. Yes, you can have them shipped directly to the house." She rattled off the address for the Ong house, which only served to piss him off more, before hanging up.

"What do you think you're doing?" He couldn't keep his anger hidden. In fact, he didn't want to, didn't even try. She should absolutely hear how pissed he was.

"What are you talking about?" Adrian watched the confusion cross her face, and it irrationally fed his anger. She didn't even know.

"Why are you ordering tile for the Ong house?"

"Because the Ongs agreed that they liked it for their bathroom today?"

"So you've already pitched the plans to them? Great. That's just perfect."

"What is your problem?"

"You're my problem. Didn't we agree that you wouldn't plan before I got you the inspection reports?"

"Yes, but—"

"And didn't we say you wouldn't show it to the clients until we agreed?"

"But—"

"I just got done with that inspection, and there is a major leak under the house. Likely damage to the interior wall."

"I'll figure it out," she said through clenched teeth.

"What if I told you that the wall you wanted to take down is load-bearing? Or that the backyard doesn't have permit clearances for your expansion?"

"I'd—"

He was too far gone down the path of this rant to listen to her response. His thoughts were spewing out of his mouth as quickly as his brain could pull them up. "I don't care what you have a degree in. You've designed one house. One. I've built hundreds. The fact that you ignore my advice shows your inexperience. Maybe it would be better to have those show designers step in. You keep making everything more complicated than it needs to be. We don't need to knock down walls and expand square footage on every house. We just need to make them livable for these people on a budget. Get your own agenda out of it. And another thing—"

"No."

"Excuse me?" Her one-word response pulled him up short.

"No. Now it's my turn to talk. I'm not going to get my agenda out of it. I'm not making them complicated to show off or to prove my skills. Hopefully, that last is a by-product. My designs take an okay room and make it perfect. I don't think *anyone* should have to settle for just okay. My *agenda* is what I'm getting paid to pursue, and that is designing rooms to be as beautiful as they are functional."

Adrian drew in a breath to refute her argument, but she stayed him with a raised hand.

"You come into my office and accuse me of breaking our deal. You weren't here with Jake and Lorena breathing down your neck and Trina filming over your shoulder, demanding something to film to fit their schedule. So yeah, I got started on the designs. I talked through minor color choice and design details with the couples for the camera. I didn't mention any major feature that I couldn't guarantee, and I've kept fifty percent of the budget open until I see your fucking reports. I'm not an idiot, despite what you think."

"Then why send—"

She cut him off, clearly not finished ranting.

"Why send you the sketches? To get your feedback. To see if there were any red flags before I create the blueprints. To see if the goddamn wall is load-bearing. I'm going to give them the best damn house their budget will buy. But that's not what this is really about. It's about your precious proposal, isn't it?"

So maybe she wasn't being as irresponsible as he'd thought, but he was too mad to back down now. Not when he was close to finally getting the truth out of her. "Have you given it any thought?"

"No. My workload has exploded, and I have gotten zero answers to the many, many questions I have asked."

"So you don't support it? You don't think I deserve to own a part of the company I've spent twelve years slaving away for?"

"Do you want me to hand away Frankie's chance at running this company someday?"

"For the last time, that's not what it would be."

"Isn't it? Can you give me any proof that after you buy in, Dad's not going to make you head contractor? Are you going to be *my* boss if I vote yes? Hell no, on all counts. You can't tell me that's not how it would be, because he hasn't told any of us anything. It's been Frankie's dream to run this place since before Gabe died." Sofia's voice grew louder and higher in pitch as she picked up steam, like a teapot too long on the stove.

"I'm not asking you to give away Frankie's share of the business."

"No, you just want a part of it. But there are only so many slices of the pie. What the hell is your proposal, Adrian? You can't tell me. Dad can't tell me. All I have asked is for you to give me the details. But no, I am supposed to just support you no matter what because we slept together a few times."

"Sofia…"

"Oh my God. Is that why you slept with me?" Her face drained of color and emotion as that nasty thought took root. "Were you trying to guarantee my vote for your proposal? Throw the big girl a little touch to clear your path?"

"No, that's not…" He couldn't let her believe that.

"Get out of my office."

"I'm not done."

"Oh, yes, you are! Do you think just because I let you touch me, you get to come in here and tell me how to do my job? Fuck that and fuck you, too. Leave the reports, and then just leave."

Adrian knew when to call it quits. He turned on his heel, his fury now directed at himself for screwing up that conversation so royally. They'd both take time to cool down, and he'd try again.

~

THE DOOR CLOSED BEHIND HIM, and Sofia dropped her head onto her hands. She couldn't stop the tears from coming. He hadn't pulled a single punch. He thought she was incompetent, untrustworthy, and frivolous. He had zero respect for the value she added through her work. He'd slept with her to gain her cooperation and pushed her away when that had failed. She'd thought that they were building something solid. In her weaker moments, she had pictured them together, raising a family and running the company side by side. Now, those dreams felt ridiculous. He'd made them ridiculous by tearing away any illusion she had that she was in a committed, respectful relationship. She didn't need him to rub her nose in it.

She was so done.

She walked out of her office, leaving behind everything but her keys.

CHAPTER 25

SOFIA DROVE and drove until she got to the coast. She didn't realize where she was headed until she got there, but her subconscious knew. She needed the water. It was already dark, and technically the beaches were closed. But she parked by the side of the road anyway and got out of her car. She kicked off her shoes and ran down the steep, sandy cliff path that wound down to the shore.

Her toes sank into the icy sand and the waves at high tide swirled around her ankles, soaking the hems of her jeans and chilling her to the bone. Letting loose the pain she'd been fighting to contain, she turned to face the turbulent waves and let out a scream that threatened to split her in two. Anger, sadness, fear, all crammed into a primal roar. Each sob pulled a painful memory or a piece of guilt to the surface, and she let them all flow into the vast ocean. Gabe, Mom, Dad, Adrian—every broken piece of her heart swirled in the eddy of her pain. Once the seal was broken, scream after scream fell from her lips, each one taking more of her, until at last she was empty.

When she came back into herself, she was kneeling in the surf, and her face was wet with salty water. Whether it was from the ocean or her tears, she couldn't tell and didn't care. With her head finally clear, she was able to think for the first time in weeks.

She wasn't happy. What would make her happy?

She held the newly empty space in her mind quietly, and waited for the big picture to materialize. From the back of her mind, where she'd buried that shiny dream after college, emerged a bright and beautiful office, with her designs framed on the wall. It was a business that she loved and was proud of. In her mind, her dad gave her a pat on the back and told her, "Good work." She drove home to a lovely old house with a loving husband and children running in the yard. She carefully kept Mister's face blank. She had to move forward, so she touched the fragile dream gently. It had lain buried for too long, and she'd gotten distracted by her father's crazy plans. It was time to bring it back into the light.

I WANT RESPECT.

I want to do what I love.

I want to be with a man I can love and who loves me in return.

SURELY THAT WASN'T TOO much to ask. Shivers rattled through her, shaking her from her soul-searching. Hauling herself back up the steep path to the highway, she picked apart her revelations. The first, she'd never get as long as she was working for her father. The second didn't seem likely either. And her hopes for the third had gone out the window when Adrian hadn't been able to handle her reaching for one and two.

She couldn't control him or his feelings. No matter how much she wanted to, either he'd have to come to the conclusion that what she did was worthy of his respect on his own, or he wouldn't. If the latter was the case, good riddance. She deserved better than that, no matter how much she missed his laughter and that dimple, his kisses and—

No, no farther down that path, or she'd crumble. She climbed into her car and turned on the heater, even though it felt like she'd never be warm again. She hadn't felt this cold and shattered since the day they'd found out Gabe was dead.

What would her life have looked like if Gabe had survived and come home?

Would she be happily designing homes as the head of Valenti Brothers' design team? The vision she'd guarded so long in her head felt like a shadow of the truth when held up to the moonlight. If Gabe had come home to run the business, she likely would still have ended up doing the lion's share of the paperwork. Gabe had never been an organized soul. And though she would like to think he'd have supported her in her dreams, he was still her big brother and would have probably bossed her around, just like Dad. This illusion she'd held on to for three years evaporated as her resentment toward Gabe faced the cold light of reality.

She'd been so angry for so long, but that wasn't fair to either of them.

"I'm sorry, Gabe. I'm sorry I blamed you for everything. I love you." She whispered the words into the silence of the car, hoping that wherever her brother's soul was he could hear them.

She'd thought she was done grieving, but the fresh tears on her cheeks assured her she was not. She was so tired. Tired of being angry and sad and guilty. She had to let it go.

Sofia resolved to give herself some grace. She was going to stop blaming her dead brother for her troubles. She knew who was causing her problems, and she was looking that person square in the eye in her rearview mirror. She could take responsibility for her own actions. And while she got her feet back under her, she'd plan, because that's what she did best.

She was done taking responsibility for things just because no one else wanted to. Her mother was right: no one was making her run the business. Certainly, no one was appreciating the fact that she'd done it. So, enough. If she wasn't going to get the respect she wanted at Valenti Brothers, she could go somewhere else.

Even just thinking that thought turned her knees to jelly. So many unknowns crowded her mind, so much uncertainty. She'd worked for her father every day of her adult life. True, she had contacts in the business world from college and conferences, but putting out feelers was a big step. She hauled in a shaky breath. A big step, but a necessary one. She went back to that happy fantasy in her mind, and she could see herself in her office, drafting table full of swatches and tiles, happy as a clam. As she let the fantasy play out and soothe her rough edges, she kept waiting for a boss to come in, but no one arrived to mar her happy planning. And then it hit her.

She didn't just want to not work for her dad. She didn't want to work for anyone. Maybe Enzo had planted the seed in her mind, but now that she'd thought it, she couldn't shake it. She wanted to open her own design firm. It had always been her goal to run her own division inside Valenti Brothers. This was the same vision, slightly shifted, and it still felt right.

With her fresh resolve to forgive herself and forge a new path still clear in her mind, Sofia made the long drive back to Menlo Park. She let the details swirl through her mind, plotting and planning, eager to navigate her way back to happiness. And she very carefully avoided any thoughts that led to a certain tall, dark and handsome lover who she missed terribly. That was another sorrow for another day. She was finally starting to feel warm again, and she couldn't afford to let anything extinguish her flame.

It was past midnight when she pulled up in front of the office again, damp but happy, ready to finish the payroll one last time before she walked away.

MONDAY MORNING, Sofia was already at her desk when her dad strolled in at eight a.m. She'd spent her weekend researching and reaching out to old friends. She was ready. She patted the stack of papers she'd assembled, outlining her plan.

"Good morning. Have you got the payroll for me to sign off on?"

His terse tone told her he was still angry at her. She might as well get him furious all at once.

"I emailed you the link on Thursday."

"I'll go check my email then." He turned to go.

"It's the last one I'm going to do."

"What is that supposed to mean? Guys gotta get paid."

"That's exactly why I'm hiring an office manager."

Arms crossed, his eyebrows pulled together like they were facing off in the ring. Before, just the sight of his angry face would have made Sofia second-guess herself and back down. Not today. Not ever again.

"We've been over this. I don't want money handled outside of the family."

"Yes, I heard you, and I believe I told you to find someone in the family to do it, then. Since you haven't, I'm going a different route."

"The expense—"

"Is necessary, Dad. And half of her salary is already covered by the flood of new business. You can take the rest of my salary to pay her a decent wage." She handed him the packet she'd prepped, including a qualified resumé and the cost projections.

"So you're just going to hand our bank accounts over to a stranger? I'm not hiring someone outside the family."

"You didn't seem to have any qualms about selling half your business to Adrian."

"That's different."

"Besides, she's not a stranger. My girlfriend from college, Meena, is looking to change jobs, and she said she'd give us a six-month trial."

"I don't like it." Dom crossed his arms over his chest, fully expecting the argument to end there.

Sofia let the silence hang between them while she gathered her courage to say what needed to be said. "Then *you* can find someone else."

"Why do I need someone else when I have you?" His placating tone pushed Sofia back into her resolve.

She straightened her spine and stood firm. There were things she needed to hear before she dropped her bombshell. "Why don't you say what you really mean? You want to keep me behind this desk because you don't think I can handle the designs."

"Now, princess, I didn't say that." He reached out a hand to brush her hair back behind her ear as he'd done when she was a child. She stepped back out of reach and glared. Why did the men in her life seem determined to keep her locked away in some safe tower? She'd scale her own walls, thank you very much. Dom sighed and let his hand drop. "Your designs are beautiful, but I don't think you can keep them in line with the mission of this company. On time, under budget, safety you can trust. That's the promise I've made to clients for over thirty years."

"Just because I want to make these homes shine doesn't mean I can't also hit those targets."

"They aren't targets. They are the foundation of my reputation. And no, I don't trust you yet. You're just getting started." His voice began to rise.

She raised hers to meet it. "Because I've been tied to this desk for three years! Meena starts Wednesday."

"I am not adding expenses right now."

"You've had free labor for over thirty years, first from Mom, and then essentially from me. You're going to have to pay for someone to handle this like a real business does, because I'm done."

Without another word, she strode out the door. Sofia sucked in a shaky breath. She'd done it. She'd stood up to her father and taken the first step to freedom. She would let him get used to the idea of outside help before she told him she was actually leaving. It also would give her some time to work out the details. This was just what she'd planned. So why did this victory feel so hollow? Where was the elation she'd expected to feel? She pushed aside the lingering churning in her gut and headed to her car. She still had a lot to do to prove herself, and she wouldn't get there wallowing in self-doubt.

"Mamá, are you sure about this?" Adrian asked for what felt like the fiftieth time that morning. Instead of his usual lazy Saturday morning routine, he was up early without nearly enough caffeine. His brain couldn't quite believe that his mother was actually ready to go through with this plan to visit her daughter and the baby.

"Are you trying to talk me out of it?" She brushed her hair with shaky hands, smoothing the already shiny and tangle-free locks over and over.

"No. Not at all. I just want to make sure you are ready."

"I am. I want to see the baby and help Mahalia. I spoke with Dr. Williams, and he gave me that prescription you picked up yesterday for when I start to panic. Besides, Sofia said it would be better for us to be out of the house while she works." She smoothed a scarf over her head that hadn't seen the sun in ten years, and tied it firmly beneath her chin.

"I still don't understand that whole business. If you wanted something fixed, why didn't you ask me?"

"Because nothing is broken, *mijo*. But that doesn't mean it can't be better. I like the picture Sofia put in my head. Do you trust her?"

A month ago that would have been an easy answer. He'd opened up his home and his heart to her because he'd trusted her, which made her betrayal even harder to bear. He'd trusted too quickly and gotten burned. But his mother didn't need to hear that right now. As far as she knew, things had just cooled down between him and Sofia because the show had ramped up.

He hadn't had the heart to tell his mother that the girl she'd welcomed at her table wasn't as wonderful as she appeared. He didn't know what that would do to her fears of letting people in, so he held his peace when Graciela sang Sofia's praises. He didn't have enough of his heart left intact to handle breaking hers, too. At least Sofia had been gracious enough to keep her promise when Graciela had finally gathered her courage.

"With the living room, maybe. But she takes everything too far. I don't want you to be disappointed. She is probably just doing this as publicity for the show."

"That is unkind, and no she's not. She told me specifically there wouldn't be any cameras."

"I want you to be happy, Mamá. If this makes you happy, I'll let her try."

"I'm sure it will be lovely. She's a sensible girl. She had good ideas when she interviewed me for the plans."

"Yeah, it all seems sensible until she wants to start knocking down walls and reversing floor plans." Who was she roping in to help with this? He'd checked with all of his guys, and no one knew anything about it. He'd have felt better about leaving if it was his crew working on it. They'd keep her in line. But she was probably going to make Seth or Frankie do most of the labor. Damn it, then he'd owe them big time.

"You are not helping." She set down the brush carefully and checked her purse for the twentieth time. "Medicine, phone, wallet, ID, keys, lipstick… You have my bag, yes?"

Adrian lifted his hands in surrender. "I already put it in the truck. It has clothes for three days, and all of the baby things you told me to pack." He dropped his hands to her shoulders. Her nerves were making them vibrate beneath his light touch. "Are you ready to go?"

Graciela closed her eyes and drew in an unsteady breath. "You are sure no one will see me?"

"Yes. You can sit in the back of the cab, and the windows are tinted."

"And you promise, you will not stop, no matter what I say, until we get to Mahalia's house?" She picked up her large, brand-new sunglasses from the counter and put them on, covering any lingering insecurities.

"I promise, and I filled up the gas tank yesterday."

"Okay." She inhaled deeply one more time before stepping toward the door. "Let's go."

In the end, it took about five tries for her to actually make it out the door. Adrian half carried her down the steps because her anxiety buckled her knees. He handed her up into the extended cab of his truck and tucked her purse in next to her. "All good?" he asked one last time. When his mother mustered a tight nod, he smiled. "There's water and snacks in the cooler at your feet. I'm so proud of you, Mamá." He kissed her hand and climbed into the front seat. Pulling slowly out of the driveway, he watched his mother crouch down in the back seat like a criminal avoiding the news crews after an arrest.

It broke his heart that she felt so afraid. Had he failed her? Had he enabled this to the point that she was terrified of life? Had he missed the signs that she'd needed more from him? Guilt chased hard on his heels as he sped up the highway toward Oakland. Even once they hit the open road, she didn't relax her grip on her purse or her active scanning of the surrounding traffic. He tried to break into her fixation with a task. If he could keep her focused here in the car, maybe she wouldn't be so tense about the world flying past outside the windows.

"Mamá, why don't you send Sofia a text and let her know that we are out of the house. I left her a key upstairs under my mat."

"Okay, *mijo*. I can do that." She pulled her phone from her purse and gripped it like a lifeline, her hands shaking like she was much older than her fifty-two years.

This excursion better be worth all of this stress. He couldn't believe he was actually letting Sofia loose in his house, but his mother wanted this, and he would give anything in this world to make his mother happy. He knew Sofia would make big changes in the space. That's what scared him. He just hoped she wouldn't go overboard, like she had on every other design, and end up ruining his mother's safe haven.

He was also grateful for this trip out of town, because it got him away from the projects for a while. He'd been working like a dog, keeping multiple crews busy on different projects, all while dancing to Jake Ryland's tune.

He couldn't deny that the resentment had been growing inside him, stealing the joy he normally felt over a job well done. Knowing that he had zero chance of changing Dom's mind as long as Frankie and Sofia were opposed was eating away at his motivation. He was going to have to leave. He hated the idea of leaving the only job he'd ever known, but if he couldn't advance there was no way he could stay. He needed to leave before things turned bitter. Part of his plan while he was up here in Oakland for the weekend was to scout out new potential contractors who might need some help. Maybe they could relocate closer to Mahalia so it wouldn't be quite so stressful for his mom to help with the new baby.

He also couldn't keep seeing Sofia every day and not have her. It was killing him slowly. No matter how many times his head reminded him that he was angry, that she'd done him wrong, that she was standing between him and his dreams, his heart still sped a little faster when she walked into the room. His blood ran a little hotter when she leaned over her desk. His soul reached out for hers when she smiled, until she saw him and her smiles faded. He'd really screwed up that whole relationship, and he'd be damned if he hung around to watch her move on.

"She says she found the key and is already hard at work."

His mother's voice broke through his turbulent thoughts, scattering them beneath his speeding tires until one remained. Why hadn't they worked harder to stay together?

"HEY, YOU GOT STARTED WITHOUT ME!" Frankie stood in the open doorway with two welcome white-and-green coffee cups.

"I don't have much time." Sofia climbed down from the step-stool where she had been removing the heavy damask drapes, letting in some much needed light. Leaving the curtain hanging from half of its pins, she gratefully clasped the hot coffee in both hands. "But now that you're here, can you help me carry these couches out to the curb? And then we need to clear as many of the bookcases as we can." After a few quick sips, Sofia set the paper cup aside and rubbed her hands together. "Okay, grab the other side of this sofa. On three..."

They worked in quiet tandem, their rhythm smooth and silent from years of repetition. They'd all grown up helping on Dad and Uncle Tony's work sites. The room quickly emptied and they laid out thick drop cloths to protect the hardwood floors, the only thing worth protecting in the room. Sofia opened a can of pale, creamy paint and passed Frankie a roller.

"Remember when Gabe decided to paint his bedroom Day-Glo yellow?" Frankie chuckled at the memory.

"It was sunshine yellow, and he said it would help him get up for school in the morning." Sofia laughed along at the memory of her cranky, sleep-deprived brother. For the first time in too long she thought of her older brother with affection instead of guilt. "It didn't last a month before he repainted it navy blue."

"He was always jumping into crazy plans like that."

"Do you miss him?"

"Of course, I do. Don't you?"

"I do miss him, like I'd miss my right hand, but then I get really angry that he left us, just like that." Sofia snapped her fingers. "He screwed up everyone else's plans without a second thought and dumped all this stress in my lap. But that's a shitty thought to have, and then I feel guilty. I hate that I feel trapped. I hate that I've had to do his share of the work for so long, and I hate that he's gone."

Frankie met this flood of words with silence, as if unsure of where to start mopping up.

Sofia focused on the repetitive strokes of her roller as the walls gradually brightened. "Does that make me horrible?"

"No, it makes you human. Does it make me horrible that I'm happy to get a chance to run the crews how I want, without my big brother looking over my shoulder, telling me what to do?"

"No."

"Because every time I think about it, I feel like I'm stealing his spot. Your job got harder, but chasing my dream got a lot easier. And I feel guilty for it every day."

Sofia let that sink in. She had been so caught up in her own messy emotions, she hadn't considered how her siblings were dealing with Gabe's death. Did Enzo have this messed-up crap rolling around behind his stoic façade? Sofia switched to a small angled brush and began cutting in the paint along the trim line.

"That's part of why I didn't want Adrian to buy in," Frankie continued. "Dad treats him like another son. How long would it be before he starts trying to boss me around? I know I'm young, but I'm not an idiot."

"Honestly, I don't think it would be like that."

"Wait, I thought we were mad at Adrian."

"Oh, I'm pissed as hell at him right now, but that doesn't change the fact that we can't afford to lose him. I was never completely against him buying in. I just needed details no one could give me. I think it could be a good idea if we do it right."

"Thanks for the vote of confidence, sis."

"Damn it, Frankie. Don't be like that. I know exactly how many jobs we've got lined up right now, both on and off the show. If Adrian walks, so does his crew. Do you really think you can run all the crews, plus hire a new slate, if both Dad and Adrian are gone?"

Frankie paused, paint dripping off the roller. "But Dad's not going anywhere soon. It would be fine. By the time he actually retires, I'll have things under control." Vigorous strokes up and down the wall mocked the calm words. A fine spatter of paint flew from the speeding roller, coating them both in buttery freckles.

"Given the full-court press from Mom, I'd bet on sooner rather than later. Even Dad never handled everything alone. He had Uncle Tony. When Seth didn't step up into Uncle Tony's spot, you did. Who's going to fill Dad's? All I'm saying is don't be stupid. Plan how to make this work to your advantage instead."

"Don't call me stupid!" Frankie spun angrily, roller in hand still spinning, catching a surprised Sofia with splatters of yellow paint to the face. Frankie's jaw dropped along with the roller.

"Damn it, Frankie! Don't you dare laugh!" Trying to suppress the chuckles only turned them to belly laughs faster, and when Sofia gave chase with her cutting brush, all effort at restraint was lost. The ensuing paint war left them both streaky and weak from laughter. Sofia swiped at the tears running down her face and her hand came away yellow. "Truce! Or we'll never finish."

Frankie picked up the roller and started the second coat. "If you and Adrian are on the outs, why am I giving up my Saturday to redo his living room?"

"Because it's his mother's living room, not his, and I made a promise. Besides, with just a few cosmetic changes, this space could be so much better for her. Just because her son is being an ass doesn't mean she should have to keep living in the dark."

And despite the fact that she was gutted by his betrayal, she still had these feelings. She'd thought they would fade in the full light of day or burn away in the flash furnace of her anger, but they remained, steady and warm in her heart. She couldn't accept that the man who'd loved her so tenderly had done so with an agenda, and she was going to have to figure out what to do about that. Clearly, ignoring the situation wasn't working.

"Saint Sofia to the rescue." Frankie's use of her childhood nickname pulled her from her worries.

"You know I hate that nickname."

"Saint Sofia! Saint Sofia!" Frankie said in a singsong voice.

"Jesus, what are you, five?"

"You always were the Goody Two-Shoes in the family. Not much has changed as far as I can tell."

"Yeah, and look where it got me."

"Poor Sofia, using both of your degrees for the family business, exactly like you'd always planned. Martyr, much? What ever would we do without you?"

"You'd better figure it out," Sofia muttered.

"What was that?"

"I said you'd figure it out. Now shut up and finish painting."

They wrapped up the second coat before lunch and split to work on separate projects. After carefully washing up, Sofia reupholstered the wingback chair. She added a thicker cushion and updated the fabric. She also slipcovered a long sofa she found rummaging through the Valenti family storage units that would fit the space better than all the smaller couches crammed together.

Frankie built in a bench seat that stretched the front width of the room and extended into a window seat. There was space for books or storage bins underneath. Once it was stained, they moved on to the window treatments together. As night fell, they wanted to make sure everything was covered and safe. The new honeycomb blinds were translucent and could be raised from the bottom or lowered from the top, allowing more light to filter through while preserving Graciela's privacy. After tightening the last screw, Sofia collapsed into an exhausted heap against the opposite wall and surveyed the results of their hard work. It would be beautiful, once she got everything in its proper place.

Frankie came in from the back of the house where the saw was set up, hands full with two beers instead of planks of wood. "Here, sis. We earned these today."

Sofia looked at the outstretched beer. "Nah, I'm okay."

"What's the matter with you?"

"I'm turning a new leaf. I need to lose this weight."

"Jesus, just drink it, Fi. I don't know why you do that."

"Do what?"

Frankie thrust the beer at her again, refusing to take no for an answer. "Get bent about your weight. We've all had a rough go since Gabe died. So you put on a few pounds. Who cares? You still look like my sister, and you sure as hell still act like her. If the food helped you get through it, I repeat, who cares?"

Who did care? Frankie clearly didn't. Adrian hadn't seemed to mind it either, back when they'd been on touching terms. Hell, even her mother still insisted she fill her plate at dinner. The only person who hated how much she weighed was her. Maybe Frankie was right. She had needed something to help her cope with all of the feelings Gabe's death had unleashed. Maybe she could stop hating herself for being human. Wasn't she entitled to the same grace she'd given Frankie earlier? She thought back to her night at the beach. Respect and love were her paramount needs. She hadn't considered her weight as a goal even once. She'd lose the weight eventually, or she wouldn't, and would still be the same person people loved now.

Her revelation took a thirty-pound weight off her shoulders.

She could lift that challenge in her own time, but no more shame. She deserved better treatment from herself, especially if she was going to start demanding it from others as well. Maybe Frankie wasn't so dumb after all. She twisted off the top and raised it in a toast.

"To not-stupid siblings. You're right. Who cares?" She drank deep and enjoyed the crisp, cool bubbles dancing down her throat. "Thanks again for your help today."

"Do you need me to come back tomorrow?"

"No, the hard part is done. Just help me get the couch inside, and I'll be fine."

"You sure? I can help move furniture."

"No, really. It's okay."

"Remember, you don't have to do it all on your own. Love you, sis."

"Love you, too. Now go on and pack up. I'm sure you've got a hot date tonight."

"Jealous much?"

Sofia looked around Adrian's home and realized that yes, she was jealous. Even though he'd been an ass, she missed him. Missed *them*. Missed being part of an *us*, even if she'd been the only one who thought they were together. She wished she knew how to fix things between them, but how could she take him back when he had so little respect for her? It was a lose-lose situation.

"Ha, you wish. Get out of here!"

CHAPTER 26

"¡Ay, Dios mío!"

Adrian stood on the front porch behind his mother. Getting her out of the truck had taken fifteen minutes of coaxing. That was down from the hour it had taken him to extract her from his sister's house. The weekend full of mothering Mahalia and snuggling little Jeremiah had brought back Mamá's smile, the one he'd inherited, the one that had grown increasingly rare. That child hadn't slept in his crib the entire time Abuela had been there. She'd spent so much time cooking and cleaning and holding the baby, Adrian didn't think she'd had time to be afraid. Or maybe the medicine from her doctor had given her back a little control. Either way, the weekend had been a good break for everyone, but he knew she was anxious to get back into her own home. They'd left early Monday morning to avoid traffic and the anxiety that would bring.

During the drive home, she'd twisted her purse straps and scanned the windows constantly for cruisers. Her smile had slipped off her face, replaced by the more familiar mask of fear and anxiety. Adrian wished he could take all of the fear off her shoulders permanently, but he didn't know how.

The fact that his mother was frozen on her doorstep instead of immediately hustling inside filled Adrian's gut with lead. What had Sofia done? Was it so bad that his mother was literally trapped between two terrifying realities? If she had ruined his mother's one safe space...

Mamá clutched his arm for support, and he pushed the door wider so he could help her get inside.

"Come on, Mamá. I'm sure it's not that bad..."

He trailed off as he got his first clear view of the room, and his jaw hit the floor, now covered by an inviting Persian rug. He froze beside her, unable to process the complete transformation that had happened in just two days.

"It's...it's...*maravilloso!*" His mother cautiously stepped over the threshold. "Are you sure we are at the right house?"

Adrian leaned back outside to check the numbers on the mailbox, but yes it was their house. His keys were still hanging from the lock in the door. He couldn't find the words to reassure her, because frankly he was stunned.

Gone was the dark, cozy cave he'd gotten used to seeing behind this door. In its place was a bright, airy retreat.

He managed to get the door closed behind them and then just stood there, arm around his mother, trying to absorb every detail.

"Look at the windows, *mijo*." Tears welled in her eyes as she pointed. "So bright, but still private."

The blinds were lowered about six inches from the top, allowing the bright California sunshine to stream in. The cream-colored paint on the textured walls fairly glowed.

"Is that my chair?" Curiosity broke through her shock, and she walked across the room to her favorite spot.

The room felt so open without all of the couches pushed up against the walls. The new couch and armchairs anchored the space around the rug, creating an inviting place to sit with friends. He'd worried about seating for the times the entire neighborhood gathered in this room, until he noticed the built-in bench and bookcase topped with throw pillows in every size and texture. Meanwhile, his mother was bouncing in her chair like a toddler at snack time.

"She fixed it!"

"It was broken?"

"Not broken, just well-loved. The seat drooped. Now it is firm again, and this fabric!" She ran her hands lovingly over the rioting poppies in muted reds and oranges with hints of green vine. "It's gorgeous and so soft! And look at this side table, with a place for my tea and books! And this light is the perfect height!"

Every new detail brought more of the joy back to his mother's face. This was Sofia's gift. This wasn't for acclaim or to show off for any producer. Hell, she wasn't even here to see Mamá's reaction. She listened to people and asked the right questions. She heard what was said and what wasn't. And then she fixed it.

And it wasn't just with her designs. The reason she was so good at her job managing the office stemmed from her ability to get the right information and act on it. Who did he go to when an order got screwed up? Who did he rely on to make sure his guys still got paid when they forgot to punch their time card?

She'd been fixing things for him for years. How often had he not noticed? He had been so busy fixing things in his own sphere that he hadn't appreciated the gift of having a competent partner on his team. Imagine what they could do together— No, he had to quit thinking about them together. That was screwed up beyond repair. But he could think about how he would say thank you.

This transformation was amazing and would definitely change his mother's day-to-day life. There was no way Sofia had stayed under his tight budget, but he wasn't even mad. That smile on his mother's face was worth every extra penny.

"She even labeled my shelves! TBR, Keepers, Lending Copies!

Oh, I can't wait to organize." She ran her hands lovingly over her beloved books.

He hadn't seen that she was fading slowly in this cave of a house. What else had he missed? He walked over to her and pulled her into a tight hug. "I'm sorry, Mamá. Sorry I didn't think to do this sooner."

"Now, now, none of that. You have taken very good care of me and this house. And be honest, there's no way you ever pictured this room looking like this. You see four sturdy walls and windows that keep out the wind. And for that I am truly grateful. Just as I am grateful to Sofia for lending her vision to us for a little while. Oh, and this couch!" And she was off, investigating the other details she had yet to coo over.

Adrian walked through to the kitchen and found two letters and a bottle of wine on the table. He ran the one with his name on it through his fingers while he remembered the last time Sofia had brought a bottle of wine to his house. What had she written? Would she laugh and tease? Or flirt and tempt him to take her back? Would she apologize for not supporting him and ask for a second chance? After all, redoing his living room was a pretty big olive branch... Unable to take the suspense anymore, he tore open the letter.

Adrian-
    Here are the receipts.
    I hope she likes it.
    -S

THAT WAS IT? His annoyance rose. Not even a "How are you"? Or an "I'm sorry"? He looked at the receipts she'd so helpfully provided and saw that she had indeed kept it under his budget. She also hadn't charged a dime for her services or labor. She'd truly done this out of the goodness of her heart because she'd told his mother she would. No self-interest. No profit. This image of Sofia clashed with the one he'd constructed in his mind of her scheming to scuttle his proposal. Which was the real Sofia?

He brought the letter with his mom's name on it to her in the living room, and she squealed a little as she opened it. When he tried to read it over her shoulder, she tucked the paper against her chest and shooed him away. He only caught a glimpse, but it was enough to see line after line of Sofia's flowing script.

"If you are so anxious to hear what she says, why haven't you brought her back over to the house? Why isn't she here today?"

"We kind of broke up." Had they ever really been together?

"How do you *kind of* break up? You said something stupid, didn't you?"

"No! She sided against me when I brought my proposal to Dom."

"What exactly did she say?"

"Dom said she couldn't see how it would work." His mother gave him that look she'd always given him when he'd said something dumb. It was just as effective at hunching his shoulders now as it had been at fifteen. "What?"

"I didn't ask what Dom said. I asked what Sofia said."

"She wouldn't give me a straight answer. She just kept asking questions and shooting it down. What about Enzo and Frankie? What about her? Who would be the boss of who?"

Graciela sat in her chair and shook her head at him. Adrian perched on the armrest next to her, resenting the comfort Sofia had dropped into his life and then taken away.

"What? What is that look for?"

"*Ay, mijo*, she asked logical questions about how this deal would work, which I assume you couldn't answer."

"She didn't give me a chance to figure out the answers."

"If you didn't know the answers, your proposal wasn't very strong, was it? Don't interrupt." He clamped his mouth closed, the counterpoint dying on his tongue as his mother continued to school him. "She asked me hundreds of questions about the living room and how I use it. I hadn't ever thought of the answers to most of them before. But she took those answers and gave me an amazing space in return." She reached both hands up to hold his face and tilted it so he would have to look into her eyes. It was the same thing she had done to him when he was a little boy and she wanted him to pay attention. "She asked you smart questions, and you decided she didn't support you? She shook her head and patted his cheek, clearly conveying her disappointment in his logic. "What is wrong with questions? Is she supposed to read your mind?"

Adrian felt like he'd just been smacked in the face with a shovel. True, Dom had been the one to say no, but Sofia hadn't argued. She'd thrown more questions at him. He'd thought she would be on his side, but she'd only added fuel to Frankie's fire. True, they were the same questions he'd been trying to get Dom to answer for months now. Had she really just been trying to gather information, not shooting his plans down? Damn it. In light of what his mother said, he realized it was true. Sofia's questions were often abrupt and rapid-fire, but he couldn't say they were unreasonable. As he'd seen over and over when she was on the phone with a new supplier or subcontractor, her questions often got them exactly what they needed.

He'd thought they were building toward a future, but when she'd asked questions about what that future would look like, he'd felt attacked and bailed. Had he really expected her to behave differently, to change her personality, just for him? He really was an idiot. His heart clenched at the thought that he'd spent over a month angry with her for his own stupidity.

She didn't owe him an apology. She didn't owe him anything. He'd let his pride and temper get in the way of his logic, and he'd blown his chance with her for good. With no chance at winning the girl, and even less at winning the company, he needed to figure out a new plan. Whether that meant accepting his lot at Valenti Brothers or working for someone else, he couldn't say. He'd signed those damn contracts, so he was locked into the show for at least a season, but he needed to get his head on straight so that he was ready when the next opportunity presented itself. He'd spoken to a few companies based up in Oakland that seemed promising, even if he'd be starting at a lower level and working his way up again. If they called, he'd seriously consider leaving, because it would hurt too much to stay. For now, he'd stay and support the show. It was the least he could do to make amends. She deserved to see her dreams succeed.

When the dust settled, his reputation would get him through the door somewhere else. It would mean moving his mother from her home, but that might be for the best anyway. He'd have to figure out what this all meant to his crew, too. Their livelihoods were tied to his own, and he hated letting them down. He hadn't honestly thought about what would happen if Dom said no. Dread and disappointment roiled in his gut.

But if he left, Sofia wouldn't be the boss's daughter anymore.

That silver lining popped into his head and stopped his anxiety cold. After everything that had happened, after all that had been said, he still wanted her. He spent embarrassingly large portions of his day wondering where she was and what she was doing, wishing he was still welcome to be by her side. He kept a running list of things he wanted to tell her, if only he was speaking to her. Maybe leaving Valenti Brothers wasn't such a bad thing. Maybe he could have it all. Maybe, like this living room, his dream wasn't broken, but it could be better. He'd have to think on that.

"Adrian." His mother snapped her fingers in front of his face.

"What?"

"This Sofia is a good girl to do all of this for me, even after you broke her heart."

"What makes you think I broke her heart?"

"You're my son. Who wouldn't fall in love with you? Don't let pride make you stupid, *mijo*. If you love her, go make it right."

~

WHEN JAKE HAD ASKED Adrian to join her on the walk-through shots Wednesday morning, Sofia had cringed. She knew that the network execs had liked the tension between her and Adrian on screen and had requested more scenes together, but this was the last thing her heart needed. They still hadn't cleared the air, and she hadn't managed to reconstruct those walls around her heart yet.

Every time she saw him, her heart pinched at her conscience. She could break the standoff just as easily as he could, but her pride stood in the way. They couldn't even talk about the little things because the bigger issue felt like a boulder in the middle of the path between them. It had been two days since Graciela had come home, and Sofia still didn't know how his mom had liked the room. She didn't know how the trip had been. She didn't know if Adrian had been missing her as much as she missed him this last month. She hadn't even had a chance to tell him how she'd modified the plans after she'd seen his reports. So now they were going to end up having this conversation on camera. Fabulous.

At least she'd been able to give more attention to this design, since Meena had gotten up to speed over the last week fairly quickly. With the bulk of the office work off her mind, Sofia had been able to really create. She was very proud of the plan she'd put together, and she tried to channel some of that into excitement for the camera.

Sofia stood with Desmond and Patience Ong on the front lawn, trying to ignore the man making her heart race, standing to their left. "So, out here, we were thinking of adding a short wooden fence, since your property does face a busy street. This way, if you have kids or decide to get a pet, there is one more layer of safety between them and the traffic. I would love to do horizontal slats to give it a more modern feeling." It would also keep the costs lower with fewer cuts and less planking, but she didn't need to tell them that. "What do you think?"

"I think that will work. We've got the post hole diggers already, and I can lend a guy or two to Enzo and knock it out more quickly," Adrian said.

"I wasn't asking *you*." *Asshole.* "Patience, what do you think of the horizontal idea? I can show you pictures if you want to see what I was thinking."

"No, I've seen them in the neighborhood. I like the fun and kind of funky look. What color were you thinking?"

"A very natural stain on the cedar to keep it slightly rustic." Patience nodded, and Sofia pressed on. "In keeping with your request to turn the yard into garden space, we will add lemon, plum, and persimmon trees to the front yard, making it into a small orchard, with benches built in around the trees for comfort and ease of harvesting. I've got some beautiful raised planters going in the back as well."

"Oh, I can't wait!" The small Singaporean woman bounced on her toes and clapped her hands. Patience clearly did not possess much of her namesake.

"It's going to be beautiful. Enzo does amazing work."

"I know. I vetted his work on his website." Desmond Ong, pediatrician and researcher at Stanford, was the more straight-laced of the two. It was clear that while he was willing to indulge his wife's design ideas, he wasn't going to commit to anything without thoroughly researching it. Sofia considered it a compliment that they'd chosen Valenti Brothers even before the show had been a consideration.

"Then you know. As for the exterior of the house, we are

going to touch up the stucco in a few places and repaint it a nice neutral."

"All this neutral. Does anything about me say neutral?" Patience gestured to her brightly colored maxi dress and grinned.

"In terms of resale value, this is the better choice for the exterior, but never fear. I've worked your love of color into the interiors."

"She's right. It makes good sense to keep the exterior in line with the rest of the neighborhood." Adrian voiced his opinion again, and Sofia couldn't help the glare that crept onto her face. Like she needed his help convincing Patience. Who did he think he was? This was her area of expertise.

Oh wait, that's right. He didn't think she had a lick of sense. She wasn't about to give Jake the satisfaction of melting down on television, so she gritted her teeth and moved on. "Let's head inside, and I'll show you what I mean."

Once inside, they all crowded into the small foyer, while Trina set up the shot from across the room. Adrian ended up behind her, while Desmond and Patience stood spooning on her right. She could feel his heat warming her even though they weren't touching. While her heart was urging her to lean back into his strength, her head reminded her that his support and comfort were no longer hers to claim. The battle inside her was exhausting. It was all she could do to keep still as she painted the design picture from memory.

"So this is your living room." She gestured with her hands as if she was literally throwing ideas at the walls as she spoke, knowing that was exactly how it would look after the special effects crew got their hands on it. "Over here, we'll have a seating area, cozy couch, lots of fabrics and textures in the pillows, the rug, the window treatments. We keep the walls a bright white so that the colors all pop. Picture reds and oranges in here. I saw the picture over your fireplace at your other house, and I'm using it as an inspiration for the color scheme in this room. What do you think?"

"I love those colors. We bought that picture on a vacation in Thailand before we married, and I would love to keep it in the room."

Yes! Another intuition validated. She didn't need Adrian to value her work. Only her clients mattered, and so far she was two for two.

"I noticed that this living room flows into the dining room, and it looks kind of small. What are your plans for that space?" Adrian asked calmly as if the answer wasn't a ticking time bomb he'd lobbed in her lap.

She waited until Trina had backed up into the corner of the space before escorting the couple across the floor. To the viewers, she hoped it looked like a casual transition question. "The existing footprint of the dining room is small, and you lose a lot of space to this wall here. I would love to open up the kitchen and connect it to this room, giving you a larger eat-in area in the kitchen, as well as providing more seating options for entertaining. I haven't quite decided if I want to take out the whole wall or simply enlarge the opening and build around it."

There, take that. No firm commitment, and she'd left herself wiggle room to make that decision later.

"Actually, in my inspection report, when I checked out that wall, I noticed that the sconces were wired in a pretty sketchy way."

"Is that bad?" Patience looked worried, and Sofia opened her mouth to comfort her, but Adrian beat her to it.

"It's bad if we ignore it, but it's good if you want that wall taken down anyway. To repair it we'd have to pull off a good bit of the drywall, and since it's not load-bearing, it would be easy to just take the whole thing out."

Sofia was so annoyed she couldn't even gracefully acknowledge that he'd just given her the go-ahead on one of her major design points. Lord only knew what was showing on her face, but it wasn't calming Patience at all.

"Is there other bad wiring in the house?"

"Whether there is or isn't, the important thing is that we found out early and we can fix it. No problem, right Adrian?"

"No problem at all. I won't let you move into an unsafe house. I promise."

Those words and that tone were tempting to anyone. Sofia was glad that Patience seemed to accept it as law, but Fi couldn't let herself believe in him. He'd made promises to her, and look how that had turned out.

"Cut!" Jake called from the kitchen where he was looking at the footage as they taped it. "Great scene, everybody. Take a break while we set up in the kitchen. Sofia, a word?"

While the Ongs and Adrian headed to craft services in the garage for some coffee, Sofia followed the sound of Jake's voice into the family room where he was moving his gear.

"What's up?"

"I was just going to ask you the same question."

"I don't know what you're talking about."

"You and Adrian. Listen, I pitched the pilot with you two snarking at each other. The sparks were literally threatening to melt the cameras. You didn't get along, but the attraction was clearly there and the test audiences loved it! Today, I get stunted politeness from him and repressed anger from you. Where did my sexual tension go?"

"My personal life is not fodder for your show. I don't owe you any explanation."

"No, but when I've gone to the lengths I have to create opportunities for your storyline, I expect it to work." Jake tossed his clipboard on his folding table desk and reached for his omnipresent coffee.

"What are you talking about?"

"Nothing. Just TV talk." He took a nervous sip and changed

the subject. "After the pilot wrapped, you two were on the verge of sleeping together. Today you won't even look at him."

Sofia cringed at the truth of that. Had she really thought she could hide her fractured feelings from the camera? "Trust me. You wouldn't like what I'd have to say if I looked at him."

"Anything would be better than what I'm getting. Just try to loosen up, okay? Fake it if you need to."

"I thought this was supposed to be *reality* TV."

"It's my reality, and I need you to stay in character."

~

Sofia cornered Adrian by the coffee station, arms crossed and eyes blazing, and his heart perversely began to pump harder.

"Okay. What gives?"

He knew it was a mistake to grin at her, but he couldn't help the smile that spread across his face. He was that damn glad to see her, now that he'd begun to make his peace with the situation, even as she poked him hard in the shoulder to drive home each point.

"Oh, so you think it's funny to screw with me on camera? What the hell, Adrian? It wasn't enough that you left me wondering how your mom liked her room? Why are you pretending to be *nice*?" She said nice like it was a dirty word, and he had to laugh again.

"Because I get it now. I'm sorry I left you hanging. I wanted to tell you in person. Thank you, Sofia. That room is beyond anything I could have come up with. It suits Mamá to the ground, and she didn't stop wandering around, touching each new thing, until I made her go to bed. She loves it."

Sofia's militant stance softened as her shoulders dropped and the clench of her jaw released. But her arms were still crossed tight across her chest. He hadn't completely repaired the bridge

259

between them. He wasn't sure he ever could, not completely. But he could sure as hell try.

"Oh. Well. Good. I'm glad she liked it. That still doesn't explain why you're being so agreeable in there. What gives?"

"I looked at the plans with a new perspective. I can see the reason for the choices you've made, having seen the effect first-hand. I think the Ongs are really going to love this house."

"I'm so glad you approve." Sarcasm dripped from her voice, but he pushed on.

"I also don't have a dog in this fight anymore."

"What's that supposed to mean?"

Adrian turned to make two cups of coffee, taking his time with the fake sugar and cream for hers. It was hard enough to face the truth without having to face her as well.

"Sofia, I screwed up. You were doing what you do best, gathering data and finding solutions, and I took it as an attack against my plan. I can see now that you didn't mean it that way. But I can also see that there isn't a place for me at Valenti Brothers. I have to thank you and your persistent questions for pointing that out to me." He handed her the coffee as a peace offering.

"Adrian, I never said that it couldn't work. I wasn't trying to shoot down your dream."

He stepped forward, needing to touch her and ease her anxiety. He counted it a win that she didn't step away from his hand on her shoulder. "Sofia, I know. I know that now. I also know that the answers to those questions mean my dream isn't going to come true. I know that the way I reacted has killed any dreams I had on other fronts, too."

Sofia dropped her arms and turned toward him, and he took a chance and cupped her cheek one last time.

"What dreams were those?"

"The ones where the boy makes the girl happy forever more. The ones where she forgives him for being an asshole and lets him try again. The ones where I earn your forgiveness."

"Adrian…"

"No, I know I screwed up. I should have trusted you, and I didn't. I should have believed that the foundations we'd laid were strong enough to see us through. Instead I pushed you away, like a fool." He stepped back out of range so he wouldn't be tempted to touch her again.

As he did, he realized they'd gathered quite the audience. The two-car garage didn't leave much room for privacy, though Trina and her crew were pretending not to notice. He was grateful she wasn't filming this and that Jake hadn't wandered in. Sofia deserved so much better than to hash this out publicly.

He dropped his voice to a low rumble. "That's why I'm done. As soon as this season is over, I'm moving on. Your dreams are on the brink of coming true, and I'd only hold you back. And the idea of watching you fall for someone else… I can't stay and watch *all* of my dreams crumble."

"But we could—"

"Sofia, stop. I get it. Finding solutions that work for everyone is what you do. But I'm going to make the equation easier for everyone. It's better if I go." He shouldn't feel gratified by the sadness in her eyes, but he couldn't deny that it felt like a balm on his scraped heart. She had cared about him once, and if he was very lucky, she would care enough to work with him through the end of the season. It was more than he deserved and likely more than he could bear.

"I wish you would let me finish a sentence," Sofia snapped, stepping back into his space, not allowing him to retreat. Why was she making this so hard?

"What's this about you leaving?" Apparently he hadn't been quiet enough. Domenico Valenti rarely entered a room unnoticed, and this was no exception. His booming voice cut through the air, startling them both. He had been lurking in the production room all day and Adrian realized he was still miked. There was no privacy on a TV set, and he'd do well to remember that.

Dom's bellow drew the gaze of every crew member in his path. Adrian winced as Trina raised her camera to her shoulder and began filming. So much for handling this quietly with Sofia. Adrian wondered why Dom was getting camera-ready, but he didn't have time to speculate. Dom clearly expected an answer.

"Hey, Dom."

"Don't 'Hey, Dom' me! Twelve years! You've been with me twelve years. Where the hell do you think you're going?"

"Dom, be reasonable. Twelve years, and what do I have to show for it?" Adrian held out his empty hands. "You know as well as I do that I love working here, and I believe in this company. But if I can't buy in and make it even a little bit my own, I have to start looking for other options. I can't keep running into walls and not expect it to hurt."

"Too damn ambitious for your own good," Dom muttered, but he didn't refute anything that had been said. "You know my hands are tied. But at least that's settled."

"What do you mean that's settled? What's settled?" Sofia asked.

"Tony and I talked to our lawyer. Since Seth and Nick have already rolled part of Tony's share into the side business, we decided to split the remaining shares three ways. You, Seth, Enzo, and Frankie will be equal partners."

Surprised by the silence from the woman next to him, Adrian turned to see why Sofia wasn't reacting. She was biting her lip and eyeing the ceiling. He now recognized that look for what it was. She was calculating something in that fascinating brain of hers. Why the hell wasn't she jumping for joy?

"I'm leaving too, Dad."

Adrian's jaw dropped when Sofia made her announcement. The bug-eyed look on Dom's face was priceless, and likely mirrored his own. Adrian was too shocked to fully appreciate the parallel. It seemed they'd both underestimated Sofia Valenti.

"What the hell is going on around here?" Dom roared.

"I'm tired of answering to someone who doesn't respect my talents and is standing in the way of my success."

"Now, that's not fair."

"No, Dad, you know what's not fair? Pushing aside work that I love for three years while filling in the gaps left by grief. Three years stuck behind that desk. I asked and asked for a chance, and I'm done waiting."

"What about the show?" Adrian asked, trying to make sense of it all. Dom was sputtering and seemed incapable of forming full sentences.

"I'm staying on the show, but I'll be doing it as SV Design. When we re-signed the contracts, I made sure it listed me by name, separately from the Valenti Brothers company list, so it shouldn't be a problem."

"How can you afford this?" Dom had found his words and was flinging them angrily at his daughter, trying to hit the right button to make her stay. "I know how much you make. Starting your own business takes a lot of time and money."

"Gee, if only there were someone I could sell some of my equity to, someone who would take good care of Valenti Brothers while freeing up my capital. If only…" Sofia turned to Adrian.

He held his breath, afraid to break the magic of the moment. He needed to hear it from her lips. Was she saying what he thought she was saying? She grinned, and his heart stuttered in his chest.

"What do you think, Adrian? I'll sell you half of my quarter of the business. You get your buy-in, and I get enough to get my own branch off the ground."

He stepped closer, caution warring with happiness, and cradled her face in his hands. He saw the truth in her eyes. "Are you sure? How can you decide so quickly?"

"Quickly? Would you like to see the twenty-page business plan I've got in the drawer of my desk? I've been plotting for my own chance ever since I realized Dad would never let me go.

Every question I asked? I needed answers so I could figure out how it would work."

"But you'd be giving away part of your legacy."

"No, I'd be selling part of my legacy to someone I *trust* to build on that solid foundation, so I can invest in my future."

Was he imagining that emphasis on the word trust? Was he hearing hidden messages his heart longed to hear where there were none? "And Enzo and Frankie?"

"They will still have majority control with Seth. You're not going to be able to override their decisions, but you'll have a seat at the table." Her eyes shone with truth and hope, and Adrian felt his own hope rising to meet it. This brave, brilliant woman never failed to surprise him. Was it any wonder he'd fallen hard?

"Sofia, I'm so sorry I doubted you. My life was fine before this whole crazy mess began, but as a wise woman once told me, fine never means fine. I thought I was happy, but that's only because I hadn't realized how much better it could be with you. Now that I've had a taste of what a future with you could be, I don't want to go back to fine. I want to work hard to build spectacular with you. It was never about the business. It was always you. I love you, Sofia Valenti. Will you give me another chance?"

"Oh, you marvelous idiot, I love you, too. God, I've missed you. I'm sorry that my questions pushed you away. I didn't realize how they sounded, and then you wouldn't even let me explain—"

He touched a finger to her lips to stem the tide of words that she'd held dammed up all these weeks. "Say that first part again."

"I love you, you idiot."

He was still chuckling when she pulled him in for a kiss, and he let himself fall into her. He ignored the clapping, the catcalls, and the disgusted snorting from the peanut gallery. All that mattered was that this amazing woman had given him a second chance. He poured his heart into the kiss, telling her without words how much he needed her.

Adrian grinned down at Sofia but didn't let her go. He didn't want to let her out of his arms now that he'd convinced her back into them. "One last question…"

"Hmm, what's that?" The bemused expression on her face delighted him.

Damn, he was the luckiest man. His dream may not have turned out the way he'd planned, but combining it with hers made it even better. "That seat at the table?"

Sofia nodded.

"Can it be the one next to yours?"

She paused, and then smiled brilliantly, the smile he'd never thought he'd see again. "Absolutely."

"Then it's a deal."

And he sealed it with a kiss.

EPILOGUE

Three months later

"HE NEEDS TO BE DIRTIER, grittier. You can do better," Jake chided Natalie as they both stood back and looked at Enzo.

"Sure thing, Jake." She reached for the small pot of soil on her makeup counter and a small jar of Vaseline. "One dirtier landscaper coming up."

Sofia watched her brother shift uncomfortably in the makeup chair and glare at the young woman who was preparing to paint him with dirt.

Whatever Natalie saw in that glare made her pause and blush, and quickly turn to Sofia. "Let me just touch up Sofia first before I get all messy."

"Fine. Just get it done." Jake stalked out of the tent, off to slay his next dragon. That man only had one speed, and it was *NOW!*

"Do you know what scene they're filming for you today? Indoor? Outdoor?" Natalie asked Sofia.

"I think it's indoor. Someone mentioned a problem in the

kitchen." Sofia settled into the chair next to her brother and grinned at his discomfort.

"Good. What you've got on should be close to enough. I'll just darken your shadow a bit and boost your blush and lips."

While Sofia sat still and let the talented artist work her wiles, she tried to see her brother out of the corner of her eye. Looking without looking, he was watching Natalie's every move with an intensity that made him fairly vibrate with energy, despite sitting still. Sofia wondered what the young woman had done to put her mild-mannered brother on edge.

"There. Good to go."

"Thanks, Natalie. You're a genius."

"All in a day's work. Okay, Enzo, let's get dirty…"

Sofia hustled to the kitchen to film the scene Jake had requested last minute. She had plans to proof and client meetings scheduled for later. As glad as she was that this TV show had taken off, she was starting to resent the drag on her time. Now that her time was her own to control, she'd gotten very protective.

Rounding the corner, she called out in her best Rocky voice. "Yo, Adrian!"

"Ha ha. Very funny."

Trina was already tucked into the corner, camera rolling, so Sofia angled herself toward the camera before she spoke. "What did you need to show me?"

"We've got a problem with the sink."

"Oh Lord, what now? Sofia leaned over the sink and peeked in, as if that would somehow reveal a solution. If they wanted her here to film this scene, it was going to be pricey and likely a major plot point for this episode. Damn it, she was going to have to return that gorgeous rug…

Adrian turned on the faucet and ice-cold water shot into her face, completely rinsing away her harried thoughts. She'd walked right into that one.

Since Jake didn't have his sexual tension subplot now that she and Adrian were a happy couple, he'd decided that practical jokes were the next best way to add interest. The shrill scream of surprise that flew from her lips didn't quite drown out the hysterical laughter from her boyfriend. The term still felt silly three months later for a man who meant so much more to her than a boy and a friend.

Regardless of how much she loved him though, he was going to pay.

"You think you're real funny, huh, smart guy?"

"Smart enough to love you." He ducked under her arm to escape as she lunged for the spray nozzle. The yelp he let loose as the cold water hit the back of his neck was immensely satisfying.

"Get back here, you coward! Can you be serious for a minute?"

"Sure, I can." He came back, hands raised in the universal symbol for truce. He leaned in playfully and smacked a kiss on her lips. "I seriously love you."

"I meant about the sink." She was trying to bring him back to the point, but he was making it really hard to stay focused. Aware of the cameras and her blush, she stepped to the side, shaking her head. He just loved to get her flustered on camera.

"Right, the sink." He knelt down and opened the lower cabinet doors.

"Good news, bad news?" Sofia brushed her dripping hair away from her forehead, praying that her makeup wasn't also sliding down her face. When he stood with a brown paper bag, she frowned.

"Good, I hope."

"What's that?"

"Your candy drawer was empty."

"How do you know my candy drawer is empty?"

"I went to grab a snack and there wasn't even a stray M&M.

You should never have to go without something you love, so I got you some candy to fill it."

Sofia reached for the bag, but Adrian tucked it back against his chest.

"Not so fast. Let me show you what I got."

Out of the corner of her eye, Sofia saw Trina move to a closer spot and wondered what trick they wanted to catch on camera now. Her nerves were on high alert as Adrian dipped his hand into the bag and pulled out one candy bar.

"Don't Snicker." He put her full-sized favorite bar in her hand, and went back in for another. "Just Take 5 and listen to what I have to say."

"What's this all about?" Sofia asked. He was up to something, but he simply raised an eyebrow and two more candy bars out of his bag.

"Sometimes, I can be a real Butterfingers with your emotions, but I will always love you to the Milky Way and back."

Sofia's heart began to melt like the chocolate clenched in her now too-tight grip. This sweet man was proclaiming his love on camera. She smiled as a roll of caramels was added to the pile in her hands.

"I want to Rolo-ver every morning and see that smile."

That sounded lovely and...long-term. Where was he going with this?

"You are one Hot Tamale, and I love your Mounds." Adrian's cheeky grin and wiggling eyebrows pulled a laugh from her, and she tried to move in for a kiss, but he stepped back and raised a hand to stop her.

"No Twix. I promise," he said as he added the caramel cookie bar to the stack in her hands before sprinkling it with silver-foil-wrapped cones. "Only Kisses every day for the rest of our lives."

Sofia's eyes were now riveted to his face. This no longer felt like a silly gag for TV. This felt like the most important moment of her life. He reached into the bag one more time, and when she saw the black velvet box in his hand, her own hands went limp and the chocolate dropped unheeded to the floor.

Suddenly the wet hair and misty makeup didn't matter, and tears streamed unchecked down her cheeks. She had put dreams of this moment aside for so long. Now that it was here, she was completely surprised. They had so much going on right now, what with Adrian taking on more responsibility at Valenti Brothers, Sofia mentoring Meena and getting SV Design off the ground, and filming the second half of the Million-Dollar Starter Home premiere season.

She'd been content in the moment for the first time in years, enjoying a challenging career and a man who loved her as is. This was a big leap. They had only been together a few months. And yet, as her mind was rapid-fire spinning through all of these thoughts, underneath was the quiet knowledge that, yes, this was the right time and the right place, with the right man. She waited for him to find the right words. As much as she wanted to leap in with an answer, she needed to hear them first.

"Sofia, I've known you for years, and I've wanted to be a part of your life since the day I met you. I know we had a shaky start, but I want to build a beautiful future with you and design a love that lasts decades. I thought my life was just fine before, but it is so much better with you by my side. Will you marry me?"

It sounded like the perfect project for the next eighty years or so. Sofia drew in a deep breath and let her heart do the thinking for once.

"Yes. Yes, I will."

He took her now empty hands in his and slid a beautiful brilliant-cut diamond ring on her finger. Giggling and giddy, she wrapped her arms around his neck and held on tight as he spun her in circles in the torn-up kitchen.

"I love you, Sofia."

"I love you, too, Adrian."

"I'll admit, I expected more questions out of you," he teased.

"Just one. Who told you it was a good idea to propose by spraying me in the face with water?" She grinned up at her fiancé, delighted when he barked out a laugh and his dimple came out to play.

"Cut! That was great, but the bit about her mounds was a little too steamy for HomeTV. Everybody hit makeup and wardrobe to dry off and we'll go again," Jake called out from his perch behind a bank of screens set up in the dining room.

Sofia covered her mic and whispered, "How long do you think he'll wait for another take?"

Adrian lifted her, effortlessly and fully aware that it turned her knees to jelly every time. With his rock-solid arms supporting her, Sofia grinned and opened up her heart to a future together. She wrapped her legs around his waist and admired her ring over his shoulder as he carried her out of the house.

"Let's go find out."

THE END

DIRTY DEMO

DIRTY DEMO

When Winston Hartwell's construction crew ends up on a reality TV show, there's no way he's going to sing for his supper, no matter how nicely the curvy camera lady asks. He's terrified of the limelight, and he doesn't trust these Hollywood types as far as he can throw them.

Trina McCallister is one last reality show away from her dream job of filming movies. She'll do whatever it takes to get the footage she needs and get the hell out. But she isn't prepared for the sexy giant with a voice of gold to demolish her carefully constructed defenses.

When lies and fear shake their newly laid foundation, only an act of bravery and trust will save them from ruin.

For all of my writer friends, new and old, published or aspiring: Thank you for making this crazy ride so much fun. I wouldn't be here without you.

CHAPTER 1

"CUT! TRINA, GET IN HERE."

"Yeah, boss? What's up?" Trina held her camera rig between them defensively. With Jake Ryland, she never knew if she was going to get a high five or a verbal slap. He was a driven producer and working with him would make her name, but he was known for his unconventional methods and quicksilver temper.

Compared to some other directors and producers she'd worked with he was a vast improvement. He'd never grabbed her tits or suggested that she film some after-hours activities to get ahead. But she still resented the hell out of having to work for him.

She should have been working on Devon MacLean's new movie. She had always planned to work her way into the movies. After a few solid years in television, she'd put in for his film crew. Her first interview had gone very well. The follow-up conversation had not. She'd been shot down. Again.

And so she was stuck in the reality TV grind a little while longer. At least she'd found a fresh show. She didn't love laboring in obscurity, or working long days on a set full of big, sweaty dudes, but she was getting the opportunity to prove herself to the

Boys' Club and that was all that mattered. That was all she could let matter.

Jake might be running the show, but she was making it great. Without her creative camera angles and inventive shots, he wouldn't have had a pilot, much less a full season request. She made this show stand out from the crowd of other home décor shows, and she did it by being a gymnast, lighting engineer, and therapist all in one.

Making non-actors look good and feel comfortable on film without intruding on the scene was damn hard to pull off, and she did it well. She didn't doubt her talent, only that she'd ever get the opportunity to use it in the way that called to her.

Ever since she'd been a little girl playing with her mom's camcorder, filming her dolls getting attacked by Monster Kitty, she'd loved making stories come alive on the screen.

Soon, Trina promised herself. She'd get there soon. She'd come too far to give up. Tuning back in to her boss, she waited to hear what her next hoop to jump through would be.

"I need more B-roll footage. We are starting to work on final edits for the premier, and I need more filler. I'm thinking we highlight a few of the more outgoing guys on the crew, maybe get some hijinks or blooper reel stuff. I can get some from the time lapse and fixed room cameras, but I want some candid shots, too. We also need to bulk up our library of location shots."

"No problem, boss."

"George is going to take all A-roll shooting this week, so you can embed."

"What? Why?" Trina had worked damn hard to earn her spot at the head of the film crew. This felt like a slap. George couldn't deliver like she could. He was steady but slow, and he didn't have her touch with the homeowners. She resented the hell out of losing her chance to film the reveal shots.

"Embed, you know, befriend them, become one of the guys.

They'll be more relaxed if they trust you off camera. Can't do that if you're always hiding behind the big rig."

Trina tugged at the hem of her oversized t-shirt, untucking it with her nervous fingers from the front of her baggy jeans. She'd have no problem fitting in with the guys. She'd spent most of her career doing exactly that, just trying to survive and get ahead in a male dominated environment. The part that made her nervous was stepping away from the lead camera spot, even for a little while. She'd taken this spec job to do the sizzle reel and the pilot and then signed on for the first season of Million Dollar Starter Home, because Jake Ryland had promised her a foot in the door with his movie producer buddies. After the MacLean shut-out, she needed more influential names on her resumé.

If she wasn't proving herself and staying in his line of sight, she worried that he'd conveniently forget his promise. But he wouldn't keep it if she openly defied him either. Shit. She would just have to play along to get along. She'd give him the best damn B-roll he'd ever seen.

"Anything you're looking for in particular?"

"I need settings, scenes of local landmarks, etc. And then the crew profiles. Find what makes them unique. You know, the joker, the screw-up, the sob story. Anything juicy you can dig up, I want you to get for me on film."

"You got it."

∼

"HEY, GUYS! HOW'S IT GOING?" Trina McAllister strolled into the room they were framing through the middle of what would be a wall with her small camera on her shoulder. Winston Hartwell set down his hammer. A guy of his size could cause a lot of damage with his tools if he wasn't paying attention, and Trina was definitely a distraction.

Winston was painfully aware of the one woman who didn't

make him feel like an oversized brute. Tall and broad through the shoulders, she easily carried the heavy equipment that her job required. He'd seen her on and off for a few weeks as filming for this stupid show ramped up, and he'd never seen her falter or complain. She wielded her camera with a strength and grace unmatched by her male colleagues, who often bitched and moaned over the strain and long hours.

With her blond hair pulled back in a messy braid and a fiercely focused expression, he saw her as a Norse Valkyrie. Instead of choosing whom to slay, she decided whose soul to capture with her camera. He cringed every time she turned that torture device towards him, but he couldn't look away as she nimbly moved through the room taking whatever she wanted.

She was beautiful and strong, and he fantasized about how she would use all of that fluid power to find her pleasure. He shifted his tool belt to relieve some pressure and tried to get his response under control. He turned his mind to music, his fail-safe calm space since childhood. Often songs attached to certain people in his mind, and now Flight of the Valkyries played for her. It made him grin. She had all the energy and power of the Wagner opera when she leapt around the room to get her shots. He wanted to take that power and use it to please them both.

Wanting was one thing. Talking was another. Words deserted him when he was near her, so he was grateful that Rico picked up the conversation from the far end of the stud wall they were building.

"Hey, Trina. Do you need to get some hot-guys-with-hammers shots for the show?"

"Yeah, that would be great. Do you know where I can find some?" Her sarcasm pulled a rumbling laugh from Winston's chest, earning him one of her rare smiles.

"Ouch! That hurts, T." Rico rubbed a hand over his heart. "Play nice."

"That was nice. Keep it up, and I'll show you something that really hurts." She bent and lifted a hammer playfully, and Rico danced away behind the wall, laughing. "I'm going to be hanging with you guys this week, getting some close-ups and B-roll footage. Just pretend like I'm not here."

Winston cringed. Sure. Forget that the woman who flipped his every switch was going to be shadowing him for a week. Easy as pie. Usually, Winston had no trouble keeping his mouth shut and his eyes on his work. He'd worked for Valenti Brothers Construction quietly for years. He hadn't been thrilled with the idea of the show in the first place, and he was still a reticent participant. He'd much prefer a spot out of the limelight. Add having to keep his cool around her on camera for an entire week, and he was in trouble.

"Everything okay over there, Mr. Strong-and-Silent?"

"Sure. Just dandy."

He tried to get back into his rhythm as she set up and zoomed in on his hands swinging a hammer, his arms flexing, then Rico's work with the saw. She snapped up every minute detail with that camera of hers, and drew Winston's attention like a candle drew a moth. He'd knocked his fingers twice with the hammer and almost shot his hand with the nail gun. She was a dangerous woman.

Winston counted the minutes to freedom. At five, he could escape and regroup. He would rebuild his defenses against her potent distractions before tomorrow. Now that he knew she'd be with them all day, he'd be prepared. But after the surprise and a full day in her camera's sights, he was frazzled. He needed to hide for a little while. He needed his music.

In times of trouble, he could always count on music to take his mind away from it all. On the bus home from a bad game, in the weight room doing rehab, even while he went under for surgery, music had soothed his frustrations and fears. It would give him the space he needed to prepare for the next day's struggle.

He'd gotten so comfortable with the guys on the crew that he usually sang along with the radio. It had been weeks since he'd sung at work because of all the new people. That was too long, and it showed in his shaky defenses. He needed to get his fix, and tonight was his chance. He'd spend some time with good friends and good tunes, and everything would look better in the morning.

"Hey, Trina, what are you doing tonight?" Rico asked.

No. No, Rico, shut up. Don't...

"Nothing. Why?"

"We're going to go sing karaoke tonight. Wanna come?"

"Who is we?"

"Me, Winston, Charlie, a couple of guys on the other crew."

Damn it. A year ago, Rico had been wooing some woman and convinced them to go along to karaoke, and Winston had been hooked. He and the guys had a standing hangout at Mitchell's Pub for Karaoke Mondays. It was so low key that his nerves stayed out of it, and at this point he was singing to a room full of friends. He'd been hoping to lose himself in the music for a little while. But knowing she was in the audience? Shit. He'd be lucky to squeak out a single note.

Trina turned to him, shock clear on her lovely features.

"You sing?"

Winston didn't respond. Couldn't. His mind froze, and his throat snapped shut.

"This I gotta see. You're on!"

Trina was pleased with her afternoon of work. She checked her list of crew members. So far she'd pegged Rico as the smart-ass flirt, Charlie as the older voice of folksy wisdom, and Manuel as the goofball kid. She drew a line under the name that had so far eluded classification. Winston Hartwell was a hard nut to crack. She hoped to make a dent in his shell at karaoke.

He was magic on camera, all shoulders and biceps for days. Just enough sweat to shine and enough grit to be real. Any woman watching would be tempted to run her hands over his arms and linger while brushing off the dirt. Lord knew, she'd been tempted to, and she was never tempted. She'd had several late night dreams that featured his battered and rough hands drawing delicious reactions from her. She couldn't remember the last time she'd let herself desire a man's touch.

Even though they'd worked the same project site for over a month, she still didn't know that much about him. The strong-silent routine was clearly his forte, which only made her job harder. The close-ups she'd gotten were gold, but she couldn't pin down the man's personality beyond sex god if he wouldn't speak. She'd been careful to keep a good distance between herself and the guys on the crew, wary of getting tangled up with a bunch of rough and tumble construction guys. That clearly wasn't going to cut it now.

These guys didn't seem so bad, though. Maybe it was the fact that Valenti Brothers was a family firm, or that the boss's daughter cut the checks and called the design shots, but she'd gotten a lot less cat-calling and lewd jokes than she'd expected. Or maybe her fuck-off shields were just that good. Either way, she was going to need to open up and get closer to these guys if she was going to get the kind of shots Jake wanted.

Even though it made her faintly nauseous, she deliberately left her camera behind. Jake wanted them to trust her and bond. He was right that it wouldn't happen with a huge camera sitting between them, but leaving it behind was like heading into battle with a gaping hole in her defenses. She deliberately kept her I'm-Just-One-Of-The-Guys armor on and tucked her smartphone into her pocket. Baby steps. She even added a baggy hoodie for good measure against the chill of the California spring evening and the interest of a male gaze.

Tonight would be her first chance to get to know these guys away from the job site. It had been so long since she'd gone out socially, she was afraid she'd forgotten how. She fell back on her work skills and ran through a mental checklist to prepare just like any other shoot. A job was a job, and she was determined to do hers well. So she'd pull up her big girl panties and brave a night at the bar with a bunch of dudes.

She could do this. Women did this all the time. She was not going to let her anxiety win. She would drive herself. She would order a few pitchers, but pour herself only one pint. She would stay with the group, and leave by eleven. Ask about their families, wives, girlfriends, hobbies. Tease out funny construction stories. This would be fun. She would be safe. She could do this.

Before fear could paralyze her, she started her car and drove into the darkening night.

CHAPTER 2

Winston was already seated at their regular table when Rico and Trina walked in together. A hot flare of jealousy licked his throat, and he swallowed hard. He stood and raised a hand and was gratified when her eyes flashed to his and held with a smile.

The first two pitchers of beer sat in the middle of the table, and he poured a pint for Rico as they made their way over. Trina sat down in the seat right next to him, and he could feel that entire side of his body flood with the warmth of awareness. He could smell the sweet floral scent of her hair over the stale beer and staler man-aroma of the bar. This was going to be torture.

Thankfully he'd already downed half a pint of his own beer, so he had a little liquid courage in his system to help loosen his tongue.

"Do you want one?" He lifted an empty pint glass towards Trina. "Or I could get you a wine?"

"He speaks!" Trina grinned at him, and his tongue tangled again. She picked up a different pint glass and poured herself a beer from the other pitcher. "Beer is fine. Thanks."

He didn't know how to take her comment or the fact that she hadn't let him pour her a beer. Still, she'd chosen the seat next to him... Jesus, he was a grown-ass man. He shouldn't be dissecting a girl's every move like he was in middle school. He should be able to speak to a woman, but her nearness tangled his thoughts.

Rico had no trouble finding words and dove into the conversation when she asked for stories, telling tales about the crew and past jobs. Half an hour in, Winston was pleasantly surprised to discover that he was enjoying himself and was more than a little buzzed. It usually took him quite a while to feel any kind of alcohol. His six-foot-four, two-hundred-ninety pound frame could hold his liquor.

Maybe it was Trina and her hair that smelled of wildflowers making him light-headed and giddy.

"So the new kid was trying to fit a pipe the other day in the Randall master bathroom, but he grabbed a three-quarter inch pipe instead of a half. What an idiot! He gets it all cut and prepped. And then from inside the cabinet, all I hear is, "Fuck! I don't think it's going to fit!" Rico was laughing throughout his story.

"That's what she said." The words flew out of Winston's mouth, stealing Rico's punch line before he had time to think twice about telling a dirty joke with a lady at the table.

Trina burst out laughing and leaned her head against Winston's arm. He froze, afraid to move and break the moment.

"Did you really just crack a joke? My goodness, maybe I should talk about inspecting the plumbing more often." She was teasing him, and he was tempted to repeat the joke, but the moment passed, broken by Charlie shouting at the announcer on the television.

"You disappoint me, Hartwell. I gave you the perfect set-up there." She leaned in closer so she could speak under the rest of the conversation. Up close, she looked so beautiful, so feminine, that it was hard to keep thinking about her as just one of the crew. She was a woman, and his momma had raised him better than he'd just behaved. Even though she didn't seem to mind the crass humor, he knew better.

"I'm sorry. That joke was out of line."

"I'm a big girl, Winston. I've had sex, and I can laugh about it when it's funny."

Holy Shit. Now that she'd gone and mentioned sex, all he could picture was her in the middle of the act, and it fried his circuits. His brain was literally melting from the vivid images his imagination was supplying. He was so far gone, he didn't even hear the DJ calling his name until Charlie kicked his chair.

"Hey, dude! It's your turn."

Winston coughed to clear his throat and his mind. He couldn't go up there with a raging erection.

"Ladies first. Do you want to sing?"

"Oh, hell no. I'm quite comfortable with my spot behind the camera. I don't do stages."

"Okay, who else is coming up with me? Group jam?"

"Come on, Winston! Show her what you've got." Rico turned his words to Trina. "You won't believe what this big guy is hiding."

"That's what she said," Trina quipped in a soft voice, turning smiling eyes on Winston. "Well? Am I going to get to see this *big* surprise?"

If she didn't quit looking at him like that, he would show her anything she wanted. Hauling in a deep breath and chugging down the last quarter of his pint, he rose and told the DJ to change things up from his usual. The only time he felt truly free with his words was when he sang someone else's, lost in the music. She wanted to see what he was hiding? He was feeling just brave enough to show it to her.

TRINA CHUCKLED INTO HER BEER. Teasing the silent giant was too much fun. He was so damn cute when that blush crept up his neck. Still, she was impressed that he'd actually gone up on stage and had a microphone in his hand. She would have lost money on that bet. This was going to be good, judging by the way Rico kept watching her, laughing, and waiting for her reaction.

Her spidey-sense was tingling. This was going to be a good shot, and her fingers were twitching for her camcorder. She pulled her phone out of her back pocket and set it to record video, holding it as inconspicuously as possible in her lap.

As the opening strains of Stevie Nicks' iconic anthem floated from the speakers, the crowd grew quiet. Gutsy choice, picking a female vocal, she mused, before she fell under his spell along with everyone else.

Spellbound was the only word to describe the crowd under the influence of his rich tenor. His velvet voice wove through her thoughts and tempted her with images of birds in the sky and a woman taken by the wind. He locked eyes with her and held her gaze as he crooned about wanting to be her lover. Trina's heart beat in her throat and her hands trembled, her response to his performance shaking her to her core and shaking the phone in her lap as well. Had she really thought he was a gentle giant? This man was dangerous. He had the power to drop panties with a well-sung chorus.

As he repeated the final verse of the song, Trina couldn't help but hope she would win. A kiss, a touch, a night in his bed. Her long suppressed libido had been lured out of hiding by his voice. It overwhelmed her common sense. She could think of nothing but loving to be his lover as he made his way through the applause back to the table.

The guys slapped him on the back and clapped along with the rest of the bar. She was probably being rude, but she couldn't manage more than an open mouthed stare as she tried to pull herself back together.

"Well? What did you think?"

Winston's intense gaze demanded the truth, and she gave it willingly.

"I think that you *are* a man hiding big talents."

"That's what she said!" Rico cracked himself and the rest of the table up with laughter, breaking the tension between them. Trina finished her beer, wondering just how big his other talents were. She couldn't keep her eyes from dropping to his lap, trying to size him up. Her fingers were aching to drop to his thigh and wander. She grabbed the empty pitchers instead and escaped to the bar for refills.

She was working. Doing research. Building trust. She wasn't here to lust after her co-workers no matter how sexy the tall, dark, and built contractor was. Rico was up onstage belting out a horrible rendition of "Rico Suave" complete with early nineties dance moves that was drawing the desired laughs from the crowd. If he kept swiveling his hips like that, he was going to throw his back out, Trina thought with a grin.

"Hey, pretty thing. There's that smile. Don't I know you?"

A very drunk, very handsy guy sidled up next to her at the bar while she tried to get the bartenders attention with the pitchers. Trina shrugged her shoulder to dislodge his grip.

"No, you don't, and we're going to keep it that way."

"Aw, come on. Don't be that way. I'm just trying to be friendly."

That hand slipped lower to her ass and gave her what she was sure he thought was a *friendly* squeeze. She smacked his hand away and glared.

"Touch me again, and you're going to lose that hand." Her mind was spinning with all of the self-defense moves she'd learned after...But before she could settle on one, bro-dude was looking over her shoulder, eyes wide and frightened. She glanced to find Winston standing directly behind her, arms crossed, biceps bulging, and jaw clenched.

"Sorry, man. I didn't realize..."

"That she is a person and therefore deserves to not have her ass grabbed by strangers?"

Trina watched bro-dude pale and stutter before sprinting for the door. She let her shaky breath go. She hadn't lost her head, and she wasn't trapped or helpless. There was no reason for the fear that was making her tremble now.

"You okay?" His massive hand on her shoulder grounded her, where the other had pissed her off. What was it about him that made her respond to his touch with pleasure instead of fear?

"Yeah, thanks."

"It looked like you told him off, but he's an ass who doesn't take no very well. Thought I'd make it easier for you to leave."

"I was debating whether or not to break his wrist, so you've saved him a trip to the ER, anyhow."

"I think I would have liked to see that." She wasn't imagining the blatant admiration in his gaze, and it drew her even further back into her body. Her heart pulsed strongly in response, reminding her that she was alive and very well.

"You get off on watching women beat up men?" She tried to diffuse the tension with a joke, so she didn't jump into his arms and ask him to take her right there on the bar.

"I get off on watching you do just about any damn thing." He brushed a lock of her hair behind her ear, sending tingles down her neck, before he walked away from her and straight out of the bar.

CHAPTER 3

BACK AT WORK, Winston glanced over his shoulder for the fifth time. Well, five not counting the eight times he stared at the door straight on, or the three times he'd changed his position for a better view. He'd laid himself bare last night, both on the stage and at the bar. Now all he could think of was seeing her again. What was she thinking? Had he completely blown it? But Trina was nowhere to be seen no matter how often he checked.

Today, he was on his own, framing the tight closet they were adding to the attic bedroom. Awkward angles made it slow and tedious work. He bopped his head along to his music, trying to distract himself from his obsession. Sweat dripped down his spine in the hot attic, making his gray t-shirt stick to his back and not doing a damn thing to help cool him down. His jeans kept slipping lower on his hips forcing him to hike them back up every few minutes. Every damn thing annoyed him today, the fact that he couldn't stop thinking of Trina most of all.

He had just cut the last two by four when that sweet floral scent, so incongruent with her tomboy appearance, tickled his senses. He turned and tugged off his headphones. Trina was standing at the top of the narrow staircase carrying her big rig.

"Hey, where've you been?" he asked without thinking about how it would sound.

"Why? Did you miss me?"

"Maybe."

"I had to upload all the video from the stationary cams and my portables from yesterday for the intern to log." She walked further into the attic, which immediately shrunk around them to include just enough space for the two of them. The rest faded into a fog. He couldn't tell if she'd dropped her voice on purpose or if it was just in response to him, but everything she said felt like it had a second meaning. "But I'm here now, big guy. I'm hoping you're ready for me."

"I'm always ready for you, baby. What do you need?"

"An OTF session."

"OTF? The hell is that?"

She grinned at his apparent confusion. "On the fly. I'm going to ask you a few questions while you work."

"Nearly done here. This is the last beam."

"Then I'll ask you questions while you pretend to work."

He swung his hammer wildly towards the already secured frame with a stupid grin on his face and felt like a king when she laughed.

"Okay, wise guy. Here we go." The red light atop her camera began flashing. "How long have you worked for the Valentis?"

"Three years." He bent with his nail gun and secured the bottom and then the top of the last beam. He didn't realize that he'd just mooned the camera until he turned around and caught her staring at his butt. She coughed to clear her throat.

"And before that?"

"Odd jobs here and there." He sure as hell wasn't going to pour out his sob story to the camera. No one wanted to hear about the young football star who'd flunked out of college and lost his scholarship. It had been his own damn fault for not studying hard enough. School had never come easy, and a lot of people had gone out of their way to make sure he passed high school so he could keep playing. He should have known he'd need to study harder than everyone else to succeed but the lure of college girls and football parties had been too potent. He hadn't made it out of his junior year.

He'd even gotten a second chance. He'd been picked up by a semi-pro football team and was being scouted by the NFL before a blind-side hit blew out his knee. After six months of rehab, he could walk and lift, but the rigors of football were out of the question. No one wanted to hear that story end badly. They all wanted to root for the miracle recovery.

Music had been his only solace while he recovered and figured out what the hell he could do with his life. His brains had failed him, and his talent hadn't kept him safe, either. All he had left was his brawn for as long as that held out. Scary thought. Construction was as good a labor job as any, and the Valentis were good people. They ran a solid company and didn't cut corners. He couldn't ask for more. He wouldn't. Trina and her prying questions couldn't get too close. He had no interest in sharing with the world what a loser he was.

"And how long have you been singing?" she asked.

"Nope."

"What do you mean, nope?"

"That's not going on the show." Talk about embarrassing. He only sang at that karaoke night because he was out with friends, and it had taken him years to even get up the courage to try that!

"Come on, Winston. Your voice is amazing! Can't you see it? The Singing Subcontractor!" She spread her hands in front of her like she was envisioning the marquee.

"No way. I don't sing." His voice vibrated with a tension he hated, and he tried not to snap at her. She couldn't know the buttons she was pushing.

"You got up on a stage yesterday and killed it!"

293

"That's different. I know those people. I've been going in there for three years. They like me."

"So you've been singing karaoke for three years?"

Winston crossed his arms and shut his mouth.

"Come on. Why don't you want to sing on camera?"

"Just because." *Oh, that's a real mature answer, Idiot.* But he couldn't tell her the real reason, that he was terrified to fail, to have his talents be not quite good enough again. He'd already lost one dream. He couldn't lose the only thing besides football that had ever made him feel alive. And he couldn't bear to have her think he was a coward. Panic licked at the back of his throat, and it must've shown on his face, because Trina turned off the camera and set it on the floor. Christ, he didn't want to lose control in front of her, but the pity in her eyes pushed him right up to his edge.

TRINA HELD her hand out and approached with a wariness normally reserved for stray dogs and hairy spiders. He'd gone awfully pale, and if he fainted it would be like felling a redwood. She'd be crushed beneath him, and not in the sexy way she'd been imagining. Despite her desire to help him, her own fears were sending out warnings. He was a big man, they were alone in this attic, and she was pushing all of his buttons. The space constricted around them making it hard for her to breathe. She was afraid of pushing him too far, but she couldn't back down now. She was too close. Jake had told her to do whatever it took to get the shot, so she stepped towards him instead of away, as her nerves were demanding. She approached and he retreated. She maneuvered him into the corner where the stationary camera couldn't see him. No one deserved to have a panic attack caught on film. She trusted that her lavalier mic would catch what she needed.

"Hey, for the record, I like you, too. Take a deep breath. Camera's off now."

He hauled in a shaky breath, and she got close enough to place her hand on his forearm, hoping to gentle him. He was as hard as steel, and she shivered to think of what he could do with that strength.

But he's not that kind of guy.

She prayed her instincts were right, or her next move could really backfire.

She reached up and cupped his face in her hands, and his eyes latched on to hers. They'd gone from blank with panic to gleaming with desire in a heartbeat.

"The way you sang on that stage last night was incredible. I can't stop thinking about it." *All true. Keep going.* She deliberately ignored the sharp voice of her conscience poking at her ulterior motives. "I laid awake all night with your voice in my head." She smoothed her hands down his neck and over his broad shoulders that bunched with tension beneath her fingers. "Would you sing something just for me?"

He tried to speak, cleared his throat, and then tried again.

"What do you want to hear?"

"What do you want me to hear?"

He silently stared at her long enough that she was sure she'd blown it. Why on earth had she thought that she possessed the kind of feminine wiles needed to pull this off? The scared, pathetic sex-starved excuse for a woman seducing the hunk with the golden voice? Ridiculous. The intense connection she'd felt the night before had probably been one-sided.

And then that voice began to vibrate in his throat, and she could feel every note rippling through her, her blood pulsing thickly in time through her veins.

He sang of shadows and valleys, of being hers if she'd be his. The popular Mumford and Sons song had never felt so sexy or so personal before. He kept his eyes locked on hers, compelling her

295

to believe that every word was meant for her. Trina was a goner. As he sang of a man who wasn't perfect but would try to change for the woman he loved, she fell under his spell. She managed to let him finish the first two verses, but by then, her belly had filled with molten lava, and she cut him off mid-chorus with a kiss that erupted with heat, surprising them both. She took advantage of his surprise and pushed him back against the frame, before all but scaling the mountain of a man. She'd get Jake his scene later, but this was for her. Directly underneath the camera they couldn't be seen. She reached behind her and clicked off her mic.

This was for her eyes and ears only, and she was going to give herself the gift of his pleasure. The fact that this big bear of a man would open his heart and choose that song just because she'd asked had put her more at ease than she'd been in years. She desperately wanted to be his to have and to hold.

She could tell the instant his surprise faded. His kiss changed from an instinctive return to a claiming. He spun her around trapping her between his massive chest and the soon-to-be wall. Before she could even think to panic, his hot mouth possessed her wits, and she was his.

Every thrust of his tongue drove her further out of her mind, and for the first time in far too long, that didn't scare her. His kiss filled her thoughts with blatant pleasure, and she drew it into her parched soul. She needed this. Needed him. It was glorious to not think about a damn thing and just feel.

He gripped her hips and growled against her mouth before he lifted her to better plunder. No one had ever lifted her before. At five-foot-nine and a hundred and seventy pounds, she was no spinner to be tossed around. She wrapped her legs around his waist and reveled in the novelty of being with a man strong enough to carry her. When he moved his mouth to her neck and began rocking his hips, thrusting his hard cock against her clit through all of the layers separating them, she moaned low and loud, startling herself.

She clapped a hand over her mouth and tried to hold it in, but the pleasure he was unleashing was too great to contain. When he cupped her entire breast in his massive hand, she groaned and dropped her head against the stud running the length of her spine, wordlessly begging for more. She wanted it all. Pinned between the wood of the wall and the wood in his pants, she ground herself against him, taking her pleasure from him. He seemed happy to oblige, increasing his speed to match her hips that were rocking to their own frantic rhythm. She desperately wanted the orgasm that sat just out of reach. When he bit her earlobe and pinched her nipple at the same time, the shock sent her flying over the edge. She was grateful for the supporting studs behind her and between her legs, because every bone in her body had dissolved. She reached a sleepy hand down between them, intent on bringing him as much pleasure as he'd just given her.

The muted buzz of a circular saw cut through her euphoria, and she remembered where they were. Fuck. She'd just dry humped a sex god in the middle of her workplace, surrounded by mics and cameras. She couldn't remember if she'd managed to hold in her cries at the end or not. Panic erased the last dregs of lassitude from her body, and Trina pushed at his shoulder. When Winston pulled back to look her in the eye with a pleased grin on his face she hissed.

"I can't do this. I'm sorry"

He dropped her quickly, and her feet hit the floor with a dull thud, driving home reality. He raised his hands, as if he were under arrest, and frowned his confusion.

"You kissed me."

"Yes, and you kissed me back. You gave me my first orgasm in over a year, and it was fucking amazing. So amazing that I am seconds from dropping to my knees and giving you one back," she whispered. "But doing this here could get me fired, and I am very close to not caring about that fact."

It took him a minute to catch all that she'd said and deliberately not said.

"So, you're not saying 'no,' just not right now?"

"And certainly not right here."

"Okay." His silly grin found its way onto her lips when he kissed her.

"Okay."

Trina grabbed her camera and escaped before her will power collapsed.

CHAPTER 4

AT THE BASE of the stairs, Trina pulled up short as Jake rounded the corner with a shit-eating grin on his face.

"Well done, McAllister. I didn't think you had it in you."

"Huh?" Her head was still fuzzy with lust, and she wasn't following.

"Getting him to sing. Inspired! Rico is shaping up to be the class clown we needed. How's it going on the local color?"

Damn it. Jake had heard Winston sing already? Oh God, her lav mic was a live feed. What else had he heard? And he'd asked a question. Shit, what was it? Local color, right.

"I'm planning to head out tomorrow."

"Great, let's talk strategy for getting the Hulk to sing on camera. He seems to respond well to you. Let's play with that. Tomorrow, he'll go along as your local guide. Dress up, wear something pretty, and we'll see if we can get him to serenade you. Go to Natalie first thing in the morning, and see what she can do with your face."

"But, I don't think..." Trina didn't like this plan, but she was already protesting to empty air. Jake was off to the next crisis on his list. The idea of tricking Winston didn't sit well. He didn't know he'd been recorded, and after what he'd said about being afraid of singing on camera, her deceit roiled in a mess of greasy black sludge in her gut.

He had signed the contract. Technically, anything caught on the job site from mobile or stationary cameras was fair game. And she had to keep an eye on her goals. She needed to show Jake that she was willing to do whatever it took. She had to get out of the brutal grind of reality TV, and no silver-tongued devil was going to lead her astray. Despite her legitimate justifications, she left for the day with guilt weighing heavy on her heart.

HE WAS IN TROUBLE. Winston couldn't remember the last time he'd fallen so far, so fast. When Trina had put her mouth on his, he'd swallowed his words and his tongue in shock. And then his world had exploded with color and light and warmth and the most glorious sounds. How did women know the exact sounds to drive men mad? Did they teach that in those separate sex-ed classes? Was there a manual? It was a powerful weapon against a man's will power, and he couldn't wait for the next target practice. His cock was still aching with the orgasm he hadn't had, and he wondered if he'd be able to resist pulling one off later. It would be painful to wait for her to finish the job, but what a sweet reward for his sacrifice. Now that she'd put the image of her on her knees in his head, it was everything he wanted. He imagined her full lush lips closing around his cock while his hands tangled in her goddess braid.

He was lost in the fantasy of thrusting into her warm mouth until he came, when Rico strutted in, singing off-key.

"What the hell are you so happy about?" Winston asked, as he picked up his tools.

"Trina just asked me to lunch tomorrow to 'discuss my arc.' I think she likes me, bro." Rico's swagger didn't usually bother

Winston, but today it unleashed his inner tigers. Twin beasts of anger and doubt chased each other's tails in his brain.

Why would she kiss him, climb him, and then make a date with Rico?

Of course, Rico was the more logical choice for a good time. He would be able to actually speak and entertain a woman.

I guess I'm good for a quick fix. Great.

"That's cool."

"Hey, you okay? You don't look so good."

"I'm fine. I'll see you tomorrow." Winston got himself into his truck without punching Rico or searching out Trina for an explanation. He counted it a win. He turned on "Creep" by Radiohead and poured his frustrations into the song.

How stupid to think he was special! What a fucking joke!

TRINA LOOKED at herself in the mirror, trying to find anything familiar to hold on to. It had been a long time since she'd seen her body in tight clothes. She was positively shocked to see her figure after hiding it away for so long. After being harassed on the first production she'd interned on during college, she'd done her best to hide. She knew it hadn't been her fault, that he'd been a power-hungry asshole, but she'd felt safer the less of a target she was. Baggy clothes, frumpy hair, no makeup, just one of the guys. It had become her unofficial uniform in the male world she inhabited.

Now, here she was deliberately trying to draw attention to herself, and it felt foreign. Digging in the back of her closet, she'd found an old corduroy skirt that still fit. It hugged her hips before flaring to her knees, leaving her calves bare. She was tempted to pull on a sweater that would cover her or maybe a parka, to her ankles…

Instead, she reached for a heather purple V-neck t-shirt.

When paired with the underwire bra she'd dug out too, her girls were well-displayed. She even found an old pair of heels that nearly crippled her, but she shoved her feet into them anyway, like a stepsister trying to pretend to be the princess. She tried to think about how Winston would see her, but she didn't have a powerful enough imagination to chase her insecurities away.

Christ, this was uncomfortable. But women dressed like this everyday. Not everyone got grabbed or taunted. Not every woman got cornered by her mentor and forced to perform sexual acts. Not everyone. But it had happened to Trina, and she couldn't ignore the fact that it could happen again. When she looked in the mirror, she saw the girl she'd been five years ago, and she broke down in tears.

But doing this, going along with what Jake wanted, this was her chance to get away from all of the bad memories, to get rid of the black-ball that had derailed her career. Before she could talk herself out of chasing her dreams, she bolted for the car.

By the time she got to work, the tears had stopped, but her nerves were still on high alert. She dropped heavily into Natalie's chair.

"Good morning, sunshine. What brings you into my lair without a camera?"

"Jake said I needed to look attractive today. Clearly, I need your help."

"I think you look lovely everyday."

"That's sweet of you to say, but my 'usual routine' is sunscreen and Chapstick. Today, I need to charm someone into doing something they don't want to do."

"You want to make him drool."

"Yes. I mean, no. Not Jake. But 'him,' yes. He should want to do anything I ask."

Natalie hummed her approval. "Okay. I can work with that."

Trina let her mind empty as she closed her eyes and submitted to being brushed and blended by the talented artist.

"Not now."

Natalie's voice was strident and startled Trina into opening her eyes. Enzo stood in the doorway of the tent blocking the sun.

"I have the…"

"I said, not now. I'm in the middle of something."

"Anything I could get in the middle of, too?"

Natalie glared at the middle Valenti brother until he held up his hands in retreat.

"Just kidding. Sheesh, it was a joke! Come find me when you're free."

He waved a sheaf of papers in his hand, and tucked them away as he left.

"What was that all about?"

"A man who doesn't know when to quit."

After what felt like an eternity of fussing, but had in actuality only been about fifteen minutes, the torture stopped.

"Open your eyes."

Trina no longer saw that young, naive girl in the mirror. A bold, sexy woman she didn't recognize stared back. Behind the mask of make-up, she was still scared, but no one else would be able to see that through Natalie's magic.

"You're a genius."

"Knock 'em dead, sister."

"Nope, just want to wrap him around my pinkie."

She hefted her camera onto her shoulder, and the straps of her rig pressed down on her larger-than-usual chest uncomfortably. She struggled to loosen the buckles one-handed.

"Hang on, honey. Come here."

Natalie lifted and tucked until her boobs were nearly tumbling out of her neckline, but at least they were out of harm's way.

"Thanks. I usually wear sports bras to work."

"Well, you look rockin' without one, but we've gotta keep the girls safe!" Natalie laughed with a final friendly pat to

Trina's chest, before turning back to organize her puffs and powders.

WALKING INTO THE HOUSE, Trina was greeted by the voice that had chased her through her dreams, belting out "Creep." The melancholy behind his words made her want to go wrap him up in a hug and make his world right again. Instead, she started recording. This was what she needed to prove her chops to Jake. She snuck the lens of her camera around the corner of the doorway where the music was flowing.

"Hello, beautiful." Rico came up behind her, carrying spools of electrical wire. "You look hot!"

"Yeah, thanks." *Dammit! He's going to fuck up the audio.* She tried to ignore him, hoping he'd keep walking.

Instead, Rico stepped closer and set down his spools. "You didn't have to get all dressed up for our date, but damn, I'm glad you did." The singing stopped. There went her shot. She kept filming just in case she managed to capture something good, but it was doubtful. The element of surprise was gone. In her annoyance, she almost missed what he'd said. "Thank God. He's been singing that damn song all morning!"

"Wait, what date?" Trina gave up on capturing the elusive Singing Subcontractor in the wild, and tuned in to the conversation at hand.

"How quickly they forget..." Rico had his flirtatious banter turned up to eleven. "Lunch? Today?"

Trina stepped back, hating herself for retreating, but she needed to be clear.

"Rico, stop. I asked you to lunch so we can talk about the show. No date."

A chuckle snuck around the partially dry-walled hallway.

"Well, we could make it a date if you're interested."

"Thanks, but no. Let's get filming. I've got a busy day."

She walked ahead of him into the room where Winston crouched by the opened interior wall, back to the door, running wiring for new lights and sockets. She had the pleasure of seeing the cheeky grin on his face drop away when he saw her. The raw desire that flooded his features was infinitely more satisfying. She turned the camera aside. Jake might be able to make her use her feminine wiles to get the shots he wanted, but this reaction? This was just for her, and she wouldn't need a video to remember it. The next time she felt awkward owning her feminine side, she'd be better armed to fight her demons.

His eyes widened and his nostrils flared as he drew a breath through his clenched jaw. His hands convulsively gripped the pliers he held as if they could somehow keep him anchored in place.

It was a primal reaction, and Trina felt the answering tug of desire unfurling within. She'd been wary of him because of his size until she'd gotten to know him better. Now that he'd blown her mind wide open with that down and dirty orgasm, she was feeling more confident. Walls she'd held up for years were being demolished left and right, and the sunshine felt good on her heart. She'd forgotten the thrill of enjoying a man's gaze instead of fearing it. She still wanted to return the favor, and that surprised the hell out of her. The asshole had taken so much more from her than she'd realized. But she'd handled Rico in the hallway and hadn't fallen apart. Maybe she could handle Winston, too.

"Hey, what are you doing after lunch?" she asked him.

"I was just going to keep running wire. Why?"

"I'm going over Rico's arc at lunch. I thought we could go for a drive, scout some local sights, and talk about your role."

"Sure. Is this a date?" he teased.

Leaning in close enough to tickle his ear with a whisper, she replied.

"We'll see."

CHAPTER 5

So, her lunch with Rico wasn't a date. That detail made Winston irrationally happy, tempered only by the knowledge that he didn't know if their drive was either. After that kiss, and her insistence that they behave at work, his brain hadn't been able to shut down his looping thoughts. He'd imagined every scenario outside of work that could involve him and Trina getting naked.

Crouching down to run wire with a raging hard-on was difficult, but he'd gladly pay the price. The scenes his imagination was supplying were too good to push aside. In his bed, on his couch, at her place... He couldn't wait to get his hands on her again.

"What's gotten into you today?" Rico dragged him from speculating on the texture of her inner thighs when he walked back into the room after lunch.

"Huh? Why?"

"You're over there humming the Jackson Five, dude. Why the sudden turn around from 'I'm a Creep' to 'I Want You Back'?"

"Shut up."

"Oooh! He doesn't want to talk about it. Does it have anything to do with the calf eyes you were making at our sexy camera lady? She is one hot piece of ass, I tell you what. I could barely sit at the table for lunch." Rico mimed jacking off and laughed.

Winston stood and crossed to Rico. He rarely used his size to intimidate, because people made assumptions about big burly men that caused problems. But just this minute, he didn't care if he caused a problem. In fact, he'd enjoy it.

Towering over the shorter man he usually considered a friend, he used his height to drive home his message.

"Don't talk about her like that."

"Come on, man. You can't tell me you haven't noticed."

"Noticed what? That she is a beautiful person, inside and out, who deserves better than to be reduced to a 'piece of ass'? Why, yes, I did notice. Man the fuck up, Rico."

"So that's how it is? You have a thing for her! You're jealous she went to lunch with me," Rico crowed.

"I'm not jealous. I don't care if she wants to fuck your hairy ass or not. You don't talk about women like that."

"Quit being so sensitive."

"Quit being a dick."

"Boys, boys, simmer down." Trina peeked her head around the corner. "Whatever you're fighting about can wait. Winston, I've got to get these shots scouted before we lose the light. Let's roll."

"See you later, sunshine." Rico teased.

Winston didn't respond because all of the words rushing to the tip of his tongue would only make things worse. He flicked off his partner and tugged his keys from his pocket as he followed her out to his truck.

"Don't you need a camera?" he asked as she settled into his passenger seat.

"Nope. Today, I'm just scouting. I do that with my phone. I'll set up time lapse and aerial shots later."

"Okay, so what's on your agenda?"

"Top of the list? A thank you."

Winston's mind stuttered. Was she thanking him for the kiss?

"I overheard what Rico said, and I heard you stand up to him, too."

"He shouldn't have said it."

"No, he shouldn't have, but a lot of guys do, and it's rare for someone with a Y chromosome to push back. So thanks."

He felt a blush, an honest-to-God blush working its way up his neck. He cleared his throat and tried to change the subject. Compliments for being a decent human being made him uncomfortable.

"You're welcome. So what's next on your list?"

"I need to get some outside shots of local tech giants. I want to see if there's a way to show iconic industry without getting into copyright troubles. I also need some forest and mountain shots, the ocean if we've got time."

"Deal, we can swing by the new Apple spaceship and the Googleplex, and then I'll take you across Highway 92 towards Half Moon Bay. You'll get all of that in one drive."

"Perfect."

She tugged her phone out of a purse, cursing.

"I hate these things. Why don't skirts have pockets?"

That, of course, made him inspect the offending article of clothing with his eyes as if she had somehow missed the helpful openings. Which in turn led him to inspecting the legs coming out of said skirt. Which in turn had him missing most of her side of the conversation she'd begun on the phone with someone and jerking his attention back to the road when she laughed.

"No, Rico is cool. He's on board with the plan. I just wanted to tell you I'm out scouting, and I stole Winston for the afternoon to be my guide and hostage."

"Katrina McAllister, I trust you won't let me down." Jake's voice boomed from her phone.

"No problem, boss."

He waited until she'd hung up and tucked her phone away, before asking, "So...Katrina huh?"

"Yeah..."

"Why shorten it? Katrina is a beautiful name."

"Thanks, but a childhood of being called Kitty Kat was long enough for me. Can you imagine what a guy like Rico would do with that?"

Winston could imagine and nodded.

She reached over and turned on the radio, effectively ending the line of questioning. She turned to her window and watched traffic flash past through the lens of her phone's camera. He dutifully drove her past the tech campuses she needed and parked while she wandered and dropped pins for her camera locations. Everything she did on set, crouching, crawling, balancing, she did out here, too. In heels and a skirt that showed way too much of her thigh for his sanity when she squatted down to set a shot. After taking what felt like a million shots, she finally climbed back into the cab and slumped in her seat.

"This is so much easier in gym shoes." She kicked off the offending heels and stretched her toes before tucking them beneath her. He maneuvered them onto the highway towards the coast, giving her a chance to rest a bit before he asked his next question.

"You said something about discussing my part on the show?"

She turned in her seat and tucked an ankle beneath her knee, clearly forgetting the fact that she was wearing a skirt. He tried not to swallow his tongue and pay attention.

"We want you to be the surprise element. Obviously, that's a shorter timeline than Rico as the jokester, but it has more potential past the life of the show."

"Wait, what are you talking about? What's the surprise?"

"Your singing. The Music Man. The Serenading Subcontractor. We're still working on the tag line. Jake loves it, and he wants to play up you singing on the job site as a personality showcase."

"No." He managed a hoarse whisper.

"The only hitch is song choice. Any chance you have a hidden songwriting talent? Original songs? Royalties and releases are going to kill us."

He cleared his throat and tried again.

"No."

"That's okay. We'll figure something out."

"No!" Before she could steamroll over his objection again, he put a hand on the thigh angled toward him, and her words trailed off. How could he explain?

"I told you, I don't sing."

"Of course you do. I heard you, and you were amazing."

"I sing for friends and to entertain myself. I don't sing on camera. And I'm certainly not going to sing for my supper in front of primetime America just to be some gimmick on your show." He slapped off the radio that suddenly felt mockingly chipper.

Trina sat back like he'd slapped her, eyes wide and jaw dropped. Winston turned his eyes back to the road, refusing to feel guilty for shutting her down. But he'd chased dreams with his talent once before, and he'd had to pull himself back up from rock bottom when he'd failed. He couldn't go there again.

"Sing something."

She lifted her phone from her lap and he froze. A cold sweat prickled his forehead in the hot truck, and his throat tightened.

"Just for me. Not for the show or anyone else. Just you and me. I want to show you what I see."

He tried to judge her intentions while keeping half an eye on the road. She was looking at him like she wanted to lick him top to bottom, and he was helpless to deny her. He drew in a shaky breath.

"Sing 'Creep' again."

"And you won't show anyone?"

"Only you."

Nodding, he opened his mouth and hesitantly began to sing an a cappella version of the rock ballad. She held her phone steady as her body began to sway to the music he made. Watching her get lost in his voice was intoxicating. He did his best to keep his attention on the road, but she kept shifting in her seat and drawing his eye. When he hit the second chorus, she raised her free hand to her neck before sliding it down to rest on the upper curve of her breast. He stuttered, and she slid her hand lower, teasing inside the low neckline of her tight t-shirt.

Rumble strips shook the car and his brain back into action. He jerked his eyes back to the road and swerved back into his lane.

"Keep singing." Her command was breathy, and her hand slid into her lap, brushing the top of her thigh where he'd touched her before. Was she imagining it was his hand again?

He manfully tried to pick up the next verse, but her hand inched up the edge of her skirt and her hand disappeared between her legs. His mouth went bone dry, and he choked on the words. He pulled off the road at the scenic overlook they were passing and slammed his truck into park, transmission be damned. He had to have his hands on her now.

He reached for her, and she undid her buckle and straddled his lap in a heartbeat, just as eager as he was.

She gripped his face between her hands and stared him down.

"You're not a creep or a weirdo. You are so fucking special. I'm not running anywhere." Then she kissed him, lips aggressively seeking his own. The memory of her lips that he'd been tending in his mind since yesterday was blown away by the reality. He hadn't pictured taking her in his truck, but never let it be said he wasn't flexible. She met him kiss for kiss, thrust for thrust, grinding her sweet core against his rock hard cock, making him curse the denim holding him prisoner.

311

Her ass was wedged against his steering wheel, and he took full advantage of her relative and willing captivity. He reached his hands under her shirt, needing to see, to touch, to taste her gorgeous breasts that had driven him crazy all morning, happily peeking out of her shirt.

When he discovered the lacy concoction that held them in place, he was surprised by the feminine detail, given her usual tomboy exterior, but so damn grateful for yet another erotic image to tuck away in his memory.

Lowering his head, he dusted kisses across her collarbone while his fingers tried to free her from the pink lace. One pert nipple escaped only to be captured by his lips seconds later. Her groans and the grip she had on his hair as she wrapped her arms around his head, holding him to the task, was all the encouragement he needed.

He was beyond thought, a mass of burning need. This woman wasn't afraid of his strength or his size. She was taking what he was giving and pushing him for more. He wanted to give it to her. The thought of giving it to her over and over until she cried out in pleasure almost set him off. He boosted her up, trying to get her skirt out of his way, and got distracted from his plan by her gorgeous bra-framed tits thrust up against his chin. When she leaned back to give him better access, he was derailed by a far less pleasant sensation. The blaring of his horn made them both jump. Startled back to reality, Trina clambered back to her side of the truck.

"This isn't working," she said, tugging her bra up and her shirt down. He hissed as she slid her skirt back down to her knees. His cock was not a happy camper. It took every ounce of restraint not to follow her to the other side of his cab. He closed his eyes and gripped the steering wheel reflexively as if that could keep him in check.

"Hey." Her voice called to him, soft and a little shy, and he opened his eyes. She had her purse and her phone in one hand tugging on the door handle and was pulling a moving blanket over the back of the seat with the other. "Are you coming?"

"Dear God, I hope so." He opened his glove box, snagged an emergency condom, and followed wherever she wanted to lead him.

CHAPTER 6

TRINA DIDN'T TURN around when she heard the truck door slam behind her. She knew Winston was right behind her, and if she saw him she was afraid she'd chicken out. She focused on the heat still throbbing insistently between her legs. She tucked her arm against her breasts, needing the pressure to hold on to the heavy pulsing pleasure he'd left behind.

She was trying desperately to keep her arousal going against the barrage of negative thoughts her brain was tossing in front of her, like landmines on the road to O-town. She wanted this. She wanted him and all of the things his massive hands promised her. When he was close enough to overwhelm her good sense, wonderful things happened. But every step from the heated haze of the truck allowed her mind to clear a little more, and her survival instinct kicked into overdrive.

All the things women were told to try and protect themselves in the big bad world flooded her mind. She'd repeated them to herself so often that it was impossible to ignore them now.

Don't go to remote places alone.
Don't leave with a guy you don't know.

Don't wear clothes that are easily removed.
Keep your cell phone with you.

She glanced down at the silent phone in her hand. Zero bars. Fuck.

She gathered her courage and turned to look at him, jumping when she found him so close. Christ, had he been that tall yesterday? She wasn't a short woman, and he towered over her. Her defenses rose instinctively, and she sidestepped his raised hand. She needed space to breathe. To hide. To run.

Nerves made her hands shake as she bundled the blanket in front of her. She desperately wanted to return to the safety of the truck and civilization. But she was suddenly afraid of what his reaction would be if she said no.

She stared blankly out at the steep hills covered in golden brush and evergreen pine and juniper descending to a reservoir, her artistic eye silent. She couldn't focus beyond him and her fear. After all, she'd gotten him all hot and bothered in the truck. She'd been as eager as he. How could she explain that she wasn't so sure she could handle this, now that the brisk breeze and bright sun had slapped her back to reality? She might have looked like a woman who could handle a casual tryst, but inside she was still the woman who had real scars and fears. How stupid to think that makeup and a different shirt had changed anything!

Trina girded herself for the coming conversation and mentally cursed her impulse control for getting them into this mess.

He came up behind her, his arms wrapping beneath her breasts as he bent his head and kissed the side of her neck. Panic flared and chased the goose bumps down her neck. Her breath stuck in her throat. He was so big. He could control her so easily. It hadn't scared her in a house full of people yesterday, but here, in the middle of nowhere, fear was winning. She froze, tempted to let him have his way as the easy way out. But she knew that regret was a cold bedfellow in the aftermath. She pushed at his arms and stepped forward, away from the wall of heat he was putting off. She let go of a breath shaky with relief when his hands dropped and slid into his pockets instead of grabbing for her.

"You okay?"

That simple question, spoken with such honest concern, nearly broke her. Gratitude flooded her eyes with tears, but she managed to keep them contained.

"No, I'm not okay. I thought I was, but all of a sudden this feels too fast."

"What changed in the two minutes since you were grinding on my lap in the truck?" He ran a hand roughly over his scalp and ruffled his hair even more than she had, but he didn't turn away from her explanation.

"I had a minute to think, and it just got scary."

"Fuck." He dropped his hand and his head. "I'm sorry. I didn't mean to frighten you. I know I'm a big guy, and the thing you said yesterday about going down on your knees...I got a little too excited."

"No!" she interrupted. She couldn't let him think that, not when everything had felt so good in the moment. "No, you didn't do anything wrong. I did. I don't...do this."

"What is 'this'?"

"Have casual sex with a man I barely know."

"My feelings for you are anything but casual, Trina." He reached for her hand, and it felt ice cold inside his warm grasp. She fought panic and was grateful for his loose grip. "I've never fallen for a girl this fast, but there's something about you. I know that going so fast can feel scary, but I promise I would never do anything to hurt you. I can wait."

∼

SHE WRAPPED her arms around herself, as if trying to hold herself together, and spoke into the space between them. "I'm sorry. Just walking up here, to a secluded spot on a mountain side, with a man…It's not smart." Winston felt his heart drop into his shoes, along with his erection. Nothing about the feelings he had for her was rational. It didn't change the fact that they were there and taking quite the beating at the moment.

"And you try to be smart."

"I sure don't try to be stupid. And I haven't had good experiences when I ignore my gut."

"That's a loaded statement." He walked over to a wooden bench facing the gorgeous view of the California wilderness. Keeping his eyes forward and his bulk on his half of the bench, he patted the empty space next to him.

"Want to tell me about it?"

"It was a long time ago."

"Whatever it was, it seems like it's still bothering you. I'd like to know, so I don't put that fear in your eyes ever again." People had always judged him an athlete or a bruiser, the distinction often depending on when he'd last shaved. They tended to forget there was a vulnerable human inside the impressive exterior. In his youth, he'd gone along with it, playing into those assumptions. Now, it all felt false, and he hated that no one could see the real him. He wanted Trina to be the one who saw him, and she couldn't do that if she was afraid. When she tentatively sat next to him, he counted it a small win. She wrapped the blue quilted moving blanket around her shoulders and spoke into the canyon, not meeting his eyes.

"I was almost done with college, and I'd just gotten an internship on a different reality show. I was basically an unpaid gopher, but I was excited to hang out with the camera guys and learn by watching. Everyone asked, 'Why do you want to haul heavy equipment around with a bunch of smelly guys all day?' But I love capturing stories through my lens. It's the way I see my world, so why not make a career of it and prove that women can do it just as well as men? Break glass ceilings, kick down doors, and all that…"

She trailed off, and Winston could tell she was getting to the part of the story she didn't like remembering. He offered his hand, laying it open next to her on the bench if she needed it.

When she took it, he felt the brief squeeze of thanks from his fingertips all the way to his heart. That she could accept his comfort, if not his passion, made him feel like less of a monster. After a lifetime of being valued for his size and strength, it felt good to be needed for his compassion. One little hand resting in his, trusting him, made him feel like a hero.

"I'm not stupid. I knew going in that I would be working in a male dominated field. I knew about casting couches and blow job interviews. But of course, forewarned is forearmed. I figured that wasn't going to happen to me. Until it did."

Her eyes were aimed steadfastly at the distant horizon, but he doubted she was seeing any of the rugged California wilderness. He held his silence, giving her time and space to continue. He didn't like where this was heading, but he'd asked to hear it, so he'd listen.

"I finally got up the nerve to ask the Director of Cinematography on the project to let me shadow one of the veteran cameramen who'd taken me under his wing a little. The DC asked what I was going to give him for the privilege. I tried to laugh it off, but it was clear what he was implying. I knew it was wrong. I knew I didn't want to do that. But he was a very powerful man in the industry, and if I ever wanted to make it into TV or the movies, his name backing me would have been a golden ticket. So I laughed again and tried to joke it away. When he kept pushing, I backed down and left, without getting my permission to shadow. It felt like my first big failure. I knew I'd chosen right, but I had taken that job to learn, and now that wouldn't be happening. I questioned my decision over and over, until that decision no longer mattered.

"He found me alone that night, sorting and organizing the equipment van. He pushed his way inside and shut the door. He had me cornered. He made me... he..." The words caught in her throat, and she began to shake.

"You don't have to say it." Winston regretted ever bringing it up. No woman should have to tell these stories.

"Yes, I do. I need to get it out. He made me touch him. He made me make him come before he would let me out of the van. And he talked the whole time. He told me I was pretty, a real distraction. He told me he'd been watching me, noticing my attraction to him. He would give me what I wanted if I did a good job. That I'd never work in the industry again if I didn't. That no one would believe me if I told. But if I kept quiet and made him happy, I could have it all."

Winston wanted to beat this man to a pulp. His fists wanted to clench and flex, mimicking the way he would punch the bastard in the balls. But her hand was still trembling in his, so he kept his impulses under control. The last thing he wanted was for her to think he was anything like that monster.

"What did you do?"

"I cleaned up, I cried buckets, and I followed that cameraman around like glue. I was determined to learn, and then I could get the hell out. What else could I do? Everything else felt impossible. I wasn't eating or sleeping, but I couldn't afford to fall apart and I couldn't risk telling. It was my big chance.

"Then the jokes started on set, guys making sly comments about my body or trying to grab me, guys who had never noticed me before. Apparently, he'd been bragging, and these guys thought that made me fair game. So who was going to believe me?"

"I believe you."

She turned to look at him, and he fought with every ounce of restraint to not pull her into a bone-crushing hug. His self-control paid off when she scooted closer to him and laid her head on his shoulder.

"The season wrapped up and my internship was over, and I thought that would be the end of it. But when I graduated, I had zero offers. No one would even return my call. Except for him. He hired me to do his next show, and I worked there for five years. He owned me."

"Jesus, Trina! How did you get through that?"

"I made myself one of the guys. Baggy shirts, old jeans, always buy the first round. The older guys took me in, and the rumors died. I kept my head down, made sure I was never alone with him, and honed my craft. And when this opportunity came by to work with an ambitious young producer on a spec project, I jumped. Jake promised me a step up and a way out. If I nail this series, he's going to recommend me to his buddies doing films. I will never have to look that smug asshole in the eye again. Win-win."

CHAPTER 7

Winston sat silent, trying to absorb everything she'd said and find words for an unspeakable situation. The toughest thing he'd ever had to do professionally was walk on to a football field, assured in the knowledge that the other team would try their best to beat the crap out of him. But he'd trained and studied and had accepted that as terms of his game. At the height of his career, he'd been able to bench press twice his own weight. He'd been hit by three hundred pounds of angry linebacker and walked away grinning. And he still couldn't comprehend the level of strength this woman possessed.

She'd not only found the courage to chase her dreams through closed doors, but she'd faced down her abuser every morning for five years. She didn't have his bulk or his reputation to hide behind. How had she managed it? She hadn't let the asshole win, and she'd become a damn fine camera operator along the way.

Hell, he couldn't even find the balls to sing for the show. She had more courage in her pinkie finger than he had in his whole body, and it put him to shame. She might not believe it herself, but his Valkyrie was fierce. He wavered between admiring her strength and wanting to protect her. He fought an overwhelming desire to beat the shit out of any man who'd ever hurt her.

"I'm sorry." Her voice was soft and full of regret.

"Huh? Why the hell are you apologizing to me?" He turned to look at her, truly confused. She worried the edge of the blanket between her fingers. He touched her hand and waited to speak until she looked him in the eye. "You have nothing to apologize for."

"But I kissed you and then got you all excited driving up here." She glanced away and her shaky hands tugged at her t-shirt hem and his heartstrings. Words tumbled over each other as she tried to explain. "It's the first time I've felt anything for anyone in years, and I got carried away. Your voice does something to me... And then I freaked out and dumped all of this on you. I'm sure this isn't what you expected on this afternoon drive."

"Oh really? I've been hoping to get to know you better for weeks. Mission accomplished. I'm sorry that you've had to deal with all this shit for years. I... Is there... God, I don't know what to say... You are just... You are the strongest person I have ever met. How can I make it better? I want to. I can't find the right words here, but I wish I could take away all that pain."

He lifted his arm when she snuggled closer, and she curled into his side. Her shivering was thankfully receding beneath his fingers stroking down her arm. His eyes were drawn to a uniquely shaped tree along the ridge line. A coastal cypress, its trunk twisted by buffeting winds cresting the peak, reached toward the blue sky, but its roots were anchored deep. Its size and shape were testament to the number of years that it had endured its harsh environment and thrived. He wondered if she could see her inner strength mirrored there as clearly as he could.

She was still quietly tucked into his side, and he was content. He'd thought she was done with the conversation, needing the time and space to recover, when she surprised him by replying.

"There's nothing that can take it away completely, but the fact that you want to means a lot to me. The fact that you can make me forget and focus only on pleasure feels like a gift." She turned to face him then, her eyes glittering in the waning afternoon sunlight. He was relieved to see that her earlier panic and tears were nowhere to be seen. Her eyes glittered with an infinitely more scary emotion he didn't dare name. But he couldn't deny the way her gaze warmed his heart. And other regions. This was getting serious again, and if she wanted to keep space between them, he needed to backpedal. He could admit he was nearing the end of his restraint.

"You can unwrap me whenever you like." He joked, trying to find a safe path back from her treacherous memories. She laughed with her whole body, a joyous release of her tension, and he fell. Anything. This brave, strong, sexy siren could ask him for anything, and he'd give it happily while dashing himself against the rocks. She turned her body and tucked her legs across his lap, before raising a hand to his neck.

"Do you mean that?"

"Whatever you need."

"Do you think you could sing to me again?"

He cleared his throat. No song choice for karaoke had ever felt like the fate of his soul was riding on it. His brain had gone completely blank. She started to slide away, disappointed, but he stopped her with a gentle squeeze of his arm that was still around her shoulders. He could only imagine what she was thinking...Ah-ha!

"Each day through my window..." He poured his heart into the song of watching and wanting. He imagined that Trina really was his girl. Every word spoke his desire, and she was listening, hearing everything he couldn't say. The Temptations were living up to their name. As he continued to croon about wanting a future with this woman, he watched her face soften with trust and desire. She shifted in her spot, trying to get comfortable.

Slowly, she reached for the top buttons on his shirt, and he stumbled over a line.

Her nimble fingers worked quickly down the front of his work shirt and tugged his white undershirt impatiently from his jeans. She ran her hands over his abs and up to his pecs, before straddling his lap. She'd resumed their position from the truck, and he could only hope that meant she wanted to resume their activities, too. She draped the blue blanket over her shoulders, shrouding them both in a makeshift tent, hiding their intimacy from the world.

She leaned forward and kissed the edge of his jaw before whispering in his ear.

"Keep singing."

Her husky voice shot straight to his cock, and he obeyed. He'd promised her anything she needed, and he was a man of his word. Her chilled hands pushing his undershirt up until it bunched beneath his armpits made his voice shiver through the end of the chorus. He wanted to run away with her, away from prying eyes and insane shows and painful pasts. He wanted to drop to his knees and worship her until she answered his prayers. When she lowered her lips to his chest, he simply wanted.

Winston had never been this turned on in his life. The way she rocked her hips against him was almost painful for the pleasure it sent shooting up his spine. When the song ended, he started another to try and distract himself. Maybe if he kept half his brain on lyrics and notes, the other half wouldn't focus too clearly on where her hands were going. He wanted to give her the power to take what she needed. That meant keeping his own needs in check until she asked for them, though it just might kill him.

Peter Gabriel gave him the words to say what he felt looking in her eyes. As he gasped for air in the spaces between the lines, he reached for her with his voice. She reached back with her touch, her light, her heat, until she took his mouth with hers, silencing his salvation. He was lost in her. It was a damn good thing she no longer needed him to sing, because when she slid her hand into the waistband of his jeans and gripped his cock, he lost the ability to form thoughts and words entirely.

He rested his hands on her hips, needing to touch her, to be with her in this moment, but he held back on squeezing or pulling her closer where he wanted her, afraid of triggering bad memories. He hated that the asshole was still between them. No, he couldn't second-guess like that. He'd go mad. But he could let her have the lead as long as she wanted.

And she wanted. Her movements became frantic as she tried to touch all of him at once. He tried to soothe her with kisses, but she refused to calm down. She tugged at his zipper and his jeans, until he lifted his hips and shoved them down to his knees. He lowered his now bare ass to the wooden bench.

"Is that what you wanted, Kat?" His cock rose proudly between them, bouncing against her lower belly, demanding her attention.

She grinned and slid off his lap, lowering her lips to continue charting new territory. Her hands eagerly explored his bare length and girth, while she kissed her way to his cock. The feel of her tongue gliding up from the base of his shaft to his dripping, sensitive head loosened his control over his own tongue, and every dirty thought he had came spilling out of his mouth. "Are you going to take me hard and fast? Or do you like it slow and dirty? Whatever you want, it's yours." She smiled and answered by closing those gorgeous lips around him and slowly pulling him in. His fantasies couldn't hold a candle to the reality of her hot mouth around his aching rod.

"Is that what my voice does to you? Does it make you all hot and horny?" She sucked him into the back of her throat, and he gasped, "Fuck, that feels good. Does it feel good for you, beautiful? Licking my cock. Driving me out of my mind." She reached lower to tug and toy with his balls and his hips jerked off the bench without a warning. "God, your hands. I'll do anything you want. Just don't stop."

She groaned in response, unable to speak around his cock, and the vibrations went straight through him. It was too much. He pulled his hips back and broke the seal of her lips around him, the cold air hitting his wet shaft and making him hiss. He needed to slow down, or he was going to blow like a fucking teenager.

"Please!" he begged.

"Please, what?" she asked, her eyes never leaving his twitching member.

"Condom. Back pocket. Or I won't last long enough for you."

His hands were cramping from gripping the edge of the bench so he didn't grip her head instead. No way could he handle unwrapping a condom in this state. He prayed for her mercy. When she had finally rolled on the latex barrier, he let go a sigh of relief. Her touch against his bare skin had been too intense, and he didn't want to ruin this for her.

"Thanks. Okay, you can go back to using me for my body now."

"Is that what you think I'm doing?" Hurt and shame filled her voice, and she rocked back on her heels.

He raised his hands to her face, pulling her up and into his lap, babbling like the idiot he was.

"No. Shit, I'm sorry." He kissed her neck and breathed in that floral scent of hers. "I'm in this with you, right here. I make stupid jokes when I'm nervous, and I am so fucking nervous of screwing this up. I just want you to take what you need. Tell me what you need, Kat. Let me give you what you need."

CHAPTER 8

WHAT DID SHE NEED? She needed to feel whole, to feel seen, to feel in control but free. And here was this big burly man willing to give that to her if she was brave enough to ask. When he called her Kat, the nickname she'd always hated, her pulse throbbed in response. He was reclaiming all kinds of pain from her past with his velvet voice and rough hands. She wanted him to be the one to bring her back to life.

"I want to touch you." As she spoke, she stood and slid her hands over his shoulders. She tested her power, pushing his unbuttoned shirt down to his elbows, trapping his arms at his sides. "I don't want you to touch me until I say."

"Okay." He grinned and tucked his hands beneath his thighs. "What else?"

Trina leaned back and whipped off her t-shirt. Reaching back to undo her skirt zipper thrust her breasts forward, and she loved the way his eyes went glassy.

"Do you like those?"

He nodded, leaning forward ever so slightly. She clucked her tongue, and he immediately sat back. She inched the skirt up her thighs, before dropping it altogether.

"Good boy, you've earned a reward for obeying." She tucked her fingers beneath the edge of her lacy bra and pulled the sheer fabric down until her breasts spilled out over her underwire. She was grateful that this small reminder of her femininity still fit. She'd always enjoyed the way it made her feel in private. Now, she was enjoying the way it made a lover feel, and it was even better.

"Why don't you show me how much you like them?"

She climbed back on his lap and leaned forward, suspending her breasts in front of his face, daring him to please her. When he leaned forward and trapped her nipple between his lips, she felt the tugging desire all the way to her core. Only one layer of thin cotton and one layer of thinner latex separated them. She rocked her clit against his hard length, teasing them both. She may have been sidelined for five long years, but she still remembered how to play the game.

"Mmm, that feels good. You know what else would feel good?" She wove her fingers into his hair and tugged his head back. He released her breast with a loud pop, and shook his head.

"Tell me."

"It would feel so good to have you lick my pussy."

He stood up so quickly she almost fell off his lap. He laid the blanket on the bench for her, before kneeling in the dirt at her feet.

She tugged off her panties and laid back to enjoy. The warm sun was no competition for the heat pulsing through her body, and she was turned on as hell by the idea that someone might come across them. Winston, half-naked and all aroused with the rugged outdoors behind him, tucked his hands between his thighs and calves. He had remembered her request; that alone about did her in. Then he bent his head slowly, reverently, over one knee and started to kiss his way north.

"My Kitty Kat needs her pussy licked? Does she like it slow or fast?" He leaned in to give her a sample of each, running his wide tongue over her quivering slit.

"Slow." She was getting off on watching him explore. In her head, she began to compose the scene. She gave in to her creative impulse and reached for her phone.

"And does she like to be licked soft or hard?" Again he demonstrated, running his tongue over her clit in a whisper light pass that tickled and unleashed a squeal and bucking hips.

"Hard! Please, harder." Having this man asking her preferences and then serving them up on a silver platter was too good to be true. She angled the camera to better capture the gleam in his eye as he rested his head against her inner thigh and gazed at her core. When he looked directly into the camera and begged, she nearly came without him.

"May I use my hands now? Please? Fuck, Kat, let me pet your pretty pussy."

"Yes, you may."

One large hand slid beneath her ass, kneading and lifting her into position. The other deftly teased one, then two fingers into her tight sheath, stealing her breath. She knew she would hear her own gasps of pleasure in the video, and she would come on the spot when she watched this again. She snapped a few stills, but it was the action of this man devoting himself to her pleasure that she wanted to be able to relive again and again, even once this insane and magical interlude was over.

"Are you recording me?"

Talky, talky, enough of that.

"Shh. This looks amazing. I'm going to watch it later and make myself come."

"No fair. I want to watch it with you and make us both come."

"That can be arranged." She looked at the phone. The shot of her breasts free, her nipples hard and aching, reaching for the brightest blue sky framed the action. Her belly clenched and relaxed as his head rose and fell between her legs. His fingers inside her felt amazing, but it was the look on his face that pushed her over the edge of her climax. She tried to hold the phone steady, but she was shaking so badly she knew she wouldn't win any awards for this camera work.

Not that she would ever show this footage to anyone. The very idea triggered her fears and tamped down the tail end of her orgasm.

When she unclenched her thighs from around his head, he rose up into frame grinning and pulled her focus back to him. God. She knew she was going to need a screenshot of that grin for her personal archives.

"What next?" he asked.

"Sit back down." She pushed herself up and offered him some of the blanket. When he was settled, she sat on his lap facing the sunset. She needed to let her pussy calm down a little before round two. She set her phone down, determined to enjoy the rest of this experience with no distance between them. As tempting as it was to hide behind her lens and her art, she wanted to be with him, present in the moment and free.

And at that moment, his hard cock was present and insistent. She moved a bit and felt him slide along the crease of her ass. Maybe she wouldn't need much time before the next round.

"Give me the camera." His raspy voice sounded forced.

"Why?" Putting it aside by choice was one thing, handing control over to someone else was quite another.

"Because your ass sliding against my cock is fucking beautiful, and you can't see it. Let me show you what *I* see."

He had a point, and she couldn't argue against her own words. She handed her phone over her shoulder and stroked a few more times. She felt his short hot breaths on her shoulder, and the gasps and groans that escaped him made her giddy with power. She teased him until she couldn't take it anymore and lifted up enough to bring the tip of his cock in line with her desperate slit.

"I want to fuck you now."

"God, please. Yes, Kat, yes."

She lowered down slowly, filling herself with his thick heat. She grinned knowing that his heartfelt moan and curse would be captured on film, ready for her to play back any time. She turned that grin over her shoulder to check in, and found the camera focused on her face and not where they were connected so intimately.

"You are so damn beautiful." He whispered, as if afraid to break the spell of the moment. Trina turned back around, a little afraid of the emotion she'd seen glittering in his eyes. She didn't want to think about emotions right now. She wanted to drive herself and him out of their minds completely.

She rode him, hard and fast, determined to lose herself in the rhythm of their bodies. Gone were the forested mountains or the sparkling water before her. Work was completely forgotten. She was mindlessly driven by pleasure. Pleasure that stayed just out of reach. She moaned her frustrations into the canyon ahead of her. He stilled beneath her.

"You okay? What's wrong?"

"I can't come like this." She looked over her shoulder fearing his frustration, but the concern in his eyes soothed her.

"Do you trust me, Kat? Do you trust me to make this good?"

He wasn't looking at the screen of the phone he was aiming at her. He was looking at her, straight in the eye, his own full of hope and need.

"I do."

"Here. Take this and lie down." He handed her the phone she no longer cared about and helped her up. His speed gave voice to his own rising desires. She kept the camera rolling, but she stopped looking at it. He captivated all of her attention. The way he straightened the blanket and picked her up so gently before laying her down on the bench, it all spoke straight to her heart and she was undone.

When he entered her again, he was a man driven. Each thrust

drove home with intent. Yes, this was what she needed. His intense focus turned her inside out, exposing her needs to the bright sunshine. Needing to capture that expression, she turned the phone slightly and chuckled.

This would be the first porno with only a face shot of the climax.

"As amazing as that feels around my cock, this is kind of a bad time to laugh, you know."

She laughed again and nodded when he raised one eyebrow at her response.

"Having trouble concentrating, are we? Let's see what I can do to hold your attention." His words were teasing, but his actions were direct. One hand on her breast, the other sliding a work-roughened thumb intently over her sensitive clit in rhythm with his thrusts, he drove her to delirium. The time for playful banter was over.

"Take me, Kat. Take all of me. Let me give you what you need." He gasped as he leaned down to replace his hand with his mouth, sucking hard on her nipple, sending shockwaves directly to her clit. It had been so long since her body had felt this kind of pleasure that she was completely overwhelmed.

Unlike the last time, these hands weren't pushing or forcing. For all their strength, they were gently insistent that she relax and enjoy the feeling they were pulling from her body.

How could she refuse such a compelling invitation?

His hips increased their speed, and she dropped the camera to her chest, too weak to keep it focused, too consumed to care. Her eyes rolled skyward as the second wave of climax crashed over her, pulling her senses down in the undertow. She tumbled beneath the onslaught of pleasure. Three short thrusts, and he joined her beneath the waves.

She wouldn't need the video to remember the way this moment felt.

THE AFTERNOON HAD FADED to evening while they'd played, the sun diving behind the mountain at their back and bringing the coastal chill along with it. They dressed, eventually, and Trina beckoned him to join her back on the bench beneath his ratty moving blanket. That old stained utility sheet had never looked so good. She leaned her head on his shoulder as night settled around them. Golds and purples faded to indigo, and he enjoyed the quiet pleasure of being with her, knowing that she trusted him to stay close.

Until she turned to him with her phone and said, "I want you to watch this."

"If you want a replay, all you have to do is ask," he teased.

She smacked him playfully on the arm and laughed.

"Not that video. This one." She tapped her screen, and his voice came flowing out of her tiny speakers. He wanted to look anywhere but at that screen.

She was unrelenting.

"Watch it. See what *I* see. An amazing performer with the voice of an angel. A voice so powerful it makes me forget everything else from the first note."

He couldn't deny her anything, not after her bravery in opening up to him. So he searched deep for some of his own courage and opened his eyes.

Watching himself on camera had always been torture. He'd had to watch hours of game footage, dissecting his every mistake, every nuance of his performance on the football field. Old habits died hard, and his critique filters snapped into place. His breathing quickened in his chest, and he lost his contented smile to an automatic frown.

She paused the video and bumped him with her elbow.

"Whatever you're thinking, whatever put that scowl on your face, knock it off! Look at it through my eyes."

She started the clip again. He heard himself singing, but it was the filming that captivated him. The way she focused on his lips, his eyes, before panning back out to get his full torso, the slight wobble and inhaled gasp when he looked right into the camera, and the rumble and shake as he nearly drove them off the road.

"Can you see it? How incredible you are? Your voice could melt glaciers. Forget global warming. You're dangerous."

"Ha ha." He could feel the blush climbing his neck at her praise.

"I'm serious. Let me use this. Let me show the world the Singing Subcontractor."

"I'll think about it. The idea of people I don't know hearing me, judging me, still gives me hives. What if they hate it? What if they laugh?"

"Then, fuck them because they don't recognize talent when they hear it. What are you really afraid of?"

He drew in a deep breath and searched her eyes for some scrap of strength he could hold on to. She'd humbled him earlier, sharing her darkest struggles. She deserved nothing less than his full honesty. For years he'd been conditioned to never show fear, never be weak, never fail. His weakness had stolen his dream. It was not to be tolerated. He was only just beginning to see that being vulnerable with someone took a tremendous amount of strength. The way she believed in him made him want to be worthy.

Could he share this deep-seated fear with someone who had already seen so much so quickly? She'd overcome her fear and trusted him with her body. Could he do the same with his heart?

The steady regard in her gaze encouraged him to summon the courage to share his history. She was worth trying for.

"I pinned my hopes on my talent once before, and I lost. I flunked out of college and lost my scholarship and my spot on the football team. I was even lucky enough to score a second chance, and I played on a semi-pro team. I almost had a professional football career, but I blew out my knee and lost that dream for good. It took me a long time to recover from that loss. Now, I have a safe, calm life that keeps me fed and housed. No one is judging me, telling me I suck, finding me wanting. I'm a just big guy who's good with my hands."

"You can say that again," she sighed, and he chuckled at her attempt to lighten the mood.

"I risked a lot before, and I failed spectacularly. I don't know if I could survive a crash like that again."

"But what if you succeed? Don't say no. Consider the possibilities. You're too talented to hide behind a hammer and a hard hat."

"I'll think about it."

CHAPTER 9

THE NEXT MORNING, Trina woke and stretched, pleasantly sore from the night before. Winston had driven her back to the job site to pick up her car, and then she'd followed him home. Rounds three and four had been just as phenomenal. It had been after two when she'd finally stumbled, lust drunk, into her own bed.

She wasn't used to any of this, so she took an extra moment to relish the sensation of an exhausted morning after, before reaching for her phone.

At some point last night, she'd changed her home screen to a cropped image of his I-just-made-you-scream grin, and she smiled back stupidly before unlocking her phone and checking her social media. As usual, the pages for the projects she'd worked on loaded first.

When her footage of Winston wiring a wall with his back to the camera popped up, she sat straight up in bed and tapped for sound. He'd been singing "Creep" that day. She would never forgive Rico for talking over that audio. But in this video, he was singing Mumford & Sons like he had before their first kiss. It didn't take long for her to realize that Jake must have cut this together from what he had. She felt a punch in the gut when Winston turned to smile at the camera, cutting off the song, before it faded to black. That smile. Her smile. The one she wasn't likely to see ever again once he got wind of this.

"Catch the Singing Contractor on Million Dollar Starter Home!" read the post. She opened the full video on YouTube to check the stats. Jake must be really confident in her ability to convince Winston to do this if he was releasing the teasers already. Four thousand views since it had been posted at four a.m. Three hours and he was already going viral. Fuck. She had to fix this.

～

TRINA ROLLED into work seventeen minutes later. Given that the drive to their current set took twelve minutes, she was looking every bit as rough as a five-minute prep the morning after would suggest. She strode into the craft services area, eyes for one man only. Jake Ryland.

She knew he needed a ridiculous amount of coffee in the morning to function on the scraps of sleep he managed, so the breakfast spread was a solid bet. Her hunch paid off.

There he was, chugging down the steaming black beverage, like a marathoner gulps electrolytes.

"Hey. We've got a problem."

He finished his cup and poured another before he replied, as he pulled his chiming cell phone from his pocket.

"Oh, really? What's that?" He texted at the speed of light with one thumb, while he slurped at the screaming hot beverage in his other hand. The man never stopped. She was going to have to talk fast if she wanted to hold his attention.

"That video you pulled together is going viral."

"I think we need to work on your definition of 'problem.' I know I had to Frankenscene it a little, but surely you're not

337

worried about a little sloppy video. Thanks." He took a binder handed off by one the production assistants and tucked it under his arm, before he turned and walked away from her. She followed right behind. This was too important to drop.

"No, I'm worried because I hadn't convinced Winston to let us use that angle yet. This is going to blow up in our faces." They walked into the hub, the trailer full of camera feeds where Jake spent most of his day. She had seconds before his day began and consumed all of his thoughts.

"No, it's not. Once he sees the view count, he'll jump at the chance to be famous."

"I don't think that…" How could she explain her fears without giving away Winston's secrets? She didn't have a chance to figure it out before Jake rolled right over her words, finally giving her his full attention. It took all of her strength not to take a step back from his intensity.

"And if he doesn't, tough shit. Everyone signed an agreement that any and all footage obtained can be used unless they checked the blur box. He didn't. So I can put whatever footage you get wherever I want."

"I don't feel good about this. He's going to be so upset."

Jake rubbed his forehead and grimaced like a grown man trying to reason with a three year old. The exaggerated patience in his voice made her feel like a child.

"I don't care how he feels and neither should you. He's a man with a silver hammer and a golden voice, and that is fucking money, but he's not irreplaceable. Do you know how many singers I could ask to come fill his empty spot on the crew?"

"But that's not…"

"Do you know how many camera operators I could ask to fill yours?" He let that threat hang in the silence of her shock. "Listen, McAllister. I took a chance on you because Bill Montauk said you were hungry and tough as nails. Don't let your attraction make you forget whose side you're on."

"Who said I was attracted?"

Jake leaned over and cued up the viral clip. He pushed play and paused it at the smile.

"Tell me you weren't grinning back at him."

She couldn't lie, so she bit her tongue.

"That's what I thought. I'm counting on you, Trina, to make this show shine. Get the shots I need. Hollywood doesn't have room for your feelings."

With that less than subtle reminder, he took another sip of coffee and turned back to his precious monitors. Conversation over. Shit. He was right. He had the rights to every bit of footage for the show. He could distribute it wherever he liked. And millions of women were going to fall for Winston singing in that voice and smiling *her* smile. And Winston was going to hate her for it.

WINSTON WALKED into work amid hoots and hollers and requests for his autograph. He saw everyone on the crew, except the one person he wanted to find. The one person he wanted to kiss and curse at the same time. Rico had woken him up from a very pleasant dream involving this person using her talented tongue on his cock to tell him about the video. Seeing Trina's betrayal online while he was still hard and wanting her in his bed made it even worse.

He'd watched the video through once and cringed at every note. His hands tingled, and his head swam. He fought the urge to smash his phone against the wall.

He'd told her he wasn't ready. He'd told her why. Jesus, he'd let her film him fucking her. Apparently, his trust had been misplaced. Was she going to sell him out to a porn site, too? Spinning from arousal to betrayal to paranoia and finally to vengeance made his stomach churn.

He had to find her.

His phone buzzed in his pocket, and he ignored it. It had been chiming all morning ever since Rico had so helpfully tagged him in the video. His notifications were going crazy. He couldn't bring himself to look, much less figure out how to turn them off, afraid he'd see something that couldn't be unseen.

What if they were all laughing? God, he looked ridiculous singing into a stud wall. And that goofy grin at the end? He didn't want to think about how stupid it made him look. And he didn't think that was the song he'd been singing either. He needed to find Trina and get the damn thing taken down.

He finally tracked her down out by the equipment truck prepping rigs for the day.

"What the fuck, Trina?" He noticed the way she backed away from his anger, but was too riled up to care. "I told you I didn't want this."

"I didn't…"

He cut her off, unable to listen to lies from the first person he'd been honest with.

"You didn't what? Didn't deliberately film me singing without my knowledge? Didn't manipulate my emotions to get more footage? Didn't trick me into doing something I didn't want to do?"

She turned away from him and spoke to her cameras as she checked batteries and memory cards. Her spine straightened, and she bit out her next words with careful calm.

"You signed a contract. It's my job to get the footage Jake needs." Somehow, she'd managed to raise her shields while his laid in rubble at his feet, and his anger pushed him to lash out, to bring her down with him.

"So that's all this was to you? Another stepping-stone on your way out of television?" He lowered his voice to a whisper, beyond caring when his voice cracked with pain. Now that he'd opened up to vulnerability, he was finding it very hard to shut that door again. Her actions whipped at his newfound hope and felt every lash. "I don't think you needed to go so far as fucking me to get what you wanted. Unless that's footage Jake wanted, too."

"Stop, Winston. Don't do this." Tears welled in her eyes as she turned back to face him, and she raised her hands intending to put them on his chest. He wavered, both craving and dreading her next move.

"I'm pretty sure that's what I said to you about filming me singing."

"Hey Trina, have you got those cameras ready, yet?" Jake's voice called from around the van and reminded Winston who she was and why he couldn't trust her. He stepped a healthy distance away from her.

"I trusted you, Trina, and you sold me out. I hope it was worth it."

"Winston! Wait!" But he couldn't wait, couldn't stay and listen to more lies. He'd laid himself bare, emotionally and literally. He wasn't going to stay and let her flay him with more excuses. There was no excusing what she'd done.

CHAPTER 10

TRINA TURNED BACK to her cameras on auto-pilot. Her hands went through the motions but her mind was a million miles away, safe behind her shields. Years of honing her ability to work while emotionally shattered came to her rescue. She was confident that no one around her could see that her heart had been demolished, a pile of shattered stone clattering around in her chest. Winston's words of doubt and anger had hit like twin sledgehammers, each punishing blow making her feel smaller and smaller.

He'd gotten so close, so quickly. She hadn't been prepared to protect herself.

She meticulously loaded crates into the back of the crew van and rounded up the guys on her roster today. She drove in silence, barely registering the happy banter in the back, as she dropped the guys off at her various scouted locations and tried to hold herself together. Winston had every right to be mad at her. True, he'd signed contracts with Jake, and she'd only been following orders. But he'd asked her not to film him singing until he was ready and had trusted that she hadn't. His fear was a real and powerful thing. She understood not wanting to leave the garden and reach for the tempting fruit, when the sneaky serpent had already bitten once. Hadn't she put her head down and dealt with abusive crap for five years, because striking out again had felt too damn scary?

If only she'd been able to warn him. If only she'd convinced him sooner. If only he could see his talent through her eyes. The *if only's* chased around her head while she chased around town dropping off the last of her crew.

Finally alone with her thoughts, Trina pulled up to the scenic overlook. She scanned the rugged beauty of their spot that she'd missed seeing yesterday. *Their spot.* It was no coincidence she had chosen to film this area by herself. She felt too vulnerable here to bring another man with her. No, there was only one man she wanted to see her that open, and he'd just walked away.

Everything had seemed so bright and new yesterday that she'd been blinded to everything else. Warm sun and blue skies had filled her vision, while Winston had filled her mind and body, but she hadn't really processed the natural beauty surrounding them. Today, that task was made challenging by a thick gray fog that blanketed all but the nearest peak, increasing the illusion that she was truly alone.

While she set her time-lapse camera to capture the eventual dramatic fog burn off, she reminded herself that the weather was not a reflection of her internal turmoil. This wasn't a metaphor or a sign from God or anything but the marine layer, even though the gray and chill seemed to seep from the inside out.

She considered leaving. She could get back in the van and just drive, leaving all of her worries behind her. A waitressing gig at a roadside diner, sleeping in the truck for a few nights, she'd land on her feet. But Trina had never quit on a dream in her life, and she wasn't about to start now. Even if Winston was content to leave things broken, she was going to try and fix this mess. It had been years since she'd felt anything close to these emotions for a man, and she couldn't let him walk away without a fight.

Even if Winston wanted nothing more to do with her, she needed him to see and hear what she captured through her lenses. He was amazing. His voice was untouchable, and his charisma fairly burned up the screen. The video was up to over ten thousand views and the comments were on fire. She could tell him from personal experience how his voice poured through her like smelted gold, filling in the cracks in her soul, repairing the damage and making her flaws all the more beautiful in the process. But after today, she doubted he'd listen to her opinion on anything...

But would he listen to someone else?

A plot began to take shape in her mind, connections snapping across synapses at the speed of light. She finished with her cameras and sat down on the bench where he'd made love to her only the day before. Made love. That's what it had felt like, if she was honest with herself.

She pulled up all of the videos she'd shot the day before torturing herself with his seductive voice and that smile that still had the power to turn her inside out. Cutting together song clips from all of them to create a quick demo reel, she made sure she cropped any sensitive footage, and tried to showcase his range. Damn, his voice was powerful. She kept forgetting that she was supposed to be editing and watched the whole clip to the end.

When she got to the video they'd shot on the bench, she couldn't look away. She had been right. The look on his face after he'd gone down on her was hot enough to melt her to the bench all over again. Trying to find relief from her suddenly sensitive skin, Trina squirmed on the bench, but that only made it worse. She had known that this video would shoot her right back to the edge on the replay. Her hands rose of their own volition, to stroke and soothe her neck, her breasts, lower, following his lead. But touching herself without him felt wrong. She'd wanted to share this pleasure with him. Nothing helped ease her desire.

When the view switched and she saw herself through his eyes, it shook her to her core. The way he held the camera, the way he framed her in the shot, spoke volumes. He'd taken a little video of his glide and penetration, and she couldn't deny that the sight of his long cock sliding against her pale ass before disappearing inside of her was one of the most erotic things she'd ever seen. She was glad she'd relented and given him the phone. But then he focused on the curve of her hip, the bumps along her spine, and finally her face as she turned around. He took her breath away, showing her how sexy he found every inch of her with her own lens. And the look on her face...*oh shit, I fell in love.*

She couldn't deny it. She'd truly opened herself up to him, and it showed on her face. Trina couldn't remember the last time she'd felt so sexy or safe. Probably never. And now she'd gone and screwed things up by doing her job and leaving him vulnerable in the process. But she could fix it. Or at least she could try. He deserved so much better than he'd gotten, and she hated to think of how she'd hurt him. Maybe if she could help him feel better, someday she'd be able to forgive herself and start to build her heart and walls back up.

Before she lost her nerve, she uploaded the demo reel and sent it off in an email. There. Step one of damage control done.

She deliberately silenced the nagging doubt in the pit of her stomach and piloted her drone camera to get the aerial shots she wanted. She still had a job to do.

WINSTON WAS STILL FUMING and laying tile in what would be the master bathroom when Jake found him.

"There's our viral star! I need to talk to you about some follow up shots. I'm thinking a mini web series. This could be huge."

Winston kept placing tiles, not wanting the thin-set to dry or the conversation to continue.

"I'm going to find some smaller indie bands who need the exposure so we won't have to pay so much in royalties. How long does it take you to learn a new song?"

Winston refused to engage. If he kept his mouth shut, they couldn't exploit his voice any further. He didn't like working in the quiet, but he didn't like being made a laughingstock even more. If he could afford to walk away from this job, he would in a heartbeat. But what else was he good for?

Jake was undeterred.

"Listen, I get that you might be feeling a little shy, but you signed a contract to let us film what we need. I need this. It's a huge boost for the show. Just let me get a little more footage, and then I'll leave you alone."

"Bullshit." Winston couldn't let that lie stand. "If it gets you more ratings, you'll keep coming back for more. I'm done."

"You know I can fire you, right?"

"You know I can quit, right?" Winston fired back.

"You won't do that. You need this job just as much as I need this show to succeed. I just need a few more scenes to sprinkle. Don't you get this could make you famous?"

"I never wanted to be famous. Been there, failed that. So, no, Trina got all you're getting from me yesterday."

Winston deliberately turned his back on the producer and went back to methodically laying his tile. This was safe. Construction, especially in Silicon Valley, was a solid career. If he didn't climb too high, he wouldn't have too far to fall. He just wished that he'd remembered that yesterday before he'd reached for Katrina's shiny star.

He'd wanted so badly to believe her, to believe that he could mean something to a woman like her, that he'd ignored his own hard-earned knowledge. He'd opened himself up to love and hope and put it all out there for her to see. And she'd filmed it and sent it off to her boss to further her own career. His heart was breaking, and it was his own damn fault for daring to believe that he might be worthwhile. He wouldn't make that mistake again.

CHAPTER 11

W‍HEN T‍RINA PULLED up to the still-bustling job site, it was dark out, but the house was aglow. Everyone was hustling to make the deadline for this episode's reveal. After a full day out setting up cameras and capturing the B-roll footage they needed, she wanted to wander through the house and see what progress had been made. But she wouldn't. She would stay away from the worksite, and give Winston his space until she had something to say. Climbing into the production van to upload the shots she'd gotten, she saved files and mulled her next steps to repair her rift with Winston. She was nearly finished when Jake bounded into the tight space of the van.

"Hey! How did today's shots go?"

"Great. I'm uploading and logging them now."

"Where are your shots from yesterday?"

"I don't have any from yesterday. I was out scouting." Trina kept her eyes on her monitor hoping her horrible lying skills didn't betray her.

"So you didn't get any more shots of our sexy Singing Subcontractor?"

"No. Just what you got on the mounted cam."

"Hmm, he seemed to think you did." Jake moved closer and leaned against the desk, his thigh almost brushing her arm. Her nerves were already jumping with flashbacks to another van, another time. *But I'm not that girl anymore. That girl wouldn't have been able to feel what I felt yesterday with Winston. And I'm not a victim anymore.* Trina stood up and put space between her and Jake, casual but on guard.

"He was singing in the car while we drove, but I didn't have a camera with me."

"You had your phone didn't you? Let me see it."

"No."

"No? I don't like that word, Trina. Give me your phone."

"No. My personal phone is none of your business."

"If you've got some idea of going around me to use his talent for yourself, think again. Anything you shot for the show belongs to the show. Now give me the fucking phone."

"I'm not giving you my phone." She edged closer to the door of the van, trying to slip past him, but Jake shot his hand out to the rack behind her, blocking her way. "There's nothing on it for the show. I did what you asked, and got loads of B-roll setups. I just uploaded the first batch." Trina hated the way her voice trembled, but she hadn't given in. She'd still count it as a win.

"Hand it over or you're fired."

Trina stared at Jake's hard eyes and did what she should have done when the pilot got picked up. Jake wasn't going to let her go at the end of this season, not if her shots were what made the show. He was going to use up the energy for her dreams himself. She was better off leaping into the unknown even if she didn't know where she'd land.

"Then I guess I'm done here."

She ducked under his arm and bolted for the door of the van, but his angry words stopped her on the threshold.

"I thought you really wanted this job. I thought I could count on you to get the shots I needed. Clearly, you are more concerned about yourself than making this show a success."

She whirled back. No way was he getting the last word.

"And I thought you were different than all the other asshole producers in Hollywood. But no, you only care about yourself and your precious show. You were never going to recommend me to your film friends, were you?" He had the grace to look away, and she had her answer. "I'm not going to help you ruin anyone else's life along with mine." That felt good. Strong. She had one more thing to get off her chest and she could leave, proud of the way she'd handled herself. "And Jake, the next time you want a tough shot, don't bring sex appeal into it, or you're going to get slapped with a lawsuit so fast your head will spin. God knows, you've never asked George to wear heels and make-up for work, and you shouldn't have made me either. Fuck this. I'm gone."

"Go ahead. Get out. You can return any extra equipment in the morning and pick up your check."

Trina stumbled out of the van, shocked by her sudden change in fortunes, but feeling lighter somehow. What the hell would she do now? All of her carefully crafted plans to overcome her past came crumbling down. But she hadn't. She had stood strong against his power, and he couldn't take that away from her. This might set her back, but it would not break her.

When her blasted cell phone chimed with a new email, she checked it on auto-pilot. The response should have elated her, but now it was a moot point.

Flipping over to her videos, she watched the clips she'd resisted all afternoon. These were certainly none of Jake Ryland's business. The look on Winston's face was intoxicating, and the thought that she'd never again feel that buzz of emotion pushed the tears past her shaky dam. She couldn't fix things back to the way they were, but at least she could give him this one last thing before she left for good. She could mourn the loss of what could have been on her long drive back to LA.

CHAPTER 12

NOT CARING about her messy hair, her tear-streaked face, or her dusty clothing, Trina strode through the front door of the house still buzzing with activity at nine p.m. Deadlines were quickly approaching, and everyone was working late to get the job done. Everyone except her. She was now unemployed.

That panicky thought sent a fresh flood of tears down her cheeks. Once the seal had been broken, it was nearly impossible to staunch the flow. She would just take care of this one thing, and then she could go home and cry herself dry while she rebuilt her future and her defenses. She just couldn't tolerate the idea of a certain talented man thinking the world was laughing at him and hating her for it.

She found him in the shower. His arms were grey to the elbow, and he had streaks of grout smeared across his handsome face, the face that had once looked at her with something softer than desire. Now, his face was as hard as the tile he laid, every emotion carefully concealed beneath a layer of cement.

He turned at her cough, but kept laying the last wall of tile in the tight enclosure.

"What do you want?"

Conscious of where she'd placed the cameras in this room, she stepped into the shower with him to take them both out of sight. It was a tight squeeze, and she pressed herself as close to the not yet dry wall as she dared. Her body responded to his nearness as she ran her hands around his waistband, invading his space and half wishing her hug would be returned.

"What the hell are you doing?"

She fumbled with the box clipped onto his thick tool belt, trying to accomplish her task by feel. She pressed a free finger to his lips, and turned them so his bulk blocked her from the hallway.

"I'm turning off your mic," she whispered. "I know you're mad at me, but I have things I need to say before I go. So please, just listen."

He nodded sullenly, but continued slathering the thin-set on the backer board.

"I did sneak video of you singing on camera. It was part of my job, but it was before I understood your fear. I'm sorry."

He didn't stop repetitively swiping the gray adhesive on the wall, though it was well covered as far as she could tell. She pressed on. She had to make him understand before she lost her nerve and her chance. Once she spit it out, she could leave this train wreck behind her.

"I broke your trust one other time, but I'm hoping you'll forgive me for it."

His eyes flashed to hers and his jaw clenched, but at least she had his attention.

"You told me you were afraid to rely on your talent, that it wouldn't be good enough, that you'd fail again. I need you to know that your talent is real and strong, whether you decide to do something with it or not. That viral video..."

He huffed out a sharp breath and looked back at his fucking

tiles. She gripped his chin and turned his head back to face her. This was too important.

"That viral video has over a hundred thousand likes in less than twenty-four hours. And the comments are insane. But I knew you wouldn't take the word of a bunch of strangers, if you even got up the courage to look. So I sent a video from yesterday to a friend of mine from art school."

His eyes widened with panic, and Trina realized what he was thinking. It hurt that he would believe that of her, but she'd broken his trust well and good at this point. Her grip on his chin turned to a caress, trying to ease his mind.

"No, not that video. That was, and will forever be, just for us. I mean," her voice caught in her throat, "for me. I'll delete it all if you want. But I did send her a demo clip of you singing in the car and on the bench. She's a music producer in charge of scouting new talent. She was blown away and immediately emailed me, wanting to know who you are and if you have representation.

"I need you to know that your talent is real and that you don't have to share it on the show if you don't want to, and there are other options if you do. Jesus, I'm rambling. Look, I'll forward you her email in case you want to contact her yourself. No pressure. I just wanted you to know you have options before I go."

She moved to push past him, unable to bear another second so close but denied the comfort of his arms.

His hand shot out, slapping into wet mortar, blocking her escape.

"That's the second time you've said that," he murmured. "Where are you going?"

"I don't know." Trina blinked rapidly, determined to keep her tears where they belonged but failing miserably as they spilled down her cheeks. Damn that leaky seal. "I just got fired, but I'm sure I'll find something else."

His hands dropped the trowel and tile, sending them clattering to the floor of the shower. When he reached for her waist, she moved into him. The concern in his eyes felt too good to turn away from. She wanted to melt into his strong chest, and when he pulled her even closer, she gave in. Sobbing, she laid her forehead on his sternum and finished her apology.

"I'm so sorry that video got around, but I'll never regret that it brought us together. I'll miss you, Winston."

"Don't go. Stay."

"I can't. I don't have a job anymore. Besides, I can't stay knowing you rightfully hate me for what happened."

"That's just it, though. I don't hate you. I've spent the day hating that I can't hate you. God help me, but I've fallen in love with you. I was going to tell you once I worked off more of this scared and mad. You can't leave before I get there."

Trina felt like someone had just tapped her on the head with a cartoon two by four, complete with swirling stars. As her emotions scrambled to catch up, she stared dumbfounded at her man. Could he still be hers? Was it possible she hadn't lost everything? He wiped the tears from her cheeks with his thumbs, and then cursed at the mortar streaks he left behind. He brushed his hands on his pants and gently cradled her face.

"How could I walk away from a woman who believes in me more than I do myself? A woman who turns me inside out with a smile? A woman who saw through my bullshit to the real me and didn't run away screaming?"

The tears started again, but this time they dripped over her smile.

"I love you, too, Winston, but I still have to go. There's not a lot of demand for an out-of-work camera operator with zero references up here. I have to go back to LA where I at least have a chance."

"Don't go yet. I've got no problem with LA. I can build anywhere, but you can't walk away from all of this progress here and your deal with Ryland on account of me."

He leaned down and pressed his lush lips to hers, and not only did she not want to leave, Trina wished they could stay wrapped up in that shower forever. Would the new owners mind if they weren't the first to christen the new bathroom with shower sex?

"Come with me."

Thinking he was reading her mind, she stepped closer and nodded, anxious to lose herself in his arms again.

"Yes."

But instead of kissing her, he brushed away the salty streams with the collar of her flannel shirt and gently took her hand to lead her from the bathroom.

"Oh, you meant…right. Of course." She followed reluctantly, not wanting to leave his embrace so quickly after regaining it. But she followed where he led, her hand trapped in his massive one, at once comforting and confusing.

"Jake!" Winston bellowed. "Where are you?"

"You yelled?" Jake came into the hallway, his face calm and controlled as if he hadn't just ruined her future.

"Did you fire Trina? Because of me?"

"I fired Trina because she wasn't doing her job."

"And her job was getting me to sing?"

"Yes."

"Hire her back, and I'll give you what you need."

Trina jumped into the conversation. She couldn't let him do something he'd regret just to save her.

"No, Winston! Don't do anything you're not comfortable with. I don't need saving. That's not why I told you all of this."

"You told me the truth. And I find that with you believing in me, it's easier for me to believe in me, too. Let me do this."

Trina was still stunned, trying to understand, when he turned back to Jake.

"It's simple. Hire her back, with a raise for putting up with your bullshit, and be grateful that she's considering staying. And I will be your singing sub or whatever you want to call it. Or don't and I'll walk away with her. You said you had a friend in LA who was interested?"

This last was directed back at her, and all she could manage was a stunned nod. Was this man really putting it all on the line for her? Having someone on her side was an incredible feeling. She leaned into him, trying to tell him without words how much she appreciated his support.

"Oh, and her original deal? The one where you give her the recommendation she needs? Consider that binding and due."

"And I get as much singing from you as I want, with exclusive option rights to a spin-off?"

Trina cut in.

"He'll want to see numbers on that before he agrees. If he's going to play a larger role, he'll need higher compensation."

If he was going to protect her, she was going to protect him right back.

"That's fair. We have a deal, Mr. Hartwell." Jake stuck out his hand, and Winston shook it. "Guess you're not fired then, McAllister."

"Hmm, lucky me." Her boss might hear sarcasm, but her eyes and thoughts were all centered on the man still holding her hand. She meant every word. She was damn lucky that she'd stumbled across this incredible man where she'd least expected to find him. Without thought for their audience, she wrapped her arms around Winston's neck and leaped. His strong hands caught her ass and held her close as she wrapped her legs around his waist and her mind around the prospect that she wouldn't have to give him up. She might rue the gray handprints on her butt later, but she would never regret opening up to this man. She put every ounce of her gratitude into her kiss and felt the last of her walls crumbling down, washed away by the flood of love pouring from her heart.

Building a fresh future on this newly laid foundation was a

challenge she'd happily spend the rest of forever figuring out, as long as she got to build it with him.

THE END

ACKNOWLEDGMENTS

This book is a community effort. I would not have finished without the support of many dear friends and fellow writers.

To the OSRBC Writers/NanoLA groups, thanks for the sprints and the laughs. OSRBC:Read More Romance, thank you for reminding me of the best part of this genre, our amazing readers! To the Legends, your continued encouragement warms my heart. My RT Lovies, you know who you are, and you make me smile every damn day. Everyone over at Friends For Eva, thank you for coming to play with me when I need a break. Life wouldn't be the same without your glitter bombs and rosé-colored glasses! To the Expanded Sassy Bitches, learning from you all about this crazy business has been enlightening. To the LeBou Crew for letting me crash once in a blue moon. The rest of my SVRWA sisters, you are my tribe and you keep me sharp. To Kara for pushing me to figure out newsletters and websites and marketing, oh my! To Ro for retreats and shenanigans and keeping me company late at night online when the words won't come.

To Jen and Julia, this book would not be worth reading without your eagle eyes and thoughtful suggestions. Lucy, thank you for your persistence in making my cover gorgeous and for your long-distance friendship. As usual, many thanks to the author friends who tended to my mental health, both on the page and through Facebook messenger, during the making of this book. Sarah, Sophie, Sonali, Lenora, Joanna, Alyssa, Alisha, Cherry, Kate and Kerrigan, thank you for creating characters and friendships that inspire me.

To Cass, for having open ears and understanding that I don't need to hear the answers. I need to speak until I find them. To Jasmine, for understanding how powerful it is to hear that what we've written isn't crap alongside the well-placed questions. Also, for giving my baby a new "best friend." To Jen and Fiona and Fiona and Andrea, for being my mom friends who get what I'm trying to do and step in to help along the way. Darcie, there aren't words to describe how grateful I am for the relationship that we have. The day all of our girls became best friends was such a blessing.

To everyone who came and visited and wasn't offended when I left my children with you and went to work, you are always welcome back! To Mom & Dad, thank you for coming every time I've called for help. I love you to the moon and back. To my three darling girls, thank you for sending me off to work at bedtime with hugs and kisses instead of tears. And to my husband, you remind me day in and day out that love is in the details and that ambition is worth chasing. Thank you for your unwavering support.

ABOUT THE AUTHOR

Eva Moore began reading fuchsia books when she was 12. Now she writes sexy contemporary romances in between soccer practices and glasses of rosé. Eva lives in Silicon Valley, after moving around the world and back, with her college sweetheart, her three gorgeous girls, and a Shih Tzu who thinks he is a cat. She can be found most nights hiding in her closet-office, scribbling away, and loves to hear from the outside world. Please visit her at www.4evamoore.com.

If you'd like to know about future releases and giveaways, you can join her newsletter here: http://bit.ly/evamoorenews

Join her fan page for rosé tastings, Target jokes, and other sparkly shenanigans at Friends For Eva Moore.

ALSO BY EVA MOORE

Girls' Night Out Series

Someone Special (1)

Second Chances (2)

Three Strikes (3)

Forever Nights (4)

Christmas Spirits (5, novella)

Exposed Dreams Series

Opened Up (1)

Dirty Demo (1.5, novella)

Stripped Down (2)

Decked Out (Extended Epilogue in Worst Holiday Ever Anthology)

Roughed In (3)

Stand Alone

Welcome Home, Soldier (novella)

#LoveItOrLeaveIt (novella in Worst Valentine's Day Ever)

CPSIA information can be obtained
at www.ICGtesting.com
Printed in the USA
BVHW031638180222
629427BV00002B/97